Early Praise for *Imaginary Friends:*

Imaginary Friends takes readers on an intellectual journey; it is the story of a protagonist's (Clay's) discovery of self, literacy, and critical thinking. Its work eloquently questions written conventions, in addition to political and religious norms, as it urges readers to not only reconsider what it means to break the rules, but also—and more importantly, to reconsider what it means to interrogate the larger societal structures that determine who has the authority to prescribe laws and conventions.

As a writing professor and educator, *Imaginary Friends* elegantly employs the precise set of skills and knowledge I want my students to acquire: I long for my students to take risks in their writing, as they push the boundaries of convention. I want my students to question where rules come from and who creates these rules. And finally, I desire for my students to obtain a sense of agency and self-discovery, as they enforce their rights to develop their own languages, stories, styles—in essence, their own senses of being, regardless of whether or not these senses neatly fit prescribed conventional forms for what society says they should fit. In reality, *Imaginary Friends* is really what the CCCC Students' Right to Their Own Language Resolution is all about. It's about having the right to simply *be.*

Staci Perryman-Clark, PhD
Associate Professor of English
Western Michigan University

Author of *Afrocentric Teacher-Research: Rethinking Appropriateness and Inclusion*

Coeditor of *Students' Right to Their Own Language: A Critical Sourcebook*

D0743311

Other Books by Michael Scott Monje, Jr:

Novels:
Nothing is Right
Mirror Project
Defiant

Electronic Chapbooks:
A Waking Narrative

As Editor or Contributor:
Barking Sycamores: Year One (Contrib.)
The Spoon Knife Anthology (Ed.)

Imaginary Friends
A Shaping Clay Novel

by Michael Scott Monje, Jr.

Owned by disabled workers, NeuroQueer Books extends the
Autonomous Press mission: Revolutionizing academic access

ISBN-13: 978-0-9972971-2-6
ISBN-10: 0-9972971-2-3

Cover art by Chris Henry

Part I: The Struggle Within

The Feast of the Maccabees

Clay wrestled his body across the bed as his eyes wrestled with the Bible on his pillow. Over the course of three months of daily reading, he had only managed to get from the creation in Genesis to the discussion of the law in first book of Samuel, and while that seemed like an accomplishment, his progress seemed barely a start when he closed the book and looked down the spine at his bookmark's place.

Mainly, this slow progress was due to the outrageous number of names and places that he needed to stop and sound out. It was maddening to have to spend fifteen or twenty minutes repeating a name to himself until he understood who he was referring to and where they fit into the story, and then to read ten verses and find that the character in question was already dead. The futility of memorization and the constant cost of getting to know these people who would lead ten verse lives made the entire book seem like a cacophony of accidents that someone was forcibly interpreting as stories.

Every day, when he finished his time with the Bible, he promised himself that he would give up. All of the good stories were already covered by the children's picture Bible that his grandmother had given him for Christmas when he was four, anyhow. The rest of the book was just a horror show of death and incest and slavery, and Clay could not understand why anyone would find such value in reading it in its entirety when the truly brilliant portions could be so easily excised from the bulk of the text. Why deal with thirty-six hundred pages, when all of the good parts could be reduced to three hundred pages with illustrations?

Clay had tried to tell his mother, after he finished Deuteronomy, that there was no point in trying to force his way through certain sections because they were just lists of names. His mother had nodded, but then she had told him to read them anyway because he might not know where the lists ended and the important stories began.

So far, Clay felt like those "important stories" mostly consisted of narrative pretexts for killing anyone who wasn't Hebrew. Not that the Hebrews had it good, it seemed like everyone around them was trying to kill them as well. When he said this out loud to his mother, she made him go read the Bible for half an hour so that it could sink in. The experience did nothing to change Clay's mind about the book, but it did make him stop talking about it.

After a point, he started to wonder if the maddening banality of death *was* the point. Maybe his mother was attempting to desensitize him to the kinds of things he would encounter when he started reading other grown-up books by giving him the worst, most tasteless one to start with.

In no time, Clay discarded that theory. If his mother felt that way about the book, she would never have built their family's life around going to church, because the whole point of church was to talk about how Jesus's death put an end to the necessity of the kind of genocide that was going on in the Old Testament. At least, Clay hoped that was the whole point of church. He was never entirely sure why he was there when it was actually happening. His parents taught him to do all the kneeling and to say the prayers. They called it worship, and he was very good at worshipping. They told him so, and everyone always seemed pleased that Clay was so good at doing the things he was taught to do. Clay had no idea why they were so impressed, though, because the motions in church weren't very complicated or very fast. The motions he had to learn to perform the sing-alongs in Sunday school were harder. Didn't the adults graduate up from Sunday school? Didn't they realize that their services were much easier to perform?

This, Clay told himself, was why he wriggled as he read, because he understood all of the stories he was reading, but there was so much that was incomprehensibly not story. He knew who killed whom and why it led to the rape of whichever's daughters, how that escalated a blood feud in a neighboring kingdom that necessitated the castration of so many young boys, and then how they led a slave rebellion to restore the worship of their particular god, who was good because he let them kill other people instead of letting other people kill them. What he did not understand was why it was that people worshipped any of the gods, idols or not. It seemed obvious that all the gods, even the one that he was supposed to root for, had nothing better to do than order the deaths of all of the other gods' believers, and Clay found himself constantly baffled by the reasoning that led the humans in these stories to believe that getting involved with gods could ever be anything but trouble.

He did not mention this observation to his mother, and he did not have anyone else to talk to about it, so he carried it around in his heart. Most of the time it just sat there without bothering him, but when he read the Bible, it made him wriggle.

At least it was just a wriggle. It could have been a scream. Clay had one of those, too, and the one good thing he could say about reading the Bible was that it kept the scream in his head from escalating and running away with his ability to concentrate. Memorizing all of those names just to understand the importance of their little ten verse lives was a pain, but it seemed to Clay that his perceptions did not work correctly unless he was in some kind of pain. His best understanding of the scream was that it was his brain creating pain out of a vacuum, to make up for the lack of pain in Clay's senses. That meant the only way to keep his brain from hurting him was to create new pain that came from outside it.

As it turned out, the Bible was very, very good for that sort of thing.

Perhaps, Clay thought, the reason why his mother was so invested in making him read it was that she knew about the scream. Maybe she had her own scream, even. Often, he overheard her repeating names from the Bible to herself the same way that he did when he was trying to memorize them. Her quiet chanting made him want to ask her about her scream, but he was afraid. If she did not have a scream of her own, then what would she think about Clay having one?

He remembered the stories he kept half-hearing in whispers whenever the adults were around. The ones about Grandpa Harry and the crazy house. He knew, from piecing together the tidbits of information they were careless about discarding, that Grandpa Harry heard the scream. Clay was also reasonably sure that the reason Grandpa Harry had gone to the crazy house was because his own scream had grown so loud he could no longer hear anything else.

Clay did not want to admit to having a scream if his mother did not have one as well, because he was afraid that she would send him to the crazy house. So instead, he read the Bible and he chanted names out loud to himself until he could remember who they belonged to and what that person's ten verses were about. The scream stayed quiet while he did that. It stirred a little when he thought about the fact that Grandpa Harry had read the Bible every day only to wind up in the crazy house after all, but starting another litany was enough to stifle it again. As long as Clay stayed away from thoughts about his grandfather and the crazy house, the scream seemed to accept his Bible study as a fitting source of pain.

So he read the Bible. Even when it made no sense. Even when it disgusted him. Even when the word 'begat' lost all meaning and became a thing he repeated to himself over and over as a verbal tic. Clay's wriggle told the story of this process, growing more and more exaggerated and also more and more necessary as he marched his way toward the minor prophets.

He decided to take a break from his normal read-through, skipping ahead to the end of the Old Testament. In Sunday school, his teacher had mentioned that this week, on the first day of August, there would be a special feast day. It would be the feast of the Maccabees. Clay decided that he was going to read about the Maccabees since they had a day. He hoped that following the church calendar and reading about events during their observational days was the secret to turning all of the blood and gristle on the page into the kind of moral wisdom that everyone promised the Bible would bring, but so far it was not working. The words that were actually in the book of Maccabees were nothing like the story that he was told in

Sunday school. According to Sunday school, the Maccabees were holy warriors who restored the temple after idolaters had profaned it. According to Clay's Bible, they were angry men who forcibly circumcised children and then conscripted them into the army as child soldiers.

Clay tried to make room in his head for both ideas, but he found that they did not have the ability to coexist in his brain. There was nothing holy about forcing circumcision on someone. Just thinking about it made Clay hurt in his private place. Besides, the boys who were forcibly circumcised were only uncircumcised in the first place because their parents had been forced to convert to the religion of a conquering army. Cutting their penises and forcing them to go off to war seemed to be a punishment for something that someone else had done. So why was it being forced on children?

Clay closed the Bible. He had read enough. The scream would not bother him as long as he was worried about the boys who were circumcised and then sent off to fight.

He got out of bed and went downstairs to find his mother, to ask her if he could go to the library. She asked him if he was done reading the Bible for the day.

He nodded.

She asked him how many chapters he had read.

He said most of a book.

She nodded. Then she asked him if it was enough for him to learn a lesson from the book.

He nodded.

Finally, she asked him what lesson he had learned.

"I learned that the ideas in the Bible can mean different things at the same time," he said.

"That's a very good lesson to learn," she replied. "Did you learn anything else?"

Clay nodded again. When he realized that his mother expected him to speak, he followed up with: "I don't know how to say it yet. I need to think about what I read."

What he did not say was: "I learned that sometimes, old people will cut the young in a private place and then send them off to die."

He knew he could never tell his mother about that lesson. If she already knew, then her making him read the Bible could only be about teaching it to him, and he did not want to appear arrogant about learning something everyone else already knew. He had learned not to do that when he had first started to learn times-tables. When he bragged about knowing all of them up to the multiples of ten, his father had rattled off a table that went up to multiples of seventeen. After he was done, he told Clay that it was good he was learning, but that showing off was just a way of inviting people to put him in his place. This made Clay reluctant to say what he knew out loud. It was better for people to see him as stupid so that he could trick them than it was to make himself a target for them to put down. Also, there was always the chance that his mother did not know that the Bible was about cutting children's privates and starting wars. Clay felt like it was really obvious, but he also knew that they never talked about it in Sunday school, so it might not be as obvious as he thought it was.

If his mother did not know about the circumcision and the war, then Clay did not want to be the one to tell her. The last few times he told her about something from the Bible that he found disgusting or surprising, she accused him of lying. Even after he cited the chapter and verse and asked her to look it up, she just sent him to bed for "sass" (whatever that was), and then the subject was never brought up again.

So Clay kept the important lessons to himself when he read the Bible. He was sure that this was the right way to do things, because it was the only way his parents gave him. They would never give him the wrong way to do something as his only choice, he figured. That was not what parents were for.

❖   ❖   ❖

Overnight at Patrick's

"So what do you want to do now?" Patrick asked the question for what seemed to be the tenth time.

Clay shrugged for what seemed to be the tenth time. "I was hungry and I just ate, so I'm satisfied. It's your turn to pick."

Patrick gestured around the room. His living room was small— much smaller than Clay's—but his parents had managed to pack it full of computers and games and a big screen television, so it had many more things to do in it. In addition to that, the kitchen at Patrick's home boasted a deep fryer and a cotton candy machine *and* a waffle iron. The computer, a Commodore 64 just like the one Clay's father had brought home a few years ago, had hundreds of disks of games to play, and most of them even had software labels instead of handwritten ones marked "BACKUP COPY." All of this overwhelmed Clay, especially since he did not know what activities might be difficult for him to learn or which games were the best ones in Patrick's collection. This made him want to let other people make the choices about what he did and when he did it, but Patrick was not allowing that to happen. Instead, he was staring at Clay with expectation.

Clay shrugged. "You pick," he said.

Patrick scowled at him. It was not the first time. Clay was sure it would not be the last.

"You can't just watch me play Nintendo all night. You won't have any fun," he said.

Clay shrugged. "I had fun doing it earlier," he replied.

Patrick leaned in and whispered. "My mom is the one who says you can't just watch me. I don't care if you don't want to play, because I just like to talk to you and I'm glad you like to talk to me. My little brother tells me to shut up when I talk to him. But my mom thinks I'm not letting you play, and she threatened to ground me if I didn't give you a turn. *Please,* Clay. Pick something."

Suddenly, Clay understood. He had been so busy trying to understand all of his choices that he had missed the obvious fact that Patrick had already gotten what he wanted—he wanted a friend who could keep him company. Clay remembered that want. He had wanted a friend until Aaron invited him over after school. Once that happened, he was much happier, and then other people also invited him places. Once his parents saw that other people liked him, they started letting him invite friends to go swimming over at Grandma Bayleigh's, and they even allowed him to have Patrick and Aaron along when the whole family went to the zoo. All of this happened after the Greenridge Days celebration, within the last few months. Now, Patrick was seeing Clay differently, and he wanted Clay's help getting from the place where they had all been at the beginning of first grade to the place where people invited him everywhere.

His mother was interpreting everything the wrong way, though. She could not tell that Clay was happy and that he was having a good time, because she expected his good time to look different from the way it really looked. He tried to figure out how to explain this to Patrick and his mother, but all that happened was that he felt short of breath and almost remembered the scream, only he caught himself before it charged into the front of his brain.

He would not be able to explain anything with it hanging there, ready to move forward. He would have to try doing what Patrick asked instead.

"I would like to play pyramid solitaire," Clay said.

It seemed like a safe request—all the game required was a deck of cards, and that meant Clay did not have to try to learn computer stuff, and he also did not have to pretend to want to try something he had never done before.

For some reason, though, Patrick went to the computer and switched it on.

Clay expected that Patrick might disagree with him or ask him to pick something else, but he had not expected that Patrick would just ignore him and go to the computer. It was a very rude thing to do, especially since he had just begged Clay to pick their next activity.

When Patrick started rifling through the bin full of floppy disks next to the computer, Clay asked him what he was doing.

"I'm looking for the Hoyle Classic Card Games disk," he said. "You wanted to play pyramid solitaire."

Clay was stunned. Not that he was surprised that there was a card game for the computer—he had seen his father play bowling and *Pole Position* and other games. He knew how sophisticated the video games were getting, especially when they were computer games and not just Nintendo games. What shocked him was the fact that Patrick assumed that Clay would prefer to play it on the computer instead of just playing with real cards.

"Why don't you just go find the cards instead?" he asked.

"What cards?" Patrick replied.

That was when Patrick's mother intervened. She had been lurking around on the same floor they were playing on forever, but she had been quiet while they talked, so it surprised him when she suddenly inserted herself into the conversation by handing each of the boys a brand new deck of playing cards, still in the packaging.

"Here," she said. "Use these."

Clay jumped when he felt the cards suddenly appear in his hand, and Patrick's mother laughed softly.

"Don't worry. Patrick is just a little enamored with the computer. You can teach him how to deal out a pyramid, and you each have your own deck so you don't have to take turns."

"How will we keep score, though?" Patrick asked. "The computer keeps score for you when you play Hoyle. How will we keep score?"

"I just count the number of pairs I make," Clay said. "Just set them off to the side. Or you can do what my dad does and keep score by counting how many cards are left at the end of a round. That means that the highest score is the loser, though."

Patrick shook his head. He seemed to be having trouble with the idea that video games might also be real games. "I don't see why we should do it this way," he said. "The computer is right over there, and there are cool sounds when you make a match, and it keeps score for you."

"Okay," Clay said. "I don't mind."

"No," Patrick's mother interjected. "The two of you played *Quest for Tires* for an hour before dinner, and I promised Tyler that he could play with the computer now."

"But Tyler went upstairs to play with his blocks," Patrick whined. "He isn't even trying to play with the computer."

"That's probably because he is assuming that you're going to hog it like you do every time someone comes over. Clay wants to do more than just watch you play your games. He wants to participate."

Actually, Clay was fuming. How did this woman know what he wanted?

All he wanted now was for the night to be over. He liked Patrick just fine, and he had agreed to stay over because he wanted to be friends, but all he really felt like doing was sitting in his bedroom and reading or building things out of LEGOs. The visit had been fun until dinner, but now it was just exhausting, and if not for the fact that his parents were having a "date night," he never would have agreed to stay all night. When Patrick had issued the invitation, Clay's mother had presented it as a choice: he could go stay with Grandma Bayleigh like his brother, he could go stay with Grandpa Harry and put up with all the aunts and uncles that always changed the channel when he watched TV, or he could go stay with Patrick. Staying home and playing with LEGO was not an option, because his parents wanted to watch R rated movies and be alone.

Clay had made his choice, and now he was stuck with it, even if that meant he had to pretend to like things he hated. Even if it meant that Patrick's horrible mother was going to sit in her living room full of toys and tell lies about what Clay wanted to do.

He felt a shivering feeling in his chest, and for a moment he was unsure whether the wind was whistling or his scream was welling up. Clay excused himself to the bathroom while he figured it out. When he came back, the computer was off and the cards were nowhere to be found. Instead, Patrick and his brother were setting up a game of

Sorry. Clay asked what was going on, and that was when Patrick's mother told him that they had decided to play a game that everyone could play together. She said that after they played *Sorry*, Tyler was going to use the computer and that Patrick and Clay could play Nintendo.

Clay shrugged.

He was upset that the woman had put so much emphasis on making him choose something only to deny him his choice, but he was also relieved that he would not have to try to argue with Patrick about the computer. He tried his best not to let any of his feelings show, because he did not feel like sorting through them out loud, and Patrick's mother seemed like the kind of nosy person that would ask him all kinds of questions. Instead, he asked Tyler what color he wanted to play as.

"Shut up," Tyler said.

"Tyler always plays as blue," his mother said.

"I said shut up," Tyler repeated. "You're annoying and you make me play annoying games with my stupid brother who can't shut up because his brain is a computer and so he talks about computers all day and doesn't know about anything but computers. This whole house is stupid."

"Apologize for that," his mother said.

Tyler went to the bathroom and slammed the door. Clay helped Patrick finish setting the game up. After a minute, Tyler came back and sat at the spot for the blue player.

"I want to go first," he said.

They played three games of *Sorry*, and Clay won the first two of them. After the second victory, Tyler called him a "punk," and then he called his mother an idiot when she tried to make him apologize. Clay was quite happy when the third game ended and she dismissed them all, until Patrick tried to make Clay choose the Nintendo game that they would play.

He insisted that he just wanted to watch for a while because he was tired. Patrick protested, but when Clay insisted that he could not concentrate on a game and talk at the same time, he happily played and talked at once, narrating the story of the game as he went. Clay, for his part, was happy to be done with both talking and playing, and while his friend kept busy, he contemplated his Bible readings.

The story of the Maccabees was sticking with him, in part because it made no sense as part of the Bible. It seemed like it would make sense as part of a history, or maybe a war story like *The Iliad*, which Clay knew about but had never read. As a book in the Bible, though, it seemed to lack the sense of miracle and splendor that the more famous stories conveyed. Abraham's willingness to sacrifice his son had been brutal too, but it had made a clear point about obedience and faith. The story of the Maccabees seemed more like it was about kingdoms and control over land.

The only exceptional part was the bit about the lamp oil, and Clay liked that part. He wished that there was more to the story about it, but apart from the fact that the lamp oil never ran out even though it should have, it went nowhere. He had asked his mother about it and she had gotten really excited and explained to him that Jewish people celebrated a holiday because of the lamp oil, but that did not make the story more satisfying to Clay because it did not change the fact that his Bible had none of the information that would let him understand why that would happen. Instead, it just made him wonder why Jewish people were able to get so excited about something that was really only the promise of a good story and not a good story itself.

He had almost finished the rest of the Old Testament, now, and he did it by skipping all the things that did not have stories in them, but his trip across both books of Maccabees still troubled him because he could not reconcile the stories as he read them with the importance that they were given. It seemed to Clay that there must have been more written about that lamp oil, otherwise the story was just too simple and boring to merit the attention it got.

Maybe Jewish people use a different Bible, Clay thought. *Maybe they get the real story and Christians just get a stupid version.*

That such a thing could be true was totally unsurprising to Clay. After all, he had seen it happen before. His illustrated children's Bible left out all the parts about fathers who had children with their own daughters and widows who became prostitutes so that their children could eat. It did mention stoning as a punishment, but it never described the process or named people who had been stoned to death. Both of those things were in his grown-up Bible, though. It stood to reason that there might be even more grown-up Bibles out there. Ones that could maybe expand on the lamp oil story.

"Where did you go?" a voice asked.

Clay looked around for the source of it and saw Patrick staring at him.

"What are you talking about?" he replied.

"You were staring at the wall for like five minutes," Patrick said. "I asked you a bunch of questions, but you just kept staring. Are you okay?"

Clay nodded. "I was just thinking about something I read," he said.

"I've been reading a lot over the summer, too," Patrick said. "Have you had a chance to check out the books about aliens from the library?"

Clay shook his head. Patrick used that as an invitation to launch into a description of the books' content, and Clay made sure to keep looking over to him periodically to reassure him that he was listening.

Patrick became so invested in his talk about aliens that he seemed to forget he was playing a video game. Clay bobbed his head to the music coming from the television while the game sat paused, and after a few moments, he asked if Patrick wanted to give him a turn while he talked. Patrick nodded, and so Clay took his turn playing with Patrick's game. It gave him something to do with his hands while the other boy talked, and that made listening easier.

Eventually, Patrick left the room for a moment, and Clay took that opportunity to turn off the Nintendo and close his eyes. He liked the other boy, but he was tired of spending time with people. All he wanted to do was shut himself in a small room where he could sit and think. It was all he had wanted to do for a while, and he was going to take advantage of the brief chance while his friend peed.

Clay's fatigue was so strong and had such a pull on his body that it made him shiver. When that happened, he found himself surrounded by a blanket, and then he opened his eyes to see Patrick's mother standing over him, holding her place in her book with one hand while she tucked him in to the couch with the other.

"I'm awake," Clay said.

"I know," she replied, "thank you for visiting us today. We've all been having a good time."

"Except for Tyler," Clay said.

"Even Tyler," the woman replied. "Tyler is easy to misunderstand. So is Patrick. I'm glad he has you to talk to."

"Patrick talks to everyone. He never stops talking," Clay replied.

Patrick's mother nodded. "He likes to share the things he learns. Most people are not patient enough to listen to him, though. It means a lot to him that you listen."

"I like to listen," Clay said, "because I don't like to talk. I've noticed that other people don't care if you are quiet as long as you let them talk."

Patrick's mother nodded. Then she walked across the room and sat down in a chair that looked like a nest because it was surrounded by half-read books and newspapers shaped like soft walls, and also because it had a groove in the cushion that was in the shape of her backside. She opened the book she was holding and started to read.

Clay read the title of the book. *The Joy Luck Club*. He could tell from the cover that it had something to do with China or Japan or with Asian people, because the design on the book's cover was written in was very similar to the graphic on the sign at the Golden Dragon Chinese Restaurant and Cocktail Lounge near Grandpa Harry's house.

He wondered if it was a cookbook. He wanted to ask, but he knew from experience that it was painful to be interrupted when he was reading, so he kept his mouth shut and continued examining the cover. After a short time, Patrick's mother looked up and tried to meet Clay's eyes. He stared even more intently at the book cover to keep her from doing so.

"Did you need something, Clay?" she asked.

"I was just wondering what your book was about. It looks Chinese."

"It is a book about Chinese people, both people who were born in China and who immigrated to American and also their children who are both Chinese and American."

"It's about children? Are they Christian?"

Clay's interest was piqued. Books about children were usually okay with his mother. Especially if the children were also Christian.

"They are, some of them. The book doesn't really talk much about God, but there are some scenes that take place in a church."

"Are there scenes that take place in a school?"

"Yes. One. It's a chess tournament."

Clay was excited. With a name like *The Joy Luck Club*, the book had to be warm and positive, and with the stories about children and parents, and also chess and school and churches, it sure sounded like something his mother would let him read.

"I like learning about foreign countries," Clay said. "Can I borrow that when you're done?"

Patrick's mother blinked at him. Then she said, "I'm not sure that you are going to understand the book, Clay. It's not written for children."

"Neither is the Bible," Clay shot back, "but as of right now I'm done with the Penteteuch and the histories, and by the time school starts I'd like to be done with the wisdom books and the prophets. I thought that this was going to take forever, but only the first five books took forever. The ones after that made more sense, so I read one every day."

"That's impressive," Patrick's mother said.

Clay shrugged.

"I just want it to be over with. I was told that I could read whatever I wanted as long as I also read the Bible, but my mom only takes me to the library once a week and she always asks me questions about the books I pick out. I don't know how to answer questions about books I haven't read yet, so I try not to pick out too many of them. That way, I don't have too many questions to answer. If I finish the Bible, though, then she will probably be happy and then I can read what I want. Can I borrow your book when you've finished with it?"

Patrick's mother was quiet for a long time. Clay considered asking the question again, but before he could, she shook her head.

"I'd like to give you my copy," she said, "but I got it from the library. You'll have to check it out there."

She did not say anything else to Clay. He wondered if he had upset her, but since she did not yell at him or send him to Patrick's room, he could not be sure. When Patrick came back from the bathroom, he was in his pajamas. He said that they had to get ready for bed because they were going to the early mass in the morning.

Clay took one last look at the cover of *The Joy Luck Club* so that he would be sure to remember the book, and then he went upstairs to get ready for bed. Patrick followed him and talked to him through the bathroom door while he changed. He hoped that the other boy would obey the rules about bed time, because all of this talking was making him very tired.

Patrick kept talking, though, long past the time when they were supposed to turn the lights out and sleep. Clay did not pay attention to what he said. Instead, he contemplated the idea of Chinese Christians, wondering if they converted when they came to America or if missionaries had crossed out of the Middle East to bring the Bible to China like the way the ones on TV went to Africa. He imagined that they must have. After all, Christianity spread to Russia and Europe. It would only make sense if it spread to China, too, since there was no ocean separating China from Jerusalem.

Sleep took him while he was trying to work out what a Chinese Bible might have to say about the Maccabees and their never-ending lamp oil.

❖   ❖   ❖

The Example of Job

Clay slammed his Bible closed. The Psalms were taunting him. They went on forever, and they all seemed to say the same thing. They did it in the most boring ways, too. Earlier in the Bible, God was proving he was great. He was tearing down city walls, causing floods, making people into angels... Who cares if he "is my shepherd and I shall not want" after *that*? Still, the job was to finish the whole Bible. That was the deal he made with his mother, and the fact that there was a long plotless section full of the worst hymnal lyrics made no difference. He still had to read it.

At least Job had made sense. Well, it had made sense until Clay started reading the Psalms. Putting the two side by side made him uneasy. In Job, God was properly horrible. He decided that he could make people love him just because he was strong enough to do whatever he wanted, and he tore a man's life apart to prove it. It was just like real life—the people who had the power to command loyalty and love did so, and everyone else bore the burden of the result. That was easy to understand, and Clay could see that Job was the way of the world when he watched his mother exercise her power to force him to read stupid things about incest and slavery just so she could control his ability to read other things that she did not know about. The idea of a God that was just terrible but had to be obeyed anyway was consistent with reality.

Job was the Bible distilled into its most concise form, and from what he could see, all of the people in his life were living by it. After that realization, the gushy, effervescent praise that coursed through the Psalms just felt like a lie. It was in no way coherent with the God that Clay understood, and it was also in no way consistent with the kind of God that he could see his parents worshiping.

He wondered if maybe the Psalms were written by people who saw what happened to Job. Maybe all their praise was just a way to try to sweet-talk God out of using their lives to prove a point. If that was so, then the Psalms made sense, but then that also meant everyone who worshipped God was really just trying to appease a bully.

Clay's father had always taught him that the thing to do was to hit a bully back, and he believed that his father taught him right, so when several other boys at the local park had called him names, he had hit them. His mother punished him for it, though, despite the fact that Clay had lost the fight rather badly. Also, his father, who always wanted him to stand up for himself, grounded him for "sass" when Clay told him that his ideas about self-defense were bullcrap that just got you punished by the nearest adult.

He did that a lot—it seemed like all Mark Dillon could do was dispense bad advice, followed by punishment for either failing to follow the advice or for pointing out that it was horrible. He even did it when Clay could prove that his ideas were wrong, like when Mark said that it was stupid to force people to wear seat belts because it was just the government treating everyone like children. After he said that, Clay told him that at school they had learned that deaths from traffic accidents decreased as soon as the seat belt laws were passed, and that they kept going down because cars were designed to be safer and safer every year. That had been a "sass" grounding, too. He had also grounded Clay for biting his brother once, even though A.J. had hit him first. He doubled the sentence when Clay "sassed" by pointing out that his father was the one who had taught him to attack people back when they hit him. Trying to understand the relationship between his father, his mother, God, Job, "sass," and bullies was a confusing thing.

Clay decided not to read the Psalms until he was less confused. Reading while he was confused would just bring the scream out, and then he would wind up smashing his head or his fist or some toys. After months of keeping himself contained, he did not want that. The problem, though, was that he had nothing else to read and his LEGO collection was currently impounded.

If he was good, he would get it back after school started, but he had lost it because he called A.J. a fucking crazy little monster after A.J. smashed up an entire LEGO city that he had spent a week building. Clay had been given a choice about the consequences he would face: He was told to either apologize to A.J. and tell his father where he had learned the fuck word or go the rest of the month without his LEGO collection.

Clay chose the first option, but when he told A.J. "I'm sorry for calling you a fucking crazy monster. I only did it because I heard Dad say it when he was having beers with Grandpa Clifton," his father called him a little shit. Then he took Clay's LEGO collection anyway. For "sass."

With no LEGOs, Clay faced a long, boring slide toward the end of summer. At least when school started he would be able to read whatever he wanted. He could borrow books from Aaron or from Patrick, and he could go to the library without his mother hovering over his shoulder. He was sick of picking up paperbacks to read the back cover, only to be peppered with questions about what his choice of a book with that kind of cover meant or why he thought it would be *positive* or *good* to read a book with a title like...

Like any title, honestly. It hardly seemed to matter whether the title was something like *Vampire Hellscape* or *The Bridge to Terabithia*. What seemed to matter was whether Clay picked the book or whether he went looking for books that his mother told him to look for. If he picked them for himself, then there was always something wrong. The book was really secretly about sex, or the way magic worked in it was secretly meant to undermine God, or something. If he let his mother pick, though, then he would be stuck working his way through the Little House books again. Clay hated those books because they were all about the same thing and no matter what the characters did, it didn't matter. The books were just an excuse to make it seem like everything was perfect during the pioneer days, when really Clay knew that people starved and sometimes families ate one another. He tried to explain this to his mother, but when he showed her the *Encyclopedia Britannica* article about the Donner Party, she told him not to be disgusting and to shut up because she was trying to watch the TV version of *Little House on the Prairie*.

No matter how much Clay demonstrated that he was done with the books and that he had in fact been done with them well before the first time he was asked to write a report about one of them, Kitty Dillon seemed fixated in a particular and narrow way on that one series. Sometimes, it was less aggravating just to read the Bible than those books, even if the magnitude the specific details of the characters' degradations gave him nightmares. At least the Bible was honest about how people moved into a new place and tried to claim it for themselves and their gods and wound up dead for their trouble.

Except now, in the Psalms, where the Bible was just giving him lot of poems about how God is bigger than the biggest thing you can imagine and better than the best thing you can imagine. Clay found the size metaphor especially taxing, because the biggest thing he could imagine was outer space, and it literally went on forever, so the idea that God could be bigger than something that was infinitely big was just stupid and so were the people who tried to tell him that such a thing could be true.

He paused. That last thought had made him feel ashamed.

He knew that he should not call people stupid. He tried not to do it, not even when he was silently talking to himself in his head, because if he let himself do it in his head, then he might do it out loud, and if he did it out loud, then his mother would put Joy into his mouth. It did not matter if what he said was true or not; if it was mean, he would wind up downstairs on his back on the counter with cold water and dish soap pouring down his throat and up his nose at the same time. It was better just to make sure he did not think anything bad than it was to risk a life filled with Joy. That meant that if the Bible was making him think bad thoughts, then it was time to stop reading the Bible, and *that* meant it was time to make his mother take him to the library. He had books to take back anyway: a couple of Star Trek novels and one of those stupid Little House books.

Clay cringed away from the word "stupid" in his head. Just thinking it made him feel like Patrick's little brother, and he did not want to feel like someone who called everyone an idiot. No one liked those people.

Before he could think another bad thought, he went downstairs to see his mother about going to the library. Kitty Dillon was nowhere to be found when Clay went looking for her, though. He wandered all over the house and out into the yard, but everywhere he went, he was alone. Clay even tried going into the laundry room in the basement, thinking that perhaps she was changing the laundry over, but it was empty, too.

He went outside and sat on the steps leading up to the front porch and cried. He was sure that his mother was gone because he had called her stupid. Somehow she knew that he had thought it, even if he did not say it. Maybe God told her. If God was real and the Bible was also real, then Clay knew that he was a bully. He probably called people "fucking stupid" and then blamed it on others, just like Clay's father did. He had known the truth as soon as he saw it. The book of Job was a warning about how God really operated. Maybe he did this to everyone until they knuckled under and started writing bullcrap like what was in the Psalms.

Realizing that he had just called part of the Bible bullcrap made Clay cry harder, and crying harder stirred up the scream in his head. He closed his eyes and fought with it, refusing to let it loose in his limbs. Eventually, he managed to squash it down without hitting anything. When he did, he found that he was done crying and that a new thought had entered his mind: If God was going to be mean to him just to prove a point, then he would prove one back. He would refuse to be afraid of what was going to happen. If the book of Job taught him one thing, it was that praising God would still lead to death and destruction, just like hating him would. God did not just tear down the walls of Jericho, he also killed the sons of his most faithful servant.

If trying to appease God was not going to stop God from torturing him, then why try to appease God?

Something switched off in Clay's head, and the scream was gone. Not quiet. Not contained. Gone. He smiled. Sometimes the world was a simple place, and not too frightening. Looking down the street, he saw that his mother was walking toward him. A.J. toddled along at her side.

"Where did you go?" Clay called out.

"I just went down the street to talk to Mrs. Jenkins," she replied. "Your father and I are going out tonight and we're going to have a new babysitter. I wanted to make sure that someone close by was going to be home in case she has any problems."

Clay nodded.

"I need to go to the library," he said.

"We don't have time for that today," his mother replied. "Just read your Bible if you get bored."

Clay stomped his foot on the concrete walkway that led up to the porch. "I read the Bible for more than an hour already, and dad took my LEGO collection away. I need to go to the library."

Kitty Dillon sighed and looked at her watch. "Clay, it's four-thirty. The library closes at five, and it's a twenty minute walk away. You won't have time to pick your book out before it closes."

Clay shook his head at his mother. "It's Wednesday, and that means they are open until seven, because they have story time at seven and then they close. How did you forget that? You're the one who makes me stay for story time. I don't like the stories."

Kitty sighed again. "I don't have time for this, Clay. Your father will be home between five and five-thirty, and as soon as he changes and goes out to pick up the babysitter, we're leaving."

"So that gives us at least an hour. Let's go."

"No! I'm not taking orders from you, Clay. I have to shampoo my hair and get dressed, and I have to do it now, before your father comes home. Otherwise, we're going to be late when we go out."

"But—"

"But no!"

She stomped past Clay and into the house, slamming the door behind herself. Clay sat on the porch. He found himself strangely unaffected by his mother's anger. Besides, she was also the one who made him read the Bible, which made him get frustrated, which made him rude. That was on her. And she had not told his father off and given back his LEGO collection even though she had also heard Mark call him a "little shit."

Clay would not act like he was the one who had done something wrong. There was nothing to be gained from accepting any more blame.

He heard the door open behind him.

"Get inside and bring your brother with you!" his mother's voice snapped like a whip. "I just told you that I was getting in the shower, and you know you can't be in the front yard unless I'm watching you."

Slowly, Clay stood and turned to face his mother. Every cell in his body felt like it was burning. This was beyond the scream, this feeling. It was so far beyond the scream that Clay felt a bit silly for ever having punched a wall over a little thing like a scream in his head.

This new feeling did not tear at him like the scream had, either. Instead, it galvanized his body, making him feel like he was made out of iron. His new metallic mind had thoughts about how to most efficiently return his mother's attitude to her. He could get himself a glass of milk and then follow her around talking until she accidentally elbowed him. Then he could dump it on her and she would think that she had made him spill. That would make her late without getting him in trouble. Or, he thought, he could obey her until he heard the shower start, and then he could take a kitchen knife outside and poke out all the tires on the car. If he did that, though, then he was pretty sure his father would be angry enough to hit him. Mark Dillon had never raised a hand to either of his children, but he told them all about how much he believed he had a right to do it. He also told them about how his own father, Grandpa Clifton, had whipped him in the front yard once for slapping Grandma Bayleigh.

Clay decided not to take a kitchen knife to the car's tires. He took a deep breath instead, and then he let his heavy metal legs march his armored body forward until he stomped past his mother and into the house.

❖   ❖   ❖

The Rules of the Game

"All right, Clay! Let's get your shoes on so we can go," the babysitter said.

Her name was Katrina, just like his mother's name. Instead of shortening it to "Kitty," though, Katrina liked people to call her by her full name.

Clay liked that about her.

"Where are we going?" he asked.

Katrina tousled his hair. She had only been alone with Clay for ten minutes, and it was the third time that had happened. Clay hated that about her, but then he corrected himself for feeling hate because it was unhealthy, like using the word "stupid." His mother said so.

He felt his skin turn to metal at the thought of his mother, but then Katrina's fingers in his hair turned it back to skin again.

"You're funny," she said. "Don't you remember telling your mom that you wanted to go to the library?"

"Yes, but I'm not used to getting what I want," Clay said.

Katrina laughed.

Clay felt himself turning to metal again, but he tried to resist it. This Katrina person was trying to give him his way, and he knew that it would be wrong to get mad at her for it, even if she *was* a chucklehead.

"Well? What are you waiting for?" she asked.

He wanted to tell her that he was waiting for his legs to turn back into flesh because he did not want to move while he was still metal. Unfortunately, he could feel that his tongue had also turned into metal, so anything he let it say would be sharp. Instead, he said nothing and just smiled so the babysitter would know he was listening.

Thankfully, she did not demand that he answer her. Instead she moved on to trying to convince A.J. that he needed to wear socks. Clay felt himself like her again, and his legs and tongue stopped being metal and became flesh.

He took a deep breath, and then he put his shoes on and gathered the books that he needed to return to the library.

◆   ◆   ◆

The five block walk was uneventful, other than the one moment when Clay was sure Mrs. Jenkins would order them back to the house. It happened just as they were turning the corner at the end of the street they lived on. Mrs. Jenkins came flying out of her house, holding her skirts up slightly so that she could run barefoot across her yard, and she set herself in Katrina's path while demanding to know what was happening and why Katrina had removed the boys from their home. After Katrina explained that she was taking them to the library so that A.J. would be able to listen to story time, Mrs. Jenkins nodded and allowed them to continue on their way.

Clay wondered why she was so nosy, but he did not have time to let himself turn to metal over it. They were on their way, and a short time later, he found himself jogging the last fifty yards through the park's forested path and up to the library's back door.

The library itself was small. It had once been a one-bedroom house, but now every inch of available space was packed full of books. He lost no time once they were inside—as soon as he saw that Katrina was busy talking to A.J., he slipped between the aluminum bookshelves that crowded what had probably been the sitting-room and stepped into the foyer where the new releases sat on a repurposed hope chest. Clay hoped to find *The Joy Luck Club* there. Patrick's mother had said he would need to get it from the library, after all.

It took him a little while to find it, but the library actually had three copies in stock. It had to be a great book if a town as small as theirs needed to stock more than one copy of it.

He grabbed one of the copies from the foyer and walked back into the library proper. Clay thought about picking out another couple of books for himself, but before he had a chance to go looking, one of the librarians spotted him and walked up to chat.

They always wanted to chat.

"So, did you find the book you wanted, Clay?"

He nodded.

"Which one did you get? We have quite a few new books out there."

Clay held up *The Joy Luck Club* so that the librarian could see it. "My friend's mom read it and she said that she really liked it, so I want to read it."

The librarian's face made a move that Clay did not understand.

"Don't worry," he said, "I know it's a new book and I'll take good care of it."

"I know you will," the librarian said. "I'm not worried about that. It's just... I don't know if you'll like that book, Clay."

"Patrick's mother says that it's about church and kids and Chinese people," Clay said. "I go to church and I'm a kid. Do you think there's something wrong with me reading about Chinese people?"

The librarian's whole head became red when Clay said that, so he held very still, keeping the book between them. He knew what happened when adults became very red: They sent you to bed without food, or else they started telling stories about why parents were right when they hit their kids. When it was his mom who got red, then it meant that all the food was going to be thrown away and she was going to scream so loud that there was no place in the house to hide from her yelling. When it was his dad who got red, it was usually the first event in a chain that ended with Clay being grounded, once again, for "sass."

The librarian did not do any of those things, though. Instead, she took a deep breath, and then she said, "You can't check that book out. I'm sorry."

"Why?" Clay could feel his body starting to harden. He hoped he could finish the conversation before he started to think about ways to get even with the librarian. He did not like the getting even thoughts that came with his new metal body.

"That's not a book for kids," she said.

"It's a book about kids."

"I know that, Clay. It's not a book for kids, though."

"So you're saying that people can just write about kids all they want, but kids should not look at what they have to say? Why? Is it wrong? Are the kids being hurt? Are the people writing these books evil?"

Clay knew that adults got mad when you asked them too many questions without letting them answer, but he could not stop himself. He had intended just to ask one question, but his mouth was hard to close because his jaw was becoming heavy with the metal feeling, and both of those things made his thoughts harder.

"It's not that there's anything wrong, Clay. It's just that there are some books that are complicated. This is one of them. You should probably wait until you're grown up to read it, because it's not just about kids, it's about how kids grow into adults."

Clay glared at the librarian.

"I know you can read a lot of adult books, but this one is not like a lot of adult books."

Clay tried to respond to the librarian's words, but all he could do was maintain his glare. His metal body was now fully formed, and he knew that if he moved, he might wind up hitting the librarian with the book. His brain showed him pictures of different ways the librarian might be hurt. It felt good to bathe his mind in them, but he worried about what would happen if he let himself move before the pictures went away, so he just glared.

Finally, the librarian sighed. "Fine. You want to know why you can't check the book out? It's because your mother said you can't. She called down here and told us that you might be in tonight, and she told us that you were only allowed to check out books from the children's section unless she was with you."

"Fine," Clay said. He lowered the book. "Nothing you can do about that."

He was proud of himself for not throwing a tantrum, but the revelation that his mother had intentionally gone out of her way to ruin his trip to the library, the only trip since school let out that she had been unable to ruin in person, made Clay's metal body heat up. He worried about how he was supposed to manage it now, since he could barely control it when it was cold and heavy. The new form felt powerful, but also loose, and he worried that if he moved too quickly the heat would make him come apart at the joints. Meanwhile, the violence in his mind kept churning, spinning itself up like a turbine. Instead of showing him things that he might do to get revenge, though, his brain started showing him ways that he might free himself from his parents, like maybe he would get lucky and they would die in a car crash while they were out tonight.

Clay waited for the shame and the guilt to wipe that thought away, but they did not come. Instead, his metal body started to cool down. To feel stronger again.

"I'm sorry, Clay," the librarian said. "I don't really know what you can and can't read. I just know you read a lot, and that your mother is very particular about what you pick out. Someday you'll be grown up, though, and then you can read whatever you want."

"I can read whatever I want right now," Clay said.

"I know, but what I mean is that your mother won't always be around to tell you what to do."

"That's what keeps me going," Clay said. Then he turned around and walked into the children's section. He still carried *The Joy Luck Club*. The librarian followed him.

"Clay, I can't check that out to you. It doesn't matter if you go to the children's checkout desk or not."

"I'm not going to the children's checkout desk," Clay said. Then he sat at a table in the children's reading room. "I'm going to sit here and read the book."

"Are you sure you want to do that?" the librarian asked.

"I'm not checking it out. Are you going to tell me I'm not allowed to sit and read?" Clay could hear the metal in his words. It flaked off his tongue and adhered to the sound of his voice, slipping into the syllables he formed and turning his childish demands into orders. He guessed that the librarian could hear it, too, because she shrugged and walked away, leaving him to enjoy the book.

The first chapter was about people meeting to play a game called mahjong. Clay had no idea what the game was, so he skipped that chapter. The next chapter was about a girl whose mother had left her alone and the ways that her family made her feel bad. Clay was not sure about how to feel about that chapter. He could see a lot of different things happening there. He felt like he would have been mad, too, if someone just parked a child with him and expected him to take care of it. At the same time, though, he could not imagine his Grandma Doris talking about his mother the way that the grandmother in the story talked about the little girl's mother.

Even though Clay knew that his mother had been a junior in high school when she got pregnant with him, he also knew that his mother's family had been supportive of her and had helped her because they always told him so. Grandma Doris told him at least once a month that he was not an accident, he was a gift. She had done this for as long as he could remember. If his family could overcome their ideas about having babies and sex and marriage to help his mother when she was pregnant with him, then why did the Chinese family in the story have to keep telling the child An-Mei that her mother was bad?

For the first time, Clay was aware that there were things in a story that he did not understand. He did not want to give up, though. After the way he had talked to the librarian, he felt obligated to work on reading the book. Clay worried that if he admitted to not being able to understand this book, then it would lead to even more extensive rules being put in place to restrict his reading choices. If, on the other hand, he managed to tease out the main ideas in this book, then he might have a chance at convincing the librarian that his mother was wrong and that he should have the right to read any book he chose to read.

He flipped back to the table of contents and read the title of every chapter. Most of them did not seem to be named in ways that made their plots immediately clear. He knew from the Bible and from reading a few books like *Childhood's End* that there were times when books were indirect, when the different themes they discussed were talked about in a kind of sideways-talk that only became apparent after you finished reading the whole thing. Something told him that this was a book like that. Still, knowing that he was missing an important element in the story did not help Clay to understand what that element was.

He looked at the first chapter again. It was about a game called mahjong. Once Clay read it all the way through, it was clear that the game itself was not the important action in the chapter. The important action was the fact that this was something the family did together. That, Clay could understand. After all, his whole family played Uno together, and even though it was a stupid game that depended way too much on luck, they all had fun. The game was not the important thing—the fact that people came together and played and talked was the important thing.

Still, it was obvious that the behavior of each of the people during the game *was* important. Clay guessed that all of the talk about the way the dead woman played was meant to tell him something about who she was. He did not know if he was right or not, though, because he did not understand the game. If he was right, then there was no way for him to interpret what the comments about her playing style meant. He went back to the table of contents, hoping to find a chapter that might explain mahjong more.

Right away, the first chapter in the second section of the book jumped out at him. It was called "Rules of the Game."

◆ ◆ ◆

As it turned out, "Rules of the Game" was not about mahjong at all. Instead it was about chess, and about a very intelligent girl and the ways that her family encouraged her and also reveled in her success. In some ways, Clay was reminded of his own family. His father had taught him chess, and he had bragged to his friends about it, because Clay was only six the first time they played.

His father had stopped bragging after the first time Clay beat him, though, and then their games turned grim and silent. Eventually, they stopped playing. Clay wondered what would have happened if they had not.

The girl in the story was nine when she started to play, and she became a genius champion in short order. Clay wondered how far he might have gone with more opponents, or at least more patient ones. He had managed to learn how to defeat his father without anyone tutoring him about different strategies, after all, and the girl in the story had the chance to study other players in depth. For Clay, the game was the movements of his pieces across the board as patterns with no names, and they teased and provoked and reacted in moments, not across great spans of turns. He sensed that this way of thinking made him very different from the girl in the story, but he did not have the words to explain it to himself.

There was one difference he did articulate to himself, though: If his parents ever actually took his chores away and made space for him to focus on doing just what he wanted to do, then he would not be ungrateful. He understood the girl's reaction to her mother's ownership of her success—one is inclined to want credit for one's labors, after all—but as someone who had to labor for the right to make his own choices, Clay envied the ease with which the Jong family made room for Waverly's talent and nurtured it. He wanted to slap her when she ruined that, and he was happy when Lindo Jong took her confidence away and made her schemes into something small and impotent. He wished that he understood how to do that to people in his own life, because it seemed like a useful talent.

He was looking in the table of contents for a chapter about Lindo when the lights blinked. He sighed and closed the book. Learning how to take someone's confidence and make their scheming petty would have to wait. He was not allowed to check this book out, and blinking lights meant that he only had five minutes to find a book and check out before they closed the checkout desk and started story time. He carried *The Joy Luck Club* with him as he set out in search of a book that he could take home. Clay barely had to glance at the shelves in the chapter book section of the children's library to realize that he would not be able to pick one out. His mind was still on chess and China and the secret wars between mothers and children, and he could not sweep those thoughts aside just because he was expected to make decisions. Luckily, the librarian saw him almost immediately and called him over to the check-out desk.

"I thought you might use up all your time reading," she said. "So I picked out a book for you. If you like it, then you can have it."

Clay smiled. First she had not yelled when he made her turn red, now this. He was starting to think the librarian liked him. She handed him a book that was quite a bit thicker than *The Joy Luck Club*. It was also shorter, in terms of height.

Clay stared at the two books, lost in contemplation about the various trim sizes and what they might mean. He also wondered why no one thought to standardize them.

"It's about children and war and patriotism," the librarian said as she gestured at the book, "and it's not really a kid's book, but since it started getting carried in the Scholastic catalog we've moved it out of the adult section." She winked at Clay after she finished talking.

Clay put aside his thoughts about paperback book sizes and looked again at the squat, thick volume in front of him. It was called *Ender's Game*. There was a spaceship on the cover.

He was sold.

"I want it," he said. "Let's check it out."

The librarian nodded and scanned the book before taking his card and scanning it. When she reached for *The Joy Luck Club*, though, Clay grabbed the book back from her.

"You know I can't check that out to you," the librarian said.

"Can I just keep reading until the end of story time?"

The librarian shook her head.

"Why?"

"I have to shelve all the books and lock up the adult side of the library while you're listening to story time," the librarian said. "I can't go home until I finish re-shelving all the books."

"So just make this one last," Clay felt himself starting to turn to metal again.

The librarian stayed cool. "If it was up to me, I would. Rules are rules, though, and we all have to follow them."

Clay nodded. He knew about rules. Life was nothing but an intersecting set of rules that other people inflicted on him. Since they each had different rules, sometimes he felt like he was expected to do two contradictory things at once. At other times, he felt bound by a set of rules even after the people who owned those rules were gone. All of the rules in life made it hard to know how to do anything. Still, they were rules for a reason, and until he got older and found out the reason, he was stuck with them.

His chest turned to metal while he thought about rules, and as his heart hardened he found himself thinking that rules were not real things, they were just ideas, and that what mattered was who had the book. For a moment, he thought about grabbing it and running. He might get into trouble, but he would at least get to read the Lindo Jong chapter. That might give him the chance to learn how to shame an enemy into making herself small.

Before Clay could act, the librarian picked up the book and walked away with it. Rules and reality fell into agreement with each other. Clay no longer had *The Joy Luck Club*.

He did have *Ender's Game*, though. He sat down to read it, wondering what it might reveal to him about parents and children and growing up.

❖   ❖   ❖

Sass and Sensibility

Clay was reading more from Psalms when his mother found him. Just knowing that *Ender's Game* was waiting after his daily Bible reading made Clay more capable of working through them. He had only barely scratched the surface of the new book, though. One thing that he did like, which jumped out at him immediately when he started to read, was the author's dedication to showing children as fully thinking and reasoning beings. When Ender fought with another child, he did so with a kind of gravity and understanding of consequences that made his decision to break the other child even harder to bear.

After that part of the book, Clay was ready to take a break and read Psalms. They continued to make very little sense to him, but the rhythmic repetition of the language present in the parallel constructions of their texts were calming. He found it possible to enjoy the act of processing them out loud without actually feeling compelled to pay attention to their content.

Clay was doing just that when Kitty Dillon broke into his concentration with an initial "harrumph" to announce her presence in his bedroom. He shut the Bible and turned over in his bed so that he could see his mother.

"I think we need to have a talk," she said.

Clay's heart dropped into his stomach.

"I heard from someone that you decided to ignore my wishes at the library. That you sat and read a book that you weren't allowed to check out."

"I didn't check it out, though," Clay said.

His mother scowled. "Don't be a smartmouth, Clay. I didn't come up here to bring you Joy, but I can still do it if that's what you want."

He shook his head.

"That's not an answer, Clay. Use your words."

"No!" Clay said.

"Without yelling," his mother replied.

Clay glared at her. The silence between them ripened.

"I said, 'no,'" Clay whispered.

His mother nodded. "I know you think I'm terrible for making you stop yelling at me, but you need to understand that you just can't do that. When you grow up and you try to get a job, you'll get fired if you yell at your boss. I'm teaching you how to fit into the world. To do things the right way."

Clay did not respond. He let his imagination play over the idea that everyone in the adult world was as aggravating as his mother. It made him want to bash his head into the wall, but he did not do that. Instead, he quietly asked his body to turn to metal, so that his mother's words would not be able to penetrate him. He had no idea whether he could control the metal feeling or not, but he did remember that he had been able to exert a level of influence over the scream, back before it melted and fused itself into his metal body. He glared at his mother and waited.

"I'm pleased to see that you're still keeping up your end of the agreement," she said.

Clay nodded. One of them had to stick to the agreement. He considered saying that, but found himself unable to form the words.

"I don't like you trying to work around my wishes, though," she said. "You just have to trust that I know what's best for you. Someday, things will be different. For now, though, you're a child and I'm a parent. I know what you're mature enough to read about. Trust me."

Clay's glare continued.

"I talked to the librarian. That's how I know about this. Don't go hating Katrina, because honestly, she did not know that I had put a restriction on your library card."

Clay blinked. Glaring was hard work, and the metal body was not forming over his muscles, so they were starting to ache from the way he held himself—rigidly, and as if he was restraining himself from jumping at his mother.

"Did you want to say something?" she asked.

"Depends. Will I be threatened again?" Clay surprised himself when he spoke those words, but he felt the metal in the word "threatened," and it gave him strength.

Kitty's eyes expanded after Clay spoke, and her lips became thin, but she did not yell or punish him. After a couple of seconds, he continued.

"I think you can't really tell me something is not good for me to read if you haven't read it, and I think that it's stupid to pretend every book in the adult section is too advanced for me. The book I wanted to read was about normal people who came to America, and about how their kids felt growing up. Is that not appropriate? Is it too—I don't know, whatever you don't like?"

"I don't know, Clay. As you pointed out, I did not know anything about that particular book."

Kitty's words shocked Clay. It was unlike her to admit fault. Then she kept talking.

"Here's the thing you're not understanding, though: I had no way of knowing whether you would pick an appropriate book or not. The adult section does have some good, wholesome books in it. It also has books that glorify war and death, and that make it seem like killing people is a good solution to life's problems. I had no way of knowing whether you would pick a good book about family or a bad book about drug dealers and shooting people. The only thing I could do, since I wasn't there, was to try to limit the choices you had, to remove the possibility that you would pick something that teaches you bad lessons. Do you understand?"

Clay wanted to scream that he understood that his mother was stupid because *Ender's Game* was all about the fact that it was right to kill people sometimes, and it was in the children's section. Then he remembered what the librarian had said—it was originally in the adult section, but they had moved it because there were a lot of kids reading it. He probably did not want his mother to look too closely at *Ender's Game*. It would be better to talk about *The Joy Luck Club* instead.

"What I understand is that you decided to punish me before I did anything wrong," he said. The metal in his words made them clang against each other. Clay hoped that his mother heard their meanings over the din.

"I don't understand," she said.

"We had an agreement about my reading the Bible," Clay said. "You said I could pick my own books out as long as I read it. I've been reading it, but you stopped letting me pick my own books out. Even though the book I picked for myself was about families and growing up and it had characters who were Christian and little kids in it and a lot of other stuff that's also in kids' books. First you agreed to let me choose for myself, then when I did and I chose something you should like, you used the excuse that I'm not old enough to choose for myself. So you punished me for breaking our agreement when I did not break it."

Something about his words felt wrong. He knew he was saying right things—true things—but they were not coming out smoothly. The metal inside each one made them clang together until they were lying lopsided against one another. Still, he was pretty sure that he had managed to get all the details in.

His mother shook her head like someone coming out of a daze.

"I don't even know what to tell you," she said.

Clay wanted to suggest that she tell him "I'm sorry," but he felt like that would be "sass," even if it was also true. He was not sure, but since most of the things he said to his parents when they were full of bullcrap wound up getting called "sass," he tried to not talk to them when they were like that. Sometimes, though, they just kept inflicting themselves on him.

Thankfully, this did not seem to be one of those times. After a long silent moment, Kitty Dillon spun on her heel and walked out of the room. She closed the door behind herself.

Clay wanted to follow her. He wanted to corner her in whatever private part of the house she retreated to when he actually managed to say things that she heard, and he wanted to take her by the shoulders and shout the truths she blithely ignored until she realized that he was not just a child, he was a person with desires and goals and a firm sense of his own needs. If he had been grown, he might have done such a thing. As it was, his need to push the confrontation with his mother into some form of resolution was tempered by the conviction that it would also lead to his father taking him outside and whipping his ass for "sass" like he always promised to do.

As Clay's metal body cooled and turned back into flesh, he promised himself that if he ever grew to his father's size, he would force the man to eat his own threats. Ender was correct—when faced with an enemy who wants to subjugate you, your only choices are to either be subjugated or to remove the presence of the enemy as quickly as possible. Rules only made war harder to win.

Clay threw the Bible across the room and opened his library book. He had no time for agreements that his mother kept breaking.

❖   ❖   ❖

Grandpa Harry Goes to the Twilight Zone

Normally, Clay liked to spend time at Grandpa Harry's house more than he liked being at home. Not only did Grandpa Harry refuse to yell at him, he actually congratulated Clay whenever he disappeared into a quiet room to read. Sometimes his grandfather asked him what his books were about, but he never asked Clay what they meant, and he never demanded that Clay explain why he would want to read a book, either.

Grandpa Harry understood things, and Clay understood that the reasons he understood things were the same as the reasons why he was frightening. He did not care, though, because when he was with his grandfather, it was obvious that the crazy house was not a punishment for anything you did, it was a punishment for who you *were*. At home with his parents, he feared his father's threats and his mother's condemnation. Here, seeing that Grandpa Harry was home and happy and no one was making him go back there, he understood that the crazy house would either happen someday or it would not.

Either way, there would be life after. Grandpa Harry proved it was so. This made him feel safe, and the gentle encouragement he received made him feel welcome. Most of the time, his aunts and uncles that still lived at home also made him feel welcome. Not today, though. Today, Clay's youngest aunt (Marci) was torturing him with the television. It was bad enough that she came home and took the remote control off the table and started randomly changing channels in the middle of Clay's show. He accepted that as a natural part of the world. Between the fact that he liked to play with toys while he watched television and the fact that sometimes he had to look out the window to understand what the characters on the shows were talking about, he knew that people would assume he was not paying attention to what was on the screen. They did it all the time.

What bothered Clay was that when Marci stepped on his fun *today*, she kept trying to watch things that he was not allowed to watch, like MTV. When Clay protested, she would change the channel over to something boring and stupid, like Sally Jessy Raphael. Invariably, Sally Jessy (who looked an awful lot like Grandma Doris and wore the same kind of glasses) would start talking about cheating husbands or pregnant teenagers, and then Clay would have to yell at Aunt Marci because his parents thought sex stuff should not be on television. It had been happening all day.

Clay had not only been through this with Sally Jessy, but with Donahue (whose show Kitty Dillon liked, just not when her son was around), Geraldo, and *Days of Our Lives*. It was clear that Marci knew what he was and was not supposed to watch, and he was starting to suspect that she was only doing what she was doing to try to make him stop watching television.

There was no way that he was going to let that work. He knew from reading *Ender's Game* and the books of the Maccabees that he had to strike quickly when his aunt was not looking, and that his action had to end with her not wanting to be in the room any more. He felt his body turning to metal as he visualized his plan.

Normally, he did not like to antagonize Aunt Marci because she always played with him, even when her friends were around. She was also the only other person in the family who understood Grandpa Harry. Still, she would not stop messing up the television, and that had to be addressed. There were no other kids on the street that were Clay's age and he had already finished reading the book he brought with him. If Aunt Marci chased him away from the television set he would have nothing to do except read the encyclopedia, and he had already read the encyclopedia twice.

More accurately, he had read the Childcraft books twice. He had no interest in the thicker, darker World Book Encyclopedia set that his grandfather liked to casually thumb through in the evenings. Its articles were boring, and most of them were about things that Clay did not care about, like types of ocean barges and exotic kinds of musical instruments. The Childcraft books were better because they covered mathematic principles, dinosaurs, and folklore, but he did not feel like reading the Childcraft books today. Today, he felt like watching Nickelodeon, because they played several hours of *Danger Mouse* and *Count Duckula* back-to-back, and when Nickelodeon stopped being good, the *Teenage Mutant Ninja Turtles* would be on Fox. He did not have the patience for Marci's music videos and grossout talk shows.

Besides, she had a driver's license. She could leave and do things in the world if she got bored. Clay was stuck in the house. It took a long time, and he watched several scenarios in his mind that all ended with him in trouble, but eventually Clay saw how he was going to get the television back. He waited until Grandpa Harry came upstairs from his home office to get a glass of soda. While his grandfather was within earshot, he asked a question as loudly as possible.

"What kind of shirt is Madonna wearing here?"

In the video Marci was watching, Madonna was not wearing a shirt. She was wearing some kind of black nightie or underwear, and she was dancing for people who were watching her from inside glass booths. Clay did not know what that was all about, but he knew that Grandpa Harry did not like his kids watching videos of people in their underwear.

Sure enough, Grandpa Harry came out of the kitchen and into the living room to see what Madonna was, in fact, wearing.

"Aw, kids, come on," he said. "We don't need to have this on. Marci, you know better."

"I have this album upstairs," she replied. "You bought it for me."

"Go play it then," Grandpa Harry said. "We already talked about what this is. You shouldn't have done this."

"She's going to make him weird," Marci shot back.

"She's already made him," Grandpa Harry said, "and it's all of our jobs to help him out. Right, Clay?"

Clay looked his grandfather square in the forehead and nodded.

"It's okay if she doesn't want to watch Nickelodeon with me, but she shouldn't be watching things that I'm not supposed to watch," he said.

"I'm on lunch break anyway," Grandpa Harry said. "Why don't we all watch something together? They usually rerun *The Twilight Zone* about now."

Marci made an "ugh" noise, but Clay smiled. He did not always understand *The Twilight Zone*, but it always entertained him. The people on that show saw frightening things that the rest of their friends and families could not understand. It felt like the kind of show that might teach him something.

Grandpa Harry took the remote from Aunt Marci and changed the channel over to WGN. Sure enough, the opening theme to *The Twilight Zone* was just starting.

Clay wondered if Grandpa Harry had actually been coming upstairs to take over the television anyway. For all he could tell, his comment had just given his grandfather an opportunity. He wished he had some way of knowing for sure if that was true. Should he assume Grandpa Harry meant to do what he did no matter what? Or was Clay discovering some kind of magic super-ability like Ender's strategic mind? He was already able to beat his own father at chess, after all.

"Clay, aren't you going to watch TV with me?"

Grandpa Harry's voice broke into Clay's stream of thought, shattering the imaginary vision of Mark Dillon crouched over a chessboard, sweating, his finger hovered above the board, twitching back and forth as he tried to decide whether or not it was time to tip his king on its side.

"Clay. Let's have a seat on the couch. Do you want a sandwich?" Grandpa Harry was looking right at him.

"No," Clay said. "Let's just watch the TV." He climbed up onto the sofa next to his grandfather and watched as the episode opened up. It was in color, so Clay knew that it was the new version, not the one that they played at four in the morning on Nick at Night. He was glad for that. The old episodes were okay, but they were boring compared to the new ones with their special effects and puppetry. The new episodes were like *Beetlejuice*, except that Mark Dillon did not get mad when he caught his sons watching them.

Clay let himself be pulled into the show. It did not happen often for him, not like it did for most of the rest of the family, but when it did happen, he forgot he had a body, and for a moment he was able to float along like God in the television, watching and judging the affairs of the mortals who could not sense his entry into their domain.

Today's episode was about a father and son who moved to a cabin in the woods. Shortly after they moved in, the little boy (Jeff) started seeing another boy in the woods. Eventually, they met and became friends. The twist was that the boy from the woods had originally been Jeff's father's imaginary friend, back when Jeff's father was a child. This was revealed, the father confronted the boy from the woods and told him to leave Jeff alone, and that's when it was revealed that the boy from the woods was actually some kind of alien or angel or something else that just looked like a white light.

"That was stupid," Clay said at the end.

"Just because you didn't like it, that doesn't mean it was stupid," Grandpa Harry said. "It just means you didn't like it."

"But imaginary friends *are* stupid," Clay said. "Everyone likes to pretend that they're real and that lots of kids have them, but they're not. I've never known anyone who had an imaginary friend. It's just like Santa. Everyone likes to pretend that little kids believe in Santa, but we don't. We say we do because we know how the system works, but we don't really believe. Maybe some toddlers do. The rest of us don't."

"Well," Grandpa Harry said, "the rest of your friends don't. You don't know how other kids are. You don't even know all the other kids in your class."

"No, but I know that they aren't stupid," Clay said. "Quit being condescending about this."

"Can you tell me what the word condescending means?" Grandpa Harry asked.

Clay scowled at him and glared. When he realized that Grandpa Harry had not just told a sophisticated joke, he opened his mouth to reply...

... and found that he had no words. He knew what he was looking for, because he had heard the word a lot and he had managed to figure out what people did that got them called condescending, but this kind of understanding was not a thing he had words to explain. Still, if he did not say *something*, then Grandpa Harry was going to keep being condescending until he did.

Clay decided that if he could not find the words for a definition, he would point to an example instead.

"It means the way my dad treats my mom whenever the long distance bill comes," Clay said.

Grandpa Harry laughed. Then he reached over and swatted Clay on the knee.

"Okay, kid," he said. "You know what it means."

"I didn't like the episode," Clay said.

"Okay," Grandpa Harry said. "But you do like Calvin and Hobbes, and that's about a boy with an imaginary friend."

Clay shook his head. He wanted to yell at Grandpa Harry, but he knew that it would be wrong.

"What?" Grandpa Harry asked. Then he elaborated. "Calvin imagines Hobbes is talking to him and you're old enough to know that he really isn't. It's just Calvin's imagination. Heck, the cartoon *shows* it. No wonder your generation doesn't believe in Santa Claus."

It was not the same. Clay knew it was not the same, but he could not make himself say why, so he did not let himself say anything.

Grandpa Harry looked at him out of the side of his face.

"Well?" he asked.

Finally, Clay found the words to say, "But Hobbes is real. Calvin might be imagining all the personality stuff and talking to himself, but he really does have a stuffed tiger. He's not just imagining the stuffed animal. He's only imagining the part where the animal talks. That makes it okay."

Grandpa Harry grinned. "Oh that makes it okay, does it? I'll make sure to tell my doctor." Then he got up from the couch and went back downstairs to his office.

Clay wondered if Grandpa Harry had just been trying to joke with him, or if something else had happened. He was very confused. He was even confused about why he was confused. He knew he was right, though. People who had imaginary friends could not be real. Pretending that the thin air was some kind of intelligence was too silly a game for there to really be people that spent their lives playing it.

Right?

❖   ❖   ❖

Decades of Patience

Clay was liking *Ender's Game* so far. Not only did it move quickly and assume children to be capable intellectual beings, it also played with a lot of ethical questions. Ender seemed to constantly weigh his choices and actions against the expectations of his teachers and parents, and while it seemed odd that every moral choice he made resulted in his being permitted to be violent, it was very easy to see how the boy drew his conclusions. After all, it did seem like everyone in his life was banding together to tell him that what he was doing was the right thing. They constantly rewarded his behavior, referred to him as strong and ingenious, and talked about his ability to decide to kill as a gift. It was not hard to see how it was that those things would help him to accept his own nature and to find a way to explain to himself why he was right to do what he did. It was much harder to find a way to identify with him, though. Clay was not, by nature, one to pick fights. He much preferred to retreat, so that he could pursue his own projects without being encumbered by the expectations of others. Fighting was a protracted waste of time an energy that made one miss out on the opportunity to accomplish one's goals.

At least, that was what he had always thought before, even when he tried to follow his father's horrible advice about bullies and fighting. Ender helped him to see why it was that he needed to fight sometimes, though. Through the boy's story, Clay was able to accept that there would be times when he could not run, when his ability to live as he wanted to live would be threatened. At those times, the book warned, he would need to be prepared to set aside his normal rules of conduct in order to do what was necessary to preserve himself and his goals. Ender also taught him how to know when those times were happening. Unfortunately, it seemed like they were nearly always happening.

He did not notice as he read that Ender's criteria for determining the application of force were all extroverted. Not once did the boy truly reflect on the choices made unless circumstance forced it through conversation. Nor did the question of proportionality ever rise in the Clay's mind as he read. It certainly did not form a major theme in the text, so the fact that Ender viewed force as the end of diplomacy and not a part of it washed over and through him uninterrupted. The concept of overwhelming force, as presented in the novel, was just too logical for the universe to be otherwise.

If one's obligation was only to one's own side in a battle, then the most moral use of force *had to be* the one that minimized damage to your side. You couldn't think about the other side.

Clay could tell that was true because his metal body woke up and made him feel strong and warm when he thought about it. The more he tempered his anxiety in its own molten glee, the easier it became to keep his words, so the message had to be true.

He would warm himself with Ender's embers.

Clay let himself repeat "Ender's embers" out loud a few times. He liked it, so he started singing it to a tune he made up as he went along. The song and the syllables made time go away, and Clay let himself drift in the narrative. The next thing he knew, his mother's voice was nearby, laughing. When he looked up, he saw her in the open doorway. She held herself against the threshold, to keep herself from being knocked over by her own guffaws.

Clay felt his metal body harden again.

"I don't laugh at you when you repeat the lines to *Little House on the Prairie*," he said, "even though you get them wrong."

Kitty Dillon stopped laughing.

Clay smiled.

"I can laugh at you all I want, I had to clean your shit out of your pants for two years," she said. "When I get old and you have to change my adult diaper, then you can laugh at me all you want. Until that day, you remember who's who."

Her words glanced sideways and rang hollow when they made contact with his metal body, and Clay could see that she truly did fear getting old because she assumed that he would do something horrible to her.

When he replied to his mother, daggers shot from the end of Clay's tongue and he could feel razor blades in his throat.

"Don't you *ever* assume that I would stoop to doing something just because you would," he said. "That's not right."

Kitty stormed over to him and stood above his bed, staring down.

Looking up at her, Clay could not see anything but her distant face and the frame of her hair at the end of her long body.

"Don't you forget who the parent is, either. I'm still big enough to put you under that faucet and wash you out," she said.

Clay heard himself speak without knowing in advance what he was going to say.

"Do it then!" he screeched. "Just fucking do it! You won't change me because you can't wash out what's already clean. Someday I'll get that chance to abuse you back because you will be *old*."

Clay grabbed himself by the throat when he finished speaking. For a moment, he thought he might have cut himself. Then he noticed that his mother was staggering away from the bed and turning back toward the door.

As Kitty Dillon ran away, she listed to one side like a wounded animal. For some reason, as Clay watched her go, he was reminded not of *Ender's Game* and its philosophical rationalization of force, but of *The Joy Luck Club* and its winds and hidden dangers.

"Lindo," he said to himself.

"Ender Lindo," he sang. Then he started to mix it up. "Ender's embers. Lindo's windows. Linder's winders. Endo's embos..."

He kept going as he picked his book back up.

◆   ◆   ◆

Kitty Dillon stormed down the stairs and into the kitchen, cursing under her breath. Almost as soon as she started sputtering obscenities, though, she started chastising herself for doing it. She did not want to be the kind of person who would curse at her own son, even under her breath. Parenthood required more than that. Still, between Clay's uncanny, fixed glare and his brother's rampaging temper tantrums, she felt like nothing she did made any difference.

Kitty stopped everything and forced herself to breathe. She knew she made a difference, and she took a moment to tell herself so. Her chest tightened against her resolve. She felt like she was lying to herself, but she knew that she was not.

Without a thought, she dropped to her knees. The cold tile hurt her shins, but it also drew the frustration and anger out of her limbs, leaving a chilling tranquility. She said a "Hail Mary" prayer.

The anxiety receded a little. She said it exactly eight more times, followed by an "Our Father."

It hardly mattered that the rosary her mother had given her at confirmation was upstairs in its leather pouch. Kitty held it in her mind, and her fingers recalled the well-worn texture of its cocoa beads. At the end of the second decade, when she remembered the proper finish was a *Glory Be*, she felt like herself again.

When the anxiety and the vulgar thoughts caught up with her, Kitty Dillon always relied on the rosary to set things right in her mind. No matter the problem, it was always there for her: When her father made her drive him to the liquor store because he was too drunk (she had been twelve); when her friend Samantha had talked her into chewing a hunk of Red Man tobacco and she had accidentally swallowed it while trying to hide it from the teacher (third grade); when her period had not come and she had made the lonely trip to the drug store, knowing the truth all the while and dreading it anyway—that she would be pregnant and it would result in a son (at the age of sixteen)...

She could see, in Clay's behavior, a dangerous tendency that she had always felt in herself as well, and she wished he would realize her guidance and her religious instruction were meant to help him manage it. She made it work for her, she married the father of her firstborn son and their small family lived in one of the more genteel blue collar suburbs that ringed Grand Rapids. The rosary worked. Trust in God worked. Repetitive behavior and quiet time alone worked. It was just a matter of helping Clay to see that. The hard part was trying to convince him to listen, because he *was* right. He was a temperamental, rude little shithead, but...

Kitty took a deep breath and said another decade.

Clay's dignity was right to be wounded, she told herself. She had done something that belittled him. And when it came to the books, he had lived up to his side of their deal, just like he said. He even made sure that he was choosing a positive, moral kind of story to read for himself, and she had overreacted because she did not trust him.

No, he just thought she did not trust him. She chastised herself for slipping into Clay's frame of reference. Mark always pointed out that she did that, and that it didn't do the kids any good for their parents to indulge them. She needed to worry less about whether her son had a point and more about how she was going to recover enough credibility to convince him that she really did know what was right for him.

She thought about the fact that when she asked about what *The Joy Luck Club* was, the librarian suggested that they read it together. Kitty could not even keep up with the progress that the boy was making in his Bible, though, let alone keep pace with his appetite for other literature. Nor did she totally understand his interests—space and robots one day, but then family dramas and folklore the next. It all seemed so scattered, and when she managed to ask him about what he was reading and why, he always seemed so sure of his choices and so offended at having them scrutinized. It was hard not to think that he was up to something. She hoped that someday he would figure out how to exercise his need for privacy without...

Without what? she asked herself. *Without acting like...*

Kitty Dillon did not like any of the suggestions her brain was giving her for the rest of that sentence, so she refused to finish it. Instead, she prayed another decade and tried not to think of anything but the stained glass image of the blessed heart in the memorial windows on the west side of St. Jude's. It was her childhood church, and her parents were still members, so she knew the stained glass that lined its sunward wall well.

◆ ◆ ◆

Ender was just getting to know his squad when Kitty Dillon walked back into Clay's room, and for just a moment as Clay heard and smelled his mother's presence but before he turned to look at her, it seemed almost as if she was striding through Ender's barracks on the space station.

The weird overlap in his perception blipped out of existence when he closed the book and looked up.

"I've decided that I was unfair," Kitty Dillon started.

Clay smiled. She held up a finger at him. Then she continued.

"I have been nervous about keeping my end of the bargain, because it wasn't really my end. Your father was the one who said you should be able to read whatever you want if you also read the Bible. I want you to enjoy your reading, but I believe that you should be talking through the things you read and comparing your thoughts to someone else's. This is what we do in Bible study, and it's what you need to do when you read books above your grade. To help you with this, I've decided to read an adult book with you. It's one I've already read, so we can talk about it as you go. It is called *The Screwtape Letters*, and it is a book that was very important to me as a teenager."

"What's it about?" Clay asked. He liked the idea that he was going to be able to read something that his own mother had not understood until she was a teenager.

"It's about sin and temptation, and the difference between good and evil. The main characters are demons."

Clay's eyes went wide when she said that last bit. Somehow, she had a hard time with nice aliens who looked like demons (in *Childhood's End*), but she did not see anything wrong with reading a book whose main characters were actual demons. She hated the idea of his reading a book about Chinese families (*The Joy Luck Club*), but she totally ignored the science fiction book that was all about how and when to commit yourself to exterminating your enemies (*Ender's Game*). He had no idea what motivated his mother, but he was excited by the idea that she wanted to read something that seemed so... fun... after trying to stick him with the Little House books for so long.

♦ ♦ ♦

Kitty Dillon's smile warmed as she watched her son's appreciation and excitement break in waves across his face. He would see—he would come to understand the forces she was working to protect him from, because now he was going to start to read about them, and she would be there to guide him. Mark was wrong about turning the boy loose in the library to fend for himself. All that did was lead to his reading novels that no one else had read, which would isolate him. The only way to make sure her son was understanding what he was reading was to guide him through it, and that meant that you had to be able to commit to reading what he read. The librarian was right about that.

That was why it only made sense to have Clay reading things that she had already read and understood. That woman had meant well, when she suggested that the two of them debate the books he read, but the idea that the debate should not have a predetermined course was unsettling, and Kitty suspected it could be morally hazardous.

No, she told herself as she hugged her son, *this is better. Infinitely better.*

❖   ❖   ❖

Pig Pen is Happier than Linus

The sun was bright enough to hurt Clay's eyes, but the day itself was not too hot, so he did not mind being outside. He did wish, though, that his back yard had a tree he could sit under. It received plenty of shade from the mature elms and maples in his neighbors' yards, but all of those trees were on the other side of the fence that surrounded his parents' property, so he could not climb them without getting permission to leave the yard, and he did not want to bother his mother in order to get that permission.

She had been very mean when she shut him out of the house. She had told him not to even bother trying to talk to her until she called him in for lunch.

Normally, he would just disobey her. She caught him at it so rarely that enduring one punishment every ten or eleven times he ignored her wishes hardly seemed like a consequence at all. Today was different, though. Today, A.J. was in the back yard with him. Clay knew it would be a bad idea to leave the four-year-old alone, and he also knew that A.J. was too unpredictable for it to be safe to bring him outside of the fence. He kicked a clod of dirt in frustration.

A.J. played in the sand box. Occasionally, the younger boy waved at Clay, and then when Clay looked over at him, A.J. would destroy whatever he had just built and laugh wildly. After the third or fourth time, it stopped being amusing.

Clay understood his brother well enough to know that A.J. wanted him to come and play, but the sand box was out in the sun, and he did not want to leave the shady corner of the yard where he could walk around without squinting, and he liked being able to kick clods of dirt in the vegetable patch that their parents never got around to planting. Sometimes, he felt guilty about not wanting to play with his brother. He knew A.J. did not have real friends because he was not in school yet, and this meant all the other children he socialized with were being babysat by their mother. He understood how that could make one desperate, because he remembered how much fear and loneliness he had felt before he started first grade and met Aaron and Patrick. At the same time, though, A.J. liked to hit people, and not just when he was upset. Sometimes, he just hit people for no reason and then laughed about it.

Unless they hit him back.

That was what Clay had done the last time A.J. bit him, and his brother retaliated by biting so hard on Clay's arm that the welt he left stayed for a week. After it finally faded away, he waited until A.J. called him a name, and then Clay bit him so hard on the stomach that the bloody ring he left around the four-year-old's belly button looked like some kind of wicked tattoo. When he did that, his brother cried so much that their mother came and saw what happened, and then she washed Clay's mouth with Joy. He was glad for that, for once—the taste of his brother's flesh displeased him. The incident taught him it was futile to try to use A.J.'s own tactics against him. The other boy's age and reputation armored him against the consequences of his own violence, and for some reason Clay was expected to meet his brother's aggravation with passivity unless he wanted to be singled out for torment.

As Clay knew from reading *Ender's Game*, the situation was set up in such a way that his only option for dealing with A.J. was killing him. If the other boy was dead, then the only side of the story would be Clay's side. His parents would have to listen when he told them about all the times that A.J. had hit him, kicked him, bit him, or destroyed his things. He did not want to kill his brother, though. He just wanted the boy to go away forever and never be a part of his life again. The killing itself was too repugnant for him to actually do it, no matter how hard his metal body became.

To Clay, that was the weakness in Ender's philosophy—it did not lend itself well to people who simply did not want killing to be an option. In fact, the book preached against trusting one's own tastes or emotions, warning that they would be used as weapons by the enemy. He could certainly see how that was true, since A.J. had managed to turn the tables on him and get him in trouble for biting, even though their parents had never believed biting to be a serious offense when he had done it himself.

Clay had been too angry to see the way the situation might play out in A.J.'s favor before, and that had been his mistake.

Recalling that fight made him angry at his brother, and he knew that he should not be angry at A.J. for something that had happened a long time ago, so the anger soon faded into shame. He tried to shake the feeling by dragging his feet through the dirt like a plow and letting the warm earth pack him in tight. Its pressure against his shins was soothing, and its heat felt like the dry version of a warm bath. He stood there basking in that feeling until he got bored. Then he started thinking about books again, and eventually, his mind turned to *The Screwtape Letters*. Clay did not really want to think about them any longer, but since his mother was still working on finishing the book, he was forced to keep revisiting them whenever she finished a chapter.

What made him view the whole enterprise of reading *The Screwtape Letters* with contempt was the fact that his mother talked about each of the letters at length as if their meaning was something that had to be slowly uncovered and worked through, when in fact C.S. Lewis was blunt about the facts of the devil's tactics and what they meant. He also wrote in a fast-paced way that made the words slide over and through Clay like the patter of a carnival barker, so the fact that Kitty was only just at the seventh letter after a week of reading was making it hard for Clay to take her seriously when she pretended to know more about the text than he did.

He had tried going back to re-read the chapters at his mother's pace after he finished the book, but the shine had worn off them, and he realized that once he knew what to expect from Screwtape's wit, the story had no heart. The "patient" whose soul the demons were after did not seem to be anything more than a cardboard person with no real sense of his own self, and the moral lessons they expounded were all things that Clay had heard in Sunday School well before he was even in the first grade.

He wondered why it was that his mother would not just talk about the book, as a whole, since he was done with it and she claimed to have already read it.

The fact was that if Clay had been allowed to discuss the points in the book that he did actually find interesting—like the idea that the mass human sacrifice of war was actually something that brought glory to God—then he might have enjoyed the process of reading more, even if he did not enjoy the book. As it was, he was forced to keep his thoughts on what those things meant to himself, because his mother's ideas about what it was supposed to mean were ploddingly dull and she persisted in chewing them over repeatedly, even though she had not found anything new to say since the third letter.

When Clay stopped hating the book long enough to think about how it fit in with the other things he was reading, he found himself struck by the fact that C.S. Lewis (and not Screwtape) seemed to agree with Ender's tutors on the subject of war, saying it was actually a good and moral thing. To Clay, it seemed absolutely repulsive to say that giving up on everything that made life safe and happy in order to protect those same things that one was destroying was a "good." It might be necessary, as Ender said it was. It might be a choice between burning society to the ground and dying, the way that a lot of war movies said. What it could not be, though, was "good." To Clay, any book that equated war with "good," even a book full of sideways talk from pretend demons, was fundamentally flawed. What Screwtape missed but Ender realized was the phenomenal *burden* of having to defend yourself. Clay was wary about the way that the adults in Ender's world manipulated him. It was obvious that even though Ender loved the war games, he did not actually love war. He described his attitude toward battle in terms of necessity, but he did not talk about God or humanity or how war provided people with a chance to be good.

One thing that seemed obvious to Clay, but that his mother seemed uninterested in discussing, was the fact that even if the things Screwtape said were not meant to be believed by the reader as true, they still had to occur to the writer. This truism, while obvious, opened new ideas up to Clay. For example, the fact that C.S. Lewis talks about the temptations Wormwood inflicted on his "patient" as if they were a running monologue of whispers, like a voice in the man's head, might mean that C.S. Lewis himself had thoughts that talked to him when he wished they would not. It was interesting to Clay that these thoughts would be attributed by Mr. Lewis to a demon. Clay did not have whispers running through his mind unless he stopped to think about something, like he was doing just then. At that point, he heard voices that discussed his thoughts so that he could ask himself questions. At those times, the voices always sounded different, but they were always recognizable. Sometimes Clay heard his father. Other times, it was Captain Picard. Or Tom Brokaw. It was always a voice he knew from his memory, though, and it always said things that were related to what he was thinking about consciously.

Clay wondered if Screwtape and Wormwood were meant to be the voices Mr. Lewis heard in his head. If so, then Clay wondered how many of the people he saw every day had voices in their heads talking to them all the time, even when they were not thinking. He was pretty sure that Grandpa Harry had to have them, because he had heard that voices in your head were a sign of being crazy. Still, C.S. Lewis was not crazy. His mother called the man a great thinker. If these kinds of threatening, petty temptations were constantly whispered to *him*, then what did it mean when someone went crazy from the voices? Was it because the voices were particularly bad in that person's head, or just that they were particularly sensitive to the patter? And what did it mean for Clay, that he did not hear voices unless he chose to? These were things that he wished he could discuss with his mother, but when he tried to, she always shut him out and focused on what she called "the morals in the story."

Clay wondered if that was because she heard the voices or if it was because she didn't. Either way, it seemed wrong that she would not talk to Clay about these ideas. She had told him that the point of this was for him to talk about his ideas as he read, but all they ever talked about were her ideas, and her ideas were just literally the same ones that were said out loud in the book. He thought that this would probably have been okay if they had been reading a book that he picked out. Then, it would have been fair for his mother to decide what they would talk about while they read, because at least they would both be responsible for part of the situation. He put his mother out of his mind. She had said that she did not want to deal with him until lunch, so he was going to stop dealing with her until that time, too. Continuing to let her behavior frustrate him would be unproductive.

◆   ◆   ◆

As he paced the yard, he kept one eye on his brother, occasionally shouting encouragement when one of A.J.'s sand castles exploded particularly well. Clay kept thinking about voices and thoughts and demons, too. He decided that whatever voice C.S. Lewis attributed to a demon was probably the same voice that made Grandpa Harry think people really had imaginary friends. The more Clay thought about it, the more it made sense. It made sense, too, that if people like Grandpa Harry heard voices regularly, then they would expect other people to hear them too.

Suddenly, he felt very anxious about the fact that he had admitted not believing there were really people who had imaginary friends. The memory suddenly made him feel naked, and he wondered whether he would be able to talk to his grandfather without having the feeling every time. He also felt very much the size and shape of the world in the thought, and in the sensations that coursed through and over him as he contemplated it. He thought about exactly how far up the clouds were, and about how quickly he would become invisible if an observer were rising into the sky over him. In that same moment, he felt the full weight of knowing there was something that the adults in his life understood as a basic part of their existence, and that it was something he simply could not comprehend experiencing.

A.J. exploded a sand castle and giggled like a baby.

"Let's ask Mom if we can ride bikes!" he shouted.

"Not now!" Clay shouted back. "She told us not to ask for anything until lunch."

"When is lunch?" A.J. asked.

"It's whenever she decides it is."

A.J. nodded then, as if he understood exactly how this whole system worked, but he could not be bothered to feel any certain way about it. Then he began loading his bucket up with more sand.

Clay wondered about the fact that his brother was always so happy. His own early childhood had always seemed lonely and full of the boredom of waiting for something while the adults around him enjoyed themselves. A.J., on the other hand, always found joy in something, even if it was just hurting someone else. Loneliness did not seem to touch him, not unless he was left in bed too long during nap time or something like that. Then and only then did Clay see his brother cry from exasperation and destroy his own toys. He wondered if A.J. had whispers in his head keeping him company all the time. It seemed like a good enough reason for the differences between them.

"Hey A.J.," he called out. "Do you talk to yourself? Like, in your head?"

"I talk to myself out loud," the younger boy replied. "I talk all the time. I just like to talk."

"Do you ever make up an imaginary friend to talk to?" Clay asked.

"Well yeah," A.J. replied. "I'm not crazy like you and Grandpa."

The words hurt, but they did not make Clay angry. He was too surprised to find out that A.J. knew he did not have an imaginary friend of his own, and that the boy was also aware of what had happened to Grandpa Harry.

Clay wondered for the first time what was happening inside his brother. For Clay, the knowledge that people around him might be hurt by something he wanted to say would often cause him to be unable to speak. A.J., on the other hand, seemed to delight in provoking and then observing anger.

He turned his back on his brother and thought for a while about imaginary friends. If most people heard voices whisper to them, and if there were actually a large number of them who really had conjured up companions out of nowhere, then what did it mean that he had not? Was this just a skill that he had never developed because no one taught him? Or was it something he simply could not do?

Maybe if I make up an imaginary friend I will stop being crazy, he thought. Maybe A.J. was trying to help me by telling me what to do.

Usually, Clay did not look to his younger brother for advice, but this topic was much harder for him to think about than most other topics were, so he was inclined to listen to anything that anyone said about it. He summoned up a reserve of whatever energy it was that he usually put into stories and writing assignments at school, and he focused it all on trying to see a person standing in front of him.

Almost immediately, it occurred to him that he had to know what the person looked like in order to try to visualize him. Clay closed his eyes and thought about what he wished his friend looked like—himself, but a little less skinny, his hair slightly darker (still blonde, but not the white-blonde that it was—he wanted it to be a yellowish-brown), and green eyes instead of blue. He toyed with the idea of making his friend grown so that he could have tattoos and facial hair, but in the end he decided to keep his imaginary companion a child. He wanted to make sure that the constant visualization of his new friend did not put a strain on his concentration at school.

Having fully visualized the friend, Clay opened his eyes. The image wavered, like his imaginary castle had wavered, but eventually it stabilized. He was happy about that. He tried talking to his friend, but he could not make words come out of the vision's mouth. It was too hard to hold on to the visual while speaking, so when Clay made a sound, the image of his new friend disappeared. Eventually, he hit on the idea of listening to his friend instead of trying to make him talk. Unfortunately, he could not keep his new friend's voice from sounding like people he knew from the TV. He also could not hear the words like they were real words. They stayed inside his head, the way that thoughts did.

After a while, Clay stopped trying. It was tiring, and was sure that he would not enjoy the outcome if the effort was going to be so draining. It was not fair. Everyone else seemed to take this for granted, and besides, he felt uneasy about the judgment of people who admitted that they heard the whispers and hints of some strange other pushing them to do things.

He looked over his shoulder at his brother.

"Did you hurt yourself?" A.J. asked.

"A little," Clay called out.

"Do you need mom?"

"No," Clay said. Then he turned and walked back to his brother. He had to accept that people were like they were. He knew that. He also knew the people around him were no different now than they had been before. It was just that before, Clay had not known that they were all having private conversations with their voices. It was the knowledge he had gained that he found frightening, and he tried to tell himself that, but even his little brother loomed large for a moment, like the demented rabbit in the *Twilight Zone* movie or the boy who could send people to the corn field.

Eventually, Clay concluded that if most people knew the voices were imaginary, then they would just treat them like a diversion or a fleeting thought. It would be no different for them than his visualizations were for him. And who knew? Maybe those people lacked some of his own perceptions. Maybe none of them had metal bodies that protected them when they needed to be determined, or picture maps in their heads to hold together all the things that they had learned. Also, he knew that none of them had screams in their heads.

Clay looked at his brother again.

A.J. was just putting the finishing touches on a new castle. It ran the entire width of the sandbox and stood up high enough that its tallest spires reached to Clay's waist. He wondered at how his brother could make such a large castle so quickly. Maybe his voices organized things for him so that he could just follow directions, the way that Clay's visual maps helped him. Maybe A.J. was just good at sandcastles.

A.J. pointed to the castle and beamed. Clay clapped for him. Then A.J. jumped into the castle, thrashing and laughing in his own cloud of dust as he reduced it to a blurry impression in seconds. At the end, A.J. sat up and declared: "Pig Pen is happier than Linus."

❖   ❖   ❖

What Will the Neighbors Think?

Clay paced in his room. He had the space for it, since his LEGO collection was still gone and his mother had just finished cleaning up the piles of broken toys that A.J. liked to leave strewn about like plastic caltrops. He was contemplating the nature of his failure to produce an imaginary friend again. It seemed like such a simple thing to do, this pretending that there were other people around when there plainly were not. Still, Clay kept failing at it. Not just today, but always.

Today, though, his failure was special and spectacular, and it went beyond merely failing to imagine himself a friend. He also failed to move, and in that failure he clanged and banged around his room like a klutz because his metal body made pacing difficult. It was affecting his concentration. Every time he tried to move, his joints creaked and groaned as his iron sides strained to bend and flex.

It hardly helped the situation that he was also creaking in the joints because of way his shoulder had gotten pulled earlier in the day. That was how he had wound up locked in his room, after all. By falling down. Well, throwing himself down. He only got hurt, though, when he failed to hit the ground.

Clay shook his head. No matter how many times he told himself what the situation was, he still had a hard time understanding. *What kind of person would punish him for trying to help them?* He knew the answer, though. His father was that kind of person, and it was hardly like today was the first time he had shown he was. He had already taken the LEGOs, and then when the biting incident made him have to choose a son to punish. What happened today felt different from what had happened before, though, if only because Clay had been getting along with everyone and doing his best, and yet he wound up in trouble anyway.

He stopped pacing and sat in the middle of his room cross-legged with his eyes closed, letting his memories play out against the green and red flares that darkness always showed him. His metal body fell away from him and he found himself back inside the scene outside, walking through the yard and picking up bits of discarded shingles as his father and uncle threw them off the roof. Every once in a while, his father would point out a spot in the yard where a lot of shingles sat, shouting out to Clay that he needed to pick them up.

His muscles started to ache as the wheelbarrow grew heavier. With each pound of sand and tar that accumulated in its bed, Clay felt another degree of annoyance at his father's micromanagement. What did it matter if he left a certain pile of shingles until his next trip into the back yard? He was going to have to pick them all up by the end of the day. His father and uncle both said so. When he ignored his father and went about the clean-up on his own, though, all it did was aggravate the man until he stopped working altogether and stood on the edge of the roof screaming for Clay to stop being "a fucking deaf idiot" and look up.

Clay did look up then, if only because he did not want the neighbors to hear how unhappy his disobedience made his father.

"Are you stupid, or do you just think I am?" Mark Dillon asked.

Clay waited for his father to continue. He was sure that this was one of those times when Mark intended for his questions to go unanswered.

"Hey!" Mark shouted. "Don't pretend I'm not here. Look at me when I talk to you."

Clay stared up at his father. The sun was over Mark's shoulder, but Clay stared without blinking. If his father wanted his attention, he would get it.

"Don't waste your time with all the little chunks. Go around getting the big ones."

Clay scowled.

"Don't make faces at me," his father said. "Speak."

Clay considered raising both of his middle fingers instead of speaking. It would get him in trouble, but so would saying what he really wanted his father to know.

"I don't have all day, Clay. Use your words."

That was it. Clay threw the shingles down at his feet.

"Shut up!" the words came out more like a screech than a shout. "Just stop fucking talking. You wanted me to spend all day picking up the yard, fine. It's hot and I feel sick and you wanted the roof done, not me. You're gonna make me pick 'em all up, big and small and everything, so just shut your mouth and let me do it. You got your job and I got mine. Stop fooling with me unless you want me to go play in the sandbox and you can do all this your damn self."

Mark Dillon did not respond with words. Instead, he sat on the edge of the roof and then, as if he was born to do it, he let himself drop to the ground. His hips and knees bounced his body as he landed, and he grunted.

Clay realized that he had made a big mistake.

"If you leave the little pieces, then we can all help you later," his father said. His voice was very quiet. "If you used your brain, instead of just saving it for your T.V. shows and science fiction novels, you might realize that we're here to help you. No one wants you to break yourself doing this."

Clay narrowed his eyes at his father. Earlier, when he had felt like his arms were going to fall off, he had asked to be allowed to go inside and read for a while. At the time, he had been told that he was being a wussy and that he could take breaks when everyone else did. Trying to make sense of his father's conflicting behaviors made his head pound even more than the sun and the weight of the wheelbarrow did.

"Do you have something to say to me?" Mark asked.

Clay shook his head. He was not trying to say no, he was just trying to shake the pain out after being made to stare into the sun.

"You really think cussing me out in front of the neighbors was right? Me, your father? And you, being eight?"

Clay kept shaking his head. His father grabbed him by the arm and put his other hand on the top of Clay's head, pressing down.

"Stop it!" He hissed. "Stop acting like a retard, and get ahold of yourself!"

Clay tried to tear himself away from his father, but the grip on his arm was like a shackle. The hand on the top of his head pushed down harder, making him feel like he needed to crack his neck. It amplified his existing headache.

"Just stop! Stop being such a baby! You're eight years old, goddamn it, and you know better. What will the neighbors think?"

They'll think you're an asshole and I'm right.

The thought popped into Clay's head a split second after his metal body hardened over his father's grip, taking the pain of it away. It was as if the words were elemental. They aligned with his emotions perfectly, but he did not feel as if he was the one who created them. He also found himself unable to summon any other words after them, or to make his throat work. The insult faded from his visualization, and he tried to snatch at it, to hold it...

Where the words had been just moments before, there was now just a hole in the center of his vision that corresponded to a raw, empty feeling in his throat. The scream rushed forth from that hole, and before Clay knew what was happening it was pushing its way out of his throat, holding his jaws open, and pouring itself all over his father. A moment later, he felt a sharp tug in his shoulder socket and realized that his body had gone limp. His father's grip remained tight, and there was motion that ended in the darkness of his room. Someone said: "If you want to throw a tantrum like a baby, then you can take a nap like a baby!" Then the door slammed.

A moment later, the voice said, "Don't let me catch you outside this room until I decide I'm ready to deal with you. If you do, you'll lose those LEGOs forever." Then Clay cried.

◆   ◆   ◆

When his words came back to him, he wished that he could call his father stupid without getting grabbed. It was reflexive, now, for him to shrink away whenever the man's voice started to flex its tone, and Clay did not like the fact that it had become so. The way that his father used his fingers to hold Clay's attention whenever he felt insufficiently respected always left burning spots after he finally let go, and if Clay complained, then he was told not to be a baby. If he kept complaining, his father would just talk at length about his determination never to hit his children because of the things that Grandma Bayleigh used to do to him.

There was no point in talking back, because his father never seemed to absorb words unless they harmonized with the ones that poured incessantly from his own throat. There was nothing to do but pace.

❖   ❖   ❖

People are not LEGOs

Clay fumbled his way through *The Screwtape Letters*, scanning the first few paragraphs of each epistle to see if any of them could help him understand what had happened at the end of *Ender's Game*. He was on his third pass through the demonic epistolary, but nothing in it seemed relevant to the issue of a society that would construct an elaborate, multi-billion dollar military operation that hinged on the ability of a handful of chosen adults convincing a very young child to commit genocide. Even while Clay was accounting for the sideways-talk in C.S. Lewis's style, and even when Lewis was speaking about the Second World War, there was nothing that really touched the scale of the horror at the end of *Ender's Game*.

He had read his way through the last third of *Ender's Game* in one sitting, and his evolving disgust for the ways that the adults in Ender's life talked about him had been growing the whole time, becoming a monster that animated his limbs and drove him to refute its grim promises. The writer made everyone speak so candidly and with such conviction that it took real effort to remind himself that they were talking about deciding to end an entire species as a retaliatory measure, and that they viewed Ender primarily as a weapon and not a person.

Clay did not have a sophisticated vocabulary of ends and means, but he had an innate conviction that people were not the same things as LEGOs, and it was leading him to want to tear the book up even though it was a library book. Then he got to the end, and the way that the dormant hive-queen absolved Ender of what he had done made Clay feel sick all over again. After that, it only made sense for Clay to check what he had read against the other books his parents had wanted him to read. The Bible seemed to have a conspicuously large number of sections that were just as revolting in their casual treatment of mass death as *Ender's Game* had been, but it also had a large number of passages about peace and love. It seemed to Clay like it was about getting along with some people and justifying the deaths of others, which meant that either *Ender's Game* was right or the Bible was wrong. Or, maybe, it meant that he had misunderstood the Bible.

That realization was when Clay decided to check his ideas about what the Bible said against C.S. Lewis's. After spending a few hours combing through *The Screwtape Letters*, though, it seemed like this particular issue, this bald-faced justification for genocide beyond the imagination of any of the world's historic dictators, was something that Lewis shied away from discussing.

Clay got so wrapped up in his work with the books that he failed to notice that no one showed up with dinner for him, and it was well after dark before he realized that there was no sound from anywhere and that A.J. had never been put to bed. When it finally occurred to him that he had been left alone for too long, he stood up from his bed and stretched. His whole body hurt, and it took him a moment to stand up straight. He wondered if his parents were watching TV downstairs, and decided to see. Clay opened his door a crack and saw that the house was totally dark. Then he realized that he needed to pee.

He stole down the hall toward the bathroom quietly. Clay was practiced at sneaking—whenever he had trouble sleeping, he would slip silently down the stairs and lie between the couch cushions, feeling the way they pressed in on him while he let his mind drift back to sleep. If that did not work, at least it got him into the television room, so it was easy to find something to watch. Sometimes, just having the extra light and the sound of calm people talking was enough to put him back out.

Once he was down the hall, Clay managed to use the bathroom silently, but doing so brought him to the realization that he would have to either leave the evidence that he had left his room in the bowl or risk the sound of the flush waking his father up. After a long moment, he bit his lip and said a silent goodbye to his LEGO collection. Then he flushed the toilet. He realized that nothing was going to happen (other than the flush) when his body forced him to exhale by shaking his breath out of him. Then he realized how hungry and thirsty he was.

If no one woke up when the toilet flushed right next door to his parents' room, then he was pretty sure that no one would wake up if he got into the refrigerator, and he went downstairs with the confidence that comes from conviction.

Examining the contents of the fridge for something that was edible cold, he found the selection disappointing. He did not want to touch the leftover pizza because there were only two slices, so his parents would be sure to notice if he pilfered them. That only left sliced bologna and a selection of different flavors of yogurt cups. He ate four pieces of bologna and two of the yogurt cups. Afterward, he made sure to rearrange them so that the gaps where he had taken his choices were filled back in. By the time anyone noticed that the yogurt was running out early, they would have eaten enough of it that there would be no way to be sure who had taken what.

That left him feeling adventurous, so he poured himself a tall glass of his father's Coca-Cola and drank it in one draught. The cola tingled in his stomach and through his limbs. Clay rinsed out his glass and put it back in the cupboard before turning all the lights out and stealing back upstairs.

He still had work to do.

◆   ◆   ◆

Kitty Dillon found her oldest son sitting up in his bed the next morning with his Bible open to Job and *The Screwtape Letters* open to the 19th letter. He kept scanning back and forth between the two books, but he did not seem to be doing anything in particular with either of them. His attention did not stay on one or the other for long enough to convince her that he was taking in the information. When he kept going, though, Kitty wondered if it was possible that he was actually reading as quickly as he appeared to be.

◆   ◆   ◆

Clay did not acknowledge his mother when she came into the room.

He was ready to surrender, or almost so, but he had to finish this one last check. Then he would be sure that neither book addressed the kind of genocide that *Ender's Game* talked about in any serious way. He wondered if any book had. His mind recoiled from both of the possibilities, refusing to commit itself to wishing for more books about atrocities, but also hoping beyond hope that there was something out there that treated the subject with the correct amount of abject horror.

He also wondered if *The Joy Luck Club* would have had any insight into the problems he was having with *Ender's Game*. It had contained deep and canny insights into the ways that people thought, even in the short sections he had managed to read. Maybe it also contained secrets about the true nature of war... secrets that would help him speak this discontent instead of merely feeling it in his chest. He wished he could know, but his mother was not taking him back to the library until after they finished with *The Screwtape Letters*, and she was reading it so slowly that it would take a month to finish the book with her. Since he was worried about the things that he was feeling in his reading and he was disappointed with his mother's progress in their reading game, Clay decided to ignore her until he was satisfied that the answers to his questions could not be found in either theology or scripture. So he let her stare, and he did not look up until he finished with his books.

◆ ◆ ◆

Kitty did not know that her son was ignoring her, but she suspected it. Clay was too hyper-perceptive not to know she was there. He might not have seen her at first, that happened sometimes, but she was reasonably sure he would have glanced over when he was panning from one book to the other.

She drank in her son's movements, memorizing them while she waited for him to be ready to talk. There was no hurry, after all, and she did not want to rush through the morning.

◆ ◆ ◆

Finally, Clay looked up at his mother. He was content with the certainty that he was going to be disappointed and unable to find answers, because he had at least exhausted his options.

She smiled at him.

"What?" he asked. "It's Saturday. You don't wake me up for anything on Saturday."

"I have a surprise for you, Clay. You're going to go on vacation." Kitty felt her voice tighten a bit when she said it, but she hoped her son did not notice.

He cocked his head.

"We need to get you packed up."

"What is this?" Clay asked.

Kitty smiled. Then she took a deep breath.

"Okay," she said. "Let's start over."

Clay nodded.

"You are going to start the second grade in a week. Your brother is going to start preschool at the same time, and that means a lot of new routines for all of us. In the meantime, your father and I need to focus on our home improvements so that we aren't in the middle of projects when the school year starts."

She paused.

Clay nodded.

"So, you are going on vacation. That way, we can concentrate on the work around the house, and you can enjoy what is left of your summer break."

"I thought I was going to get in trouble," Clay said.

Kitty put her hands on her hips, but she did not say anything.

"Because of the way I was put in here," he continued. "And then the way that A.J. didn't even come to bed."

"I already sent A.J. to stay with Grandma Bayleigh for the week. He gets his own vacation, and you get your own."

Clay smiled. He felt incredibly lucky, and for once, grateful toward his mother. Eventually, his mother harrumphed at him, and he realized that he had probably kept her waiting for some time.

"I'll get packing," he said.

"Good," his mother replied. "Patrick's mother will be here to pick you up in an hour. Be packed with enough clothes for a week. I'll look at your stuff before you go to make sure. Don't be late—I want to surprise your father with a quiet house when he gets home."

Clay nodded and slammed his books shut. Then he paused.

Kitty Dillon bit her lip. She did not want to take questions about this, she just wanted her sons and her husband to be apart for a while.

"What about the book?" Clay asked. He waved *The Screwtape Letters* at her.

"Leave it here, along with any other library books you have. I'll take them back while you're gone."

"We're not going to finish it?" he asked.

"No time," his mother replied. "I didn't expect to have to do the roof this summer, Clay. I'm sorry."

Clay nodded and pushed the books away from himself. He was glad that his mother seemed to be oblivious to his relief at being let go from his obligation to her book. He was also glad that he would not have to see the librarian, because he did not want to have to talk about *Ender's Game*. This way, he could just put both of those terrible books behind him.

When he looked up, his mother was already gone from the room.

Clay got out of bed and started packing his things.

❖   ❖   ❖

Part II: Between the Hammer and the Anvil

Bill Watterson Knows Things and He's Trying to Warn Us

Clay tried to have a good time at Patrick's house, but it was not easy. Patrick's mother was doing the same thing she always did, meddling in the boys' play to try to force Clay into decision-making that he did not want to do. He understood it better now, and he knew that she liked him because she talked about the friends Patrick had brought around that she did not like, and all of those stories ended with "and that's why it was just impossible to invite him back."

This was Clay's third visit to Patrick's house this summer, and his second overnight visit, so he knew that Patrick's mother liked him. He found himself wishing that she would like him less, though. Or, more specifically, he found himself wishing that she could like him from a greater distance.

Clay remembered the way that they talked about *The Joy Luck Club* last time he visited. Patrick's mother had not pretended that he was too young or too ignorant to understand the book, and she seemed pleased at his curiosity. Neither of those things were particularly common in Clay's experience with adults. Even Grandpa Harry acted like his understanding of what happened around him was some colossal joke. Clay only had to remember their talk about imaginary friends to remind himself of that. The problem was not Patrick's mother on her own, then. It was Patrick's mother's ideas about what was "nice."

For example, Patrick and Clay playing Nintendo while Tyler quietly read to himself in his room was not "nice," because everyone should feel included all the time. Instead, "nice" was forcing Tyler to come out of his room, letting him call everyone and everything stupid, and then taking away the Nintendo and making everyone play five hands of euchre.

From Clay's seat at the table, the only "nice" thing that happened during the game was that the two brothers stopped fighting. The only reason that that happened, though, was because both Tyler and Patrick decided to spend the entire game complaining that the rules were stupid, the fact that more than half the deck was not used was stupid, and that their mother was stupid because she did not like their jokes and she asked too many questions about the TV shows that they liked.

Clay was shocked, not only because he had rarely heard Patrick call anything stupid (much less five things in ten minutes), but also because he felt the cold terror of his certain knowledge that at any moment Patrick's father would come into the room and start whipping both of his boys with a belt. That was what was supposed to happen, after all. Mark Dillon had always made sure that both of his boys understood that. "Sass" was washed out with soap. Insults were beaten out with a belt. Hitting a woman, especially one's own mother, was solved by a fight in the backyard that would only end when one person could not stand back up.

Not that hitting had ever happened at Clay's house, of course. The occasional bump when someone tried to grab a child and missed, yes, but never an outright hit. Not unless it was A.J. hitting Clay, at least. Still, Mark made sure that both of his sons understood how close they were to an assault at every moment, just in case they decided to start assaulting their mother.

Finally, he could not take it anymore. His heart pounded in his chest, and he felt his fingers aching as he held on to the table with all of his strength.

"Stop calling your mother stupid, you assholes!" he shouted. "Do you want to get beaten with a belt?"

Time froze when Clay spoke. Tyler stopped halfway through rising from his chair. Patrick held the card he was about to lay down, keeping it in the middle distance between his hand and the table.

"No one gets beaten with a belt in this house," Patrick's mother said. "No matter what they do."

Both of her boys relaxed visibly when she said this.

"But," she went on, "I don't expect to hear anyone being called an asshole ever again."

Clay nodded.

"Do you get beaten with a belt at your house?" Patrick asked.

"No," Clay replied.

"Then why did you think we would get beaten?"

Clay sighed. "I don't get beaten with a belt because I follow the rules. I read what they tell me to read. I get top marks in school, so that they don't ask me why I didn't. I even keep my mouth shut when my parents are wrong because it's not my place to sass. I sure don't call my mother stupid. That's why I don't get beaten with a belt."

Tyler spoke up next. "You have to have done *something*, sometimes. Everyone misbehaves sometimes."

Clay felt the blood drain out of his face.

After what seemed like ten or fifteen minutes, Patrick's mother reached out and gathered up all the cards. "Let's call it a game, boys," she said. "I think Clay might like to get some Nintendo time in. Isn't that right, Clay?"

He nodded. Then he let himself be led out of the dining room and into the television room. Patrick asked him some things about games, and he knew he nodded through them, but he did not really pay attention. It was only when he felt an elbow in his ribs that he realized Patrick had run out of lives. It was his turn to play.

Clay's turn was over quickly. This game was challenging, and much different from *Super Mario Brothers* and *Duck Hunt*. He did not know what it was called, but he seemed to be a robot with a blaster arm that could turn itself into a ball, and he was supposed to shoot tentacle monsters and explore a cave system full of technology upgrades. He liked it, but he was also bored by it, because there were a lot of areas that were too hard with the equipment he inherited from Patrick's turn. He set down his controller and looked at his friend.

"What?" Patrick asked.

"I want to go outside," Clay replied.

"Okay, but there's nothing to do out there, and my mom won't let us go anyplace she can't see from the porch."

"Aren't there a bunch of other kids from school in this neighborhood?" Clay asked. His own neighborhood was all old people and teenagers.

"Yeah, but they don't like me," Patrick replied.

Clay nodded.

"You still want to go outside?" Patrick asked.

Clay shook his head. Then he picked the controller back up and kept playing.

◆　◆　◆

"Did you ever have imaginary friends?" Clay spoke the question into the dark, hoping that Patrick would answer.

"No," he replied from somewhere in the sky and to the left of Clay's sleeping bag.

They were in Patrick's bedroom, and everyone else was asleep. This was the part of sleeping over that Clay liked. The part where he could talk to his friend without having to do anything and without worrying about whether or not Patrick was staring at him. He wished that he had the chance to talk to more people in the dark, but so far Patrick was the only one who had invited him to stay over. At home, A.J. talked to Clay, but he was not very responsive when Clay talked back. On the rare occasion when his brother did want to listen to him, Clay always heard snores before he was halfway done.

"I didn't have imaginary friends either," Clay said to the dark. "Do you ever wonder why that is?"

"Not really," Patrick said. "Tyler had an imaginary friend for a while. It was really stupid. He just wandered around all day, talking to it like it could talk back. He even made my mother serve it a snack once."

"I bet he just wanted seconds," Clay said.

"Yeah, I thought so too," Patrick replied. "Except he didn't eat the snack. He just left it."

"Are we weird?" Clay asked.

"Definitely. But so what? My brother's not weird, and all he does is complain and throw tantrums. I'll take weird."

"When I was really little, before we moved into the house where we live now, my mom used to tell me stories about one of my stuffed rabbits. I don't have it any more, but she used to wave it at me and do funny voices to make it talk."

"That's nice," Patrick yawned as he talked.

"I used to think she was just telling me stories to get me to go to sleep, but now I think she was trying to give me an imaginary friend. All the stories she told were about places we actually went and things we actually did, only in her versions, my rabbit was always along. He was the hero, really. He told me to do things that saved me when I got lost, and he helped my mom when she was stuck and sad."

"My mom told me stories like that too, only they were about my Grandma," Patrick said.

"When I was really little, like when I was two or three, I didn't think anything about the stories. They were just fun. Now that I'm older and I'm reading about things, I'm really worried. What if my mom wasn't just telling me stories? What if she really thought that stuffed rabbit was talking to her?"

Clay heard giggles.

"Sorry," Patrick said. "I didn't mean to do that."

Clay did not say anything in response.

"I really didn't mean it," Patrick said. "I just couldn't help thinking like your mom should be in Calvin and Hobbes."

"I think that too, only I don't think it's funny," Clay said. "I'm really worried that maybe Calvin and Hobbes is a warning. Like maybe Bill Watterson knows things, and he's trying to let us know about them too."

"What kind of things?" Patrick asked. His voice was suddenly very quiet.

"I don't know," said Clay. "But I think they're the same kinds of things that made C.S. Lewis think that the voices in his head were demons instead of imaginary friends. Only, you know, Calvin and Hobbes is for smart people."

In the dark, the silence seemed to be drawing neon tracers of Patrick nodding in the air over Clay's head.

"I think I know what you're talking about," he finally said. "That's why Calvin talks to space monsters and stuffed animals, right? Because everyone else is doing stuff he doesn't understand because of things they see that he can't see. So he does it back to mess with them."

"I think so," Clay replied. He had actually never thought of things that way, but it made sense for a moment. Then he changed his mind.

"It might also mean that the voices are there, whether you know it or not," Clay said. "It might mean that we only think we don't hear them, and that everyone else is watching us talk to ourselves and wondering what the hell is happening."

The dark grew heavy after that, and Clay found himself climbing out of his sleeping bag and taking off his shirt to try to relieve some of the pressure on his chest.

"What are you doing?" Patrick hissed. "They will hear you."

"They didn't hear me talking," Clay replied.

"Yeah, but they don't care what you say. They're gonna know you're getting up, though. They always know if we get up."

Clay shrugged. He wondered if Patrick knew that he had done it. He did not get the chance to ask, because the next thing that happened was that the hallway light flicked on, and Clay saw Patrick's father in the doorway. Even in silhouette he managed to be skinny and pudgy at once, and his posture was gentle but unflinching.

"What are you boys doing up?" he asked. "I don't want to hear you again. You're going to wake up Mary and Tyler."

"Sorry dad," Patrick said. "Clay just had trouble getting to sleep, so he was rearranging his stuff."

"I don't want you up," he said, "but if that's how it's going to be, you can come downstairs and watch *The Mary Tyler Moore Show* with me. I'm doing overtime next week, so I'm staying on my third shift schedule."

"That's okay," Clay said. "I think I can sleep now."

"Okay then," Patrick's father said.

The lights flicked off. It was only seconds before Clay heard snoring. He wondered briefly if it was Patrick faking for his benefit or if the other boy was actually asleep. Either way, it was clear that their conversation was over. He climbed back into his sleeping bag and closed his eyes.

The next morning he was sure that he did not sleep, but he still woke up. When he did, he had an odd idea for a comic that looked a lot like Calvin and Hobbes, but it was about C.S. Lewis and Orson Scott Card. Lewis was the stuffed tiger. Card kept building gross snowmen doing horrible things to each other and drawing treasure maps that went nowhere. Somehow the dream made him feel much better.

❖ ❖ ❖

Something About Moses and Something About Jesus

Clay sat on a stool watching his grandfather get dressed for church. He was in a suit coat and tie himself, despite his having brought a polo shirt for church and having already worn it when he went to mass that morning.

That was the only problem with Grandpa Harry, from Clay's point of view. If he was going someplace, then he expected everyone in the house to go with him, and if he dressed up, then he expected all of them to dress up just as much. Since Grandpa Harry wanted to go to church on Sunday night in a suit, it meant that Clay was to wear a suit, too. Since he did not have a suit, it meant that he would have to wear some wide-lapelled junior monstrosity from when his uncle Curtis was a child.

Curtis, now eighteen and conveniently away to college for the year, had come of age during a very unfortunate era in men's clothing. Not only did his old suit look funny, but the dark brown color felt like it was going to stick out. It was still summer after all, and most people did not wear jackets inside the church due to its lack of air conditioning. Let alone dark-colored ones. He was torn between being mad at Grandpa Harry for making him go to church twice just so he could be uncomfortable and being mad at Curtis for never having gotten himself a robin's egg colored suit when he was a child. As a general rule Clay hated wearing any clothing beyond the mandatory minimum for public decency, but if he did have to dress up he at least wanted to pick out his own colors.

Grandpa Harry was trying to insert his own cufflinks into a shirt that had buttons on it already.

"Why do we have to go to church tonight?" Clay asked. "My mom told me that only Protestants have to go to church twice a week."

"That's right," Grandpa Harry said.

"So I went last night with Patrick's family. It was nice. We went to St. Sebastian's, like during the school year."

"Well there you go," Grandpa Harry said. "You didn't go to St. Jude's yet. Protestants go back to the same church twice on Sundays. You're going on Saturday and Sunday, and you're going to two different churches, so there's nothing to worry about."

Clay frowned. Something was not right about this situation. "Aren't the readings all the same? The reader with the bible stories for the month is the same in both churches. That's why mom picked out St. Sebastian's when we moved into our house."

This time, it was Grandpa Harry's turn to frown. "So you figured that out, huh? Okay." He turned and started fussing with his tie in the mirror. "Did you really go to church with Patrick?"

"Yes," Clay said. "I told you that."

"So, then... what did they read during the readings?"

"We read something from the Old Testament, one of the stories about Moses. And then the second reading was from Corinthians, and the gospel was the story about one of the times that Jesus was healing people."

Grandpa Harry smirked at him in the mirror. "So that's it, eh? Something about Moses and something about Jesus. I don't think you really remember it."

"I remembered that the second reading was from Corinthians."

"The second reading is always from Corinthians. Or Philippians. You've been around long enough to know that—first we read from the Old Testament, then we read from Paul's letters, and then from the Gospels. Give me some details."

Clay blew air through his lips.

"Paul wrote a lot of things that were about just a few topics. Tell me one thing he actually said today, and I'll let you stay home instead of going to church."

"How will you know if I'm telling the truth or not?" Clay asked.

"Oh, I went to church this morning," Grandpa Harry said.

"Oh," Clay replied.

Grandpa Harry finished with his tie and turned around.

"What do you think?" he asked.

"I think we don't need to go to church if we both went already," Clay replied.

"I know that," Grandpa Harry replied. "What do you think about the tie?"

"It looks straight," Clay said.

Grandpa Harry shook his head. "Sometimes, kid, I think you're pulling one over on all of us." He grabbed a bottle of cologne from his dresser and dabbed it onto his wrists. "You don't even get how smart you are, do you?"

"Oh, I know," Clay replied. "I just don't get a chance to do anything with it."

"That's going to happen," Grandpa Harry replied. "You just need a bit of time to ripen." He shot his cuffs and then checked his watch. "Now, to answer the question you haven't been asking. We're going to church tonight because a friend of mine is having his grandson baptized, and then we're going to a party. So yes, you have to go. Your mother will be there, too."

"I'm supposed to be on vacation from her," Clay replied.

◆ ◆ ◆

The church was hot, and Clay fidgeted in his uncle's old suit. He already felt sweaty under it, and they had just found their seats. He had no idea how he was supposed to tolerate this for the whole hour that mass would take, much less the party afterward.

So far, there had been no sign of his mother. Clay wondered if she was going to sit with them or not.

Grandpa Harry and Grandma Doris were busy shaking hands with their friends and congratulating the relatives of the baby who was getting baptized. Clay knew that this meant they would not want him to make himself the center of attention, so he flopped himself down into the pew and stared at the liturgical book. He knew what the readings were going to be, but since he did not say the words about them right, he had to listen to them again. Maybe that was good. Maybe it was like at school when it was time to review things. He hoped that the baby he had already seen was the only one getting baptized. The shorter the mass was, the happier Clay would be to sit through it.

Eventually, he heard a commotion that included a number of adult men and at least one woman happily greeting a newcomer. A moment later, a hand rested on his shoulder. Clay looked up to see his mother standing over him. She wore a plain white dress that flowed loosely around her frame, along with a patterned shawl over her shoulders. For just a moment, Clay wondered why his mother was dressed like the women in the pictures that his great-grandfather had sent home during his service in World War II. He was too young to know very much about why his mother, who was barely twenty-five years old, would be wearing a fashion that went out of style while her own mother was still in diapers, but he found it noteworthy nonetheless. The only difference between Kitty Dillon's appearance and the appearance of the women in those old photos from the back of the family albums was that she eschewed brightly colored makeup in favor of pale pink lipstick and muted hues of eyeshadow. This stood out against the backdrop of big-haired, heavily painted women

in the church the way that her dress stood out against the bright
colors and abstract but clinging designs they wore. All in all, it looked
to Clay like he was watching a character from *The Many Loves of
Dobie Gillis* waltz through the room during an episode of *The Facts
of Life* where all the girls had dates at once.

"Hi, Clay," his mother said. "Are you having a good time?"

"I was," Clay replied. "But then I had to put this suit on."

His mother laughed. Clay felt hot for a moment, but when she
told him he was funny she touched the back of his head, and that
made the heat from his embarrassment go away before his metal body
could form around it.

"I know Curtis's hand-me-downs are a bother," she replied.
"Don't worry. You can take the jacket off as soon as mass is over."

"Why are you here?" Clay asked.

"I went to high school with the woman whose baby is being
baptized," Kitty said. "And your father used to date her, so he stayed
home."

"Okay," Clay replied.

Shortly after that, the mass started. He managed to hold on to his
quiet during it, despite the increasing heat under his clothes and the
itching that was starting up from his belly sweat. When the readings
came, Clay found that he was able to repeat them to himself even
though he had not been able to remember them until the first words
left the speaker's mouth.

He closed his eyes and recited the first reading. When he opened
them again, Grandpa Harry and his mother both stared at him. Clay
thought about stopping, but they did not tell him to stop, so he kept
going. When the reading was over, Grandpa Harry nudged him in
the ribs.

"Why didn't you do that at the house? I would have let you stay
home with Grandma Doris. I only made you come along because I
thought you probably didn't pay attention when you were at church
with your friend."

"I couldn't do it at the house," Clay said. "I could only do it after
the song, when it was time to do it."

Grandpa Harry and Kitty Dillon looked at each other over Clay's head. They both shrugged at once.

"Okay, kid."

Grandpa Harry touched the top of Clay's head. Clay leaned in to the touch, trying to get his grandpa to massage his scalp, but Grandpa Harry pulled away before the hairspray in Clay's hair started to come apart.

The rest of the mass was uneventful, so he spent the time thinking about Screwtape and all the things that he might have to say about the people in church. Most of them were funny in one way or another, but the kinds of judgments that Screwtape wanted whispered to Wormwood's patient were just stupid. Who would care if someone else was funny looking, or if they needed to tap their feet in church? Clay often needed to tap his feet. It was nothing he got excited about. He did it in the church, just to prove it.

After a moment, Grandpa Harry's hand clamped down on his leg and forced it to hold still. Clay yelped in response.

"Shhh," Grandpa Harry said.

"Ow," Clay replied.

"I'm sorry," Grandpa Harry shot back. "I don't care if you fidget, but you can't be tapping your foot so loudly or it will distract people."

"I can't help it," Clay replied.

Kitty leaned in then.

"Clay, get up and go to the bathroom. If you need to, you can take a walk in the basement. This has got to be boring, since you just went to church yesterday. Try to be back before they dunk the baby, okay?"

Clay nodded. His mother was a lot easier to deal with when they were not at home.

As he made his way over set after set of strangers' knees so that he could walk to the back of the church, he heard his mother hissing at his grandfather that he should never grab anyone and hold him still.

"That's what his father does," she said. "And it never goes well."

❖   ❖   ❖

Motherhood as Disaster Management

Clay's first day of second grade did not start off any better than his first day of first grade had. While he did not have a meltdown and refuse to get dressed the way he had before, the fact that his brother A.J. was supposed to be starting preschool created its own set of problems. First, the younger boy tried to convince Kitty that he was going to wear his swim suit to school on the first day. When she picked him up and pulled his bright red trunks down, looking to take them away so that he had to wear blue jeans, she discovered that he had not put on any underwear. The shock made her let go of her son, and he took advantage of his momentary freedom, hitting the ground with his feet already in motion and scurrying down the stairs and out the back door.

Clay tried to help by bringing his brother's pants and a fresh pair of briefs into the backyard. A.J. put on the underwear, but he demanded that he be allowed to wear shorts. When Clay told him that they could not wear swim suits because the school would not allow it, his brother finally agreed to put on the jeans and come inside. That was not the end of the battle, though. When Kitty brought the boys their morning oatmeal, A.J. ate half of his and then tipped the rest into his lap. It made a wet mess all over the front of his jeans. His mother screamed.

Clay put his fingers in his ears. Kitty's scream sounded so familiar in its uncontrolled desperation that, for a moment, he wondered if his own scream was just something everyone had to deal with. It made him feel good for just a second, and then his mother threw a dish towel at A.J. and stomped out the front door. She was only gone for a few seconds, but Clay heard the screams soaring back into the house through the windows before she came back.

Not wanting to give his mother's scream the chance to invade him and reinforce his own, he went around the house shutting windows. That way, the scream would stay out there instead of following her back inside.

A.J. played with his spilled oatmeal.

When Kitty came back, she immediately took the dish towel she had thrown at A.J. and started cleaning him up. It was not so much an attempt to save his clothing: she was scraping the excess oatmeal off and into the bowl so that it would not run onto the floor when A.J. stood up. Then she sent him upstairs to find a new pair of jeans.

A few seconds later, shouts of "Where is my swimsuit?" filled the house.

Kitty looked at Clay.

Clay shrugged. His brother was a mystery to him. The only thing he could really say he knew about the four-year-old was that he enjoyed destruction to a degree that was really only possible for professional demolitions experts, soldiers of fortune, and future dictators. What was he supposed to offer as advice to his mother, who was both an adult and the reason for A.J.'s existence in the first place?

"Just go catch your bus," Kitty said. "Just worry about yourself. You know what to do."

Clay nodded. "Where's my lunch? I can't leave without my lunch."

Kitty sighed.

"I don't have time to make your lunch right now," she said. "Just get some money out of the box in the handyman's drawer."

Then she bounded up the stairs to deal with A.J.

Clay went into the kitchen and opened the extra-wide drawer where his parents kept a mixture of tools, garbage, batteries, pens, and (most importantly) his mother's walking-around money. She usually kept it twisted up into a roll inside of a dingy old jewelry box at the back of the drawer. He found the box easily, but when he took it out of the drawer and opened it, there was nothing inside except for a roll of dimes. Not sure about whether or not his school would take the dimes, or even whether they had the resources to make change from five dollars (the lunch cost seventy-five cents), he froze.

While he stood still and contemplated his situation, he listened to the thuds and muffled shouts that told him the story of his brother's resistance to pants.

School had not even started yet, but Clay already felt so tired that the effects of his week at Grandpa Harry's house were gone. The easy relaxation he had felt after coming home the night before was gone, and his bearing was just as rigid as it usually was after bearing one of his father's drawn-out and threat-filled lessons about life and honor and conduct.

Eventually, movement on the stairs caused Clay to look up. He saw his mother standing there, with A.J. tucked under one arm, staring at him.

"Why are you still here?" she asked.

"There's no money for me," Clay replied.

"Take the dimes," Kitty said.

Clay just shook his head. No one paid for lunch with a roll of dimes. He did not even understand how to pay for lunch with a roll of dimes. Rolls of change were for exchanging at the bank, or for using to buy things from neighborhood children who needed to go to band camp. That was all Clay had ever seen them used for. How was he supposed to go about paying for a school lunch with them?

"Dammit, Clay," Kitty said, "I don't have time for this today."

"But I can't go without lunch!" Clay felt the desperation of the scream straining his voice. He thought about letting his metal body take over, but he did not want to go to school in that cruel frame of mind, even if it would help him to hold still. It would also sour his lunch and make him mean to Aaron and Patrick.

Outside, a bright yellow mass filled the street, blocking the Dillon family's view of their neighbors' perfectly maintained raspberry garden.

"Shit," Kitty said. "Forget it. I'll make you lunch. Just watch your brother."

She set A.J. down on his own two feet, but she did not let go of him until Clay walked over and took his hand.

"Come on, A.J.," Clay said. "Let's go watch TV until it's time for us to get in the car."

Clay was grateful when his brother followed him willingly.

"Transformers," A.J. said.

"If it's on," Clay replied.

"Whatever, punk."

Clay sighed. He wished he could understand his brother's point-of-view, if only to know how to get him to shut up and sit down. Luckily, *Transformers* was on, so there was no more trouble from A.J. until Kitty called for them to get in the car so that she could take them both to school.

◆   ◆   ◆

In the car, A.J. would not shut up. He kept on about wanting to stay home to watch more *Transformers*, about being hungry because his breakfast was spilled, and even about how much he hated having to play with kids he did not know. Every time he complained, it made Clay's seatbelt feel tighter, until he could not help himself and he had to pull against the shoulder strap and push himself up off the seat to try to loosen his bonds.

"Don't fidget, Clay," his mother said.

"Tell A.J. to shut up then," Clay replied as he twisted himself into his seat belt more. He felt its pressure on his neck, and then he started to feel light-headed.

"Shut up you!" A.J. shouted.

All at once, Clay felt his metal body spring into being, replacing his flesh in a flash and forcing his thoughts into rigidity. He felt the scream echoing inside his hollow metal chest, but it could not force its way out through his steel teeth.

Even though his mother and his brother were both still shouting, Clay felt like he was in the middle of a wide, open, quiet space. He could still hear them, but even though they were loud, their noises did not affect him like they normally would. Instead, they interacted with his metal body, which made their chaos bearable by translating it to Clay without overwhelming him. He let the seatbelt go slack and sat up straight. Then he turned his face toward A.J. and let his jaw open.

What came out were words that were sharpened by his tongue and laced with the edges of his scream.

"Stop being an idiot. If Dad was here, you know you wouldn't act like such a sack of shit. You know what he would do if you were like this in front of him, and you know that you can't keep tricking him into loving you best if you misbehave so much. You remember how nice he used to be to me? You know how he started to like you best? That happened because I got in trouble at school and he missed work. He stopped loving me because I made myself a problem. Do you want to be his problem? Do you want him to think of you like he thinks of me?"

The car screeched to a halt. Clay wondered why. Then his mother turned around in her seat to face him. Tears streamed down her cheeks, making oily black mascara trails from her eyes to her chin.

She said nothing. She just stared.

After a long moment, she turned back around in the driver's seat. Then she opened the door, leaned her head out, and vomited all over the side of the road.

A.J. did not make a sound.

After she finished vomiting, Kitty Dillon closed the door and kept driving down the road.

"Do you even know what you just said?" she asked.

"No," Clay replied. "My thoughts went hard, and now my head hurts."

It was not a lie, but it was not the truth either. Clay knew what his words were, but he found himself wondering why he had spoken them. They came without intent, from a place where he knew what he felt but did not know what those feelings would make him say. Their amplification in his metal body was only an echo of their feeling, and that echo made the meaning unclear to Clay. If he was asked to repeat himself, he was sure that he would not know what to say.

Kitty Dillon stayed silent as she drove.

When A.J. started to shout about *Transformers* again, Clay felt his metal voice coming back. Finally, when they were just a block or so from Greenridge school, he felt himself start to speak.

"Can't you just stop? Don't you see that you made her sick?" he asked his brother.

A.J. leaned over in his car seat and punched Clay in the face.

When Clay grabbed his brother by the throat, the car stopped again. He felt sound pouring out of his throat, but he did not know any words in it. In fact, he barely noticed when the door on his side of the car opened, and he barely struggled when his mother undid his seat belt and pulled him out.

Kitty held Clay by his shoulders, keeping him from jumping back into the car and onto his brother's throat. She leaned around him, though, grabbing his backpack.

"Are you okay?" she asked A.J. as she worked.

"Better than him," A.J. replied. "Let me outta my seat."

She ignored her younger son and turned back to look at Clay's face.

"You just have to walk from here," she said. "I don't have time for this monkey business. Tell the office they can call me at home if they want to know why you're late."

"Why do I have to walk?" Clay could see the words cutting his mother's face as he spoke. "*He* hit *me*. Make *him* walk."

"He's not going to Greenridge. He goes to preschool."

"So what? He's the one that made you sick. Make him walk."

"No! Take yourself to school *now*, Clay. Right now."

"My face hurts," Clay replied.

"It's going to be fine," Kitty replied. "Now go."

She slammed the car door for emphasis. Then she walked around to the other side of the vehicle and climbed back into the driver's seat.

Clay watched as his mother pulled away from him, leaving him at the curb. Greenridge School was close enough that he could hear the sounds of kids on the playground. If he hurried, he might not even need to explain to the office why he was late.

He ran, and he made it to the line to drop off his backpack before the whistle blew to call everyone inside. Chucking it into the pile that sat under his new teacher's name card, he turned to run back out to the playground and almost smashed through Mrs. Brecker's legs.

She grabbed him by the chin and made him look up at her.

"What happened to you, kiddo?" she asked. Then she licked her lips.

Clay still thought she looked like Miss Wormwood, and Mrs. Brecker still wore the same track suit she had worn last year. It was a little bit nice, to see that some things would be consistent from year to year.

"Well?" she asked. "Who boxed your face?"

"No one," Clay said.

"No, it was someone," she held his chin firmly as he tried to wiggle away. "What happened? Your parents finally haul off on you?"

Clay wanted to stomp on her foot because he could tell that she was playing a game with him and he did not understand why or how to stop it. He kept himself in check, though, because he was pretty sure that he was already going to be in trouble and he did not want to make it worse.

"It was my brother," he said. "My brother hit me in the face."

Mrs. Brecker's grip finally loosened.

"I'm sorry," she said. "It looks like quite the shiner. Do you want to go to the office and put ice on it?"

"No," Clay said.

"Are you sure? It would probably be a good idea. You don't want it to swell shut."

Clay stared at her.

"Suit yourself," she said. "I'm sorry I asked."

"You should be," Clay replied. "My family shit is none of your business."

"Fine," Mrs. Brecker said.

Clay felt grateful that she ignored his swear.

"How old is your brother anyway?" she asked.

Clay screamed at the top of his lungs until she put her hands to her ears and blew the whistle for everyone to line up. When he saw the wave of children approaching both of them, he stopped screaming and let himself blend into it. There was safety in the crowd, even if it surged with a kind of riotous noise that took his words and his thoughts and left him twisting with the effort of containing his scream.

Clay wished for his metal body to come back, but it did not. Instead, he seemed to be softer than ever, and everything was so intense it hurt.

He tried to ignore everyone else as he grabbed his backpack. That was all he could do.

❖   ❖   ❖

Adapted Curve Corrals

After the encounter with Mrs. Brecker, the rest of Clay's first morning at school went very much like it had the year before. Despite the fact that the children were in the second grade and that they had already internalized the rhythms and the conventions of the adults who were in charge of the facility that indoctrinated them, they still had to sit through many of the same presentations that were used to threaten the first graders into compliance with the school district's particular interpretation of educational theory and child development.

For Clay, this meant that much of the morning was free for him to spend consoling himself about his black eye. In the large-scale gathering that was an assembly at a suburban elementary school, none of the adults cared to peer deeply into the huddled masses of children they had herded into the gymnasium and commanded to sit on the floor, knee to knee and with less than a foot between their kneecaps and the back of the person in front of them.

The sounds and smells of the other children were difficult to deal with, but the concealment that came from the protection they offered was valuable for Clay. He forced back his tears by intentionally trying to re-create his metal body, to help keep himself from behaving in ways that would attract attention. After dealing with Mrs. Brecker, he did not want to have to explain his eye again. Not everyone would let his swears go like she had.

As the morning ground on, he did start to notice small differences between the last year's presentation and this year's. For starters, Principal Chitwood, spent time talking about "leadership" and "setting an example" to the first graders. Even though it was only the first full week of September, he brought up the issue of snowball fights, and he called on the boys in the group to remember that tackle football was strictly forbidden. He explained that they were in charge of helping the first graders understand all of these rules, because they were the oldest group at Greenridge school now and so they were expected to know how everything worked.

Despite his discomfort and shame, Clay could not help noticing that Mr. Chitwood's confidence in the maturity of second graders and his assurance of their competence at transmitting school culture still did not lead him to extend them the courtesy of being spared a thorough reading of the rulebook. He did not tell himself this in so many words, though. Like all of Clay's thoughts, these feelings came through in large, warping structures that bled into multiple senses, rather than chaining themselves to an interior monologue. As Chitwood talked, the light in the room seemed to hit him in a funny way, exaggerating his facial features and making them seem slightly lopsided. There seemed to be something hungry in his expression, and Clay could not help feeling like the very things that were making other students sit up straighter and pay more attention to the man were warning signs, and that if he followed those signs, then he would be safe. It also felt, though like that safety would involve surrendering a part of himself that he did not have a name for, and that he would therefore be unable to reclaim.

Clay's metal body agreed with his eyes. It hardened his ears, and the discord in Chitwood's words began to sound like silverware clashing. By the time his eardrums were metal, all he could hear was the sound of pots and pans banging against each other, and all he could see was a man in a suit who wanted everyone to give him his way even though he did not feel obliged to find out if they liked his way first.

At some point Clay realized he was sweating. At another point, he realized that the experience was over and people were standing. He did not want to stand because he did not want to bump into other students. He was afraid of what would happen if they touched his metal body and cut themselves on him. It would probably lead to his getting in trouble. Since his mother was already vomiting from the burden of dealing with A.J., that would lead to Mark Dillon missing more work and learning how to hate Clay more. So he stood, and he let himself be led, single-file, out of the gymnasium and through the hallways to his new classroom and his new teacher.

As he walked, Clay looked at the brightly colored posters that decorated the walls of his school. They were detailed and educational, and each one was the size of an entire section of hallway wall, from support girder to support girder. Each was dedicated to a different subject, too. The math poster detailed different names for large numbers, all the way up to a googol, and explained how those names had been arrived at. The social studies poster talked about Russia and something called "glasnost", and Clay wished he had more time to stop and read. The line was picking up speed, though, and it also caused him to miss the details of the dinosaur poster on the science wall and the poster about chapter books that both came quickly after the wall about Russia.

So far, the posters were the only thing about the day that made Clay feel happy, and as he progressed through the building and found himself without enough time to appreciate them, they also started to feel like distractions. At the point where they were just interesting colors that he did not get to read, he began to distrust them.

Eventually, Clay realized that he believed the posters were only put there to keep him slightly distracted. The fact that there was so much information on them, yet he was not allowed to just stop and read... it weighed on him. The other children seemed happy, though, and many of them pointed to the bright colors and the illustrated Russian tanks or the Tyrannosaurs hunting and giggled to each other. That was when he decided that the real purpose of the posters was to keep the children occupied so they would not focus on the way their classmates smelled as they shuffled along, all packed together. They also helped divert attention from the fact that they would soon be trapped in a room for hours at a time, unable to leave without the say-so of an adult that they had never met before.

It suddenly occurred to Clay that whoever could conceive of a way to bring him to that room in a docile way must be a monster. He already knew what the experience of school would be like, after all, so hiding it would not serve to keep him ignorant. It would only make him deliver himself to his fate cheerfully, an act that benefitted the people who wanted him there but did nothing to either persuade him that he *should* be there and even less to liberate him *from* being there. The posters were not for him, they were for the people who were ordering him around. They were designed to make that task easier, and all the children who pretended otherwise were being tricked into hurting themselves.

Suddenly, his metal body went away and Clay became very nauseous. He felt like a pink worm exposed in the sunlight, waiting to know if he would be eaten, stepped on, or slowly baked into a dry film on the pavement. The idea that adults would preoccupy themselves with ways to distract people until they did things without thinking was a repulsive one, and Clay feared growing up in a world that would revere the kind of person who thought in the ways that the school's leaders thought. There could be no good from a mind whose only purpose was to ceaselessly increase the efficiency of a process without regard to the morality of its results.

He averted his eyes from the walls and tried to focus on counting the number of tiles on the floor. He might not be able to stop himself from being delivered to the ends that others designed for him, but he could refuse to express gratitude toward them for what they did.

❖   ❖   ❖

TV on the Playground

"You came to school with a black eye. Did you have to fight your dad?" Patrick's question caught Clay off guard, not only because it so abruptly burst the bubble of thought that he had constructed to keep other people from noticing his eye, but also because the other boy seemed to be able to see Clay's face even though his own gaze was locked intently on a Game Boy screen. He watched Patrick's thumbs play across the buttons for a moment before answering.

"It was my little brother. Don't tell anyone."

"Okay," Patrick said. "But I got to sit next to Aaron in the assembly, and he knows about your eye too. You might not want to tell him about it, but he's already worried."

"Okay," Clay said. "Thanks."

Patrick kept playing with his Game Boy. Clay paced around him.

"When did you get a Game Boy?" Clay asked. "You didn't have one last week."

Patrick just nodded, without answering Clay's question, so he sat down on the pavement at his friend's feet and listened to the music coming from the Game Boy's speaker. He needed to rest. It sounded like Patrick was playing *Tetris*. He wondered if the other boy had managed to play his Game Boy during the assembly. It certainly would have helped Clay if he had been able to do a puzzle or something while Chitwood droned on and on. The remainder of the morning, after the assembly and after the children had been shuffled around through the hallways like so many animals to slaughter, had been nothing more than Clay's new teacher introducing herself to the class and slowly sorting all of the children into a seating arrangement.

The new teacher's name was Mrs. Hudson, and she seemed nice enough. She was a lot more particular than Mrs. Nesbitt had been. When it was time for the class to line up against the wall while she read the seating chart out, she waited until everyone literally had their backs against the classroom wall to start. Then, whenever a child stepped forward or turned to talk and stopped leaning against the wall, Mrs. Hudson stopped everything to redirect the entire class back into formation. Normally, this kind of attitude would frustrate Clay. Watching someone try to behave this way with thirty children instead of just one or two made it comical, though, and that made it easier to bear. When everyone was finally arranged, it turned out that the class was just going to sit in rows in alphabetical order. This meant that Clay Dillon was seated far away from Patrick and Aaron, in the second row from the back of the first column. The other boys, the ones who played football, wound up all around him, in his column and in neighboring columns and rows.

Clay spent the morning hoping that Mrs. Hudson would rearrange the room often, like Mrs. Nesbitt had. The way she acted during the seating assignment made him believe that this would not happen, though. After they were seated, she spent the morning mostly repeating what Mr. Chitwood had already told them, but while calling the rules "classroom expectations" instead of rules. She also talked about making the children learn cursive and about the fact that they would have science classes two days each week, and both of these announcements were new to everyone. In first grade, they had occasionally read about scientific topics, but the lessons themselves were all based on reading, writing, and math.

Despite the fact that Mrs. Hudson acted like the most anxious babysitter Clay had ever worked with, he was looking forward to being in her classroom because of the promise of science lessons. He knew what he thought was a lot about science already, having read the Childcraft encyclopedias for bugs, dinosaurs, animals, the ocean, and plants. There was nothing else he could do to teach himself, now, and he was glad to see that the teacher had anticipated having students like him. Still, waiting for her to finish telling the entire class what they had already heard was draining. By the time she excused them to lunch, Clay did not have the concentration left to cope with the demands that Mrs. Brecker and Mr. Hanson made as they tried to maintain order in the cafeteria. Because of that, he was shuffled to a table with Noah the Nosepicker while Patrick wound up being sat down with a bunch of first grade girls. Aaron was, somehow, not even through the lunch line before the two of them finished eating.

Clay had been disappointed by the fact that he did not have a chance to sit with his friends, and he resolved to make sure that they found a way to enter the cafeteria together from then on, so that they would have a better chance of getting to sit together. On that first day, though, all he could do was eat quickly, get out on the playground, and then look for Patrick. He found him with very little effort, huddled against a wall right by the doors where he could block his face from the wind while he played with his Game Boy.

Even without speaking, the two boys relaxed in each others' presence. Clay did not mind that Patrick kept his Game Boy to himself. Even though he liked video games, he did not really feel a need to play them all the time, and he was able to enjoy the music coming from the tiny digital speaker. It might be tinny and somewhat flattened, but it was at least pure music. There was no lesson in it, no silly group activity to do with your hands, and no one who wanted him to dance. He was free to enjoy himself in it in ways that the school prevented whenever music was part of a teacher's lesson. The two stayed in their silence until Aaron reached them.

"The lunch line was really slow," he said as he walked past Patrick. "I need to walk around. Let's walk around."

Clay picked himself up from the ground and followed Aaron. Behind him, Patrick called for them to wait and to let him finish his game. He stood still, looking over his shoulder at his friend. Aaron kept walking.

"Wait!" Patrick yelled again.

Clay hesitated. He wanted to wait, but he also wanted to walk, and besides, Patrick was playing with something that was just for one person. Why should everyone wait for him to finish playing a game that they could not play?

"Walk while you play!" Clay shouted. Then he trotted after Aaron, who was halfway across the soccer field already, headed toward the baseball diamond and away from the playground.

There were no rules saying that the kids could not play on the sports fields. Still, no one usually did. If there was any activity there, it was tag or football on the soccer field. The baseball diamonds remained empty, and the downhill slope behind them that led to the schoolyard fence created a place where children could hide without being out-of-bounds. The only hazard out there was missing the recess whistle because you did not hear it, but Clay had good ears. When he caught up to Aaron, the other boy just said, "It was so loud in the cafeteria, I can't be on the playground. I have to walk around where it's quiet."

Clay nodded. Eventually, Patrick caught up to them. He was still playing with his Game Boy.

"So," Patrick said, "what are you all watching on TV? My dad likes *Booker*."

"I watch *The Wonder Years* when I get to stay up, but that's not very often," Clay said. "And I like *The Cosby Show* and *Family Matters*, but I have to go to bed at eight. They rerun them before the news on the weekdays though, so at least I get to watch them sometimes. The old ones."

Aaron did not say anything.

"Aaron," Patrick said, "what's going on?"

The other boy kept pacing. It looked like he was going to cry.

Clay shrugged at Patrick, but he made a point of zipping his mouth up like a zipper and pointing to Aaron. Patrick nodded, but Clay was not sure that the other boy actually understood.

They followed Aaron around the perimeter of the schoolyard. Eventually, as they came near the swings, Aaron started to talk.

"I don't like school this year. I have to wake up early because my brother's special school has funny hours, but that's normal. My mom decided that she doesn't want to drop me off anymore, though, and now I have to take the bus. I don't like being alone in the house after she leaves. It's different when I get home from school, when the house has been empty for a while. When I am in the house as it empties, it feels like the house attaches itself to me. Sometimes it whispers."

Aaron's words brought the whistling, keening sound of Clay's scream to life. It was a distant sound, like wind in a hollow valley far away, but it was there. He wondered if Aaron was hearing the far-off sounds of himself and misunderstanding it. Before he could say anything, though, Patrick spoke up.

"That's nothing. Your house is settling. Mine does it all the time. It sounds like groans in the middle of the night. It's nothing."

Aaron scowled at Patrick, but Clay suddenly felt very silly. He had almost admitted his scream out loud, but if Patrick was right, then he was not experiencing the same thing as his friends. If his scream was something that only he experienced, then Clay did not want his friends to know about it, because that might make them think he was crazy like Grandpa Harry. They might even make him go to a different school like they had done to Aaron's brother when he had trouble with math and talking. The teachers and Aaron's mother had done that even though he was good at reading and writing.

Clay fidgeted as he walked, flinging his arms around and spinning alongside his friends. It was good to exercise his whole body, even if his friends did not want to do anything but walk.

They were walking back toward the sports fields again, skirting around the playground so that they would not have to run through masses of other children, all of whom were always shouting, when Patrick started playing with his Game Boy again. The field was muddy in that spot because there was a large depression in the hilltop that Greenridge School sat on, and it collected water so easily during the rains that it rarely dried out completely. Clay was surprised to see Patrick walking calmly through it with his eyes locked on his screen, since both he and Aaron needed to keep their arms out at their sides to stay steady while their feet slipped and glided through the loose, sloppy ground.

Then Patrick fell down. He let go of the Game Boy as he did, and it landed screen-down on soil that oozed liquid as the device's weight settled it into the surface of the earth.

Patrick planted himself on his ass in the muck, and before Clay had a chance to help him up, he launched himself at the game, turning his muddy bottom into a full mud suit as he dived on his belly to save his toy.

Aaron almost fell down laughing at that, but he saved himself.

Patrick tried to pick himself up, but he kept slipping. Clay reached out to give him a hand, but all that accomplished was Patrick pulling him to his knees and coating the lower half of his jeans in the mud.

"Give me that Game Boy," Clay said.

"It's still working," Patrick replied. "I think it's okay."

"Give it to me!" Clay snatched it out of his friend's muddy hands.

Surely enough, it was still working. Clay did not care, though. He wiped the mud off its face and switched it off, using his shirt to scrub the dirt from around the buttons. Then he handed it to Aaron.

"Hey!" Patrick shouted. "That's mine!"

"SHUT UP!" Clay yelled. "Just shut up!"

He could feel his metal body clanging shut across his skin, like some kind of ablative armor deploying from hidden caches in the creases of his joints. It jerked him up to his feet and put his arm out to Patrick. This time, when he took the arm, Clay's metal body was rigid enough and strong enough to pull the other boy up without falling.

Patrick winced as he took his feet.

"Clean yourself up. You look ridiculous," Clay said.

The hurt on Patrick's face made him wish he was being nicer, but the metal encasing him kept his words from working right. Didn't Patrick realize that this was a special situation? That getting up and not being so dirty that he got sent home was more important than whether or not someone had *touched* his *toy*? Suddenly, the scream was inside the metal body, bouncing off its interior and creating ricochet wounds all over Clay's insides. He put his hands to his head and dug his fingernails into his temples.

"Stop! Stop! Stop! Stop! Stop!" Clay did not realize he was screaming until Aaron put a hand on his back and another one on his shoulder. Normally, he would have startled away from sudden touches, but something about the way Aaron's hands lay on his back was different from the way other people touched him. The other boy was not trying to push or control or hold Clay, just to make sure that he knew where they both were, so that if he moved he would not accidentally hit or run into his friend.

He took a deep breath, and suddenly the metal and the scream were both gone, and he felt very tired and cold. Aaron walked him to Mr. Hanson and told him about what happened. Patrick came with them.

Mr. Hanson declared that Patrick would have to go home for the day and made him go to the office. "Whatever you do, don't sit down until your mom gets here," he said. "I don't care if the office lady says to, don't do it. She doesn't have to clean up after you, and she's just being nice anyway."

Clay, Mr. Hanson decided, was able to return to class. He told Aaron that they could go inside early and clean up in the restroom. He heard this, but he was busy watching Patrick walk away, so he was not surprised that Mr. Hanson talked to his friend instead. It was good, he thought, that Aaron was able to pay attention for him, because he did not feel like pretending that he was less tired than he was. He did clean himself up, though. He let Aaron bring him paper towels, but he scraped the mud from his own shins and rubbed his own jeans with dry napkins to try to keep them from being clammy and cold and wet.

Aaron, for his part, seemed to understand when he was and was not needed, and for that Clay was grateful. He was also grateful that Patrick was not going to be there at the next recess, because he was angry at the other boy for ruining lunchtime with his Game Boy. It had been pleasant for a while, but when Aaron had said that he needed quiet, why had Patrick kept playing? The music was not that loud, but someone had asked for quiet, and the boy was too busy with his game to even care. The more Clay thought about what had happened, the angrier he became at Patrick, although he could not explain to himself quite why that was.

❖   ❖   ❖

Self-Restraint

After lunch, Mrs. Hudson continued her introduction of herself and her material in a much more personable way. Not only did she forgo any further discussion of the rules that the children had already heard at least twice, she also started telling stories about her own kids and family to illustrate her points as she told the children about the kinds of things they would learn during their second grade year. Clay enjoyed the performance, which was almost like watching shows on PBS (and not really as bad as school usually was). Soon, he got to thinking that he might actually be able to enjoy this year, even with Mrs. Hudson's bizarre and demanding behavior, if she was planning to spend most of her time telling the lessons like a TV show.

Then Noah the Nosepicker started kicking his chair. Noah's last name was Doornbos, and it was right after Dillon on the class roster. He was not a bad kid or a mean one. He was just that child in any classroom who fails to understand that the laughter accompanying his grand performances, from kicking other children to coating his entire desktop in boogers, was not intended to show solidarity. Being totally mistaken about why people laughed at him, he tended to repeat and escalate any behavior that resulted in his receiving feedback, whether it was gentle, sarcastic, coaching, condescending, or indirect.

And he just kept kicking Clay's chair. Right in the ass. The first time, Clay ignored it. The second time, he shifted his weight, to show that he had felt it. Then Noah began timing the kicks to a beat, delivering two per second in perfect rhythm and concussing Clay's rear until he could feel his tailbone jangling.

He turned to tell Noah to stop, but he got no further than a firm "Don't."

"Clay Dillon, face forward and pay attention when I am presenting!" Mrs. Hudson's voice cracked like a whip.

Suddenly, Clay's words were gone.

"Was there a reason that you needed to talk during my presentation?" Her words sounded like she knew there was not.

Clay wanted to tell her that he was being kicked over and over. He wanted to say his ass hurt. He knew doing so would make the class laugh, though, and Mrs. Hudson's crystal blue eyes were examining him in a way that made him very sure that she would hold him criminally responsible if a round of unscripted laughter broke out.

Noah kicked his chair again.

Clay tried to gesture to Mrs. Hudson, but she just told him to sit still, and then she kept moving on with her presentation. Clay heard the scream bloom into his mind. It did not come up from his stomach or jump into his esophagus through a hole in his voice box like it usually did, nor did it attempt to tear itself out of his mouth so that it could pour all over the people who would not let him be without pain. Instead, it seemed to exist only in Clay's imagination-space, affecting his ability to decode the teacher's examples by driving itself through any visualization or associated personal memory he attempted to use as he thought through the lesson.

And Noah kept kicking Clay's chair, still. After the teacher's scolding, it happened intermittently and only when Mrs. Hudson was facing away from them. After a few minutes, though, Noah was beating out a rhythm that once again threatened to turn Clay's lower spine into powder.

Suddenly, the scream jumped for Clay's voice box. He jerked forward, hitting his ribcage against the edge of his desk as he tried to hold his lips tightly shut. The kept scream forcing its way through his teeth, even so. He felt his jaw giving way, and he drummed his fists on the desk.

Mrs. Hudson stopped talking.

Noah kept kicking.

Suddenly, Clay's mouth was open and his metal body was deploying.

He felt the scream start to emerge before his armor was able to get inside his mouth and cover over his tongue and throat. When the cold metal visor closed over Clay's eyes, he was already facing Noah. His hands were gripping the front of Noah's desk like it was the edge of a cliff, and he heard himself speak.

"I will take that foot off your body!"

The last syllable rose as much in volume as it did in pitch, as it was the last little bit of speech to escape a larynx that was rapidly converting itself into a set of steel guitar strings.

"No Threats." Mrs. Hudson's words carried the familiar edge of bladed speech delivered through a mechanical voice box, but they were exponentially more deadly than even Clay's most effective salvo. It was like he was a warrior version of Pinocchio and she was one of those super-heroes with an indestructible skeleton and a head made out of computer parts.

Clay turned himself around and faced the teacher. He made himself put his hardened gaze against hers, just for a moment, just so that she would know him and know that he knew her. It satisfied him that she broke the gaze before he did. It also satisfied him to feel, deep within himself, a twinge of suffering. He knew it was because he stared directly into her eyes. He drank deeply of the hurt he caused himself, though, and it made his armor thicker and his vocal chords sharper and stronger. The pain coursed across his skin, just under the metal layer, forcing contortions out of muscles and sending small rippling cramps up his arms and legs and into a strange, warm place in his torso, where they began to twist his innards.

He heard his breath getting louder and faster, but he did not feel it. He was too taken with waves of sensation he did not understand. It was embarrassing to be feeling it here, with other people all around.

He knew that. He also knew that the hurt was under a layer of metal, so other than his breathing, there was nothing to would make anyone else think anything had happened. In fact, he could probably blame the breathing on the fact that he just got yelled at. Clay understood that this meant that most of the other kids would not even worry about his breathing as long as he did not keep calling attention to himself. It made him feel a little better.

Then Noah kicked the bottom of his chair again.

Pain blossomed like tulips of white fire in Clay's lower back, and he heard a moan that escaped through his nose to get around his vicelike lips.

Everyone stared at him.

Suddenly, everything from the lights to the sounds of their questions became sharper and more painful while the original pain from the kicks became overwhelming, sending waves of pleasure through Clay that forced him to close his eyes. His toes curled. He struggled to avoid making extra sounds, and he was not sure if he was successful, but he had to close his eyes to even feel like he was able to try.

Only after he heard Mrs. Hudson start talking again did Clay re-open them. The pain turned bad and made him feel like he was going to vomit. It was the light, when his eyes opened and let it into his head. To fight this new pain, he tried to make sure the old one kept its tantalizing edge, so he ground the base of his spine against the bottom of his chair.

"If you like it, I can keep doing it." Noah's whisper did not sound like it was meant to be vicious, but Clay felt like it was. He shook his head. Then Noah kicked him again anyway.

Before Clay had a chance to decide whether he liked the pain or not, his hands were behind his back, grabbing Noah's foot. The metal reinforcing his frame made it easy to hold onto the boy even though his grip was awkward.

Clay forced a pleasant smile onto his face to help cover his concentration.

Noah's leg shook, trying to free itself even as he lost the ability to control it. Clay responded by wrapping his fingers in the cuff of the boy's blue jeans and pulling them tight. Noah's shaking grew stronger after that, but it was also easier to control.

The part of Clay that felt embarrassed about moaning in class threw itself against his metal body as the scream tore through his insides. The tighter his grip on Noah's leg became, the more the two forces tore each other apart. He felt his pleasure rise as he realized that he was going to extract physical pain from himself while taking his revenge on Noah.

His innards twisted and railed as he turned Noah's ankle to the side. Just a little. Just until there was serious resistance to turning it any more. He made himself breathe slowly through his nose while he did it, but he could feel his flesh body inside the metal one, and it was shaking with fury. His thighs kept cramping, sending pangs of noncompliance into his brain, but the hurt converted itself into an uncomfortable satisfaction that carried with it a kind of slow-motion clarity of vision.

Clay had managed to lose his words without losing his control, and the only way he knew to maintain himself was to feed on the feelings available in his environment, and he did so without judging them. That this made the scream tear huge chunks of thoughts from his mind and dispose of them in a way that negated their existence did not matter. All that mattered was that breathing steadily was painful because of the control it required, and the pain felt so fantastic that it became the reason he was so determined to breathe steadily.

When he heard Noah drum his fingertips on the desk, Clay almost lost control again, but he managed to swallow his gasp as he concentrated on twisting that leg as much as he could.

Then the world exploded. The room tilted forward, violently, and all sound went away. Clay's limbs went slack. Then his forehead hit the desktop, and it was only after he felt the cool Formica and the dull ridge of the aluminum trim on the edge of his desk that he realized the back of his head hurt.

He heard Noah screaming, and after a few seconds, that screaming grew more distant. Then Mrs. Hudson was in the corner of his vision. She was talking softly, with no metal in her voice. Her questions were about whether Clay was awake or not, so he sat up. Then he had to close his eyes because moving made him feel queasy. He said as much, so Mrs. Hudson assigned Aaron to take him down to the office. She said she would call them on the intercom, to let them know that Clay was not in trouble but that she wanted him to see the nurse.

As Aaron led him down the hall toward the office, Clay felt his body protesting the movement. Every joint creaked with exertion, and his muscles kept trying to relax themselves while growing heavy, the way they did when he was about to sleep. As he moved, he came to recognize this for what it was: Just another episode of losing his words. He knew this state for what it was, even if he did not have words for it. It made him simultaneously dreadfully light and dreadfully heavy, and it always came after he had finally hit his head hard enough to make the scream go away.

In the office, there was no nurse. Mrs. Hudson, they said, was a new teacher, so she did not know better. Mr. Weir was summoned to talk to Clay while Mr. Chitwood talked to Noah.

The counselor looked worried when Clay did not reach out to shake his hand, but he did not ask Clay to do anything but answer questions. Then, he waved a hand in front of Clay's face and asked him how many fingers he saw, relaxing visibly when Clay gave what had to be a correct answer. After Mr. Weir was done asking questions, he asked Clay if he wanted to call his mother for a ride home.

He kind of did, because he had a very bad headache and all of his muscles hurt, but he also remembered how Kitty vomited out the side of the car and the way she had made him walk the last block to school, and he shook his head no to the call. Then Aaron led him back to class while he kept his eyes shut. By the time they returned to the room, the pounding headache had firmly lodged itself in his eyeballs, which at least made it manageable.

Mrs. Hudson did not say anything when Clay laid his head down on his desk and listened to her lesson with his eyes closed.

❖ ❖ ❖

The Kindness of Strange Children

Clay Dillon wandered around on the playground, but he did not play. His head hurt too much for that. So did his stomach.

Other children swarmed around him on the playground in packs that failed to acknowledge the random outsiders that struggled to pass through their midst. Clay struggled to cope with their ignorance of his confusion, but really, every thoughtless collision with some screaming chucklehead made him want to lash out violently.

Where was Aaron? He had said something about needing peace and quiet, and then he had disappeared completely.

Clay searched for his friend, but the playground seemed oddly unfamiliar. He walked by the same slide twice without recognizing it either time. He sat down under the slide and cried, but he did not cry alone for long. While Aaron did not magically appear to bring friendship and support, other children eventually found him, and some of them found him interesting.

The first group that stumbled across Clay was a trio of boys from Mrs. Hudson's class, led by a kid named Sully. Clay did not know Sully well, but he knew that the boy was one of the group of boys whose entire world seemed to revolve around their fathers' sports fandoms. To Clay, this did not necessarily make him bad, but it did make him completely indecipherable.

When Sully and his friends came up to Clay, he stood up.

"You okay?" Sully asked Clay. "It looked like Noah hit you hard."

"I guess," Clay said. "They didn't send me home, but I have a headache."

"I guess that makes you pretty tough," Sully said. "But if you're so tough, why did you pretend Noah hit you for no reason? Why didn't you tell Mrs. Hudson what you did?"

"He kept kicking me," Clay said. "I only wanted him to stop."

Clay was suddenly aware that Sully's two friends were on either side of him.

"You twisted his foot really hard," Sully said.

Then one of Sully's friends pushed Clay, hard, into the other one.

"Hey!" The third kid yelled. "Don't hit me!"

"I—" He never finished his objection. The two nameless boys kept yelling at him to stop being clumsy as they shoved him back and forth between them.

Clay's headache intensified. He had to hold his gorge down by force of will.

Sully laughed.

"That's enough!" The new voice was firm, but so tiny that it almost had to be shrill. At the same time, though, it was brassy with authority.

Clay could tell it was a girl's voice, but it was also a bugle's voice. He tried to look around for the bugle-girl, but the playground kept spinning. The other children stopped shoving him, though.

"Good," the bugle-girl said. "Now go find something else to do."

No one moved. Bugle-girl shrieked.

"What's going on over there? Is someone hurt?" Mr. Hanson's voice carried from somewhere nearby, but not too nearby.

Sully and his friends vanished.

"Everything is fine!" Bugle-girl called out. "Clay almost fell down and it startled me!"

A second later, Clay became aware that Mr. Hanson was standing a few feet from him.

"Are you sure you don't want to call home, Clay? You're kind of walking lopsided," he said.

"No," Clay said. "I just got dizzy from spinning around too much."

"You sure?" Mr. Hanson's voice grew a little harder. "There's nothing wrong? You haven't been sick this whole afternoon, have you?"

Suddenly, Clay felt exposed. How much did Mr. Hanson know? What would he do? It worried him to be caught like this, in a lie. He knew what he should tell Mr. Hanson how he felt, but at the same time, he was pretty sure that if he told the truth, then he would just wind up in trouble at home. That tended to be how things worked, in Clay's experience. From the roofing day fight with his father to biting A.J. back, other people would torture him, hurt him, or work him until he felt very tired. Then, when he finally collapsed or lost control over his own frustration, he had to be punished for his attempt to protect himself.

Mr. Hanson watched him expectantly.

Clay told himself to keep his emotions under control. He reminded himself about how angry his father had been last year when Mr. Foster made him leave work to come to a conference. Mark had not blamed his son for the incident, but his anger was still palpable, and once they were home, he and Kitty had taken their tempers out on each other. He had heard them through the air ducts. The house they lived in was full of ways to listen to other rooms. He knew all the times they blamed him for his own hurt.

Finally, he made himself look Mr. Hanson in the face.

"I am fine," he said. "I was playing around and I got dizzy and almost fell into her."

Mr. Hanson raised an eyebrow.

"It's okay," she said.

Then he nodded and wandered off. When Mr. Hanson was out of earshot, bugle-girl turned to Clay.

"Hi," she said.

"Hello," Clay replied. "Who are you?"

"I'm Hillary," the girl said. Then she made a little curtsy. Her floral dress did not bend with her body. It was pretty, but the fabric was thick and stiff. Along the collar, rigid lace held the shape of her even as her body itself moved.

"Your mom makes your clothes," Clay said. "My mom made some of my clothes once. They didn't last very long. She makes a lot of her own clothes, though, and she's good at it."

"My mom too," Hillary said.

"Thank you," Clay said.

"I'm in Mrs. Hudson's class too," Hillary said. "I sit kind of behind Noah. I saw what he did to you. He's a creep."

"How do you know him? I don't remember you from Mrs. Nesbitt's class."

Hillary shrugged. "I wasn't in Mrs. Nesbitt's class last year. I was in Mrs. Conrad's."

She spun around a little bit.

Clay closed his eyes so that her motion would not make him feel ill. It was too late, though. He got dizzy, and then he fell down with his eyes closed.

When his knees hit the ground, he grimaced at the sensation of them sinking in and the earth settling around them.

"Oops," Hillary said. "You got a little muddy."

Clay wanted to scream. He did not feel the scream welling up inside himself, which was a relief, but he wanted to create it and turn it loose anyway. He knew that courting the scream was dangerous, though, so he tried to make his metal body harden around himself.

Nothing happened.

Well, not nothing. His dizziness got worse, and only Hillary reaching out and holding him by the shoulders kept him from falling onto his face and turning his dirty knees into a full-on mud suit like Patrick had done.

"Let's show Mr. Hanson," she said. "He can let us in to clean up."

Clay nodded, remembering how Mr. Hanson had proven to be helpful at the lunchtime recess. He let Hillary help him up, and the two went to see the playground aide together.

Mr. Hanson made a weird face at Clay when he saw the boy was muddied up again.

"You're sure you're not dizzy and falling down because of the way that kid cold-cocked you?" He asked. "Because, I gotta be honest, when I see a kid who keeps falling down and getting hurt, I get worried."

"I'm worried too," Clay said. "I don't want my pants to get stained."

"Fair enough," Mr. Hanson said. Then he unlocked the door to the first grade wing and opened it.

Clay and Hillary walked inside. She walked him up to the door of the boys' bathroom before stopping.

"I'm sorry," Hillary said. Then she walked back outside.

"Wait!" Clay called. "I need help!"

"I am sorry," she called over her shoulder as she went through the door. "I want to stay with you, but I can't go in there."

The door closed behind her, and Clay was alone, with mud up to his knees, in the dim light from the overhead windows. He walked into the bathroom he had used so often the previous year, the one that had been his safe haven when he needed to clean blood off his legs or to hide from his scream. He tried to clean himself up there, but the mud was stickier and harder to wipe away in the late afternoon than it had been earlier. When he left to go back to class, there were still half-dried clods falling off him. Mrs. Hudson sniffed derisively the first time one of them hit the floor of her room. Clay felt too hollow and too tired to make any sense of the changes in her mood, so he put his head down on his desk and listened to the rest of the class. Luckily, there was only an hour between the final recess and the end of the day.

❖   ❖   ❖

New Routines

After meeting Hillary for the first time, Clay seemed to find her everywhere. She one of the most vocal people in Mrs. Hudson's class, which surprised no one more than the teacher herself. Often, Mrs.

Hudson would follow comments from Hillary with instructions to the rest of the class about what they might learn from her. Sometimes, they were general, like when she said, "You could all stand to speak up more. I know that more people know the answers, and you should show me that." When she started telling Hillary "I don't know how it is that you didn't get picked up by the gifted and talented group" in front of the rest of the class, Clay started to chafe. The things the teacher was saying were not really praise to Hillary, and he wanted to say as much. He also wanted to tell her that he was not stupid just because he did not like to talk.

Whenever he tried to speak up, though, he felt like someone was holding him by the throat. Worse than that was the feeling of that imaginary hand. It was the viselike claw attached to his metal body. Clay wanted to be able to control it, to turn it outward and use it the way that he had when he faced down the librarian, but he could not. Somehow, the metal body had ceased to be protection and strength. Now, it was a prison.

When it took over his regular skin now, it did not sharpen him, nor did it grow hot. Instead, it stayed cold and heavy, like any old hunk of scrap would be. He twisted inside of it, trying to get out, and every time he felt like he was going to be able to force his metal jaws to open so that he could speak up, someone would say something to him that shut him down and made his iron feelings heavier. Mrs. Hudson and her not-praise that was really meant to shame everyone except Hillary did it. So did his mother asking him what had happened that made him stop being easy.

This continued for weeks, which is not to say that Clay realized exactly how long the span was. He knew that time was passing, and he knew that it was a fairly long span of time, but he lost track of the exact number of days fairly quickly. Between the ways the metal weighed his thoughts down and the ways that it hardened them, counting days was just not possible.

During this time, he avoided Noah, who was out of school for a long time anyway. He also tried to avoid Sully, but that was not so easy. The boy seemed to be everywhere, friends with everyone. Even

Aaron knew him (through a summer day camp), and Patrick had been in his Sunday school class the year before. Neither of them was particularly fond of Sully, but neither had seen him do anything like what Clay described either. When he tried to make them understand, they told him that they believed he was exaggerating.

Clay stopped trying to make them understand. After that, everything got easier.

The way that time passed reminded Clay of the grinding monotony that he had been forced to endure before starting school. Then, too, his days had been spent in the presence of other children, some who hated him, some who did not, and some who were simply so much better at everything than he was, so he had no idea how to talk to them. He felt like Hillary belonged to this last group, which was why he found it difficult to keep a conversation with her going. She kept trying to talk to him, but what was he supposed to say back? He felt like he should know, but he did not. His heavy metal thoughts seemed at first to be to blame for this phenomenon, but he quickly realized that this was not right. He could tell that his frustration was something else, even if he could not tell what it was.

Whatever it was, it made his understanding harder to achieve by making his feelings both more intense and less intelligible, which made speech even harder than it had been before. Eventually, all Clay could do was answer questions that were put directly to him. Luckily, Aaron and Patrick seemed to understand this, or at least, they seemed not to hold it against him. Instead, they filled in the cracks his silence created with their own interests, narrating them to Clay and filling his head with their knowledge. Most days, this meant that he learned more on the playground than he did when he was in class.

Such was the situation in October, when Hillary started making a point of sitting with them at lunch. It happened slowly, over the course of a week or so. First, Clay found himself separated from Patrick and Aaron because his mother gave him money for a hot lunch instead of packing his meal. Since Patrick never ate the school's food and Aaron was on the free lunch program, this meant that the three of them had to go through three separate lunch lines while making sure that they wound up entering the actual cafeteria at the same time. It was the only way to ensure that Mr. Hanson assigned them to the same table, and it did not work. At least, not consistently. When Clay could count on sticking to Patrick, then Aaron did fairly well on his own. When Clay had to navigate through a lunch line alone, especially one that involved so many people asking him questions about food, though, he became confused.

That first day, when Clay was still trying to learn how to work the line, Mr. Hanson sat him at a girls' table, and it just so happened that it was the same one Hillary sat at. She seemed glad to see him, and she asked him if Sully was still giving him trouble. The fact that she did not accuse him of overreacting made him feel relieved, and so he shared his concerns about Noah and Sully with her. Neither boy had really done anything to Clay after that first day of school, but he was sure both of them were planning something.

Hillary shared his concern and promised to let him know if she heard anything from either of them that indicated they were planning trouble for Clay. Then she talked about seeing him at church, which surprised Clay. He let her know that he had not even noticed her there before, and she giggled.

"Yes," Hillary said. "We've been going there for years. I remember when they announced that your family had just become full members. I even remember back when Patrick's family was new."

"What about Sully?" Clay asked.

"I don't know him well, but he was also born here. His family was never new."

"Oh," Clay said.

"Did you know his uncle is on the school board? He ran for election before Sully was born, and he keeps getting re-elected."

"Okay," Clay said. He hoped that Hillary realized that he was actually very interested in what she was saying.

She seemed to, because she kept telling him more secrets about things that she knew about Greenridge and its schools. She told him how people said that Mrs. Hudson was an atheist because she did not go to any churches in town and she insisted on teaching science class even though her students were only second graders. Hillary knew that she actually belonged to a Presbyterian church in Grand Rapids, though, and that the reason she traveled so far each Sunday was because it was the same church that she had grown up in.

Knowledge like this was a completely new phenomenon to Clay, who had previously only had the opportunity to absorb what the television, his parents, and Aaron and Patrick told him. From that, he had concluded that the world was a place where non-Catholics only pretended to love God, where aliens and Bigfoots lurked around every corner, and where fascinating trivia about the nutritional content of foods or the season's best new Nintendo games made up the majority of peoples' discussions about current events. These stories of people and places that Hillary told were not only novel, they seemed important in ways that those other pieces of information did not, and Clay was glad to be listening. He was also glad that after so many failed attempts at conversation, he was able to keep Hillary talking to him. When she realized that his taciturn responses did not indicate a lack of interest, she became warm in a way that reduced the intimidating parts of her intellect to positive quirks by deflating Clay's expectations about how she would respond if he failed to reciprocate at her level. By the time they were released to the playground, he was telling her stories about Grandpa Harry.

After that, Hillary made a point of sitting with him on the bus. Before she found him, he did not know that they actually rode the same route, but once she pointed it out, Clay realized that she was right.

She lived in a small house near Pine Island Drive. It was a nice place, and only about as old as the house that Clay lived in, but it was farther from town than Clay's house, so she could not walk to the park or to the grocery store like Aaron and Clay. In the morning, when Clay was the first stop on the bus route, he got to see her mother escort her up to the bus, and they would talk during the long ride back into town. In the afternoon, though, Clay's proximity to the school worked against him, and he was dropped off after only a five minute ride. Hillary still sat with him every time, though.

A few days later, she showed up at his lunch table, sitting down next to Patrick and across from Aaron. After that, everyone ate in silence. Clay wished he knew what to say to his friends to get them to start talking to Hillary, but his words fled before his attempts to brainstorm. Luckily, Hillary said something herself. What she said was:

"We have catechism class today, so you should eat quickly. We need to get on the bus to go to St. Sebastian's."

Clay had no idea what she was talking about. He said as much.

"Your mom signed you up for it. My mom told me so. All of us are going to do it—we go to the church every Wednesday so that we can take religion class."

Clay shook his head. His mother had never mentioned anything like this. Why was Hillary telling him what to do?

"Come on, Clay. Don't just shake your head. My mom told me today that I had to make sure you got on the bus."

Suddenly, Clay felt very differently about his friendship with Hillary. He could not find words to articulate this difference, but it was so abrupt that it made his metal body fully deploy.

"Don't you tell me things," he said. "No one told me to get on the bus, and I'm not leaving school just because. I have science class."

"Not today," Hillary said. "Today we have religion class."

Clay shook his head again.

"Come on, Clay. I haven't ever said anything mean to you. Why would I lie about this?"

"If I was supposed to go, then my mom would have said something." Clay felt his metal body heating up and becoming more flexible. He tried to control it, but instead he cut the inside of his mouth with his tongue.

"Fine. Go talk to your mom about it. I'll get whatever you need —worksheets or homework or whatever. I'm not fighting with you about it."

Finally, Clay broke.

"Just because you're so smart you already know everything doesn't mean you know about me," Clay said. "It doesn't mean you can boss me, either. I'm going to science class because I already go to church and only an idiot would expect me to miss learning about real things to go hear Jesus stories I could just read for myself whenever."

Hillary nodded. Then she stood up and left. That afternoon on the bus ride home she did not sit with Clay.

❖   ❖   ❖

Metal on Metal

Kitty Dillon was waiting for her son when he arrived home from school. Clay could see her through the picture window, staring out into the front yard as he trudged toward the door.

He had not realized how much he relied upon Hillary's company until it was gone. Aaron and Patrick were good friends, and they were nice to him, but when Clay spent time with them he did not feel like they really understood how hard it was for him to keep up. More accurately, he felt like Patrick did not really understand. Aaron was usually pretty okay when Clay got to see him one-on-one. It was only when Patrick was around that it seemed like Aaron lost track of how much work it took for Clay to visit. Patrick could be exhausting that way. Clay knew that, but he also knew that Aaron was not really a happy person normally. Neither was he. That was what Patrick brought to the equation. He was the only one of the three whose ability to have fun was completely untainted by any kind of tendency to brood.

What neither of them did, though, was accept Clay at face value. Patrick always assumed that Clay's discomfort was at least partially feigned so that Clay could get his way more. It was evident in the way he refused to accept that Clay did not need "turns" with video games and computers that he did not understand. Aaron's assumptions were a little less over-reaching, but he always acted like it was his job to tell Clay different ways that he could have said what he was trying to say.

Hillary did neither of those things. She just told him what she thought and then she reacted to what he actually said, not to what she thought he meant or what she thought he should have said.

Clay had ruined that. He was sure of it. Why else would she have avoided sitting with him on the bus? She had sat with him every day since she first started talking to him at the lunch tables.

This was the truth Clay Dillon lived as he walked into the house to face his mother. She did not turn away from the window when he opened the door or even when he crossed the threshold. Clay hoped that meant she was bothered by some thought that had nothing to do with him, and he tried to take advantage of that hope to scurry up the stairs with his backpack so that he could place himself firmly outside the radius of whatever foul temper she was sure to wind up unleashing soon.

It did not work. As soon as Clay's foot touched the first stair, his mother's voice rang out from the living room.

"You need to come in here and have a seat," she said. "I have a bone to pick with you."

Suddenly, Clay's mind leapt to make meaning out of the unfamiliar words.

"A bone?" He set his backpack down on the stairs. "Why?" He walked into the living room. "Are we getting a dog or something?"

That was when his mother turned to face him. As soon as Clay saw her eyes, he knew: whatever her comment had meant, it did not mean anything so hopeful or so generous as he had assumed it would. It meant that he had been "not easy" at the very least, and that she probably thought he was intentionally doing something to make her life harder.

Clay braced himself for whatever it was.

"You skipped catechism class today," she said. "And I want to know why."

Clay shrugged. "I didn't know that I was supposed to go."

"That's bullshit, Clay. What happened?"

Clay scowled. "Hillary told me I was supposed to get on a bus and leave school, but that was a prank. People play pranks at school all the time. I got pushed into the mud a few weeks ago."

Kitty sighed. "That wasn't a prank, Clay. You were supposed to get on the bus."

"Don't be an idiot. I would have missed science class, and I would have left school in the middle of the day. Who would be stupid enough to schedule church time on a Wednesday?"

His mother's expression hardened. "Me."

Clay realized then that she had her own metal body, right before realizing that it was very likely he was about to be cut by it. He tried to reason with her before she did that.

"I'm sorry," he said. "How was I supposed to know that, though? You didn't tell me anything about having to go. And why am I supposed to miss science class to go to church? I already go to church on Sunday with you and Dad. You set aside the whole day for it, so that I have to stay there and play with the loud stupid children I don't like. I shouldn't have to do all that in the middle of a school day when I already have to do it every Sunday."

"Go to your room," his mother said. "Just go."

"Why? You can't ground me for disobeying something you never said to do," Clay could feel that there was something wrong with the way his words were coming out, but he seemed to be unable to do anything to change them. It did not help that his mother's sharp inflections were making his own metal body respond.

"I said get the fuck out of here!" his mother screeched. "Why can't you just follow directions for once? You're just like your father, always thinking you're right. You knew that you were supposed to go to catechism and you didn't. Quit pretending that you're too stupid to know what you were supposed to do."

Armor plates slammed over each other as they sprang from every joint and crease in Clay's body to cover his vulnerable parts. This time, the metal body was not solid. It was instead a mosaic of small shields, capable of bending and flexing as Clay needed. He could feel how seriously it had been improved, and that feeling made him confident.

"Everyone is stupid when the one running things is stupid," he fired back. "If you're not smart enough to know that I need to be told what I'm supposed to do, then I shouldn't have to listen to you and you shouldn't be a parent yet. There's a reason that none of the other parents in my class are only twenty-five."

"GET OUT!" Kitty Dillon rushed at her son as she screamed.

At first, Clay's instinct was to crouch, so that she would have to bend over to hit him. He had seen people do it on television. The crouch would let him hit her with his full weight while she was bending over, so that he would have a better chance of knocking her down. Then, he would have a few seconds to get away while she tried to stand back up and orient herself.

At the last minute, he remembered his father's words. If he hit his mother, then his father would take him outside and beat on him until he could not stand up. He had always said so.

Clay rose from his crouch as his mother bent over him and reached for his collar. The result was that she did not so much grab him at the junction of the neck and shoulder as she punched him in the chest with the combined force of both their inertia. The wind left Clay's body before he lost his balance. As he fell, though, he thought that it was his sudden inability to work his lungs that was making him collapse, and that frightened him. Just before his head hit the floor, he realized that he could not feel his body, and he assumed that he was dead.

◆ ◆ ◆

It was dark when Clay opened his eyes, but he knew that they were open because he could feel the muscles in his eyelids working. His head protested their every twitch and he felt like someone had replaced his brain with a bag of sand, but he could feel. That meant that he was not dead.

He sat up, and the bag of sand in his head was replaced by a pain so large and so deep that the only part of it Clay could attach a word to was the throbbing. He let himself lie back down. There was no point to investigating the room if his head was going to be that way. Instead, he waited. Eventually, he heard the door to the room open. Not sure who to expect, Clay decided it would be best if his visitor thought he was asleep, so he closed his eyes.

Footsteps approached the bed. They were soft on the carpet, but Clay could still hear them, or at least, he imagined that he could. Whoever it was, they were breathing audibly but not panting, and they smelled a little bit like oil or gasoline, but not the kind that went into cars.

"I am awake," Clay said to his father. "My head hurts."

"You knocked it pretty bad," Mark said. "You probably don't want to try to wrestle with your mom. She isn't big, but she's twice your size."

"I wasn't trying anything. She ran at me because she didn't tell me what to do and then she got mad."

His father took a deep breath.

"Do I really have to go to church class instead of science class?" Clay asked.

"Yes," his father replied.

"But I already told you two that I don't want to go to Catholic school. I thought that was settled."

His father sighed. "It was. That's why you need to go to catechism. That's the deal."

Clay said nothing. It did not seem like a deal to him, that he had said he did not want to be involved with this and yet, he still was.

"Your mother is adamant. The only way you're not going to Catholic school is if you go to this catechism class on Wednesdays."

"Go ahead and put me in Catholic school then," Clay said. "I'll hit the teacher and break windows until they don't want me."

Suddenly, the air in the room was colder. When Mark Dillon spoke again, his words cut Clay up.

"Do that and I'll let the cops deal with you, you little vandal. You think you can threaten me? I'm your fucking father. I made this deal with your mother to respect your wishes, and now you're going to live with it. Got it?"

Clay nodded.

"Good. Now quit pretending that we don't listen to you and we don't give you choices. You can come downstairs whenever you're ready."

The smells and sounds of his father retreated. When Clay heard the door close, he lashed out with his fist, driving it into the drywall next to his bed.

"What was that?" The shout came through the door.

"I rolled over and hit my elbow!" Clay yelled back.

"You will watch your tone, or you'll spend the next week in there! Every day! After school!" was the only reply he received.

Clay rolled over and screamed into his pillow until his headache bloomed into unconsciousness.

❖   ❖   ❖

Gang Up

Clay spent most of the next week with a headache. He was used to that, or at least, he was partially used to it. Headaches were very common in his life, and they seemed to be caused by everything: excessive light, sudden loud noises, too much movement, too little movement, being forced to listen to people he could not understand, being forced to listen to people long after he understood what they were getting at... everything caused headaches.

Those things that all caused headaches, though, they did not all cause the same type. Nor did the same stimulus always cause the same type. To Clay, it seemed more like his tendency to have a headache was like a microphone's tendency to produce high-pitched, whistling feedback. The more noise he had to process, and the more sensitive he was to that processing, the louder his headache became. Like the microphone he imagined, he was unable to control his own level of sensitivity—that seemed to be variable and directly tied to an outside source.

That was normally. The headache he had after his fight with his mother was not normal, though. It was more like the kind of headache he had after the scream had taken him over, a kind that permeated his bones and kept him from moving correctly when he tried to walk. This particular headache made him feel as if he was only wearing his body, or perhaps driving it from a remote location. It removed his seat of consciousness from his eyes, eliminating the agitated warmth that usually felt like it emanated from his forehead, making him feel as if all of the things he touched were very far away.

Clay was not used to this, because after the scream he would only suffer until sleep took him, and it seemed like the headache itself made him numb to the memory of it. This time, though, it stayed with him for days and he was unable to tell whether it was even getting better as time went on, because it kept him from feeling like he was properly inside his body. During the week of the headache, he found it nearly impossible to want to do anything. At home, he flipped listlessly through books he remembered reading, hoping to find something that would make him feel like reading them again. At school, he managed to will himself through the work only to arrive at recess with a depleted sense of his friends' presence. Most of the time, he did not even speak. Instead, he followed Patrick around, listening to the music that emanated from his Game Boy speaker.

◆　◆　◆

Wednesday came, and Clay knew that he would have to face the bus ride to catechism. He had not seen Hillary since their falling-out, and he dreaded climbing on the bus. He would have to apologize, which was hard even when he felt he should be doing it, and now he would be apologizing for something that he felt strongly he was right to do. Hillary made it easier, though. After having avoided him for the last week, she sat herself right beside him on the way to school. She did not ask about catechism, but she did ask about how his week had been, which games Patrick was playing on the Game Boy, and whether or not Clay was going to go to the church's fall harvest picnic in the middle of October.

Clay did not feel much like answering, but he tried his best to do it anyway, since Hillary was the only person who seemed interested in trying to know how he actually felt. Everyone else either asked him why he was not acting normally or demanded that he give them attention while they talked about the things they wanted to talk about.

He tried to explain to her about the headache and about the incident with his mother, but all Hillary could do was ask him about whether or not he had been to see a doctor. Clay did not understand why she thought he needed to do that. He was not sick, he had not been vomiting or feverish, and he had no cuts or broken bones or anything. He could move all his parts. Why did she ignore the way that Kitty treated him to badger him about his headache? He had headaches all the time. He wanted to yell at her, but he could not figure out how to explain the disappointment and betrayal he felt when he discovered that his mother was taking away science class to make him go to extra church. He felt like yelling would just make Hillary go away again, too, so he stayed silent.

She still kept asking him about the headache and doctors. Eventually, he realized that he would need to respond, because there was no other way to get her to stop.

"It's not really that bad," Clay said. "I think if I needed to see a doctor my parents would know. They spy on me pretty close. They don't even let me read what I want."

Hillary stopped asking him about doctors after that, and Clay enjoyed the rest of his bus ride with her.

♦ ♦ ♦

The morning dragged on. Clay found himself stuck staring at the clock, constantly counting the number of minutes before he would lose half of his lunch time and all of his science lesson to the church school. As he counted down, he thought about the work that he had put in over the summer to read the Bible and *The Screwtape Letters*. Maybe the reason his mother wanted him in this class was because she sensed that he understood things that she had not explained well. He doubted that was true, because he knew that Noah the Nosepicker and Sully also attended church school, and he did not think that they would bother themselves with extra readings. At least, they never talked about anything like that. He would never know for sure if he did not go to check things out, though.

On the other hand, Clay felt that if he acquiesced and attended religion class this once, then his mother would be able to claim that he chose to go along with it, which would make it harder to stop her from forcing him to keep participating. It was hardly like this would be the first time she tried such a tactic, either. The entire reason he had attempted to read the Bible was because his parents had tried to get him to agree to something, and then when he kept his end of the bargain, they used his actions against him, forcing him to keep going even though they did not keep their end of the deal. It was also the reason that he still had not read *The Joy Luck Club*, and it was also the reason why he had been forced to endure his mother's thoughts about *The Screwtape Letters*. If she was willing to lie so baldly and so boldly about something like reading, then what would she do once she had the idea that he was going along with this whole church school idea? She might even use it to badger his father about putting him in a Catholic school again. She had threatened it before.

If he went to church school, then he was just giving her the ammunition she needed to claim he had agreed to something. As the red second hand swept around the clock's face and the minutes slowly bled away, Clay's resolve hardened. He would not comply. He would tell Hillary that she did not know anything but what her mother told her and that he did not want to fight with her, but he would not do what she said he should do.

◆   ◆   ◆

Clay found himself on the bus as it pulled out of the Greenridge school parking lot. He did not immediately remember how he wound up there, but Hillary was beside him, and his head hurt a lot.

"I'm glad that you decided to come along today," Hillary said. "Last week it was really boring without you."

Clay looked around the bus. Sully and his gang, including Noah the Nosepicker, were the only other children from Mrs. Hudson's class. He also saw Shawna, from his first-grade class with Mrs. Nesbitt, sitting in the front. Everyone else was unfamiliar.

"I thought Patrick went to church with us," he said. "Where's Patrick? Why do I have to go when he doesn't?"

"I don't know," Hillary said. "I guess his mom didn't sign him up."

"Why?"

"I don't know. Maybe he goes on a different day."

"There's no day when he is out of class. If he can go without missing science, I want to go to that class."

"I don't know anything about that," Hillary said. "All I know is that my mom asked me to remind you to come to catechism because it's better for us to buddy up if we are going out someplace."

Clay nodded. On the rare occasion that his mother allowed him to leave the yard unsupervised she always made him take A.J. with him, and her reason was usually the same.

Hillary kept talking, but Clay was indifferent to the meaning of her words. His mind kept turning over the problem of Patrick's participation, looking for ways to dismantle his mother's attempt to keep him from science class.

The bus ride was calm, and Sully's friends did not bother them. They did keep looking over, as if Clay's presence was a sudden shock to them every time they noticed him, but they did not attempt to bother either of the two children as they shared a seat.

That, unfortunately, did not last. After the bus arrived at St. Sebastian's and the children disembarked, Noah and Sully took an interest in Clay. He ignored them when they called out to him, following Hillary to the classroom and taking a seat beside her. They came along.

Hillary grabbed Clay's hand and squeezed it as they sat down. He was unsure why, but he assumed that she also disliked the idea of being in a classroom that was made up entirely of Sully and Noah's friends.

When minutes passed and no teacher appeared, Clay whispered to Hillary to ask what was going on. She whispered back that she did not know—the teacher that she had seen the previous week had been a substitute.

Eventually, the sounds of other children in the hallway went away, but there was still no teacher in the room. Clay kept silent, but Hillary kept whispering to him. He tried to hear her, but her words seemed to slip away from him unless he mouthed them to himself to make them sink in. He wanted to ask her to be louder, but he also did not want Sully and his friends to inject themselves into the conversation.

"Are you talking to anyone? Or do you have to keep yourself company now?" Sully's voice sounded like a horn on the other side of the room.

"I'm just trying to listen," Clay said.

"Well, you're listening with your mouth moving," Sully replied. "That's not really listening. That's rude."

"You don't need to care," Hillary said. "You aren't part of this."

"I care because I have to sit across from you all year long and I don't want you muttering about me, you little queer." Sully spoke to Clay as if Hillary was not even there.

Clay had no idea what Sully meant by 'queer', but the way Sully spat the word out of his mouth made Clay's metal body deploy. He had to shout to make himself heard over the clanging of the armor sliding over itself to lock into place.

"You don't talk about me," was all he got out.

Sully and Noah both started laughing.

"Or what? You'll shriek me to death?" Sully climbed up on the table. "Or are you gonna twist my foot and then blame me for hitting you back?"

He put his leg out and shook it at Clay.

"Go ahead, you little psycho. Try one of your homo tricks on me."

Before Clay knew what he was doing, he was on his feet, lifting the end of the table up and dropping Sully back into Noah's lap. When the two collided, Noah and his chair shot backward and slammed into the wall.

"Get off my junk you queer!" Noah screamed as he shoved Sully.

Sully careened forward, stumbling into the up-ended table. His other friends laughed. It seemed like they did not care who was getting hurt as long as it was someone. Once, they helped push Clay into the mud on the playground, but now they seemed just as happy to see Sully fall down.

Clay felt his metal body shift, flowing like he was made of mercury. His arms seemed to grow longer as he shoved the table (and Sully behind it) back toward Noah, pinning them against the wall as they called him a queer in chorus.

Sully saw Clay's fist coming and ducked under the table to avoid it. Clay tried to swing downward, and even though he made contact, the blow had no power. As soon as he heard Sully giggle at the ineffectiveness of his punch, his body hardened again, and he found it difficult to make himself move.

Sully pushed back against the table, and with Noah's help he did manage to move Clay. It took the both of them though.

Clay stared at them. They laughed.

"Look at the little faggot, all puffed up like he's going to hit us!" Noah bleated. "Are you just gonna stare, or what? I'm not afraid of you. I'll kick your ass."

"Enough!" Hillary's voice dismantled the armor protecting Clay, and suddenly he was very tired. He sat back in his chair, watching as she and Sully righted the table.

"You need to leave him alone," Hillary said. "We all know that Noah got what he was asking for."

Sully rolled his eyes. Noah scoffed.

"I mean it," Hillary said. "You know Mrs. Hudson's rule—if we get in trouble here, we also get in trouble at school."

"If we're bug-eyed little faggots here we're also bug-eyed little faggots at school though," Noah shot back.

"Keep using that word. I'll tell everyone you learned it because that was what your dad called you and Sully when he found you kissing," Hillary said.

The sound of Noah's teeth grinding carried in the room, but he said nothing. Sully seemed to take the hint as well, and he started putting the room back together. Soon, the rest of the children joined in.

After everyone rearranged their chairs, the only sign of the conflict was a small hole in the drywall where Noah's chair had hit. Unfortunately, when the teacher came into the room a moment or two later, it was the first thing she saw.

"Who did this?" she asked.

Clay opened his mouth to admit fault, but Hillary spat out "Sully" first.

"He and Noah were fooling around, and he shoved Noah into the wall," she added.

"We'll deal with this after class," the teacher said. "I'm going to need you to stay here while we call your parents," she added to Sully.

"I didn't do it!" he shouted.

Hillary made a face and then stared at Noah.

"We didn't mean to do any damage," Noah said. "We were just bored and fooling around. We weren't fighting."

The teacher eyed them both.

"I thought I heard some language as I came down the hall," she said.

"Nope," Sully replied. "A lot of us were talking though. It might have been hard to hear what we said."

The teacher nodded. "I'll let it go this time, but don't make me regret it."

Clay leaned in to whisper to Hillary.

"What's a faggot? And a queer?"

"They're the same thing," Hillary whispered back.

"But what are they?" Clay asked.

"Don't worry about it," Hillary said. "Just keep an eye on Noah and Sully."

Clay did as she asked, but even so, he felt the tip of the scream licking away at his consciousness. This time, it was not incoherent. It was made out of the words that Noah and Sully had used against him.

❖   ❖   ❖

Emergent Behavior

"I tried it and I hated it so I am not going back." Clay Dillon planted his feet in the entryway to the house and tried to make his face as serious as his words.

His mother laughed a little bit before she caught herself. Clay could not see her, but he could hear her voice carrying up the stairs.

"I mean it. You can't make me miss school to sit around with a bunch of turds. I won't."

"Don't call your classmates turds. Just tell me what happened," her voice called out.

Clay kicked off his shoes and set down his backpack before stomping down the stairs to confront his mother. When she heard him, she ordered him to walk up and down the stairs ten times without stomping before she would listen.

As he did it, Clay felt his anger growing with each step. His mother often raised her voice to him, or else she stomped around, cleaning with such a heavy hand that the clattering of dishes in the drainer sounded like a deliberate attempt to break the plates against the pots and pans. What right did she have to demand different behavior from him?

By the time he finished his punishment, his entire exterior was a shining titanium monument to her work. His vocal chords felt like a woven garrote, and he cut his tongue against his razor teeth as he contemplated the ways his voice would carve his mother into chunks.

"Okay, so what's the problem?" she asked as she folded clothes and stacked them on the washing machine.

"Patrick doesn't have to leave school for catechism and I don't know anyone in my class. Why does he get to stay for science class when I don't? He goes to St. Sebastian's too."

"I don't know," Kitty replied.

"Well fix this," Clay shot back.

His mother sighed.

"Clay, you're already signed up for class and the sessions have started. I can't just pull you out and put you in another group. Besides, I have a lot of housework to do and this allows me to make sure you go to catechism without having to take an hour out of my day to drive you around."

"Patrick's mother takes an hour. She takes whatever time she needs to take. And she works. And she makes homemade French fries. And she doesn't yell at Patrick and his brother, even when they call her stupid."

"Well maybe you should just go live with Patrick's mother then!" Kitty shouted.

Clay licked his lips and imagined the blood from where he cut his tongue was making them bright red. Then he smiled.

"Okay. Let me go pack," he said as he stomped up the stairs.

"Get back down here and go up and down the stairs ten times!" Kitty yelled after him.

"I don't live here," Clay shouted back. "You can't talk to me like that."

His mother followed him up the stairs and into his room, where she saw that he had already started to take clothes out of the dresser and stack them on the bed. He made sure to put together at least a week's worth of each item: socks, shirts, underwear, pants.

"Stop," Kitty said. "You aren't going to be able to move in with Patrick."

That was when Clay carved the air with his vocal chords.

"So you're just lying about everything, then," he said. "You lie about what you want me to do, you lie about sending me to school by making me quit my favorite subject. You lied about what was in the Bible—you said it was about God when it was really about conquering people and killing and making children into sacrifices. You lied about *The Screwtape Letters* being good and then you made me listen to your stupid blathering about it for a month even though it's a baby book and you can read the whole thing in an afternoon. You lie all the time, and then you tell me not to get mad. I have never not been mad at you. Not since you told me to use my words when I was upset and then yelled at me for yelling at you. You want to know which time? The first time. I have been mad at you every day since then. You're stupid, and you shouldn't be telling me what to do because I am in second grade and I already know more than you."

He felt his mother split apart as he talked. Her face got very red while her hands turned white, and it seemed as if the pieces of her body were floating away from each other. Then everything about her changed, and she was in motion.

Clay felt himself being pulled through the doorway and into the bathroom. This time, there would be no Joy. Instead, his face was pressed into the porcelain sink before there was water running. He felt something slimy on the side of his head then, and a second later the sound of rushing water filled his ears before being followed by the blast from the faucet. He took a deep breath when he realized that his other ear was over the drain. Then he was submerged.

Clay went in and out of the water a few times as his mother wrestled him. Each time, she tried to force a bar of soap between his teeth. He bit her, at some point. Then the soap managed to get in. He tried to spit it out, but she was holding it there.

At least she did not put him back under the water.

"You learn some respect," she said. "I am your *mother*."

"Could've fooled me," he muttered around the soap.

"Just hold that there until I'm done talking with you," she replied.

Clay tried to open his mouth, to drop the soap, but Kitty held his jaw. Then she forced him to look at her.

"You might know more than me about what's in those books, but you do not know more than me," she said. "You do not know what will happen if you grow up with nothing but hatred and entitlement. You do not know what happens when mothers let their sons run a household. You do not know what it is like for other women to see you and then to talk down to you or treat you like trash because they were older when they had their children. You. Do. Not. Know."

"I know you're a liar. You don't keep promises." He wanted to add: And you want me to pretend the stuff in the Bible really happened just because you're afraid.

Clay could not make his mouth keep working around the soap, though, because it was making him queasy. Every time his lips and tongue moved, they coaxed more suds off the bar, and those suds had already filled his nostrils and started trickling down his throat.

"You will go to that church school as I tell you, or you will go to Catholic school. Those are your choices. You won't run away because you are eight and you don't know where to go. You won't get expelled from those schools because I will just put you in other schools."

Clay felt his gorge rising. He tried to push the bar of soap out of his mouth, but his mother still held his jaw.

"You will get raised right until you are eighteen, and then to hell with you if you want to act like your father's brother."

Clay's chest heaved as his stomach tried to force the soap suds up and out of his throat. He tried again to spit the bar out too, but instead he wound up shoving himself into his mother. She grabbed for his arm, as if she was going to keep him from hitting her. As soon as she let go of his jaw, though, his mouth opened.

The bar of soap hit Kitty Dillon in the nose, propelled as it was by a stream of projectile vomit and soap suds. Then her son's body collided with her midsection. At first, she tried to fight him off, but then she realized that he was not hitting her, he was convulsing with round after round of heaving nausea.

She slipped and fell. Her head hit something, and then she remembered that the towel rack was behind her.

"I'm sorry," she said as her butt hit the ground.

Clay fell on top of her. He wanted to tell her that apologies meant nothing, but he could not make words and his mouth muscles were busy trying to push as much soap out of his body they could.

When he gained control over his legs, he ran. He did not keep track of where he was going, but in a moment he discovered that he was at the front door. He decided to keep running.

As Clay was putting his shoes on, he heard his mother shout: "Do not go out that front door!"

He reached for the doorknob, but as he did, a fresh wave of nausea hit him. He ran upstairs instead, and then he shoved his body under the bed and cried.

I do not hate my mother, he said to himself. He felt the lie in it, but the truth made him ashamed, so he kept saying to himself that she was trying to be good to him, but she did not know anything. He kept saying it, and he felt the scream growing as he did.

Eventually, she tried to talk him out from under the bed. He retaliated by pouring the scream all over her until she grabbed the back of her head and moaned. Then he burst forth from under the bed, scrambling on all fours. She tried to step back from him, but he head-butted her aside, ramming his skull into her stomach as hard as he could before he ran into her bedroom and locked the door. He did not stop there, either. Clay took every item he could find and stacked it up against the door's frame, so that it could not be kicked open.

All he wanted was to be able to pick some things for himself. His books. His time at church school. Or better yet, he should be able to pick to skip church school if he wanted. He did go to church every time they asked, after all. And he read the Bible more than they did.

When he had started Maccabees, his mother admitted she had never read it. He thought about what she had said about knowing things, though, and he wondered if she had gone out and read *The Joy Luck Club* after all.

"Linder's winders," he muttered to himself between sobs. "Endo's embos."

He kept thinking about the books he had read, or read part of. All of the ones that were about the kinds of fights he had with his parents or the kinds of hopes he had for his future were the ones that his mother hated. They were also the ones the rest of the adults tried to keep him from reading. At the same time, though, his mother did not want him reading the more aggressive books that taught him about how adults hurt children in their private places, whether those private places were on their bodies or in their minds. Instead, she only seemed to care to have him read simple stories.

When she had tried to talk to him about the Little House books and he had asked where all the Indians in the books were, she had not known. Clay knew, though. He knew from reading the World Book Encyclopedias with Grandpa Harry. He knew that the cute family that his mother wished everyone would read about, that they were able to wander around in such blissful pioneer abandon because all the people that used to live in the places they lived had been killed.

Even if she did not believe in having him read *Ender's Game*, he realized, his mother believed in Ender's game. He wished he could vomit the stuff of his parents out of him like he vomited soap suds. He tried to imagine how to do so. When he heard heaving sounds, he thought for a moment that he might be succeeding. He realized, though, that they were coming from another part of the house. Clay tried to shut them out, but he could not. Then the moaning started, and he knew the one who was heaving was his mother.

He resolved not to go to her, but her noises tore away at his insides like shrapnel. When his brain felt like a giant empty tin can that was slowly folding under the pressure of the air around it, he finally broke, tearing through his barricade and unlocking the door.

Clay Dillon found his mother in the bathroom with one arm around her stomach and the other one snaked around her head so that she could touch the back of her own skull. She looked up at him and then her chest heaved.

"I'm done throwing up," she said. "But my head hurts a lot. So does my stomach."

"Did I hit you?" Clay asked, suddenly afraid of what his father would do.

"It was just a push," his mother smiled, "a push. And I pushed you first, so your father doesn't need to know." She heaved again.

"I need you to call him at work. Tell him I fell down and hit my head. Tell him I knocked into something and hurt my stomach. Tell him to come home."

Clay felt himself shaking.

"It's okay," Kitty said. "Just call him. Don't tell him anything else, but tell him that I knocked into something and then I fell down. My stomach hurts and so does my head."

Clay nodded. "Should I call 911?"

Kitty shook her head. "I'm not bleeding. It just feels like a lot of cramps. Tell him that too."

Clay did as his mother asked. When his father finally came to the phone, he said exactly what she had told him to say. His father asked how it happened. When Clay realized that his father could not see him shrug, he said, "I don't know."

"Call Grandma Bayleigh if she doesn't want 911," his father said. "Tell her to get over there right now and it's an emergency."

"It's not an emergency," Clay said. "She's not bleeding. She just has some cramps. You know how cramps happen when you bump something. Charlie horses." He knew he was not explaining things correctly, but his father's urgency and his mother's moans were making it hard to concentrate.

"Your mother is pregnant, Clay," his father said. "You're having a little sister soon. At least, you might. When pregnant ladies get hit in the stomach, it can be very bad. Now call your grandmother."

Once again, Clay Dillon did as he was told. While he described the situation to his grandmother, he kept feeling his head collide with his mother's stomach. Over and over again, he felt that spot where his head always hurt after he knocked it. He felt it drive the wind from her, and he felt it ache with the aggravation of old wounds. Clay Dillon realized then that he might have killed his little sister before she was even born.

After he hung up the phone and told his mother that Grandma Bayleigh was on the way, he crawled back under his bed and cried.

❖   ❖   ❖

Part III: Imitation of Life

Secrets, Silence, and the Coming of Baby Sis

Kitty Dillon did not lose her baby after Clay head-butted her. She stayed in bed for three days, but she did not lose her baby. While she stayed in bed, she did not talk to Clay or even ask for him to be brought into her room.

Clay, for his part, did his best to stay out of everyone's sight. Grandma Bayleigh came to stay with them during this time, and because he did not know what she had been told about Kitty's illness, he tried to avoid being alone with her. His mother had promised, in a way, not to tell his father about their conflict. That did not mean that she would not talk to his father's mother, though, or that word would not get around to his father in the end.

He knew this from experience.

◆　◆　◆

When Clay was four years old, he had a dream about being held prisoner in a closet until he soiled himself. He knew it was a dream, and he tried to escape from it, but the dream held him as tightly as the confines of the closet within it. He screamed and thrashed, begging for whoever had locked him away to listen and let him out, but his words did not come. Instead, he was forced to scream with his fists as he beat against the walls, wondering which one was actually a door.

His release from the dream had come only when he gave up in his desperation and stopped fighting against his body's growing physical needs. As soon as his bladder opened and he felt the warmth and the wetness of his own urine flowing against his thighs, his eyes opened and he was back in his room. From there, tried to pull his bedclothes free, to take them downstairs to the laundry. After he managed to pull them all into a ball, Clay became very tired and laid down to rest so that he would have the energy to carry them down two flights of stairs. His mother found him sleeping on the floor the next morning.

When he woke up and saw her, he cried from the embarrassment of seeing his mother handling his soiled things, but she promised that she would not tell anyone. A few days later, though, he overheard his father laughing about it after he went to bed. The man's guffaws sifted their way to him through the house's heating vents, just like all the other information that he gathered when his parents thought they were alone. Since that time, he had never believed his mother's promises when she said she would keep a secret, and so he feared the day that his father would learn the truth about Kitty Dillon's sudden malaise.

◆ ◆ ◆

Clay's fight with his mother happened in the evening on a Wednesday. All of their fights happened on Wednesdays, it seemed, and this was not surprising because those were the days when he was forced to go to catechism, so they were also the days when he was most angry at his parents.

That Thursday, he managed to make it through his morning classes without crying, but he could not hold himself back at recess. He also felt like he could not tell Patrick or Aaron why he was crying, so instead he ran away from them and hid inside a monster truck tire that had been placed on the playground for the children to play on and around. The tire was damp and filled with gravel and moss, but it was also dark like the space under Clay's bed, so he felt comfortable there. When he tried to hide again at lunch time, though, he found himself pursued by Hillary. She crawled down inside the tire with him and asked him why he was upset. Clay pushed her over so that he could get a head start running away from her. Then he found himself a pine tree and climbed inside. She found him again before the end of the recess, but she did not try to follow him into the tree. Instead, she stood in front of it and tried to see him.

Clay did not say anything to her, and she did not call out to him for a long time. When she finally did, she sounded angry.

"I don't care if you don't want to talk to me," she shouted. "I just wanted you to know I'm sorry you feel bad. I also wanted you to know that I have to go. My dad got a new job and we are going to move. My mom says I don't need to go to catechism because we will move at Christmas break and I will have to start it over again, but I can keep going if I want."

Clay cried harder, but he tried not to make any noise that would let Hillary know.

"If you want me to go with you, I'll still go with you. At least, until I stop going to school here."

He did not answer her. After a long time, she went away. Clay knocked his head against the trunk of the tree while he waited for the whistle that would end the lunch recess. He liked the cool, rough bark when it dug into his forehead. He did not like thinking about Sully and the other boys being around him after Hillary was gone.

♦ ♦ ♦

On Friday, there was only a half day of school because the teachers had an in-service. This meant that Clay did not have to worry as much about crying in front of his friends, but it also meant that he had to spend much more time with Grandma Bayleigh before his father came home.

Clay liked his grandmother as much as he liked anyone in the family, but sometimes he had difficulty understanding her ways. She always laughed and smiled like she was joking, but most of her jokes felt sharp, and she always watched to see how people laughed at them. This made him feel uneasy whenever he laughed with her, but it also made him reluctant to stop laughing at her jokes, even when he felt like they were unfunny or even unfair. His father was the same way sometimes, but when Mark Dillon told mean jokes, they were never vague in their intentions. He threw around terms like idiot or even fuckwit to emphasize who was meant to be the butt of his sentiments.

Bayleigh was very different, though. Because of that, Clay was always left wondering whether she was cruel or just incapable of detecting the pain that her words could cause sometimes. It was this tendency toward probing remarks that made him uneasy about spending an extra half day with his grandmother. His mother might never tell anyone about their fight, but Clay was relatively sure that if he spent enough time around her, then she would somehow divine the truth and tell his father. In the end, though, Clay found that he was less anxious at the idea of enduring the joking interrogation than he would have been if he stayed at school and thought about her being alone with his mother.

The afternoon with his grandmother was a pleasant surprise. She busied herself with the laundry and did not have much time to play jokey games with Clay. What attention she did give to him was cheerful, and not nearly so searching as he had expected it might be. Instead, she chided him about taking turns picking out television shows with his brother so that he would not feel left out.

Grandma Bayleigh went home Friday night after Mark Dillon came home from work. The next day, Kitty came downstairs to eat breakfast with her children. When Clay woke on that day, he ventured downstairs to find her sitting at the kitchen table while his father made pancakes. She smiled at him and then motioned for him to take a seat with her. He was afraid at first, but his mother's smile was too open to deploy his metal body, and that helped him feel more at ease, so he took a seat next to her.

They waited patiently together while Mark finished cooking. After he was done, he disappeared upstairs for a moment, and when he came back he was carrying A.J. Clay noticed that his younger brother was still scrubbing the sleep from his eyes when their father set him down in a chair. Both of them kept their silence while they watched their parents dish out the pancakes and top them with syrup. A.J. seemed unable to quite understand that he was expected to stay awake. He kept nodding off, dropping his forehead to the table, and he only jerked himself back upright when Mark's hand touched the back of his head again. This happened two or three times while Clay watched.

It was only after all of the food was dispersed that the parents spoke to their children.

"I want you both to understand that your mother has not been sick. Not like you're used to. She's not feeling bad, really, and there's nothing for you to worry about."

Clay immediately stopped believing what his father was saying. He knew, even if Mark did not, that his mother was actually feeling bad. At least, he hoped she was, because otherwise she had spent three days in bed for no reason other than to spite him for their fight.

Kitty smiled.

"Clay already knows this, but we wanted to tell you both anyway. You're going to have a baby sister."

"Who will?" A.J. asked. "Me or him?"

"You both will," Mark replied. "Your mother is going to have another baby."

Clay nodded. They both knew this was no surprise to him, so he did not think they expected him to be very excited.

"Nope," was all A.J. said.

"What do you mean?" Kitty asked.

A.J. shrugged.

"You're going to have a baby sister!" Mark exclaimed. "Aren't you happy?"

"Nope," A.J. said.

"Would you rather have a brother?" Mark's enthusiasm was already flagging.

"Nope," A.J. said. "Dog." Then he dug into his pancakes.

"I'm happy," Clay said. "I just hope a sister works out better than a brother did."

"Clay! That's mean!" His mother giggled despite her words.

Clay shrugged.

"Apologize to your brother," Mark said.

Clay stared at A.J. He did not want to apologize. A.J. had not been made to apologize for saying he wanted a dog instead of a sister. Why should he have to apologize for admitting he had no love for the wreck of a brother that his parents had shoved at him?

As he contemplated his brother's face, he felt his metal body deploy.

"Clay, apologize." There was iron in Mark's words.

"I'm sorry that I said what I did," Clay replied. He made sure to drive his words home by pretending that the "I"s were nails.

Mark grimaced, but he did not demand more.

"I'm sure he didn't mean anything by it," Kitty said.

Clay glared at her.

"Anyway," Mark said, "we're talking today because this new baby is going to require some adjustments. You see, the doctor has said that your mother needs to get a lot more rest. That's why she has been having a hard time. Not enough rest."

"This means that you will both be spending a lot more of your weekend time at Grandpa Harry's," Kitty said.

"Good," A.J. said around his pancakes. "Grandpa gets the good TV."

"And during the week, Grandma Bayleigh will be coming over to see you off to school. She will also be here when you get home, and she is going to want some help keeping the house up." Mark smiled then. "You will both need to do what she says, so that your mother does not have to worry about all the housework herself. That way, she can get the rest she needs. Remember, your mom resting is the same thing as the baby resting."

Clay nodded. A.J. chewed his food.

"Any questions?" Kitty asked.

Clay looked at her for a long time. Then he said, "Do I still have to keep going to church school?"

"Of course you do," Mark replied. "I already paid for it. Now shut up and eat your food."

❖   ❖   ❖

Breakfast with Bayleigh

It was only an hour or so after breakfast that Grandpa Harry came to take the boys away from their parents for the rest of the weekend. Clay enjoyed his time away because it provided him with the opportunity to forget about school entirely. Not only did he stop worrying about church school, he stopped thinking about Hillary's revelation that she was leaving town. In fact, he stopped thinking about all the kids at school. Instead, he focused on his aunts and uncles, who seemed to be very grown-up indeed, with all of them being old enough to drive. On top of that, only Marci was still in high school.

Grandpa Harry mostly had to work, but Clay's uncle Curtis was home from college for the weekend, so he took to entertaining his young nephews by taking them out on long drives and discussing the state of the world with them. From Curtis, Clay learned that college was very difficult and that it was very expensive. He also learned that his uncle was pleased with the way that his college girlfriend helped him plan for a future beyond his degree, and how her own plans were to attend a medical school if she could find a way to pay for it. Medical school appealed to Curtis as well, and he said as much to Clay when A.J. was not around to hear them. He made the child promise not to tell anyone, though. After that, he became much shyer about explaining the world to Clay, which made him wonder whether or not his uncle was ashamed of his ideas.

On Sunday, Grandpa Harry drove the boys home. They were allowed to stay until after dinner, but once Curtis climbed into his used BMW and drove away from the house, they were returned to their parents, who put them to bed almost immediately.

When Clay woke up the next morning, he was surprised to find that the lights in his room were still off and that the door was open. He usually closed the door when he was trying to sleep because otherwise, the sound of his parents' voices carried through the house, keeping him awake. Then he heard the sound of the sink running downstairs, and he realized that he was awake because of it, so he rose from his bed and went to investigate the sound. He was sure that it was not his mother, who seemed to be unable to leave the bedroom for any length of time. If it had been her, then she would have turned on all the lights in the room and talked until the boys were awake.

He found Grandma Bayleigh downstairs, and then he remembered that he should have expected to find her. She was doing the dishes and listening to what sounded like a breakfast time news program, the kind that never actually discusses the news because all of its air time is taken up by the anchors' giggling and telling stories about their children. The noise came from a portable television set that sat on the counter.

"Hiya kiddo," Bayleigh winked at her grandson as she dried a frying pan. "I was just taking care of the pans from when I cooked your dad his breakfast."

"Dad doesn't eat breakfast," Clay said.

"Yes he does. He just doesn't cook breakfast. You've got to get up with him if you want to make sure that he doesn't run off without it." She winked at Clay again.

Clay nodded.

"What about you? Do you want some eggs?"

Clay made a face at his grandmother. He hoped that it was not just a grossed-out face, because his father told him that grossed-out faces were rude. Instead, he tried to make a face that communicated that his grandmother was either lazy or forgetful if she thought he was going to eat eggs.

"I was just asking," she replied. "I didn't think you were my egg eater. Your brother, he likes eggs. Still, I had to ask. Otherwise, you might have gotten mad at me for making a hot breakfast for your dad and your brother and not for you."

Bayleigh set the pan down on the counter and spun away from Clay. He tried to see what she was doing, but her wide frame and her billowing sweatshirt blocked his view.

"I've got something for you, since you don't like the mushy foods," she said.

Clay leaned harder, craning his neck to try to reach his gaze around her suddenly-wide elbows. Then, as if out of nowhere, she spun around. Her hands gripped the sides of a bright red box.

Cap'n Crunch grinned up at Clay from his perch on Bayleigh's matronly belly. His ears were hidden by her fingertips, but he was smiling all the same. He clapped for his grandmother, and then he took a seat at the kitchen table.

"I thought you'd like that," she said. "And I won't tell your mom if you want to eat it out of the Pyrex bowl."

Clay nodded, so his grandmother opened up the cabinet with the baking dishes and retrieved a miniature ceramic casserole dish with blue flowers on it. He recognized the bowl as part of a set that she usually used to heat and serve canned vegetables at her own house.

Before Clay could ask why his grandmother had brought her dishes with her, she filled the bowl with cereal. It was easily two or three times what Kitty would have allowed him to have at a meal. His eyes went wide.

"Too much?" she asked.

He shook his head.

"I didn't think so. You need to eat if you're going to keep growing."

She poured in the milk and slid the bowl in front of him. When he tried to ask for a spoon, Clay found that she was already laying it beside him.

"You're really good at this," Clay said.

His grandmother grinned back at him before turning to finish the dishes. Clay dove into the cereal. While he was eating, his brother joined him.

Bayleigh winked at A.J. as he rubbed the crust from his eyes. Clay noticed that it was the exact same wink she had delivered to him.

"Hiya kiddo," she said. "Want some eggs?"

A.J. smiled and nodded, but he was not very curious about his grandmother's process in the kitchen. Instead, he sat himself down across from his brother.

"What kind of eggs?" Bayleigh asked.

"Sunshine up," A.J. said.

"Sunshine up it is," Bayleigh replied. "How are you doing with your cereal Clay?"

"Good," he said through a mouthful.

"So boys, how is school?"

"Mine is good," A.J. said, "but Clay hates church so he fights with our mom."

"I don't hate church," Clay said.

"I do," Bayleigh replied. "Never had any use for it. God is fine by himself, but his pep squad pisses me off."

"What do you mean?" Clay asked. In his mind, he saw Sully and the rest of the catechism class clapping and performing cheers for God. That was not quite how it worked, at least as far as he knew, but he also sensed that his grandmother was telling a truth, even if it was not quite *the* truth.

"We used to go to church when I was young," Grandma Bayleigh replied, "All the kids in town went, but the kids whose parents read the book every week always acted like they were just a little bit better than everyone. They let us know it every chance they got, too. By the time we had to leave the farm, I figured out that that was all church was. They talk a big game about helping people, but you try going for help sometime. You'll get it, but only after you embarrass yourself in front of all the other families and grovel about being a worthless husk. I'd rather starve."

To Clay, that description did not sound as much like church as it did like what happened whenever Grandma Doris and her sisters got together. He had witnessed the three of them descend on his aunts Marci and Diane, and it had been like watching the vultures on the National Geographic close in to pick at the bones left behind after a hyena raid. He supposed that since Grandma Doris and Grandma Bayleigh were the same age, that when they were both children

Doris's people might have acted exactly like Bayleigh described. From there, it was not hard to understand that other people might have been the same way.

That description also fit in with C.S. Lewis's description of the temptations Wormwood whispered to the Christians he sought to turn. For the first time since his mother had bludgeoned him with *The Screwtape Letters*, he began to understand that the overly simplistic narrative might have been disguising a more complicated revelation. It was not that the text was complex so much as that it was a simple explanation for a complex and distasteful event.

He began to wonder if that was the key to the entire business of religion. If so, then his mother's insistence on forcing him to submit to the church schooling was even worse, because it sought to force him to pretend that the complications were real and not merely the pageantry of people who had the ability to force him to pretend that their whims were the foundation for reality.

"So," his grandmother started, "why is it that you're upset about church?"

"I'm not upset about church," Clay said. "I just don't think I should be leaving school in the middle of the day to go to church school. I do fine with church when it's on a Sunday, but I don't want to give up science class for it."

"Gotcha," Grandma Bayleigh said, "For a minute there I thought you'd gotten some sense, but I guess it takes time to develop. Don't worry, though. Your mom can't make you go forever. When you get old enough, the priest will talk to you about doing something called Confirmation."

From the way she said "Confirmation," Clay could tell that it was meant to be capitalized.

"Anyhow, if you don't want to do that, then they're not supposed to be able to make you. But that's in high school. Until then, you just have to put up with your mother's stupid ideas."

Clay nodded. He was glad that there was at least one person who understood him in the house.

"I don't have to go," A.J. said.

"That's because we already know you're going to hell," Clay replied.

A.J. scowled at Clay, but then Grandma Bayleigh put a plate of eggs down in front of him, and he seemed to forget about what his brother had just said.

❖   ❖   ❖

You Really are a Dick

Grandma Bayleigh's breakfast treats were just the beginning of the changes around the Dillon household. She also expanded Clay's television privileges and stopped forcing him to spend extra time watching A.J. in the backyard. Clay, who had always been told that children were meant to be outside whenever it was not raining or freezing, suddenly found himself with a good deal more time to read and to play with his LEGOs than he had ever known before.

Still, he did not stop playing outside, despite the fact that no one forced him to do it anymore. He did, however, start bringing his books from the school library with him when he went outside. Kitty Dillon usually kept him from doing this because she believed that it would make him less active, but Grandma Bayleigh believed that it was enough that he wanted to be outside, and that no one should ever be discouraged from reading. On Tuesday, she told him that she herself was an avid reader, even though she had not finished high school the regular way and had instead taken a test to get her diploma after Clay's father Mark was born.

Sensing an opportunity, Clay told his grandmother that the school library only allowed him to take out one book per week. He also showed her his progress in reading the Bible, and then he described the agreement that he had made with his father about reading more grown-up books. Bayleigh responded by promising that she would take both of the boys down to the library in the middle of Greenridge sometime before the end of the week.

This was how Clay found himself, only a week after the fateful fight with his mother that had resulted in her disappearing from the household to spend her days in bed. He was happier than he could remember being, even if he felt a sinking sense of responsibility for his mother's illness, and he was finally seeing that the things he had been promised were coming to him.

Suddenly, he found it much easier to get himself moving in the morning and to concentrate on tasks. Each morning, after his bowl of Cap'n Crunch, he got himself dressed and out to the bus before Bayleigh had a chance to say anything to him. His lunch box was already packed when he came downstairs, and he was pleased to see that instead of an apple, he had a packet of the fruit snacks that Bayleigh kept in her own pantry. Likewise, instead of having to worry about a pudding cup, he had a small slice of cake.

On the bus, Hillary was nowhere to be seen. Clay hoped that she was not out of school already, since there was still about a month to go before Christmas vacation. He did not know how long it took to move, though, so he thought that maybe she would have to miss a month of school to help out at home.

Without her, the ride was lonely, and no one tried to talk to him. No one was mean to him, either, and that was a welcome relief. For some reason, Clay usually felt like people were being mean to him even when they were ignoring him, but that was not the way he felt on that day.

When the bus arrived at school, he stowed his backpack in the usual place with the rest of his class and headed out onto the playground to fill the time before classes started. Usually, this was when he met up with Patrick and Aaron, but on that day they were nowhere to be found. Clay did what he normally did when he was alone and feeling good. He went to the swings, and he endeavored to jump off them from the greatest possible height, so that he could feel himself slam into the hard-packed earth. This was something he did often enough that his body had begun to form its own imprint, preventing the regrowth of grass in a skinny oval just downhill from the playground equipment.

After five or six jumps, Sully started swinging next to him. At first, the other boy did not say anything, but after Clay jumped three or four times, he saw that the other child was slowing down his swing and dragging his feet in the gravel.

Clay picked himself up from the ground and dusted himself off. Sully stopped his swing entirely.

"How do you do that?" he asked.

Clay shrugged.

"I mean it. I used to do that a lot, but when I was in kindergarten I landed wrong and I broke my wrist. How do you do that all the time and not get hurt?"

Clay looked at the ground. He did not know how to answer the question, because Sully was wrong to think that he did not get hurt. He got hurt every time he jumped. He ached with the hurt, and sometimes it felt like his bones were being ground into powder at the joints. He knew how to land, to spring back so that he could go again, and to keep himself from getting bruises. None of those things meant that he did not hurt.

He wanted to tell the other boy those things, but he did not know how. They were not part of the answer to the question he had been given, and the question he had been given did not have an answer that it was possible to make sense out of. Clay stared at his shoes instead of answering, hoping that if he put his gaze on himself instead of the ground, that Sully would not draw any conclusions for himself.

"Fine. Don't talk. I knew you were a dick."

Clay felt the sting of the words. He knew them. All the kids knew them. They knew that the teachers would punish them for using the bad words, but no one ever punished their parents, and so the children used the language of their parents whenever there was no one around to prevent them.

He knew how to respond to those words, at least.

"Go fuck yourself you stupid monkey. No one asked you to talk. I'm a dick? You're a dick. I never did shit to you."

Armor deployed over him. The metal body did not need time to form. It sprang whole from the patchwork quilt of movie lines and Mark Dillon's epithets that Clay vomited over his classmate. His outburst was enough to make Sully take a half step backward.

"Noah's got problems at home," Sully replied. "You didn't help him out when you got him suspended."

Clay narrowed his eyes at the other boy. "He kicked me and laughed when I told him to stop it."

"Yeah, but he didn't get it," Sully replied.

"He kicked me and he didn't stop till I stopped him and then he hit me in the head."

Sully shrugged. "Does it make you happy then? Sending him home so his dad would hit him with a belt every day? That what you wanted?"

"I just wanted him to stop kicking me. If *I* hit my mom, my dad will hit *me* with a belt. He says so all the time. Why shouldn't Noah get hit with a belt if *he* kicks *me*?"

Sully did not say anything back to Clay. Instead, he just started swinging again, pumping his legs and puffing his cheeks as if he was working against some kind of strong resistance.

♦   ♦   ♦

Class was uneventful that morning, and both Aaron and Patrick were present for it. Clay did not know why he had been unable to find them on the playground, but he looked forward to catching up with them at lunch even if he would not be able to join them for recess because of catechism class.

At the lunch table, he learned that there was a morning reading group that one of the other second grade teachers put together. Aaron and Patrick were a part of it, but they did not enjoy the book that was chosen, and so they were thinking about quitting. Neither of them had seen Hillary there. Her disappearance remained a mystery.

When he got on the bus to go to St. Sebastian's, he found that Sully and his gang were already aboard. Even Noah was there. He took a seat as far away from them as he could, but once he was settled in, the other boys moved to surround him. None of them tried to share his seat, though. Clay was glad for that.

"I'm sorry," Noah said. "I didn't know about your dad."

Clay shrugged. He wanted to say that he never actually got hit because he listened to his dad, but he knew that it would make Noah back into his enemy, and he did not want another enemy when he was already alone and surrounded. Still, his metal body sang beneath his skin, begging to be let out.

"Why don't you ever come and talk to anyone? Why do you just hang out with those two goons that talk so loud all the time?"

Clay shrugged again. "They're my friends," he said. "No one else has really tried to talk to me, either. I'm used to that, though. None of the kids my mom used to babysit liked me."

Sully's eyes widened. "No one dislikes you," he said. "I haven't heard a thing like that, except when you twisted Noah's ankle or did something else to be mean."

The metal body sprang to life and responded to Sully before Clay could.

"Sticking up for myself isn't mean. Just because you're all too stupid to stop yourselves from hurting other people doesn't mean that we all are."

Noah nodded. Sully looked ashamed.

"Look, we just wanted you to know. You can play football with us. We didn't try to leave you out. It just happened," Noah's words were a little shaky.

"I don't play football," Clay said.

He did not say that no one had ever taught him about football, or that he was often confused about why so many other boys and their fathers seemed so preoccupied with it. Nor did Clay admit that he often hoped that his grandfather would explain the game to him, since he was always watching either the Detroit Lions play on the weekends. He did not want to let these boys to know, either, that his father only watched football when he had bet on it or that he had never been taught why the thing had such an odd shape. Instead, he just left things at "I don't play football."

They offered to teach him, and to explain the positions, but it was all very confusing to Clay, and it seemed like he would be very stupid if he tried to play the game because he did not understand anything they said. He already felt very stupid a lot at school, since he was never allowed to participate in the gifted classes, and people like Shawna played tricks on him when they were supposed to be helping him with classwork. The dog treat he had been coerced into eating in the first grade still came back to haunt his memories when he tried to think about making friends at school. Only the metal body made him feel better, and it only worked when Clay resolved not to ask questions and not to give other people information about himself.

He shook his head at their every offer, insisting that he just did not play football. They asked if he would be interested in another game, and he shrugged. The truth was that he did not know very many games. His father had taught him chess and checkers, as well as baseball. When Clay started beating him consistently at chess, though, he began to find that his father was too busy to play that game, even though he was not too busy to play baseball. When Clay kept stepping away from the ball that always seemed to be sailing directly at his head, though, he then found that his father was too busy to play baseball anymore. The only games they played now were things like Uno and Monopoly, and that was with the whole family.

Eventually, Sully just offered to give Clay a chance if he ever changed his mind. Clay replied that he was not about to change his mind, and that was that.

After everyone else got off the bus, Sully looked Clay in the eye.

"You really are a dick," was all he said.

Clay felt the heat of a good many cursing replies boiling away at his vocal chords, but before he let loose with a tirade, he noticed the bus driver watching them. He resolved not to let Sully trick him into getting into trouble, and to remember the lengths that the boy would go to in an attempt to coerce him into behaving badly in front of an adult.

❖   ❖   ❖

Real Friendships in Imaginary Castles

Clay never did learn what had happened to Hillary, because she never returned to school. Without her to keep him company on the bus, the lines between his time at home and his time at school grew more distinct, and it became easier and easier for Clay to navigate through the school day. His newfound understanding of other boys, as supplied by the likes of Sully and Noah, also helped him. He came to realize that they said they did not think poorly of him because they believed it to be true as long as he was not around, but that being near them made him the focal point of their disdain. Clay combated this tendency by simply staying away from them and from any other children he did not already know.

When Aaron and Patrick were busy with their reading groups or other activities, he found trees to climb. When he could, he brought library books out onto the playground with him so that he could read while he was safely hidden in a tree. It was a lonely way to pass the morning time before school, but it was also a way for him to collect his strength. As he read the books that he kept hidden inside his coat, he removed it and let his skin taste the morning air, chilling itself into a hardness that was very like the metal body, even if it was very different.

Over time, Clay found ways to induce his metal body by combining the cold with other sensations. Scraping his cold arms against the trunk of the tree until he accumulated red welts and, eventually, bloody streaking tears in his skin would do it. So would saying all the things he felt like saying to his parents out loud, even if he did it quietly.

Patrick and Aaron never knew about his time in the trees, but Clay was certain that the other children, the ones who also had to stay outside in the morning, knew all about it. They started to keep their distance from him when they saw him walking back toward the tree line, after all. Sully's gang never seemed to play any games near him either, even though he often picked trees near their regular field. On those days, they magically seemed to choose other activities that took them away from him. It made Clay feel powerful when that happened, and his empowerment kept his skin hard, developing his metal body further than he had imagined it could go. By Thanksgiving, this morning ritual began allowing him to keep the metal body willfully deployed throughout the day. It was difficult to keep his vocal chords from cutting people when he did this, but it was much easier to focus on finishing his work and on keeping other people from playing tricks on him, so he practiced silence as much as possible.

Patrick and Aaron did notice this, and Clay could tell that they noticed because they kept asking him if he was upset. When he told them that he was not, then they told him all about the television programs they liked, most of which were on past Clay's bedtime. He felt like they were providing a bridge for him, taking him from the limited understanding enforced on his world by his parents' habits, and he was grateful for it.

Still, every so often Patrick would say something that reminded Clay about how narrow his attention was, and how the other boy only cared about his own special projects and his own special games. When that happened, Clay's tongue lashed out in an attempt to cut chunks of Patrick's being away, so that he could hold them when his friend floated far away from him. He felt bad about this, but he also felt like the only way to get the other boy to focus on anything outside himself was to hold on to a piece of him in such a way that when Patrick looked at Clay, he saw himself.

The occasional harsh word from Clay never seemed to bother Patrick, but it did wreak havoc on Aaron when he had to see it. Sometimes, that led to the two of them asking Clay to go somewhere else during recess, and then he would retreat back to the trees to practice forging his metal body.

The more perfectly Clay shaped himself into a robot warrior, the more often Aaron seemed to need breaks from him. On the other hand, though, there came a point in mid-December where Patrick began asking Aaron to wander away when he wanted a break, because he wanted to stay with Clay. When that happened, the metal body began to soften. He was not sure why, but something about Patrick's loyalty, even in the face of his own emergent sharpness, made him want to be a person again.

During those times, Patrick prodded Clay about the stories he had begun to write in the first grade. He had not touched them in over six months, and he was surprised to find Patrick remembered them so vividly. The other boy's admiration inspired him, and he began to bring his notebook with him when he climbed trees, instead of bringing something to read.

When Clay wrote about Van and his battle against the Scream, his metal body fell away, and he found himself transported back into the castle that he had constructed around himself back in Mrs. Nesbitt's class, when he thought that he could defend himself from his own terror. It was the only time that he had the ability to access it, though. The high-ceilinged, wide halls made of golden blocks that snapped together like LEGO but felt like granite under his hands had, at one point, been real to Clay. Now they were just something inside his story. Parts of a place he could visit, but where he could no longer live.

Van could live there, though. He could live like Clay had never been able to live: as a leader, with friends and people he could help protect, who could also help protect him when he was wounded in a fight or when he faced a puzzle that he could not piece together on his own.

At Patrick's suggestion, Clay gave Van a new friend. He named him Blur, and wrote a story about how Blur had crossed the wasteland in a ship that was able to outrun the Scream, only to find that the wall around Van's castle was too wide and too high for him to get around. Pinned against those ramparts, Blur had turned his ship's weaponry against the scream. Somehow, his missiles exploding into the wind had an effect. Their explosions change the breeze around the castle, keeping the Scream from blowing so close and allowing the people to come outside on occasion.

When Van saw how Blur's weapons were useful as a way to permanently retake territory, he welcomed the other warrior into the castle and made a friend of him. By that time, Clay had been forced to invent many other people for Van to live with: computer technicians who were smart enough to fix his ship, doctors to patch him up, and even a group of children that looked up to Van. Blur was his first friend, though, and through the story Clay began to understand something about the peculiar triangle that he created when he was with Patrick and Aaron at the same time.

Eventually, Patrick's interest in the stories about Van and Blur spilled over into the time that they did spend with Aaron, and his enthusiasm spilled over into Aaron as well. Shortly after that, Van and Blur found that they could not manage to hold their territory without help coordinating the battle, and so they met Jules, who would stay within the castle and provide them with information from the radar and computers. Since Clay could not maintain his metal body when he was talking about Van, he no longer spoke sharply to Patrick and Aaron, and they no longer asked him to go away to his trees. In fact, they stopped attending their reading club in the morning so that Jules and Blur could spend more time with Van.

Outside of the storytelling time, Clay found that his body reverted more and more to metal. It was as if his ability to reach back into the place where his imaginary castles were real came with a boomerang effect. As a result, his joy was rendered invisible except when it caused his body to warm enough that his joints loosened, and then he would turn pink as his chassis sought to keep itself from overheating.

It was only when he was alone that he became Clay again. Eventually, he realized that it was because Van was becoming the metal body. Time at school was a battle that required him to wear robotic armor, and once he and Patrick designed it for Van, the newly minted cyborg started to silently extend himself through Clay's being, turning the sharp metallic transformation that had already begun into a highly effective protection against the ravages of everyday life.

Clay never wondered whether Patrick knew about the transmutations of his body, and he never needed to, because when they were together he no longer had to spend time with Patrick, who could not stop talking. Instead, he got to spend his days with Blur, whose taciturn loyalty matched Clay and Van's needs perfectly.

❖   ❖   ❖

The Advent of the Storm

It was mid-December, just before Christmas Break, when Clay discovered that his mother and his grandmother hated one another. In the weeks before that day, Kitty had made herself invisible while Bayleigh was home. Clay assumed she did this because she was resting, but as he soon learned, it was not so. He might never have made this discovery, except that on that day, the weather became quite terrible at the middle of the school day. The frozen landscape that descended over Greenridge's aptly named geography after Thanksgiving suddenly turned bitter, and snow that had already kissed the ground was churned up by new winds that were so strong some of the kindergarteners were knocked down by them during recess.

Normally, Mr. Chitwood would never have entertained the idea of sending children home if they were already in school. Why would he? The concrete and cinderblock bunkers that America built to house its youth were every bit as sturdy as those that had protected him from bombs and napalm attacks in southeastern Asia, so they were naturally impervious to something as simple as Mother Nature throwing a temper tantrum. This was his firm conviction, and his resolve rarely weakened. That day, though, he changed his mind because the National Weather Service called the school directly. They advised him that the winds were only just beginning to pick up, so things would only get worse. This was enough to make Chitwood bite back his pride and send the children home while the weather was merely dangerous. His emergency preparedness binder (written by himself, of course) said that the children who were being bused home had to have their parents notified.

So, at ten-thirty in the morning on a day just three days before Christmas Break, Mr. Chitwood called Mr. Weir and the receptionist into his office, and the three of them divided the list of families whose children attended Greenridge. They then called the aides, and once those five people were organized, they proceeded to make their phone calls. With each adult being asked to call roughly eighty homes, they kept the announcements brief. Children who normally walked home would be held until their parents came to retrieve them, due to the high winds. The others would be sent home if there was a parent waiting for them, and the parents were discouraged from attempting to drive to the school because of the weather. The buses were sturdy, each of the staff was instructed to say, and their monstrous tires would not lose purchase on the roads. It was what they were built for.

Because there were so many calls to make, Mr. Weir never thought to ask Bayleigh if one of Clay's parents was home. She was listed as one of the two emergency contacts in the child's records, after all, and he assumed that her presence at their home was just the way their family worked.

◆   ◆   ◆

Clay arrived home about an hour and a half after Mr. Weir called his house, and he immediately started to worry, even before he walked up the street from the bus stop. His was the only stop that was empty when the bus pulled up to it. Everyone else's parents were waiting for them, to walk them back home.

"Sorry kid," the bus driver said. "I would drive around the corner and up the street for you, but we're pointed the wrong direction. Are you going to be okay?"

Clay nodded. Not because he was sure he would be, but because he did not know what else to do. Adults usually disliked it when you gave them negative answers. After he got off the bus, he did manage to make it up the street without falling over. It was not easy. His boots slipped against the snow, even though it was up well past his ankles. This was something Clay was unused to. Normally, the snow felt like it was holding his feet rigid, keeping him from pushing forward against the ground.

He wondered for a moment how treacherous these winds would be if there was no snow, and then he was home. Grandma Bayleigh's car was in the driveway, and so was his mother's. Why, then, had neither of them come down the street to help him home? His mother, he understood, was resting. At the same time, though, Bayleigh's entire reason for being around the house so much was to do these things so that Clay and A.J. would not be neglected while Kitty focused on her own health.

Clay heard the answer to his mental query as soon as he entered the house. His mother's voice and Bayleigh's were carrying throughout, and they spoke so loudly that he could not tell where they were coming from or what they were saying. All he heard was the razorblades in the words. For a moment, he felt the armor under his skin and considered coming between them. Then fatigue hit him.

Not having had the chance to visit the castle with Patrick and Aaron today had cost him. So had walking up the street. Now, thinking about the fact that it would be the next day before he was able to rest and spend time with his friends, he realized that he simply did not have it in him to interfere.

Instead, Clay put his coat away, took his boots off, and retreated. He walked carefully, to avoid the adults hearing him and bringing him into whatever was happening. Once he was in his room, he left the door open so that he could keep listening to the fight. Even without knowing the words to it, he could still understand who was winning and whether or not they were getting closer to his hiding place. While he listened, he buried himself in the blankets on his bed and tried to imagine his way into Van's kingdom. A few times, he almost made it, but whenever he reached out to feel the texture of the bricks, the images slipped away, and he was stuck inside his bedroom once again. Eventually, the sounds from the adults quieted, and that also made them clear to his ears. He found himself eavesdropping.

What his mother and Bayleigh were arguing about was him. Their shouting was disorganized, but in it he heard mentions of his own protests against catechism class, of the idea of a hot breakfast on school days, of the fact that Clay's bedtime was still the same as his brother, who was in preschool, and even of his mother's sense of humor.

"Nothing's saying you can't say the rosary while still lightening up about the fact that your kid likes to read about stuff you don't," came out of his grandmother at one point.

Clay wanted to be happy that someone was sticking up for him, but through it all, he found himself stuck in an uneasy place between gratitude and fear. Grandma Bayleigh seemed to be trying to make the rules even though his mother did not want her to, and while Clay hated his mother's rules, he feared the precedent that Bayleigh might set. After all, if she managed to keep his mother from having her way in her own home by asserting the weight of her familial seniority, then that sentiment might get passed down even harder to him, making the unreasonable ideas of his own parents that much harder to argue against. The other side of the situation beckoned to him, though. If his mother's ideas were suppressed by Bayleigh, then he would not need to worry about arguing that he should be allowed to make his own choices, because Bayleigh's ideas were pretty much what Clay wanted to do anyway.

He kept listening, flicking his attention back and forth between those two thoughts as he heard the two women exchange the upper hand with one another. Clay began to gather that the argument was not just about the way things were done around the house, either. He heard his mother call Bayleigh mean-spirited, and she said several unflattering things about herself that did sound a bit like the way his grandmother phrased things. For her part, his father's mother kept pointing out what she had actually done around the house, from the laundry to bringing Kitty hot meals, and she also kept asking at what point she would have done enough to be allowed to finally speak her mind. Clay did not hear his mother's reply, but he did hear the sounds of bodies moving from the lowest floor of the house up to the entryway. Keys jingled, and then the door slammed. He pulled the blankets further around himself, wondering which of them had fled the house but not wanting to reveal himself to whoever was left.

A few minutes later, he heard the door slam again, and then Bayleigh shouted, "I don't like you at all, but I'm not going to kill myself getting away from you. The weather stinks and you're supposed to be on bedrest anyway. I'll get myself away from here once things clear up, but until then you're just stuck with me. I guess you can pass the time thinking about what I'll look like burning in hell!"

Kitty Dillon did not answer. At least, not in any way that Clay could hear.

♦ ♦ ♦

That night when Clay came downstairs to dinner his grandmother was hard at work in the kitchen. She winked when she saw him, but she never mentioned anything about his being sent home early or about her fight with Kitty. As far as Clay knew, neither of his parents were even aware that school had been canceled in the middle of the day. The next morning, she gave him Cap'n Crunch for breakfast again.

❖ ❖ ❖

Autocyborgography

Van stood on the playground and stared at Patrick. He refused to become Clay again, because he knew that if he did, he would cry. Patrick refused to become Blur, though, because Noah the Nosepicker was shifting back and forth uncomfortably and trying in his own way not to show how close he was to tears. Van could tell anyway. He did not care.

The scream licked away at his thoughts. Luckily, his entire body was a metal body.

He had spent hours on his armor when he was alone in his room and his castle was out of reach, and he had found magic phrases in hidden places that helped him to strengthen it by holding on to words when the scream came for him.

"We need another person or two," Patrick said. "This is a great game to play at recess, but it's boring to always do the same things. Besides, Aaron is always the radio person. He deserves a chance to fly."

Van held himself rigidly stiff. He heard words in his head, about coming not to create peace but with a sword. About not being afraid to turn away from your loved ones when they were unrighteous. About the destruction of people who had wronged you. Some of the words belonged to people from the Bible. Some belonged to Ender, or Wormwood, and more than a few came from Waverly Jong. He chose to listen to Waverly, who always knew hidden motives in the wind, which made him think that she had heard the scream as well.

He failed to listen to Amy Tan, or he might have known better.

"It's okay," Noah said. "I can just play football."

He nodded. Football was a good choice. Noah knew football. Van knew how to change himself back and forth from a cyborg warrior to a child. Neither of them belonged in the other's business.

"No," Patrick said. "I want to hang out, and I can't play football because it makes my asthma bad."

Noah shrugged.

"Why do you even want to do this?" Van asked.

Noah shrugged again.

"It seemed like fun. Like video games on the playground. I like Sully, but all he wants to do is pick on people. He says it's a joke, but if you don't laugh at yourself, he can be pretty mean. The only time I've seen you be mean is when someone else was mean first."

Van felt himself start to change. He flexed all the muscles in his body to keep his metal body deployed. He would not become Clay, because that would release Patrick from the story, and then he might actually get away.

"It's not like we're going to play without you," Patrick said. "Noah will be gone at catechism whenever you're gone, so we can't play then anyway."

Suddenly, the metal body was gone. Clay sat down hard in the dirt, tired. He tried to bring up Van's castle so that he could start to talk Noah's way into it, but he could not.

He managed to say, "Fine. Just not today." Then he fell sideways. That was when Aaron found them.

"Are we going to the castle before school?" He asked. "Clay has catechism today, so we can't do it at lunch."

"I don't think so," Patrick replied. "I don't think this is part of the game."

Clay moaned. Noah got down on the ground with him.

"How can you sit here?" he asked. "The ground is freezing my ass and I just sat down. Let me help you up."

"I'm tired," Clay replied.

"He's doing this because I brought Noah to play," Patrick said. "He's been like this."

"Well why did you bring him?" Aaron asked. "He hit Clay."

Patrick shrugged.

"I wanted to play," Noah said. "It's okay. We don't have to play today. Want to go to the swings?"

Aaron nodded. Clay let Noah help him up, but when he walked he felt dizzy and off-balance, like Van had not quite put his body back together the right way when he converted back from being a cyborg to being a person.

"Can I keep coming back?" Noah asked.

Clay felt himself nodding. Sully was the one who had called him a dick, after all. All Noah did was hit him in the back of the head really hard. That was nothing, and besides, he had apologized for it.

Headaches happened so often that having one smashed into you was hardly even an event. There was no point in holding a grudge over them.

◆ ◆ ◆

That morning in Mrs. Hudson's class was uneventful. Clay did his best to pay attention to the lessons, but he still felt very tired because of the strain that the before school playground squabble had placed on him. Noah kindly refrained from kicking the back of his seat or fidgeting enough that he could hear it, and this made him think that perhaps he really had been the one to escalate things too much with the other boy. The only real problem that morning was that Sully was incorrigible. He was too far away from Clay to cause him any direct distress, but every time the teacher stopped class to make them re-focus, it seemed like she was having to talk to him. By the time the kids were let out for first recess, he had not only been threatened with a call home, his name was on the board. This meant that he had to stay inside while the rest of them went out to play.

Patrick grabbed Noah by the elbow as the kids streamed out of the classroom and down the hall. Clay did not hear what he said, but he saw Noah shaking his head back.

"No, I think I want to play football if he won't be around to wreck things," he shouted back.

Clay realized then what Patrick must have asked. He was a little glad that Noah did not have any intent to join them, because he did not feel like having to do anything. At the same time, though, it bothered him that Patrick would invite someone into their game who might drop in and out without any consideration for the rest of them. Why bother playing at all then?

Outside, Aaron was the first one to talk.

"So what are we doing today? Castle stuff? Or are you two going to fly around a bit?"

Clay just shook his head.

"We can't do either one," Patrick said. "Noah can't come with us."

"We didn't do anything before school either," Aaron said, "and we won't be doing anything at lunch, because Clay and Noah will be gone. Why don't we just go to the castle now?"

"I'm tired," Clay said.

"It wouldn't be fair," Patrick said.

"Noah could have come with us and he didn't," Aaron said. "Why should we wait for him? He hasn't even started to play yet, so it's not like he would know if we did things while he was gone."

Patrick shook his head.

"I don't know why you're up in arms about this but fine," Aaron said. "Did anyone watch *The Simpsons* over break?"

"Not allowed," Clay said. "My dad says it's a bit gross, and it's on after I go to bed."

"They sang the best version of 'Jingle Bells,'" Aaron said. "The one the music teacher threatens to kick you out of class for."

"It's going to be a good show," Patrick said. "I saw it. It's funny."

Clay shrugged.

"You'd like it," Patrick said. "You should watch it at your grandparents' house if your dad won't let you."

He nodded. They kept talking about television shows he did not know.

Clay kept walking along behind them with the scream whistling away in his ears. He tried to go to the castle without his friends, to see if he could make it appear without them, but his head started throbbing right in the place where Noah had hit him all those months before. He reached for Van then, but he found nothing there. He tried to get angry about it, but his metal body refused to come. Even the version of it that had not been Van, the one that had kept the scream inside him and forced him to endure it, was gone. So far gone that he could not even make himself hear the cyborg's voice.

He hoped that would not last for very long. In the meantime, he kept his feet moving, remaining barely aware of anything except the fact that it felt very odd to be taking a nap while he was still walking.

❖   ❖   ❖

It Was Written...

On the way to catechism class that afternoon, it occurred to Clay that Blur and Jules were his imaginary friends, and that therefore he was wrong to believe that imaginary friends were an impossibility. He had never thought of them that way before, but it made a lot of sense. He was, after all, the inventor of their appearances and the author of their words. They were born in his head, and while his friends controlled their actions, he had been responsible for the world they lived in and the rules that governed their lives. They were his, even if they were not always under his control. He knew that his handing them off to others created new versions of them, because Patrick was always thinking of what to do with Blur next, but he was also aware that there was always a version of Blur he carried, and that it had to be periodically reconciled with Patrick's or else they would diverge and become different entities.

Suddenly, Clay became convinced that either God was everyone's imaginary friend or else they were all His. It was the only explanation —either they were living in a world like the one Van lived in, with a hidden auteur that dictated their rules and their environment but left them to do for themselves in the bodies he had manufactured for them, or else God was invented by them and existed in their heads, occupying some kind of fantastic realm like the one Clay had built first for himself and then later turned over to Van. If everyone was right about God, and they were all actually thinking about the same thing, then God had to be imagining them. It was the only way to explain how so many people could have the same idea at once.

On the other hand, though, he recalled that people did not have all the same ideas about God. The fact of that was plain, because Clay's mother often belittled people for having the wrong ideas about God even though she herself believed many things that the priest had spoken differently about. She never seemed to notice when she did this, but Clay noticed everything, and so he knew that even though people like his mother pretended to all have the same ideas about God, they really did not. Like Patrick and Aaron pretended that they all had the same ideas about Blur and Van and the other cyborgs in the castle, even though they had to stop and fight sometimes about which versions of those same ideas were best.

Suddenly, something fell out of Clay's insides and he felt a chasm open within himself that was so deep and wide it felt as if he could hold the world in it. As he considered the way he had envisioned and populated Van's realm and the way he had recruited its population, he started to realize that at some point the stories of ancient Canaan and Judea had been envisioned in exactly the same way. Even if they were real places on the earth, and even if events had occurred at those places that were very similar to the events in the Bible, the lands of the Bible were not the lands of Earth. They were instead a kind of magic castle that was shared not only among a small group of friends, but among everyone who helped to hold the idea of them in their thoughts. They could not be anything else. By their very nature, the versions recorded in books had to be capable of being turned in at the corners, folded over, and stuffed into a human being's imagination. That person might fill them with giants and armies, and he might punish the fathers who lusted after their own children because they were vile, but he was also choosing to spend time envisioning a world wherein fathers lusted after their own children. Whether these things had happened in the outside world or not, the people who had enshrined them in books made them into attempts at reflecting imaginary friends into the minds of others. They meant for those concepts to sear themselves deep into the past history that informed continued play in that realm, only that realm was meant to be the real world at the same time.

Clay began to feel a little ill and wanted everything in his mind to slow down. His thoughts did not slow themselves to accommodate him, so he put his fists together and looked at them. This was the size of his brain, according to Mrs. Hudson. Any God that existed could not possibly reduce himself to the size of his two fists without losing the properties that allowed Him to be supreme. Nor could any human communicate with a creature they could not find in the world, unless that creature was one that they had created the way that Clay created Van's friends. The God his mother prayed to must be her imaginary friend, then, because even if there was a creator out in the universe, he could not be so small that he fit inside the kinds of thoughts that Kitty Dillon usually had, even if he did manage to force himself into a space the size of her two fists.

Of course, Van was something different from an imaginary friend to Clay, because he was a cyborg, and he made a good number of his own choices. Still, he might be an imaginary friend to Patrick or to Aaron. To Clay, though, Van would always be a suit to wear or a profession he could embody, except for the fact that the cyborg's behavior would be whatever he wanted and not necessarily what he was told to do. Clay had invented Van, yes, just like he invented Van's imaginary friends. But there were times when he was Van and he did not know what he would do next, so he knew that he could not be making him. At the same time, though, he knew that Van was something he had started by writing down stories that were meant to map his castle and show it to others.

Suddenly, Clay felt afraid. He could not stop thinking about the crazy house and the way Grandpa Harry kept warning Kitty and his other daughters to take care of themselves, lest they wind up there. He found himself now feeling like going to a place he had created probably meant that he was in the crazy house every time he went there. What if his grandfather had been warning everyone about what might happen when you lived too long in that space where you could create people?

He never felt this way when he was with Grandpa Harry, who took great care never to fight with his children or anyone else and who always approached temper flares and crying tantrums as problems to be solved. It was when he was away from his grandfather, when his parents talked about Harry, using his first name without any embroidery, that he began to feel his panic rise.

He realized then that his parents had made Grandpa Harry into God-stuff by shaping Clay's ideas about his grandfather. They must have built a cyborg version of Harry, or else an imaginary one. They used it to control his ideas about what Grandpa Harry was and what he could do by passing Clay a version from their heads, the way that Clay had passed a version of Blur to Patrick. They still controlled that version, even if Clay made it do things and added to it with his fear, he realized. They did it by defining Grandpa Harry to Clay, the same way that Clay had defined Blur and the rules of his world to Patrick. The same way that they were trying to pass an idea about God to him.

The thoughts disgusted him. At the same time, though, he felt elated as he began to understand why the Maccabees' lamp never sputtered or went out, and how it was that Job was still able to love God even after enduring His trials. It was so simple. The Grandpa Harry that Clay feared was like the Van that was in Patrick's head, or the God that his mother Kitty prayed to. He might be fully formed by the decisions and stories that Kitty absorbed, but he was still something that she had made, the way Clay had made the imaginary castle. And the God that Clay found in the Bible was no one so much as He was the process by which the book's contents had been shaped over the centuries. Like the contents of a human brain, a book could no more contain a supreme being than it could the actual land of Canaan.

Clay realized the implications then: There were different Gods that were purported to be the same one, despite their having been changed in makeup and meaning by translations, errors in understanding, and the imaginations of the creatures that brought them into existence. None of those Gods were anything but an imaginary castle at their least intrusive, or a personal cyborg at their most, but that did not mean that there was no God. It only meant that there was no God in the books that sought to simplify and explain, to turn things in at their corners and to let the texture of existence be supplied by whoever happened to stumble across them. If there was a God that was imagining Clay, then, he would be as unknowable to humans as Clay was to the Van that existed in Patrick's mind. People would be limited by being discrete points swimming inside God's greater imagination, and limited again by the fact that they were swimming in their own re-imagined cyborg selves and those the people around them used to filter their ideas about God.

Such a God as could actually exist would see them in the same way that Clay saw his characters, and while he might even be surprised by the ways they steered themselves, he would ultimately find himself no more capable of communicating with them than they were of truly communing with him. That also meant that the God of the Bible was nothing more than the sum of the choices its writers had made, a kind of emergent intelligence that reflected who they were and that was then reflecting Himself into the minds of people like Clay's mother, who built him up further before attempting to pour Him into their children's brains. The dashing of babies' heads against the stones, the killing of the children who made fun of the prophet's baldness, and even the passions and temptations of Jesus Christ himself were, in some way, the execution of the plan of all the people who had made the God that Clay was being taught to hold within himself.

He vomited then, and as he did, he felt a bitter taste in the back of his mouth. Clay knew it was Wormwood, and he regretted having allowed his mother to force the demon into him because he was such a poorly designed source of temptation. Still, this was a lesson itself, because it proved that Clay did not have to choose to accept the thought transplant when other people reflected their imaginary friends into him. It would happen whether he wanted it or not.

This also meant that Clay was living with Ender in his head, and that knowing Ender was a foul genocide, worth even less attention than a demon, would not be enough to shut him out. Clay would need to be careful to pay him no attention, or he might find Ender popping up in thoughts that Clay did not choose to allow him into. Meanwhile, Wormwood was the source of his immediate discomfort. He could not be tolerated, and the only way to be rid of him would be for Clay to make himself dislodge the construct from his thoughts. He closed his eyes and let himself be disgusted over again by the brute simplicity and the haughty regard for his own cleverness that Clay had detected in the voice of C.S. Lewis.

Lewis had been such an imperfect God, obviously flawed and fooling only those who expected that since he was purporting to be in the service of a bigger God, his words were guided toward a purpose defined outside of himself. None of them expected that his service was only to a piece of himself that he refused to own, or even to admit to having invented. His creating such an oily and obvious demon felt as silly to Clay as the idea that the giant green head in the Emerald City was living. The child's ability to see Lewis behind the curtain told him that there was no way Clay would ever build his life around the messages that his text pretended were profound. And yet, Wormwood had still entered Clay's ear and found a home in his brain. Perhaps it was not Lewis, then, who created this version of the demon, but his mother. It was not Lewis, after all, who had made the creature tenacious and profound... That idea had come from Kitty Dillon.

He panicked at the realization. If his mother could put demons in his head that controlled his feelings, and feeling his metal body was the only way to protect himself from the scream, then what?

Van's armor slammed itself over every inch of Clay's body, and his joints suddenly felt strengthened, like someone had added steel to his spine. The collision between his thoughts and his metal body pulled him back out of himself, bringing the bus and the scenery outside it into sharp focus and dashing the vertigo of his thoughts against the pain of direct sunlight in his eyes.

The first thing he did after feeling himself gain control over his armor was look around to make sure that no one would be able to tell he had thrown up. Luckily, Sully and his friends were several seats away, and the pool of vomit was quite small. On top of that, the bus driver had her eyes on the road, and the back of her head did not seem exceptionally perceptive.

He looked down into the vomit, and he realized then that he knew what he had to do. He had to treat the God his mother had created for him the same way he had treated Wormwood. He had to expel it, before its brutality and its sacrifice of its own son determined the way he related to the world. He would not wind up with children that he felt the need to shout down and fill with Joy the way his mother did to him.

Van grinned. He had never been able to understand what made up the body of the scream, only how to push it from place to place. Now, though, he began to feel confident that he would be able to find a way to expel it forever. How else could it be? He could not allow himself to make his choices under the guidance of a fictional entity created by his parents. Especially not one that demanded the pain of disfiguring young people in their private areas and sending them to die. Nor could he fathom worshipping the ineffability of a creature that would create a man only to prove the point that the man would worship him no matter how badly he was treated. His mother could go on believing that. She could think he was Job, but he would spit her forth in the same way that he had ejected Wormwood onto the floor of the bus.

Job would demand that God meet his own moral standards, and he would challenge his maker to either create a just world or to obliterate the masses of sycophants that no longer bowed to his will. Van smiled at the thought.

◆   ◆   ◆

When the bus reached St. Sebastian's, Van relinquished his being back to Clay. He could not stand against people who did not visit his castle. He was not strong enough. He could straighten the spine of this child whose mind was capable of making and unmaking worlds, though.

◆ ◆ ◆

Clay went into catechism with the love of creation in his heart, and never once did he question how Van could know his mind or what the difference might be between his cyborg and the imaginary friends that others reflected into him. Nor did he think about what that might mean about his own ability to know the mind of God. Instead, as he looked at the other children, he saw them for the first time as they really were—potential deities, all of them, whose only imperfections were their inability to unmoor themselves from their immediate impressions and consider the ways that words could make and unmake the world.

"How are you today, Clay?" the priest asked as he passed the children in the hallway.

"*In the beginning, there was the word, and the word was I am,*" Van replied.

◆ ◆ ◆

The priest tripped over his own feet as his mind wrestled with the content of Clay's message and what it meant to hear a voice like that emerging from a child who was too young to have even completed the catechism. He tried to recover before anyone noticed, but he felt the Dillon boy's eyes on him as he did, and they seemed to push him just enough to make him shaky for an extra step or two.

Other children around them giggled, so the priest looked over his shoulder to see if the boy was having fun at his expense. He saw nothing but cheerfulness and joy on Clay's face.

Had the child been saying anything earnestly? Or just babbling, as so many of the children tended to do?

In the decade since he had left the seminary, he had never felt like a child was playing games with him, but it certainly seemed like this one was capable of that kind of thing.

❖ ❖ ❖

The Judas Goat

"He did it."

Sully's finger loomed larger than anything else in the room, despite being on the other side of it. It was as if the refraction index of the air had suddenly changed, and now the resulting distortion was making the single digit aimed in Clay's direction loom.

That was how it looked, anyway. He wondered if that was because of Van's cyborg eyesight or if it was just because he was nervous. Then he looked from Sully to the hole in the wall. It was bigger than the last time they had damaged the room. Then, a little divot in the drywall from a collision with a chair had marred the finish. This new hole was the size of a child's fist, which was fitting, given the circumstances. It had not been his fault, though. He wanted to let them know that. Instead of telling anyone, though, he stared at Sully's finger.

Slowly, the other boys nodded along with Sully. All of them except for Noah, who just kept still. Clay felt a growing awareness in the back of his head. They were making him guilty just as surely as the church was collectively making a God and forcing it into his consciousness. Resisting one was the same as resisting the other. Even though Clay had never really thought about whether Sully was smart or not, even though he really did not think much about him at all, the other boy had discovered god-making and god-thinking and mastered using it on him while he was still occupied with arguments about why he should have to participate in this silly exercise. Now he knew. If one did not learn the secrets of god-thinking, then those who knew them would find ways to use their skills against you, and you would never be able to fight back.

"Come on Clay," the teacher said. "Let's go. We are going to have to call your mother."

His joints froze up as the teacher said that. Even if he wanted to follow her, he did not think he could.

She walked out the door and held it open. "I will drag you if I must. Your mother will understand. We're quite friendly with each other."

Clay managed to pull himself forward at that, and he heard snickering as he did so.

As he walked down the hallway toward the church office, he thought about how Sully had egged him on while they waited for the teacher. The boy had gotten wind of Clay's stories about Van and about the game that Patrick had helped him develop from them. Whether Noah had been the source of that information or not, Clay did not know. The Nosepicker had not joined in when Sully started calling him names over it, though, and he had spoken out when things escalated to the point where Sully beat his chest and started saying Clay's name in a muddled, drawn out way.

Clay was not stupid. He had seen that kind of mockery before. His uncle Curtis used it as a way of indicating people that he considered subhuman, like those who allowed their dogs to kiss them on the face. There was a word that went with it.

He had shouted that word in Sully's face, ignoring the fact that Noah was between them, and when Sully tried to push through his friend to attack him, he seized the opportunity to push things further. He grabbed the wrist on Sully's left hand when it sailed over Noah's and he bit it as hard as he could.

As soon as he felt the slackening in the other boy's muscles that came with the shock and sudden pain, Clay understood why his little brother loved to rely on it as a tactic. Sully started to thrash and twist under his teeth, so he gnawed as hard as he could to stop it. This led his victim to try to punch himself free. That did manage to successfully mash enough of the inside of Clay's mouth to cause an involuntary unlocking of the boy's jaw, and it was when Sully swung his hand away from Clay's face that his fist plunged into the drywall.

"You did this!" he screamed.

Clay smiled, wondering whether the blood he tasted was from his teeth being ground into his gums or if it belonged to Sully.

Noah jumped in then, convincing both boys to sit down and shut up. He also tried to sit in front of the hole, to help obscure it, but that did not work. The teacher saw it as soon as she stepped into the room, and that was when Sully pointed at Clay with his uninjured hand and said:

"He did it."

◆   ◆   ◆

Clay knew that his mother had been the one to pick up the phone. He had been able to hear her react to the reports of "his" behavior and had dreaded seeing her. When his grandmother showed up instead, he smiled. Bayleigh could be mean sometimes, but she was generally mean in private. Publicly, she enjoyed taking apart anyone who leveled accusations at her people, and she never seemed to care to sort out who was right before she did it.

Clay was not comfortable with the way his grandmother navigated the world, but he was happy to be able to benefit from it. Before they got to go home, though, he had to wait in the main office while Bayleigh went in to talk to the priest. Mr. Weir was also in there because the church had called his school before they called his house. Clay was not invited to join them, not at first. Not until after his grandmother spent a few minutes in the office with them, speaking loudly enough for him to clearly hear her side of the conversation. A moment later, Mr. Weir came out of the priest's office and led him back to the adults, and they asked him to explain what happened. He stared at them, unsure what to say. Words about the god-language formed in his mind, but he could only see them, he could not hear them or make them in his throat. Also, he felt like he should not have to explain Sully's god-thinking to adults, especially not to the priest.

Not knowing how to start without wasting their time, he waited.

"Well, did it happen the way Sully said?" Bayleigh asked.

Clay shook his head.

"Well, what happened then?" The priest leaned over his desk at Clay.

Clay opened his mouth to speak, but suddenly his mouth was dry, and it only moved at well-defined hinges and pivot joints. A moment later, he felt the rest of his metal body slide into place, and found he could not speak as his words were replaced by images of himself in a straitjacket. He looked like the unfortunate dog in the Tom & Jerry cartoons or Daffy Duck after a fight with Bugs Bunny. He tried to make the words, but his jaw ached, so he could not.

Instead, he asked Van to explain to him why he could not talk. There were no words to the response, but suddenly Clay felt like saying that he had bit the other boy might be the worst thing he could do. What else was there to say, though? If he made something up and it came out later that he bit Sully, then he would be in even more trouble. No matter what he did, he was going to wind up losing.

He cried. A moment later, he felt his grandmother's arm around him.

"I can't help with this situation if the only information we have is Sully's side of the story," Mr. Weir said. "We will not get involved with this on our side. It didn't happen at school, this was an extra activity that parents negotiated with their church, and all we did was agree to excuse their time out of the building. Unless another incident happens at Greenridge, I don't see why we should have to interfere. I also don't imagine Clay will want to come back today, but he is welcome tomorrow. Whatever your two," he waved at the priest and at Grandma Bayleigh, "decide, well that's a church matter."

With that, Mr. Weir departed. He did not say anything on the way out. Clay wondered whether the silence was because of what he supposedly did or if Mr. Weir just disliked his family. He tried to quash that last thought when he felt it coming, but it cut him and the scream seeped through the gash.

After Mr. Weir was gone, the priest raised his eyebrows. "Well, let's talk," he said.

◆　◆　◆

Kitty Dillon was livid when she heard the news. Her body went rigid, and it felt like the weight in her belly was getting heavier, petrifying itself into position. Her son stood before her, and she could not help but remember that he had also pushed her down and hurt her just a short time ago. And now this... biting. Like his brother.

Her thoughts turned to flame as something in the front of her head exploded. How was she supposed to keep herself healthy for the new baby and manage A.J.'s aggression if the good one was going to suddenly give up and start acting like the rest of Mark's family?

She burned slowly as she watched her son, and she could not help thinking that her heat was what was needed to temper him.

◆ ◆ ◆

Clay could not hear his mother over the cacophony caused by her anger. It made his metal body hot and fluid, but it also threatened his integrity. He felt like he needed to move, to shed his heat into the world around him, or else he might fall apart. He could feel damage setting in from exposure to her, and the onslaught meant he could not open himself enough to strike out with anything sharp. Instead, he had to wait and to plan, and also to hope that he had the strength to hold himself still as the metal bent around and under him.

Van winced, and then suddenly the metal body was cold and rigid again, but a howling echo of the scream started in the core of Clay's suddenly empty chest. The boy swayed and tried not to retch as his interior was torn apart and chewed up, but he managed to hold on through his mother's heat.

◆ ◆ ◆

Bayleigh heard her daughter-in-law's voice through the floorboards. She made faces and tried to keep herself from intervening, but she knew that Kitty was being too hard on the child. His hands had not been bruised, and she had felt them when she had comforted him at school. She was sure that he could not have punched through a wall, been confined with no way to wash his hands, and still have no plaster residue or dust, no scratches, no impact bruises... That arrogant priest and the mewling, ineffectual

school counselor had missed Clay's hands. She was almost totally sure
that they had not bothered to look at the other boy too closely either.
Even as her rage took her, though, she never really wondered why she
had not spoken up to point it out.

◆　◆　◆

"Go," Kitty Dillon finally said. She had just finished explaining
the ways that temptation demons tried to undermine children three
times in a row, and she knew at this point that she was just making
her son bear repetition to see if he could.

Clay nodded, but he did not move.

"You're not listening!" she shouted.

"Yes I am!"

She would normally have shouted down the boy's defiant tone as
disrespectful, as Mark taught her to, but Clay spoke first and sounded
amazingly like his father and that plucked the ability to reply clean
from Kitty's throat.

Clay sensed her temperature cooling and let himself throw razors
from his mouth.

"I heard you tell me that I must never, ever protect myself from
people who come after me, just like I hear you tell me that I have to
protect A.J. even though he hurts me. Even though he breaks things
and talks garbage. Just like you want me to get hit in the face so that
the wall doesn't break or else I will be punished. You just keep
believing whatever the telephone brings into your bedroom. You're
not in the world. I don't need you."

When Kitty's voice came back to her, all she managed to say was:
"Get out." She did not shout it.

Clay got out. She heard the door slam behind him. Then, before
she could do anything, she heard it begin to open and close quietly,
ten times, with her son's voice counting softly with each repetition.
Kitty took deep breaths while she waited for him to finish, and then
for a while after. When she felt her voice get strong again, she called
for Bayleigh. Her words to the woman were simple.

"Get out. Now. I don't care if I can't manage my children without help. I have my own people, and I can send Clay there."

"They can take both of them?" she asked. "Because you can't take care of A.J. In fact, you might be able to let Clay run free if you put a food dish out for him and you leave the TV on, but you really can't take care of A.J."

The older woman's body posture seemed to scream that Kitty Dillon never had been able to take care of him, in fact. She fought down the urge to scream.

"Fine. You're right. A.J. needs to be supervised. Go ahead and take him with you. But the boys should see each other and their father on the weekends." Her mother-in-law nodded. "And once my health is back and their little sister is safe, they are coming back. They both need to know that."

Bayleigh turned around and left the room. A few minutes later, after telling Clay that she was going to take A.J. and he needed to watch his mother, she left the house.

❖   ❖   ❖

Step on a LEGO

After Grandma Bayleigh took A.J. out of the house, Clay was alone for an hour or two. He lost track of exactly how long it was because he did not watch TV or play downstairs where there were clocks. Instead, he stayed in his bedroom with his LEGO collection. The bedroom door was open so that he could hear if his mother shouted for him, and he did his best to pay attention to sounds so that he would not lose the thread of alertness that allowed him to respond promptly.

At first, this task was not difficult and Clay was able to find his center in the bricks, moving them in slow, tidal motions that shifted and scraped in odd, soothingly painful ways. He began to sort the bricks, pulling all of the double-wide yellow ones to form the wall of his castle. Later, a Van would need to be put together out of minifigure parts and accessories, but for now the task was just to work up a floor plan. As he progressed, he needed to go fishing for parts less and less, and silence crept in. Beneath it, like the high whistle of voltage in the walls that never quite went away, was a crackle that he knew longed to turn itself into a scream. Once he recognized it, the thing never went away. Instead, all the other noises became louder. Then the sound of a car door outside made him jump and race out to the landing, even though he knew by the time he got there that it was too far away to be coming from a vehicle in his driveway.

Clay's discipline cracked. He felt the scream pour its way out of the cracks in the white noise of the world around him, and he knew it would soon be tearing itself through his throat, ripping up his vocal chords and summoning his mother from her room, which was sure to make her angry. Even as his hands shook, even as they tried to reach out and hurl his baseplate into the wall, complete with his castle's foundation, he forced them into his bin of bricks instead, and he dragged his arms through the ocean of plastic as quickly as he could, relishing the small bites against his skin and wincing at the cacophony of plastic screaming that came from his motion. When the scream finally did tear itself out of him, it was cut down quickly by the buzzing swarm of scratches, pokes, and pressures the bricks inflicted. Drowned under the noise and finding Clay's nervous system already overloaded, it dissipated into the background.

Afterward, Clay sprawled across the floor on his back, panting. He did not understand why going elbow-deep into his LEGO bin had been so satisfying, but it had, and now he found it hard to concentrate on building his castle.

As his mind drifted, his body suddenly started to feel funny. It was like when he was uncomfortable, except he was not uncomfortable, he just knew he could be less uncomfortable than merely being comfortable. He had no idea about how to realize whatever it was that his limbs were asking for, though, so he tried to ignore the strange feelings. He found it impossible to relax into his own exhaustion, though. There was still something he could do.

He held his arms up in front of his face and looked at the red welts that marked thick, angry lines across both of them. The impressions from the bricks had changed the geometry of his skin's surface, and oddly artificial trenches and circles still showed in the patterns of red and white.

Suddenly, the craving resolved itself into an understanding in his head. A moment later, Clay stood in his LEGO bin in his bare feet, with his blue jeans rolled up to his ankles. His soles cried for him to get out even as the mass of bricks against the sides of his legs helped to hold him up during the contortions and spasms caused by the full weight of his body pushing him into the bed of sharp edges that sifted and swirled against him. When his nerves calmed enough to let him be still, he gulped air. Tears streamed from his face. He had never felt so happy in his life. That was when it occurred to him to hop. Just a little, and just for a minute.

He did it.

His feet were hot and white and he could feel that they were, so he did not even need to look down to see them. They were also making the back of his mind hot and white, even as he looked out the window at the wind in the trees. The heat was visible, and even though his skin was actually starting to feel clammy, it filled him with a kind of mental push, the same way that the fun part of a flu did.

Outside, someone was crying. Clay felt sorry for them, but the LEGO assault was sending waves of pleasure up his legs, and his all-over body feelings were getting stronger. His knees were getting loose, too, and it felt like he might fall down. He did not realize that the sobs he heard were his own until he wiped his face and found that his hand was drenched in a swampy mix of sweat and tears. Then he remembered to breathe, and he took in long, gulping breaths.

He did not feel upset, and he did not want to cry. He wondered why it had happened when he felt overloaded before, but he was also feeling tired again, and pursuing that thought was more than he had the energy for.

Throwing himself onto carpet again, this time on his belly, he aimed for the pile of yellow bricks that he had been using earlier. They bit into flesh where his shirt had ridden up. Clay grunted into the carpet. He needed to sleep, but his brain kept turning the possibility of his mother's need over and over. Then he heard a car door close in his own driveway, and he was out the door and into the hallway before he even realized he had stood up. His metal footsteps clanged against the floor, and the joints in his hips and elbows whined as they moved faster than they had been designed to work.

Clay's sharpened tongue was flicking steel licks at steak knife teeth and trying to decide how to greet whoever had arrived when he stood at the top of the stairs and found it was just his father.

"What's all that?" Mark asked as he pointed at the LEGOs on his son's belly and tried to stifle giggles.

Clay looked down. His shirt was still riding up, and several yellow bricks stuck out of his flesh.

"*That's my armor,*" Van said.

❖   ❖   ❖

Exodus

When Kitty Dillon told Mark that she was sending the boys away, she made sure to call attention to the noise that Clay made while he was playing in the LEGO bin. He knew this because he could hear her, and some of the things she said made him want to cry. The exact words slipped through his grip, cutting and burning him as they did. He knew that they were designed to wear his father down so he would be enthusiastic about having a quieter house too.

Some words stuck out more than others. Nasty. Tantrum. Vindictive.

Clay could tell that she was making it seem like he had tried to keep her from resting, but he did not know how to explain what he was really doing to his father. He suspected that his parents might treat it as something even worse than antagonizing his mother if he did so, anyway, so it was easy to give up on it. His despair was driven by the fact that his need for painful noise, or even just for play, was not figuring into their discussion about him. The omission left an impression of taboo, and it left him worried that he might have happened across something so awful his parents would not even think to mention it as a possible cause for his behavior. Torn between wanting to defend himself from accusations of malice and fearing the ways in which his parents would pick apart and examine his attempts to protest his innocence, he felt he could not do anything but wait for them to decide what would happen next. Lucky for him, what happened next was something he had long dreamed about. He was sent to live with Grandpa Harry.

It was explained to him that he would be grounded from visiting friends' houses because of the extra work involved in transporting him back and forth, but that his mother needed the chance to rest if Baby Sis was going to be born healthy. On the weekends, he and A.J. would both come home to spend time with their father, since he would not see them at all during the week.

Clay went along with the plan cheerfully, figuring that he would have enough peaceful time to himself at his grandparents' house to make up for his inability to escape his brother on the weekends. It was all he could do not to be smug about the fact that he was receiving something that he could never have asked for. After his father asked him why he was staring off into space, though, Clay realized that it would not go well for him if they thought that he wanted this. Based on the way his parents usually behaved, they might even assume that he had intentionally manipulated them into it.

He did as he was told and packed all the clothes he would need for a week, along with his toothbrush, library books, and school backpack. Clay made sure that he had his lunchbox and that it was cleaned out, and he also stashed a few toys in his clothing pile. It was only when he pulled his oversized box of LEGO bricks out of his bedroom and toward the stairway that he understood exactly how much the situation had strained his parents.

"What is that noise?" Mark shouted up the stairs as Clay worked.

"I'm just getting the rest of my stuff," he said.

"I see your backpack and a grownup-size suitcase," his father shouted back. "How much stuff do you have? Are you planning on bringing a whole bag full of makeup like your mom does? Or fifty pairs of shoes?"

Clay pulled the box of bricks and grunted.

"It's my LEGO stuff," he said between breaths.

"Oh no," Mark said back. "Just stop where you are. You're not bringing all those."

"It's mine, and I want it. I'll be there all week."

"It's too much stuff," Mark barked back. "It's too heavy, and your grandparents have toys you can play with. Leave it here, you can play with it on the weekend."

Clay felt like he was going to hyperventilate. Why was it so important to his father that the LEGOs stay? He never used them.

He pulled the box further.

"Don't make me come up there," Mark growled.

Clay snarled back. It was a wordless thing, sharp and almost metallic. There was something too uncontrolled to be constructed in it. Mark recoiled from its sting.

"You can bring some, but only some. Put them in your lunchbox. No more than what fits in your lunchbox."

Hearing his father relent brought Clay's world back into focus. He tried to reply, but he could not. His throat still wanted to snarl, and he could tell it would if he opened his mouth, so he did not.

"You're welcome," his father's lazy contempt dripped from the soft consonants. "Put that trunk back in your room now, and then hurry up and finish so that you don't keep your grandfather waiting when he comes for you."

Clay did as he was told, putting all his weight into shoving his burden back in the direction of his bedroom. In his head, he was thinking about how quickly he could pick out the yellow bricks and the spaceship parts from the rest of his collection.

◆   ◆   ◆

At Grandpa Harry's, things turned out to be not much better than they were at home. In the car, everything was fine, the jokes flowed freely from Clay's grandfather, and they both felt happy to be together. Still, Kitty's pregnancy troubles had disrupted the family's usual social patterns, and Clay immediately felt the distance that brought when he got into Harry's Buick. It closed as they drove, but it was still there, a reminder of the way that his lack of control had affected the entire balance of the family and the fact that now even bedrest was not enough for his mother.

When they got out of the car and walked into the house, it became clear that the distance had grown even greater than Clay realized. The entire place felt foreign to him, despite his being able to trace the shapes of the patterns in the woodworking with his bare hands. It also seemed darker than usual.

Harry had built the house from architectural plans that were made to order. One of the things he had specified was the presence of a large number of wide, picture-style windows in various rooms in the front and back of the house. It usually had to be dark out before the house became dim, but on that day, it looked like Mrs. Hudson's classroom did before she came in and turned everything on for the day.

As Clay walked through the entryway from the garage to the kitchen and thought about the schoolroom quality that the house had taken on, his footsteps echoed like they did in empty classrooms. He stepped through the house, checking each room on the main floor to see if they were all equally dark.

Grandma Doris stood in the kitchen, and somehow her presence absorbed the light, pulling the room toward herself. Her tightly knit brow sucked the warmth from the environment as well, leaving her surroundings as flat and desolate as a cloudy day in the back part of February during that week when even hope freezes and only ice fishers are happy. Clay tried to flee from it by taking his things to his room and unpacking, but dinner was served very shortly after he arrived, so he was forced to plunge back into the family.

At dinner, only Aunt Marci joined Clay and his grandparents. He was glad for that, and for Grandpa Harry's humor, but any positivity that came into contact with Grandma Doris was absorbed so thoroughly that it might as well have never emerged. At one point, he was so desperate to change his grandmother's bearing that he even tried to flex his metal body. That stopped because when he reached out for his silverware, he felt his joints creaking, so he retreated.

Marci tried to help.

"You know, I can take Clay to school tomorrow so that neither of you has to miss work," she said. "It's no problem."

"No," Grandpa Harry said between bites. "Clay doesn't even go to school until you're in second period."

"I don't have the first three periods because I'm at the tech center for beauty school. It's no problem for me to change things around and do my practice hours in the afternoon instead of getting up and going in every morning."

Harry shook his head. Clay wondered what the problem was.

"I'm not having you miss class," he said. "And I don't want you to get your schedule all rearranged so that you think you have an excuse to stay out late on weeknights. You already go out every weekend."

"I'm not going to be missing class," Marci said. "And I won't be able to sleep in much, because he's still going to need to go someplace early."

"No," Grandpa Harry snorted a little as he replied that time, but he did not raise his voice.

"I can't take him either," Doris said. "I have a job driving other people's kids to school already, and I have to be there two hours before he's even getting up."

No one replied to her for a long time. Then, finally, Grandpa Harry smiled. "Well I guess that just means I get to play hooky to make sure Clay gets where he needs to be, doesn't it? What do you think about that, Clay?"

"You can drop me off at the bus stop instead of school. That way, it will go faster," he said.

"I don't think I'll need to do that, kiddo," Harry replied.

"Of course not," Doris said, "you'll just work later, so I'll have to start making dinner ready at eight o'clock if I want to keep you from going down to Mr. Burger."

Grandpa Harry winked at Clay. Clay smiled at him, but he could feel his grandmother trying to pull the smile away so that she could absorb it, and the perception of that emotional current drawing against his grandfather hurt him. The strain put on his metal body by resistance to his grandmother's gravity made groans in all his joints like dull metal screams, and something in the back of Clay's skull became heavy.

❖　❖　❖

Disrespecting the Lord

It took several days for Harry to get Clay to start talking about why he was fighting his parents over catechism classes. Bit by bit, though, he managed to get longer responses from his grandson. By the time the two were entering their first full week of driving to school together, the child had finally started to open up.

Clay decided to talk to his grandfather about Sully because the boy kept making faces at him on the playground, but he did not try to talk or fight or do anything other than make faces. If not for the hope that Grandpa Harry would have some idea why Sully would keep behaving in this way, he probably would have continued his silence. It turned out to be worth sharing, though, because Grandpa Harry told him that Sully was probably upset that he had not managed to get a bigger reaction out of the incident. He asked Clay how long Sully had been bothering him, and Clay told him, only leaving out the original incident with Noah that had touched it all off. For whatever reason, whether it was the phrasing of Harry's questions or Clay's belief that he was only supposed to respond to his Grandfather's exact prompts, it just never came out.

Clay kept thinking about things, seeing them over and over again in his head, but he did not want to volunteer the information. Noah had been nice to him for a long time now, so he did not want to see the boy suspected of anything, especially with the way he had just tried to protect Clay from Sully.

Harry knew that his grandchild was not being forthcoming, and he had suspicions about why, but he was not quite ready to articulate them yet, so he remained silent for the rest of the drive. After his grandfather went quiet, Clay looked out the window but failed to register any features of the neighborhood because none of them had changed since the previous week, so there was nothing to provoke new memories.

◆   ◆   ◆

Harry did not give up on Clay, although he did wait for a day or two before reopening the subject. No use in having the boy feel pursued. He knew what it was like to be attempting to tell people things and to have them constantly stop him to ask him to make minor changes instead of letting him finish. Doris had worn him down from a diamond in the rough to some kind of flat skipping-stone with those same kinds of demands. He stopped himself at that thought, and backtracked. The idea had slipped out without intent, but it was still a telling sign that he was starting to justify instead of taking responsibility for his own actions. Looking into his full-length bedroom mirror, he started adjusting his dress shirt. It was crooked already, and he had not even gotten into the car yet. By the time he dropped Clay off at school, it would look like it had never even been ironed.

Harry loosened his clothing and started rearranging it. While he did, he reminded himself about why it was important to take responsibility. The other path... well, it had led to this house and a company car, but it left Doris unhappy and made his children call him mean.

He took a deep breath. Maybe it was time to talk to a sponsor. It had been a few years since he needed it, but...

...maybe Kitty could use it, too? Harry had not seen her drink in years, but some of her reactions to her sons made him wonder if maybe her problems were more like his own than he had previously acknowledged.

While he thought about the ways that having a sponsor might help his daughter, Harry tried to visualize the woman he could ask to do that for her. It definitely should not be Doris—if such a thing were possible between the two, it would have manifested already—and he was fairly sure that it should not be anyone as blunt and flatly calculated as her mother-in-law, either. A knock on the bedroom door startled him out of his reverie. He quickly finished re-tucking his shirt and, adjusting the location of the fly, he buttoned his pants and zipped them quickly. Everything was in a neat row, now, and he felt much better. While he finished fixing his belt, he shouted for whoever it was to come into the room.

◆   ◆   ◆

Clay pushed open the door to his grandfather's bedroom and stepped inside. It was bad enough that Grandpa Harry was running so late that he had been forced to pour himself cold cereal instead of having waffles like he had been promised. Now he was starting to get nervous about missing the beginning of class time. The best he could hope for was missing most of the before class outdoor time, and that meant missing his chance to visit the castle with his friends. It made him want to shake his grandfather and shout, but it was not an emergency yet. It would not be an emergency as long as he got there before class started.

In the room, his grandfather just appeared to be straightening and smoothing his suit. Nothing was out of place in the room, and there were no signs he had been in the middle of anything. Why was he hiding upstairs then?

"We need to go," Clay said.

Harry started untying his tie. The knot was not straight any more. "We'll go when we need to go. I have to finish getting dressed."

"We're late, and I already ate cereal," Clay said. "We need to go."

"I can't go to work like this, just wait. Your school can't get you in trouble if it's my fault that you're late."

Clay did not believe his grandfather. He was also pretty sure that his mother would still punish him if she knew, since it was his responsibility to help remind the adults when they forgot. No one was perfect and everyone forgot sometimes, that's why it was his job to remind them and his own fault if he did not. He remembered the way his mother smiled when she told him that. Then he remembered it had been because he was crying about missing his class field trip due to the missing permission slip.

Besides, Van thought, ***not everyone forgets. They know that— why do you think they make it our job to remind them?***

Clay's fingernails bit into the palm of his hand.

"We need to go," he said.

"Who is the adult here?" Grandpa Harry demanded. "It's my fault if we're late, so let it be my problem."

He started taking deep breaths to stay calm so that he would not yell at his grandfather, but soon he was hyperventilating, and that did not help, so he made himself stop.

"Don't hold your breath to try to get your way," Grandpa Harry said. "It's not healthy, and you're too old to do it."

The scream came roaring up from Clay's belly so quickly that he did not even know what it was, he just knew the hollow, nervous echo from before was being replaced by something filled with vibrant force. Just before it slipped out of his mouth, the ablative plating deployed over his entire body, inside and out, turning him to metal through-and-through. As guitar-string garottes replaced his vocal chords, his esophagus became stiff and unyielding, his shoulders lifted, and the scream forced its way toward the top of his head. When it found the crown of his skull, it pushed so hard that Clay had to put his hands on the sides of his head to keep it from changing shape under the pressure. Then the feeling moved down and forward, eventually settling in the tight knot of muscle behind his eyes. A split second later, that knot was on fire, and the scream was pouring out of Clay Dillon through his pupils. It felt like going to the doctor and getting blood drawn, only if it was drawn out of the center of his vision in bright lights and snaking, shimmering patterns.

"I am going downstairs to make sure I have a lunchbox in the fridge. After that, I am calling my mom to let her know that I tried, and I am going to sit in the car," Clay heard Van's voice coming out of his mouth, but he felt curiously apart from it.

This is not how the metal body works, he thought.

Yes it is. The reply was so swift that it felt automatic. Clay shivered, but he saw through the scream that his grandfather was finally moving toward the door.

"Lead on," Grandpa Harry said. "I am ready."

His body turned and lurched forward. His movements were not under his direct control, which made him uncomfortable. On top of that, he was becoming very tired. It was easier to trust that Van had good reasons for wanting the same things he did than it was to try to stay in control. Giving up was restful.

◆　◆　◆

In the car, Harry approached the issue of catechism class again. He hoped to find out more about why so many of his grandson's problems revolved around it, and what might help the boy realize how important a step in his faith the church schooling could be.

"So, today you go back to catechism class," he started.

"Really?" Clay's voice remained flat and cold, like it had been in the bedroom.

"Well, they only just sent you home for the rest of last week, right? So today, it's time to go back."

"I was hoping that was over for me now," Clay replied. "It's obvious that they don't have anything to teach me. It's all just the same Bible readings we already hear in church over and over again."

"Those readings are important. They tell us what we need to do and why," Harry replied.

"Not really," Clay replied. "I've been reading through the Bible. We don't even use a sliver of it, just the same hundred or so stories out of thousands. Stories that make sense. Stories that don't. Stories that teach us about being hurt and being made to do things for God, only to find that he does not like the way they were done and punishes us for accomplishing his goals. It's not very good, and reading it gives me nightmares."

Harry stopped the car.

"I have had enough of that," he said. He could already hear the pitch of his voice rising. "You do not disrespect our faith to me."

"I'm not disrespecting anything. Didn't you read it? Don't you know what it says? Or do you just listen to what they read on Sundays? Most of what the priest tells you to do isn't even in the book, and a lot of what is in the book is about having babies with your own family. Church and the Bible are not the same thing."

Harry felt his smile turning. He felt drunk, and he could not stop himself. He stuck his finger in his grandson's face and shook it.

"This! This is why your mother is making you go to catechism. Because you do not understand a thing about religion, and you think you're smarter than everyone. Well you're not smarter than God, and you need to go until you understand that."

He dropped the car into drive and jammed his foot down on the gas. They were late, and it would not do to unsettle his daughter by giving her a reason to be upset at the two of them. Harry looked over at his grandson in the passenger seat, expecting to see him braced and grimacing the way that his own children always had been when his need grew great and he began to drive the way he drank.

Instead of looking nervous or fearful, though, Clay had the smallest, most severe Mona Lisa smile Harry had ever seen. It was unsettling, to find something so deeply introspective on a child's face.

"Knock it off," he said. "You're not impressing anyone."

"*I never meant to*," Van replied. "*I'm just happy to be going to school.*"

Clay shivered, unable to relax completely into place inside the metal shell. The scream was taking up too much room in his head and eyes, and his stomach was unsettled. Where did Van expect him to go?

Visions of the castle came to him. He tried to look out of his eyes, but the scream made it very painful, and he did not want to see his grandfather that badly. He was feeling disappointed because he had been sure that Grandpa Harry would understand what Van had meant about the book and the god-thoughts. He had counted on it, in fact, and on being able to talk about why Clay did not want the God his mother was giving him. He had even gotten himself ready to discuss his fears about Wormwood.

He desperately wanted his grandfather to understand that he wanted to keep these things that let him have Van and build LEGO in his head, and that he could feel them being unbricked and put back together in frightening shapes whenever the others pushed God-thought into him. Instead, every time he tried to talk, he just felt the distance between the inside of his armor and the outside of his skin.

❖   ❖   ❖

Isolated Incident

On the playground during morning recess, Patrick asked to speak to Clay alone. At first, Aaron seemed disappointed, but when he was reminded that Wednesday was the day Clay left at lunch for catechism class, he nodded and then left the two of them.

It felt funny to be asking Aaron to go away, and Clay wondered what Patrick did not want the other boy to hear. He was not used to keeping anything from either one of them that he did not also keep from the other, but Patrick seemed to work differently than he did. Then Patrick asked him to stay overnight again.

For a second, he felt like his metal body was in mid-deployment, but when Van did not suddenly take control over the situation he realized that there was no problem, but that he would need to explain things to his friend. Patrick watched him warily. Despite the fact that the two boys spent a lot of time together, he noticed that his friend never really seemed easy around him, and he felt quite the same way about the other boy.

Even if Patrick occasionally did annoying things or pushed him around a little, he was never really mean about it, and most of the time the two were in sync about what they liked. And even if his tunnel-vision focus was always turning itself in unpredictable directions, Patrick shared Aaron's ability to help Clay see how the lessons fit together and what deeper connections could be made between them and the things like television shows and books that existed outside of the narrow range of educational materials in Mrs. Hudson's classroom. Still, he could feel the tension oozing out of him. Eventually, Patrick started speaking again. When he did, his words sounded like he was answering a question, even though Clay had not spoken.

"I didn't want Aaron to feel bad about the fact that I am inviting you over because I promised him I'd try to invite him next. It's been a long time since I got to have any friends over, anyway, and I don't know if he even remembers that. If he does, I don't want to disappoint him, but he already said he was going to be busy until spring break because of his family, and I don't want to wait to get to have friends over, so please don't make him feel bad."

Clay nodded. Then he looked at the pavement. He was still trying to figure out how to explain the fact that he was grounded for not living at home even though his parents were the ones who made him leave. The more he thought about how to say it to Patrick, the more frustrated he got, because he was sure that Patrick would understand it in a hurtful way. Whether it would be because he appeared to be so terrible his family no longer wanted him or because he came from a family that was so terrible it would not take care of him hardly seemed to matter. Having to explain was shameful enough, no matter how it was interpreted.

When the words finally came, he felt like he was supposed to feel like someone else was saying them, but since they clearly came from himself and not from Van, he knew it was not so.

"I can't come over on the weekends for a while," he said. "My parents have us doing family stuff every weekend until my baby sister is born. And I can't do stuff during the week because my grandpa is bringing me to and from school, and I am just supposed to make it easy for him."

Patrick nodded. "That stinks," he said. "I was really hoping you'd be able to be there."

Clay nodded. "I don't get to pick what happens to me," he said. "Want to get Aaron and go to the castle?"

Patrick nodded again, but this time he said nothing.

❖   ❖   ❖

Finding Joy in Surrender

When it came, the air was clean and sweet, sweeter than the cloying artificial lemon taste that filled the back of Clay's throat before running up his sinuses and into his brain. He understood that he was having the Joy put into him, but not in so many words. Words failed to materialize during the moment, only disorientation came. Besides, even if the words presented themselves, one blast from the sink sprayer would flush them out of his head. When the air came, it came with a deafening rush of undifferentiated noise, and that felt like metal spikes going into his temples. Clay understood temples as places where headaches started, and he knew you could kill people by punching them. His father had said so once after he hit A.J. in both of them at the same time (his brother having done the same thing to him just moments before).

The rush of noise kept pounding, but he could breathe. Visions of his parents dying in car crashes obscured Clay's vision as the noise ensured he remained oblivious to the rest of his surroundings, and this made him anxious because he could not tell what was going to happen next. What his... mother... would do.

It took effort to remember which parent was on the sprayer.

Clay coughed, and then his gag reflex triggered. When he spewed soap bubbles out over the sprayer, though, the water filled his mouth again.

"I guess we still have a little soap to get," Kitty said.

Clay choked, and then he tried to kick away. It was a feeble attempt, hopeless because he was lying with his head below the level of his feet, so "away" would only bash his skull into the stainless steel drain.

"Fuck!"

His father's voice. He remembered then: They were both there. He had been fighting with one of them when the other stepped in to gang up on him, because neither of his parents could hold their own on an argument with an eight-year-old.

Clay tried to laugh, but when he did the water realized it had a route to somewhere other than his sinuses. He choked and dry heaved again.

"Mark! You have to use that language, now?"

Clay imagined his mother trying to put the Joy into his father. However that turned out, one of them would get what they were due.

"He's kicking!" Clay's father grunted between syllables.

Then it was all over. The sprayer was gone and Clay tipped upward, which caused all the extra fluid that had been rushing through his sinuses and out his nostrils to suddenly run down the back of his throat. He burped, gagged, and retched a bubbly mix of saliva, soap, and snot into the kitchen sink.

"There, there," Kitty said. "You know what happens when you can't make joy come out of your mouth. Joy has to go in."

Clay did not allow himself to scowl at her. Instead, he let his metal body encase him. Inside it, he imagined up a film projector so he could watch movies of his mother's funeral on the wall of Van's castle. His body hiccoughed more soapy water.

"He only makes such a big deal about it to guilt trip you out of using this as a punishment," Mark said. "If you give in and baby him, he wins."

Kitty shushed Mark and waved him out of the room. Then she held her son.

"Your father just doesn't understand," Kitty said. "He thinks that just because you were punished, it means that it did not really hurt you. Or that you need to be alone with the hurt to learn. I'm not sure which one. But he doesn't understand what you need like I do."

Clay watched his mother pull his armored suit closer to herself. He tried to make his skin deploy ten inch spikes so that she would be finished when she hugged him, but he could not make it happen, so he just watched movies of it.

◆　◆　◆

Earlier that day, Clay was reading alone in his room. All of his good books were at Grandpa Harry's house because his mother asked him to only bring his homework with him over the weekend, and to leave his other stuff so that he would not need to keep packing every time he went back and forth from one house to the other. This meant that the only thing he had around the house to read was the Bible.

He was trying to work his way through the gospel of Mark without kicking a hole in the wall. What was the point of telling the Jesus story four times, in contradictory ways, while swearing that they were all true at once? Was it just a way of testing to see if people would obey an impossible order just because they feared the punishment? If that was the foundation of his family's god-thought, it was awful. At the same time, though, it shed a brutal and clarifying light on why all the grown-ups around him were so terrible and untrustworthy. He thought about giving up on the Bible again, but his brother was napping on the room's other bed, so Clay could not do anything noisy, ruling out his LEGOs. If he left the room, then his father and mother would probably put him to work doing chores so they could spend "quality time" together. Clay did not want to be home with his parents, let alone doing chores with them, so he stuck to his Bible and tried not to choke on it.

As he read, he kept remembering that Patrick had invited him over for the weekend. If his parents cared about whether or not he kept his friends and learned to know people, then they would have let him go. He was sure of this, as sure as he was that bringing it up to them would be terrible, nothing but another excuse for them to unload piles of words that made no sense, except perhaps as brooms to sweep concerns away without taking responsibility for their own failings.

At some point, Clay realized that he had come upon the loaves and fishes story. It was one of the most major readings included in the church liturgy, one that was repeated at least three times each year in Sunday school, on top of its annual inclusion in the reader. That recognition made him backtrack and review the entire gospel to that point. As he scanned the section headings throughout each chapter, he came to realize that unlike the Old Testament or even Matthew, Mark seemed to have written entirely and only stories that were repeated regularly in church. There were tiny anecdotes he did not remember in between them, but each major episode was something he could recall seeing included in the liturgical reader, even if the versions of them read in church were actually from the other gospels.

That was interesting, especially since so many of the stories in Mark were as fantastic as the stories in any of Clay's science fiction readings. Why was it that he was expected to believe that praying would make one boy's lunch feed hundreds, but that exploring the galaxy was an unattainable fantasy? Or that telling a blind person to see would work? Clay could remember meeting friends of his mother who were in wheelchairs, but he could not remember any of them going into a church and then being able to walk back out of it.

As he contemplated how the most unbelievable parts of the Bible seemed to be the foundation for his parents' belief in it, he wondered how much different things would be if they admitted that those stories were just science fiction from people who did not know about science. What if, instead, they spent time asking themselves why it was that Romans ruled the Jews, really? Or what if they questioned what was going on in those moments when the book claimed God turned his back on his people to let them be conquered? It seemed to him, as he read, that there were probably much more useful lessons in the stories about which decisions by which rulers resulted in the fall of David's kingdom than there were in the way that Jesus pulled all the same magic tricks that Steve Martin had used in that movie about the preacher who lives on a rock n' roll travel bus.

Some time later, his mother came in to check on him or to see if A.J. was up from his nap. Clay was unsure which it was, but by the time she showed up he had discovered that the so-called loaves and fishes story was actually something that happened twice in Mark, and he wondered if that was intentional. It seemed, since the numbers of people and of fishes were so similar and the other details changed just a little, like it should probably have been in Matthew, with the other embellished and changed stories from Mark that he had already spotted.

Kitty Dillon disappeared from Clay's vision as she sat on the lower bunk with A.J., but she was soon hovering just off his elbow as he read. His brother, he realized, must still be asleep.

"What are you reading?" she whispered to him.

Clay tapped the gilded leather cover of the book impatiently, wondering why his mother needed to ask when there was only one four thousand paged onionskin book covered over with gilded leather in the house.

"Which book?" She whispered.

"Mark," Clay replied. "I'm at the second story about feeding people with a small boy's lunch."

Kitty frowned. "Second?"

"Yeah, it's in there twice. Once in Galilee, like we learned in church, and again when he's preaching to Gentiles."

"Are you sure?"

Clay held out the book for her to see.

After his mother read for a moment, she said, "That can't be right. He didn't feed four thousand people with seven loaves and a few fish. He fed five thousand people with five loaves and two fish."

"That part is here too." Clay flipped back to the sixth chapter and showed his mother. "I think maybe they accidentally forgot to delete the one they didn't want."

"What do you mean?" Kitty was frowning again.

"When they decided which one was going to be the story they published. Whoever wrote the final draft. They forgot to get rid of the old version when they put in the new one."

"That's not how the Bible was written," Kitty said. "That's the word of God. People didn't just make it up."

"All books are written the same way," Clay said. "Someone had to figure out which words to use to talk about what God said to them. It's not like he just gave them words. Words come from people."

His mother scowled. "I think you might need more than one catechism class."

"What? The words have to come from people. How else would they show up on paper made by people? And why would there be differences in them? If this was the word of God in his exact words, then wouldn't it be a sin for the liturgy to use different words for the story than this Bible does? Or what about the old Bibles that used language that's hard to read like 'thee' and 'doth?' Those can't be the word of God at the same time this is, unless someone is getting the message without words and then finding the right ones. And then, that person had to choose how to tell the story. So it got written like any other book."

"We're going to talk about this later," Kitty said. Then she took his Bible.

"Hey!"

"Hey you!" She hissed like a whole pile of snakes. "We will discuss this with your father after you nap."

"I'm not tired. That's why I was reading."

"You sound tired to me," she said. Then she left.

◆ ◆ ◆

Clay had no idea how long he was forced to sit on his bunk without anything to read, but he knew he did not sleep, because he spent the entire time planning the various ways he might be able to steal things his mother would miss, just to make her understand how it felt.

When she returned, she still held his Bible.

"I don't believe you're really reading this," she said. "There's no way you can follow it for page after page and understand it."

"Liar." Clay could not help the word. It was the only one he had, and it was determined to be out in the room.

"What did you just say?" his mother demanded.

"Liar." The word came again. A moment later, Clay found a few more. "You don't know. You don't ask. You tell me what I don't understand, but I am the one who read it. I know I understood."

"You don't understand anything. You think there's no difference between any of the books you read, but someday you will grow up and understand that there are big differences. Some books have true facts in them, and some have important lessons, and it takes time to understand what they are. And you need people to help you. No one can just read the Bible and understand how it all fits together at once."

Clay felt his eyes bug out, and his lungs it felt like they were going to vomit. He wondered why there was food digesting in his lungs.

"Don't you make faces at me like I'm an idiot," his mother rasped as he fought to parse his sensations. "You might be able to convince everyone else, but I am your mother. I know what you're up to."

Clay's stomach twisted, and it felt like it was inflating. He wondered why there was air in there, but it seemed like that's where the air needed to be if there was food in his lungs. Everything was wrong. He had no idea how to decode his mother's words, his metal body would not come, and his regular body was not acting like it was possible for it to function the way it felt.

"Admit it. You didn't really understand what you read, you just wanted an excuse to read all your science fiction books. It's okay. We can start over together, like we did with *The Screwtape Letters*."

"Fuuuuuuuuuuuuuuuuck YOU!" The words seemed to be independent of Clay's mind. They just appeared, formed from something in the modified processes of his body, and then they were there, confronting his mother. Clay wondered if they came from his god-thoughts trying to resist hers, or if they had been born out of some other process.

He did not even feel the palm of his mother's hand when it connected with his cheek, but he let his body cry because he understood what had not been apparent before: The metal that was making him stronger was not in his body, and it did not have to be something he allowed to happen to him. He could resist it, and if he did, she might see that he was just a kid.

Then, suddenly, they were both inside the castle. He was taller than her.

"*You don't get to do that,*" Van said to Kitty Dillon. "*They'll lock you up like they did to grandpa if you do that.*"

His mother said nothing back. Instead, she grabbed Clay by the wrist and pulled him out of his LEGO castle, through the door of his bedroom, and down the hall so that his father could hear what he had threatened her with. After that, they put the Joy back into his life, and then she hugged him and left him alone again, without his Bible but finally tired enough to nap.

❖ ❖ ❖

Hypocracy

It was Sunday before Kitty Dillon tried to talk to Clay again. After the Joy had been put into his life, she put him to bed, and then she left him because clearly, he needed more rest. The strain from going back and forth to his grandfather's house must have caught up with him. Around 8pm, she did get worried because he had not come out of his room at all since the incident.

When she took a plate of cheese, salami, and crackers up to him, she saw the covers pull tight just as the door opened. The next morning, the same thing happened, and then she took the empty plate away. Kitty thought about sending Mark in to retrieve the boy for mass, but it hurt to think about how that was likely to go. She did bring a plate of breakfast foods upstairs and then got A.J. ready to go. Before they left for church, Mark protested leaving the boy alone. Kitty knew, though, that this was just another one of his excuses to avoid going himself, and she also knew that Clay would not leave that room until she found a way to get him talking to her.

He was her son. She understood the way he worked.

♦   ♦   ♦

When his mother came for him, Clay did not know that it was around one in the afternoon. He did know that they had gone to church without him, and that he was hungry again and out of food. When they were gone, he snuck out to get extra milk and orange juice, but he did not want to eat anything that would leave dishes behind, so he did not have cereal.

After he had enjoyed what seemed like an infinite time alone on the main floor, a car rumbled down the street and startled Clay. It was navy blue, like his parents' station wagon, and he slammed himself to the floor when he saw the vehicle. When belly made contact with the cool linoleum in the kitchen, Clay realized he was naked. By the time he spider-crawled to the stairs and rushed back to his room, his heart was beating so loudly in his ears that he could not hear whether his family was home now or not. It was only later, when he did hear them arrive, that he realized he had made a mistake about the car outside and that there was no chance anyone had witnessed his nudity.

When his mother finally came for him, he was dressed. He realized at some point that he must be, or she would use it against him. He also made sure that his LEGO sets were all put up, as well as anything that she might assume he had been reading. Clay did not know how long after that he was made to sit on his bed alone, but he knew it was long enough to complete one of the simplistic and laughably brief chapter books that she thought were appropriate for him. Three times.

If Clay had been in possession of a clock, he would have been able to tell time, but that would only have served to increase his distress because his frustration with the stilted dialogue of the writer's imagined fourth-grade students would have been compounded by his emerging understanding of the fact that the book was actually so woefully undersuited to challenge him that he was finishing its hundred and two page stretch in just around thirty-five minutes. As it was, he wanted to throw the book overhand at his mother's forehead when she walked in with his Bible. As frustrating, inconsistent, and disturbing as that book was, at least it was a challenge. The "appropriate" chapter book only had characters with language skills more in line with actual second graders than fourth graders, and since it was an adult who wrote the book, he did not have much hope for the author's ability to understand the skills and knowledge that children possessed. He did not throw it, though, instead he held himself very still and tried to deploy his metal body.

Van was no longer responding to him. Somehow, Clay had lost the ability to control when the cyborg came and went.

"Clay, I wanted to come and talk to you about what you were thinking while you were reading this," she said as she caressed his Bible. "Because I'm thinking you don't really understand how it all fits together, so we should get on the same page."

He made room for her on his bed. There were no chairs in the room, and he needed her to stop standing between himself and the door. She hugged him. The metal body deployed then, and Clay felt himself unwind inside of it.

"See, I knew you just needed some extra rest," his mother said.

Clay watched her hand tap, trace, massage, and examine the textures in his Bible's leather cover as she talked about the fact that it could be hard to understand. She also discussed how its language was so stiff and outdated that you needed other people to help you decide what it meant, but he was far more interested in her hands.

When she was holding the book, it was clear how much it mattered to her, and that made it easier for Clay to listen as she circled back and forth over the idea that he could not possibly be smart enough to understand plain words written in correct grammar and printed clearly on the page. Her assumptions made the metal body harden, and he felt the razors on his tongue, but he made himself cut his palate instead of spitting them into his mother's face. He did not want to destroy the ballet of hands that was keeping him from forgetting she was human. They tapped the cover insistently.

"This is the history, Clay. This is thousands of years of people remembering what happened, what it was like before God stopped talking to the world. Understanding how it was handed down is complicated, which is why you can't just arrogantly decide you understand what you read in it. That's why I do my Bible study, even though I'm grown up and I took all the classes. To learn that history, and to understand the lessons in events like the flood."

"You know that isn't history, right?" Clay asked. "That's a story."

"Yes," Kitty spoke even more slowly than usual, and it made Clay's arms try to reach out to bash her, but he managed to hold them still. "It's our story. The story of where we come from, all the way back to before it was called Catholic, and before it was called Christianity. And it's about the promise God made to us, which is why we need to remember it. He might destroy some of us sometimes, but he won't kill us all again. You need to know that, so that you don't spend all day afraid like that character in *Annie Hall*."

Clay had no idea who Annie Hall was, but he was suddenly very afraid of his mother, to the point where it left no room for anger. If she was convinced that the stories in the Bible were just like the stories in his history book from school, then he was convinced that she was dangerous, but he had no words for why. When Kitty grabbed his shoulders and kept repeating that God made them a promise, he started to scream. At first, Clay thought that the scream was just in his head, but then he realized that his ears hurt and he knew it was everywhere.

"You idiot! There isn't enough water." Van's voice interrupted the scream, squelching Clay's panic and cutting off his ability to control his arms and legs. They kept moving anyway, and as the cyborg's voice continued, it all began to seem coordinated. *"You know that Adam and Eve were not real people, right? Look at a map of the Middle East. Look at a globe. The Tigris and Euphrates don't meet. I saw it at school. I saw it on the map at church. Your dumb stories about people who didn't exist took place where two rivers who never cross crossed. How can that be history?"*

Clay was relieved that Van kept him from feeling the slap when it came. He did not like the way the laughter came afterward, though. *"Keep hitting me for telling the truth. I know you. I know the kind of people who do what you do. I understood what I was reading."*

He felt nothing when she left the room, or even when his father came to bring him back to the kitchen for more Joy. His mother was crying too much to say her little saying about Joy going into his mouth, too, and in the end, she just stuffed the sprayer into his mouth and let it go until she realized he was drinking. An hour later, Grandpa Harry came to pick him up for the week.

❖   ❖   ❖

Bad Influence

Clay hid at the top of the stairs. He did this quite a bit when he was at home, because his parents often talked most honestly about what they were planning to do to him when they thought he could not hear. He was unused to needing to use the strategy at Grandpa Harry's, though. He never overheard people making plans for him when he was with his grandparents. Well, not unless Curtis was in town from college, but Curtis was the kind of person who spent his free time deciding what was best for everybody else, so he would have felt a little left out if his uncle had not concocted various schemes to improve his life through positive attitudes and exposure to the Right media. Today was different, though. Today, Clay was not only having to eavesdrop from the top of the stairs like he did at home, he was having to eavesdrop on his own parents just like he did at home. The worst part was that he knew Grandpa Harry was sitting downstairs in his office and pretending to work while the house's furnace ducts carried the whole conversation down to him.

The subject of his parents' argument was why Clay should not be coming to see his grandfather any more. The reasons for their disagreement were unclear, but it seemed like his father wanted him to go see Grandma Bayleigh sometimes so that A.J. could have a turn visiting Grandpa Harry. Clay did not see why there was a problem with that, but apparently his mother did.

"I'm not saying that A.J. can't come over here instead of seeing your mother," Kitty said for the third or fourth time. "What I'm saying is that I don't want Clay going over there. Not with the way she spoils him and then says nasty things about my family and about the church."

"I don't think A.J. heard those things from her. And you know she's been cleaning up after him for weeks, and she could use a break."

"Yeah, well, I want to give her one," Kitty said. "By not sending my other son over there. She won't get a chance to unravel his discipline."

"No one's unraveling Clay," Mark said. "He's really started to toughen up this year. I think we're over all the little kid tantrum bullshit."

Clay felt a little surge of pride when his father talked about him growing up, but he also felt a pang when his mother did not say anything back for a very long time. Finally, Kitty spoke again.

"You know your mother is a bad influence. She's so judgmental, and she doesn't respect other people. I'm sure she's the reason that A.J. calls everything stupid, and I wouldn't be surprised if she taught

Clay that trick he does where he just stares at you without speaking until you're sure he wants you dead."

Clay knew that his mother was describing the way the metal body came out to protect him, and he was not entirely surprised to find out that it looked as hard as it felt. He felt a change in himself when he heard his mother describe him as possibly homicidal, though. Something shifted, and suddenly he was able to feel how the metal body could be used to do so much more than just protect himself. This realization called out to him, and he felt a pull toward it as he realized that he could pay his mother's mistrust back by realizing her predictions. He was relieved when those feelings started causing him to panic, though, because as soon as he retreated from them, their existence made him feel ill and he realized what they were. The problem was, now he was a sack of wet oatmeal on the floor, unable to make himself move except by punching himself, over and over again, directly on his sternum, in a grim imitation of the way his uncle mocked people. After a few hits, his heart skipped a beat. Then his lungs refused to expand.

The panic was complete. He no longer had a name, just a desire to fight to keep breathing, and he no longer had a mother or a metal body, just a scream that forced soggy muscles back into action until—

A breath.

Fuzzy darkness.

Arms.

"Are you okay?" Mark Dillon spoke to him from just above his face.

Clay decided his father must have picked him up. He waved.

"That wasn't an answer," his mother said. "We should take him to the emergency room. I think he hit his head."

Knots in Clay's chest tightened at the mention of the emergency room. He did not want to have to talk to doctors about the bruises he was sure he would have on his chest. He knew that hitting yourself was one of the ways to go to the crazy house, and he did not want his parents to send him there. Also, they seemed like they were in a mood to blame his grandparents for things, and he did not want them to think poorly of the way Grandpa Harry took care of him. That meant he could not afford to get caught doing things that would make his mother want to keep him at home again.

"Wind knocked out," he wheezed. "No head."

His father set him down. It felt like he was being placed on a couch. His vision started to clear soon after that, and he saw that he was downstairs, in his grandparents' living room. He could see the landing in the corner.

"Did I fall down the stairs?" he asked.

"No, honey," his mother replied. "It looked like you tripped on the upstairs landing and just fell onto it. Kind of. I don't know how you managed to land on your back, but you did, or else you rolled there."

"What's the last thing you remember?" Mark demanded.

"Being asked questions," Clay replied.

"This isn't the time to be a smartass."

Clay shrugged. It brought pain in his head that made everything dark and foggy again. His chest throbbed.

"Grandma Doris says she can't have more than one of us at once," Clay said. "So if A.J. needs a turn, he can have it. I like it here, but I have not seen my other grandma in a while."

He felt his father's hand on his forehead, and it felt like a smile. Then sleep took him.

❖   ❖   ❖

Decades of Hope

Clay's fingers worked the beads quickly, the way he always saw his mother do it. As each ridge on the pad of each fingertip became intimately acquainted with each blemish, imperfection, and ridge on the cheap plastic rosary he had received last Easter, he began to feel some of the calm that his mother was always promising prayer would bring him.

The words to each invocation still caught in his throat awkwardly because Clay was embarrassed by their obsequious and superficially self-denigrating language. It seemed out of place to confront a supreme being about a matter that you felt was very important in language that was pleading the unimportance of anything as small as yourself, and if he let himself think about that, then his metal body deployed and his thoughts turned in on themselves, becoming ugly. That made praying out loud hazardous for Clay, but his practice every week in church came in handy, allowing him to mouth the words without breath so that he could say each decade without having to hear himself speaking. It was easier, that way, to pretend that he was not trying to speak to a deity whose existence he doubted with every fiber of his being.

The plastic seams on each of the rosary's glow in the dark beads pricked his metallic senses into being so that the conviction pushing him, saying he must bear through to the finish, that conviction became more real to him than the prayers. This focused his intent, until he was sure he was praying even if he did not speak, and even if the thing he prayed to was also something he was making within himself.

Clay Dillon prayed for his mother to be gone from his life. He prayed to be spared her decisions about his education and her embarrassing attempts to talk to him without having to listen. Mostly, he prayed that something would come to protect him from her Joy and her ever-present cheerfulness, which seemed to always float above a cushion of pleasure that did not dissipate or change, even when she was screaming and lamenting her own decisions to demonstrate remorse for causing Clay to display more pain than she had intended when administering her discipline.

The things that made him want his mother gone reminded Clay very much of the way that the large, mean girl in his preschool class had always made people eat sand until they hit her, only to run crying to the teacher, confessing about the sand and claiming that it was a misunderstood joke. More often than not, the poor sand-eating child whose will finally snapped and connected with Roberta's jaw was the one sent home. Even when that was not the case, she was never gone for much longer than a week, and then it took only days for her to fall back into her old patterns.

There was a new feeling in his throat and in his hand, and Clay realized that he was on another large bead. He had shifted prayers to the *Glory Be* without registering any of the words.

Sinking into that place where intentions formed polyhedral arches and words comfortably popped from the lack of pressure, his will worked its way through visions of himself at Grandpa Harry's house. In them, he was being picked up in the morning by the bus Grandma Doris drove. There was no metal body, and uncle Curtis didn't even come home from college unless there was a holiday that required presents and enough of his siblings to keep him from talking rudely.

As his fingers paced through the beads, the inside of Harry's house refracted, folding itself away into the arches. Clay found himself in a cold place where vision did not seem to be the right term for his method of perceiving, but where visual representations of things that were usually invisible stood frozen in the landscape of his memories like gigantic extrusions from the bodies of the people in his life. He stared at them each before he started screaming.

As soon as he let loose, the metal body closed around him. Still, the scream shattered many of the archways in his thought complex, causing his family's bodies to sag like someone had cut their strings.

Be silent, Van commanded. ***And be protected.***

Clay continued to scream. The pure need of it, along with the revulsion that always poured through its center, propelled him forward. The metal bent around him, and it felt hot and alive. He continued to push, seeing his mother's mental doll crumple.

She's dangerous. Clay had no idea how he spoke to Van while screaming. ***I have to save you.*** *You don't understand what will happen if you don't stop her.*

His pickup throat opened then, and razorblade arpeggios of incoherent need broke Van open, shattering the integrity of his metal body as if Clay had found a miracle frequency to shatter him with resonance or some magic sonic power that simply dissolved molecular bonds. The last of his mother's polyhedrons faded out then, and her form sat shrouded in darkness.

Sleep took him.

◆　◆　◆

The next morning, Clay woke with his fingers still pinching one large bead about halfway around the rosary. As soon as he felt the jagged edge of the plastic ball's seam, he remembered how important his prayers had been, and he kept praying. He knew that his mother must not be allowed to keep him from his grandparents, and she must not be allowed to make decisions over top of Grandpa Harry. Harry never made Clay eat soap, and he asked questions instead of telling him how he had to be.

The visions from the night before were clear now. The geometry was simple; his grandfather was able to see children as people. It was vital that he continue to be the one that made decisions about how Clay would make it through the day. Harry also had to know about Bayleigh and about how Kitty Dillon wanted her children cut off from half their family. He was sure that his grandfather would make sure his mother could not cut them up and keep them apart. His grandfather knew about family. He kept working the beads, not even praying but just feeling them in his hands and letting them sting him with their rough edges, hoping that they would reveal to him some plan, some great way of enacting his grandfather's guardianship without Mark or Kitty stopping it.

◆　◆　◆

Days later, when he was in church with his grandparents and his mother came to sit with them, she remarked on his devotion, his lack of leg-bobbing and other fidgeting, and his general happiness as signs that better discipline was winning. When he heard that, Clay squeezed the jagged plastic crucifix until his blood trickled down his fist and dripped onto the church floor from his wrist.

❖   ❖   ❖

Wind Patterns Sometimes Whisper Like Answers

A long time after he finished the rosary, but not so long after that he forgot he had done so, Clay found himself being picked up from school by Grandma Bayleigh. He itched at the thin scar inside his palm where his scab used to be and thought about those beads and the way they seemed to make his prayers stronger as they cut into him. Then the worry started. His grandmother was not taking him away from his mother, after all. She was just picking him up from school instead of letting Grandpa Harry do it.

Clay knew that his mother had not relented and agreed to allow the Dillons to take care of him because she grew louder and louder as his father continued to push the issue, and the last couple of times it had even sounded like she was throwing things. His father ran out of their bedroom once when it happened.

Bayleigh smiled when she saw him.

Clay shrank inside, suddenly worried about all the things his mother had said about Grandma's propensity for cruelty and hatred. Maybe she was a bad example. Maybe his mother was right.

You know her better than anyone. You know she isn't right about anything. Van's voice was soothing.

Clay ran to his grandmother and hugged her.

"Your grandpa had to go to a sales meeting. Its time got moved on him," Grandma Bayleigh said. "So he asked me to come and get you."

"Is A.J. in the car?" Clay asked.

Bayleigh shook her head. "Marci came by to pick him up at lunch. She's been planning on that for a while. Said she wanted to take him to the zoo, and honestly, I'm ready for that. Your little brother is good at digging in the dirt, but if I can't keep his muscles working and his attention on a project, then he gets wild."

Clay nodded. It felt like his soul was in that nod.

"He likes animals," he said.

"So, I'm about to go home and make Clif some pizza. Do you want pizza?"

Clay nodded again.

Somewhere, Van went to sleep.

⁕   ⁕   ⁕

The thing that was in front of him was not a pizza. It was covered with cheeses, somehow combining slices of deli Colby with the soupy remains of shredded cheddar and a little of what, from the smell, had to be artificial nacho topping they had at the 7-11. He wrinkled his nose at the smell before he realized that it was due, at least in part, to the Coney sauce, kidney beans, and canned mushrooms embedded in the pizza's surface.

Bayleigh chuckled.

"I bet you never saw pizza like this," Grandpa Clif said. "We only eat pizza at home when Bayleigh is trying to get rid of leftovers. I don't eat leftovers, but I eat pizza."

Clay grimaced.

"Next time she asks you if you want pizza," Grandpa continued, "You make sure to ask her if we're going to Fred's. That's the only place she likes to get real pizza."

"Okay," Clay said.

"I forgot to ask today, or we might not be having this talk," Grandpa said. "It's okay, though. I like chili and I like nachos. What about you?"

"I like those things," Clay said.

"Then eat up," his grandfather pushed the plate closer to him.

The smell drifted up. It wasn't bad if he closed his eyes and thought about chili and nachos. It was only bad when he was expecting pizza.

Grandma Bayleigh cackled.

Clay took a bite.

"This is really good if you stop calling it pizza," he said.

◆   ◆   ◆

After they finished with the pizza, Grandpa Clif went outside to work with his tools in the garage. He asked Clay if he wanted to help, but Clay did not feel like listening to the saw and the yelling, and he did not like the way the sawdust bit his skin. He was very grateful, though, that his grandfather wanted to give him a choice. At home, his father either demanded his help with home improvements or commanded him to stay away.

Instead of going to help with the tools, Clay watched daytime television with Grandma Bayleigh as she clipped coupons.

"The trick," she said, "is that the mail-in rebates give you your best dollar value. You give 'em a week or two after the coupon comes out but before it expires, and then you use it when the item's on sale and you wind up getting all of your money back. Or else, you wait and then they offer a rebate in store, and you use a discount coupon for the same thing. How do you think you got all those coloring books? Your mom and dad didn't buy those. They got them from me, and I got a dollar more than I paid for them once I got my rebate check."

Clay watched, fascinated. His grandmother's ability to turn the newspaper into money seemed very useful. He wondered why Grandma Doris called the newspaper garbage and threw it out every night. It seemed to be worth using. He knew his mother used it, and he knew she learned that and canning from Bayleigh. She never taught him, though. His grandmother was the one who taught him. Why did she think her mother-in-law was evil when she taught the family all these things that made life easier and set aside food for the winter?

As he wondered, his grandmother kept clipping coupons. She wasted no motion, sliding the scissors forward without even closing them and then snipping the short side before setting each one in a stack. Food, office supplies, cleaning supplies, doodads, and candy. Those were the piles. The scissors she used to cut them were from TV commercials that Clay had seen when he woke up in the middle of the night and snuck downstairs to see *The Many Loves of Dobie Gillis*. Grandma Bayleigh did not have cable, though, so he wondered where she had gotten them if not from the commercial with the ordering information, but then his vision tracked to the pile of doodad coupons and he knew.

Sitting there, listening to the rich people on television kissing while he watched his grandmother find ways to make money out of the newspaper, Clay began to wonder if he had perhaps been wrong about God. In this place, with people who liked teaching and learning and who knew how to be quiet, he could almost believe that there was something capable of protecting him in the universe. He tried to go to that place where he was sure of it, like he did in science class when concepts made sense, but it eluded him. In his mind, he kept pitching his field of perception forward, searching for the polyhedral arches that would allow him to hold onto God like other concepts. Everything he found was still himself, though, even when he ran into Van in the castle. It was odd to be there while still watching polyhedrons, because the two states each made the other less opaque, even though only one was, strictly speaking, a visual phenomenon.

"Do you believe in God?" he asked his grandmother. "I know you don't go to church, and you always make jokes, but you also pray."

"That's how you know I believe in God," another coupon in another pile interrupted her speech. "Because I don't believe in churches."

"At church, they say they feel God, and that's how they know. I don't feel anything."

"I don't feel anything either," Bayleigh said. "I just realized that when I believe in God, I don't need to feel anything. It's just something I do, and it works. See this house? My good husband? Do you have enough to eat? I don't need evidence that God is real, because I got what I needed already."

"Do you think you'd stop believing in him if you lost those things?" Clay asked. His mind flitted back to Job.

"Wouldn't you stop believing in the president if he started losing wars?" Bayleigh shot back.

Clay did not know what to say to that. He supposed he would stop believing then, if it mattered, but he did not believe in the president anyway. President Bush talked like he wasn't sure of himself, and every time he smiled he looked a little confused. The last president had also looked a little confused, but he never sounded like it.

He felt a difference between the two ways his grandmother used the word 'believe,' too, but he was not sure whether she felt the difference or not and he was afraid to point it out. Grandma Bayleigh did a lot of things and taught a lot of things, but she did not tolerate sass, and Clay knew that his own father's approach to the subject had been honed and refined in the laboratory of his grandmother's childrearing.

Instead of answering, he thought about where he was, and he wondered if it was enough reason to start supposing that God was something more than the story in his head that resisted the pressure to change when others tried to retell it.

❖   ❖   ❖

Thunder Under Ground

Clay tried to pull away, but her hands stayed with him no matter what he did. They felt like cobwebs, not fingertips, because they did not pull him with force. Instead, they caused him to freeze and panic with their drag and their persistence. If he twisted, then they restricted, and the reaction was so instantaneous that he wondered if the hands knew his muscles were going to move before he even made the decision. His mother's hands were his entire world now. He was aware that she was arguing with Bayleigh in the distance, but as long as he could not free himself from them, they were keeping him from being able to hear what was being said.

A moment later there were other hands. They were rougher, and they pulled more insistently, but when they broke Clay free from his mother's cobweb fingers, they also released him and allowed him to hurtle out of the orbit of the two women, before crashing himself into the couch hard enough to prompt Grandpa Clif to shout "Hey, that's new!"

It would wind up being the only thing Clif said during the exchange.

"You knew I did not want this, and you went behind my back just to prove a point," Clay's mother had daggers in her voice, but luckily Bayleigh was capable of wielding a shield with hers.

"Your father called me and asked me to do him a favor. If you want to accuse someone of disobeying your wishes, you should call him."

Kitty tried to step past Bayleigh at that point, and Clay was sure it was so that she could lay those dusty fingertraps on him again. His grandmother managed to stay in her way.

"I suppose you just happened to have found a way to get rid of A.J. for the day, too. Like that wasn't something you planned for, even after you promised to take care of him."

"I let your sister take him out. They'd planned it for several days in advance, and she promised to talk to either you or Mark about it. I'm sorry if she didn't, but you really don't have any reason to come in here like this, and I don't want you to come further into my living room until you decide that you are going to stop accusing me of things."

"You can't tell me what to do. That is my child, and I'm here for him."

"He's also my grandchild," Bayleigh said, "and I don't want you to take him while you're still out of sorts. What are you doing, anyway? Why are you out of bed, when you know you're supposed to stay there until the delivery?"

"Don't you make this about me," Kitty was no longer throwing knives. She rushed forward with a heavy sword instead. "Don't you dare change things without telling me and then leave me wondering where he is and make me out to be the crazy one. I was worried."

Clay could not listen to his mother any more. "How did you know to be worried? You aren't due to see me again for three more days."

"Don't sass your mother," Bayleigh fired the thought off almost without registering what Clay said, but she glared at Kitty after.

"Well, this is a joy..." Kitty let the words trail.

Clay threw himself into the couch over and over, trying not to let the scream out of his stomach and into his head. He could feel Grandpa Clif's eyes on him, but thankfully he said nothing in reprimand.

"Just take him," Bayleigh said. "Take him home, or take him back to your father's. Should I call to tell Harry that Clay won't be going back there tonight?"

"No thank you," Kitty replied. "It's been taken care of."

◆ ◆ ◆

In the car on the way home, Clay felt dizzy, but when he tried to look at his mother instead of looking out the window, he felt even dizzier.

All of his school clothes were at Grandpa Harry's. He wanted to tell his mother this, and to insist that she go get them, but the way she held on to the steering wheel and the pull he felt drawing him toward the edge of the car as they rounded every corner made him incapable of raising the issue. When he tried to imagine saying anything, his body attempted to scream out his terror.

"You know you're not innocent in this," Kitty said. "I know what you're up to, and I know that you planned it all out with your father. What part of this did he want you to do? Were you supposed to turn my dad against me so that I wouldn't be credible anymore? Was that it?"

Clay dug his fingernails into his arm, but his terror kept rising. The scream forced its way into his throat. He bit his tongue and ground his teeth.

"I know you're keeping something from me, so what is it?"

His mind went to the rosary, to his prayers that his mother would go away. Suddenly, he was terrified that she had.

"I just saw you think about it. Spit it out."

He did, then.

When he had to stop screaming to breathe, his mother's hand found its way over his mouth and nose, and he pulled away, trying to find air. The car jogged, and Clay realized how much his mother needed to win, so he sat still and willed himself to forget that he needed to breathe.

"I know just what to do about this kind of defiance," she said. "There's really just one thing, but it will teach you how to be honest and respectful."

She put both hands on the wheel then, and Clay sucked in his breath.

"Oh, quit overdramatizing everything," his mother said. "You'd think we hit and abused you."

◆   ◆   ◆

Clay felt heaviness in his knees that had no relationship to the amount of time he had spent kneeling. In all honesty, he knew that his mother tried to make that part comfortable, recognizing as she did the length of time it took to say a rosary and insisting that they move into the carpeted living room and lay down pillows beforehand.

"There's no reason that adoration needs to break us," she said.

Clay concentrated on not groaning. Rounding his third decade, he was still concentrating on it. He tried to go through the prayers silently, the way he had taught himself to do, but his mother was demanding he speak them so she could hear.

"You know God can hear everything, but if your voice joins with mine, he will really know that you're trying to make sure your father respects me and you really want God to help us."

It was hard to speak prayers at the best of times, since Clay felt like he was unable to find a way to really believe them, and they seemed like things you should not speak without believing. Now, it was onerous, and when his voice showed signs of the strain, he was accused of disrespecting God in a way that impressed upon him the fact that this was much, much worse than either swearing or manipulating his mother by following directions from other people.

Still, she dragged the rosary out of him, bead by bead. The only way out was through, and she made sure not to let him go any way but hers. She even took time after every *Glory Be* to re-dedicate the string to helping her husband find his way back to honesty and respect.

Clay found that the best way to keep himself talking was to make sure that it hurt him more than the scream would. The scream could not take control from him then, because his brain stayed focused on the hurt.

He wanted to tear at his skin with his fingertips or jump up and down in the LEGO bin to help with this, but his fingers had to be glued to the rosary, and his mother was making him use her perfectly smooth cocoa bead chain, so there was no roughness to distract him.

That led him to do the only thing he could. He chewed on his cheeks. At first, it was just a little, to keep himself aware and in control. Soon, though, he started playing games, sucking them in so that he could work away pieces of flesh and imagining that it made him look hollow and duck-mouthed like the women on TV who did it. Clay wondered what they did about the taste of the blood afterwards, but he supposed there were just some things you had to do to be on television.

The chewing and the blood did the trick for at least twenty-five beads before Clay started slurring because his mouth was so full. His mother reprimanded him then, but his "Sorry" caused blood to trickle down his chin and onto the carpet. When Kitty Dillon noticed what was happening, she shouted at him, pulling him to his feet and then into the kitchen, where she held his jaw open with one hand and a flashlight that appeared to come from thin air with the other.

"What are you doing?" she asked him. "What did I do to deserve this?"

❖   ❖   ❖

Accepting What Descartes Rejected

So, with his grandparents on both sides having undermined his mother's intentions, Clay Dillon moved home. It happened at once, and Clay did not dare to argue with the decisions, because he did not have Grandma Bayleigh's couch to throw himself against any more, and even if he did, his father was not like Grandpa Clif. He would not say something once and then let things be. Home meant being aware, at all times, of everything he did. Or else.

That night was tense, even after he was done with the rosary and his mouth was cleaned back up. He spent part of it wondering what would happen to all the toys and clothes he had left at Grandpa Harry's. He also wondered how long it would be before he had the opportunity to see his grandparents again. His only other experience with his mother's repudiation of a place had been when she declared that she would not wait in line for more than twenty minutes at the grocery store and then left, depositing her two carloads of food in the line and walking out the door. That was before they moved into their house, when A.J. was still in the kind of baby car seat that could be carried with you when you went into places. They had never returned to that particular grocery store after Kitty's walkout, either.

Later that night, Clay heard his father and mother arguing about keeping him at home. His father rightly pointed out that it was strange to be so adamant that Clay be kept from his grandparents while also forcing A.J. out of the house. He worried out loud that Baby Sis would be affected by the strain of Kitty's taking care of Clay, too, which was odd because it had nothing to do with the first topic. His mother, in response, told his father that Clay was too often underestimated. She said the chance to learn how to work would balance out his "book knowledge" until he managed to "get to a place where his development would be normal." She also blamed his father for having caused this, pointing to his habit of reading to Clay from books she considered to be for adult eyes only. Her complaint totally ignored the fact that *The Hobbit* was also a cartoon movie and that it was the only book aimed at adults that Mark had ever read to Clay. She used the opportunity to push more books by the overbearing but faceless old man who had written *The Screwtape Letters*, too, insisting that those books about witches and sorcerers were what children were "supposed to read."

That night Clay dreamed of Grandpa Harry's house, where no one questioned his reading choices and there were enough encyclopedias that he never ran the risk of needing to go to the library. The next day, he went to school normally, and his mother even found the energy to put a bagged lunch in the fridge for him. He almost missed the bus because he was busy re-packing it into his lunchbox, which was freshly washed and sitting in the drain pan by the sink. At the last minute, though, he managed to get the latch closed over the half a family sized bag of potato chips and thermos full of diet Mountain Dew that his mother had left with a lumpy peanut butter sandwich. It all happened so quickly that Clay did not even register thanks for her giving him the good snacks from his father's lunch and sparing him the regular rice pudding and apples.

School the next day was fairly uneventful, aside from Clay's receiving an unusual amount of attention from kids who noticed, for the first time, how much they liked him. Things went back to normal after half of Mrs. Hudson's class helped him polish off the half bag of chips, though. Sully was the first to stop being polite. Most of the others followed him quickly, which left Noah standing and watching

them walk away as Clay and Patrick started to discuss Van's plans for
the lunch recess.

When he got home, his mother sat him down for a talk. It was
right after Grandpa Harry dropped off Clay's things, and it was about
the fact that Kitty was not supposed to be getting up and doing
housework. She made him promise to help and to remember that
even if something was not his chore, it still needed to be done. and he
was the only one to do it. Then she showed him this new way of
doing things by sitting in a chair that she dragged into the kitchen
from the dining room and giving him step-by-step directions while he
did the dishes.

Clay already knew how to do dishes. It was, in fact, a chore that
he was expected to do once per day, and the only reason he usually
did not accomplish that feat was because no one ever told him when
"once" was supposed to be. As a result, he was constantly
remembering the chore, only to find the sink empty except for a loose
butter knife and a coffee cup or two. He was also constantly getting
in trouble for the fact that his mother usually did all the dishes after
dinner even though she had cooked. This made the whole process of
managing his choices very confusing, but it was not the kind of
confusion that required him to listen to step-by-step directions, so he
wondered why his mother thought the solution for his forgetfulness
was to demand that he only did what she said, when she said to do it.

He thought about throwing the plates at her, but he did not
want to risk hurting Baby Sis again. It took until the next morning
for Clay to realize how much things were going to change for him.
He was shaken awake while it was still dark out, and by the time he
asked what was happening, his father's voice and shadow were
retreating from him. Just as he slipped through the light in the
doorway, Mark said, "Time to go to school. Get up."

When Clay finished washing his face and made it downstairs, he
was still in his underwear and he had barked his shins against the
furniture a few times. No lights were on. He heard his father moving
as if it didn't matter.

"Why aren't you dressed?"

He looked at the digital clock on the microwave, the only source of light on the entire main floor.

"It's four-thirty," he said. "I don't go to school yet."

"No, but I go to work yet," his father shot back. "Come on."

"I get to go to work with you?" Clay asked.

"Don't be a smartass," his father replied. "You have school. I'm just taking you to Patrick's so your mother can sleep. She doesn't need to be getting up at six to make you food."

Clay shrugged and went back upstairs to get his clothes on. Twenty minutes later, he stood in the entryway at Patrick's house, trying not to stare into Patrick's mother's cleavage as she bent over him in her nightgown and told him that she was happy he could come over to visit. Then he was told to have a nap on the couch, which he pretended to do until he heard the sound of meat in a frying pan.

Patrick's mother stood in the kitchen making eggs and sausage. He could see her from the couch when he tilted his head up a bit.

"Wow," Clay said. "You have time to make hot food in the morning? My grandma does that, but my mom says only grandmas know how."

"I wouldn't be able to do it except my husband is about to come home," Patrick's mother said. "So he will do the dishes and make lunch for the boys after I go to work. He works at night and sleeps while they are in school."

Clay nodded. His father had talked about the men that worked all night in the tool & die industry. Some of his stories made him nervous about Patrick's father, even though the man had always been nice and gentle.

"What does he do?" Clay asked.

"He's a shipping clerk in a warehouse," she replied. "At night, he takes all the orders that people put together for stores and he loads them into a truck so that they can get delivered and people can buy them."

"What kinds of things?"

"All kinds. He works in a place that provides cold storage for a lot of companies, and they distribute all sorts of frozen foods around this side of the state."

Clay nodded again. He understood now. Patrick's father might be strange enough to work at night, but he was not the same kind of strange that worked at night in his father's own industry. Satisfied, he watched as Patrick's mother cooked the entire meal without saying anything. When it was all ready, she gave him plates and asked him to set the table while she went upstairs to wake her sons. She did not give him directions, though. That made Clay happy at first. As he tried to set the table, though, he kept wondering if Patrick's family set the table the same way his own did, and what to do if they did not. He worried about making them angry by not knowing how to do it their way.

He was still staring at the stack of plates when everyone came into the room. No one said anything, though. They each just took their own and sat down while Clay stood there, staring at the ever-shrinking pile in front of him. That was when Patrick's father came in. He touched the top of Clay's head, but then stopped himself and withdrew.

"Sorry, I didn't see which one you were," he said.

Clay said nothing. Patrick's father took a plate and sat down. Then his mother asked Clay to sit, so he did.

"Someone's not quite awake yet," she quipped.

Clay ate the eggs and sausage he was given, as well as a piece of toast. He wanted a little more, but not because they had guessed wrong about how much he needed, just because he liked hot breakfast and did not get it often. Even though there was plenty on the table, though, he found himself unable to ask for it.

"Did you need something?" Patrick's mother asked.

Instead of asking for food, Clay asked this: "Did you like *The Joy Luck Club*? Was the ending good? I only got to read a couple chapters."

Patrick's mother nodded. "It was very good, but I'm surprised you liked it."

"Why? I play chess. And I'm about Waverly's age. Why wouldn't I like a novel about kids my own age?"

As he asked his questions, Clay began to feel something loathsome toward Patrick's mother. He did not know what to do with it. The thing in him that felt her assumptions about what he would want to read was as painful as a razor, but it was slick and sticky too, and he could not stop himself from feeling covered with it even though he tried not to touch it. When he asked Van for the metal body, it came, but the gooey feeling from Patrick's mother stayed with him inside of it.

"It's not really about the children, that's all," she said. "I can see why you'd really like those chapters, but if you had read the whole book, you'd see that a lot of it is about women. Mothers and daughters, especially adult daughters. I was just surprised because of that."

The thing became harder to separate himself from, and it hurt more.

"Why?" he could hear the tears in his own voice. "Why surprise?"

Patrick's mother shrugged. "My boys are both advanced readers, but they like adventures. And Patrick says you like adventures. So, I was just surprised that you would be into a book that is small and quiet, and that focuses on family relationships."

Clay threw his fork down on the table. It made a terrifically metal sound as it collided with the ceramic plate.

"Family relationships are adventures," he spat. "Excuse me. I need to poop."

Then he excused himself from the table. The last thing that registered in his mind was his friend Patrick standing up with him, followed by Patrick's mother holding her son in place so that he could not chase after Clay.

❖   ❖   ❖

Flashes of Insight

Catechism class was not going well for Clay, but he no longer really expected that it would. In fact, he no longer really expected that anything would go better than his average weekly religious instruction class. Since it had been, for some time, the single worst hour of his school week, it meant something that his new state of being was so universally low that being in that place was no longer better or worse than anything else. In the weeks since his mother started keeping him home, she had put him to work cleaning, washing dishes, folding laundry, and simply carrying things because she said she was not allowed to lift that much weight. Clay would not have minded so much if it was just the work, but every time she asked for his help (and that was the turn of phrase she insisted on), she also found it necessary to totally re-train him and to monitor each individual step taken, just like she had done with the dishes, lest he think originally or depart from the order of her commands in the slightest.

These demands were the most tiring aspect of the entire experience, and Clay could not understand the point of asking him to do something and then spending more effort monitoring him than it would have taken for his mother to do the thing herself. He understood that for some of the chores, his mother might really be unable to do them and that for others, he really was unsure how to proceed. The majority of the time, though, her presence seemed almost purposeful in its tendency to break his concentration and cause the very deviations she punished him for. When he slowed down and explained it to himself, suddenly it made sense that he should not feel any differently when he was home with his mother than he did now, in the small church classroom with Sully and his gang.

That day, they were inflicting as much damage as they could before the teacher arrived and brought the room to order, changing

Clay's trials to tedium and breaking up any predations that began during their wait. That day, the problem was that Sully decided to interpret Clay's lack of engagement with the other boys and his lack of enthusiasm for their discussion about the Raiders as looking down on them and wanting them to know it. To prove to Clay that he was not actually better than them, they kept kicking him under the table and dropping elbows into his sides and back as they moved past him.

It was less overtly cruel than some of Sully's past taunts, but at the same time, it was constant. The worst part was, Clay could not even tell if Noah was participating or not. When he looked to the other boy, his face was drawn and apologetic. Still, whenever they had to pass close to each other, unwanted prodding and kicking made him wonder if Noah was keenly trying to fit into both social worlds or if Sully was attempting to make Clay accuse Noah of something he was not doing, to escalate things further.

Clay exhaled hard when the teacher came in and started the day. He was sure that, as usual, Sully's torments would cease before they ran the risk of getting the teacher's attention. Unfortunately, the constant kicking of his shins under the table revealed that not to be the case. When he shouted in surprise at the first one, the teacher hissed at him. The second one earned a grunt, and then the teacher glared at him until his vocal chords shrank and dried up, deploying his metal body. He did not get the razors in his throat, though, and when Van realized that there was no way to defend Clay, he let their body soften again.

The kicks kept coming.

He put his head down on the table and waited to be yelled at for sleeping. Tears streamed from his eyes, and the kicks slowed down, but became stronger as they sought to surprise him during lulls in the teacher's patter. As Clay waited for each new assault, he tried to anticipate where it would come from. In his mind, the brightly colored arches that made thoughts rearranged themselves, giving him flares of light from directions that seemed intensely located, yet indistinct. He moved his feet according to the lights, and then he heard someone grunt as they kicked a table leg.

The teacher shushed whoever it was. Clay giggled. The teacher shushed him too.

The next time, he was kicked in both knees at once. The simultaneity of the flashing arches confused him, and he could not tell what he should have his body do, so they both connected. After they did, he realized that the flashing lights were the sounds of other children at the table moving their hips, but he still did not know how to move enough to avoid two at once without getting in trouble for getting out of his seat, and he still could not will himself to speak.

The flashes began to appear less reliably after that, and in many cases, they coincided with the kick so that Clay had no time to move, just a split second of panic before having to actually feel the pain. He worked to keep himself silent, both because he did not want to give his tormentors the satisfaction of a response and also because he knew the teacher would only blame him, the source of the noise, without actually investigating the problem at hand.

To keep himself silent, he sucked his cheeks like he had when he was with his mother, and he teased the site of the wounds from the last time he chewed. Then he bit down. Hard. Repeatedly. Consistently. It did not take long for him to taste blood, and when he did, he began chewing. The taste did not bother him, not until his mouth was full and the consistency of his saliva changed.

Why was blood, even wet blood, so infuriatingly dry? He could feel his cheeks and tongue puckering even as he swallowed to make more room in his mouth.

"Ewwwww..."

The sound penetrated his concentration, forcing him to realize that he had not been taking in sounds. He did not know how long had been like that, and he wondered briefly how long that had been going on. Before he could get lost in that thought, though, another sound made him go all the way back to the classroom.

"He's drooling. It's bloody." It was Sully. "Gross. What an animal."

The teacher stared. Her eyes kept widening. Clay tried to smile for her, to show that he was all right, but that just made him drool more blood.

"Go clean up in the bathroom," the teacher said. "And then go to the office. I will phone down to let them know why you're coming."

Clay nodded.

"Are you okay? Do you need me to look in your mouth?"

Clay shook his head. The teacher stepped toward him, and he realized that she did not know which answer he was giving, so he ran.

The bathroom was a single-person unisex installation at the end of the hall, so he was able to lock himself inside while he washed his mouth. Once he was rinsed and he stopped chewing, there was actually very little blood coming through. Instead, the cool air from breathing dried the open wounds, igniting them with a new kind of pain that made Clay's knees weaken and forced his body between himself and his thoughts. He tried to make words, but when his lips moved, his cheeks pulled. Then his brain, stomach, and feet all felt like they were being drilled into from many different directions at once. Only grabbing the sink kept him from falling over when the onslaught began.

It was better not to talk.

Once he was sure that the blood had stopped coming, he drank enough from the tap to rehydrate his mouth, and then he went to the church office. The secretary told him that they had already reached his house, and not to worry because his father would be coming to get him.

Clay froze. He wanted to start chewing on his cheek again, because he still remembered the last time his father had been forced to leave work and come to his school. Then, the fact that Mr. Weir had made him lose consciousness meant that it was the school counselor who got in trouble. He also remembered that his parents left him alone to feel bad while they fought about making him go to Catholic school. He did not want to go to Catholic school, and he did not know if his father would still defend him now, since this time it was probably his own fault he was being sent home.

"Are you okay?" The receptionist's question seemed very stupid to Clay, but he nodded. It was best to always answer adults when you did not want them to keep talking to you.

❖   ❖   ❖

To Give of Oneself

Mark was not so hard on Clay after he saw the inside of his mouth. Being forced to show his father was uncomfortable and awkward, but at least it was brief. He did not mind so much that his father wanted to look at the wounds, but having to stretch his mouth and expose the insides of his cheeks to the air strained the feeble healing already in progress, sending sickly trickles of blood down onto his tongue.

"Let's get you home and get you some ice chips. That will help keep the swelling and bleeding down while your body gets the healing started."

That was all Mark said as he leaned over and stared down into Clay's mouth, pulling lightly on his cheek to move it in the light. Then he released his son, who bolted to the drinking fountain and filled his mouth with cold water, sloshing it around until it stopped coming out pinkish and he spit clear.

The drive home was silent, and when they arrived at home, Mark made a short statement to Kitty about the bleeding in his mouth. She scowled, but she assured him that she would make sure Clay was well taken care of.

As he listened to their conversation, it seemed like he was eavesdropping through a long tunnel, the way he had when he overheard them through the air duct. The sensation was quite odd, happening as it did while he was in the room with them, but as they discussed their plans without asking him anything or acknowledging he was in the room, their conversation seemed to elongate and echo of its own accord.

"Okay?"

It took a moment for Clay to realize that his father was now speaking to him.

"You need to pay attention to things, Clay. If you don't, then you might accidentally walk into traffic or get hurt."

Clay nodded.

"I'm going back to work, but your mom and I agreed that today is not a day you need to do chores. She can't do chores, either, so you just leave everything until I get home. All right?"

He nodded again. His father's voice was coming into focus now.

"I will see you tonight. There is ice in the freezer. Eat some of it if your bleeding starts up or if the pain gets to you. Okay?"

Clay hugged his father. It was spontaneous, and it felt strange, but the news that he was not going to be asked to work overwhelmed his decision-making process and pushed his body to act on its own.

Mark Dillon peeled his son off his leg and walked out through the main floor of his house. He was worried, and it showed in the way he stepped through the space.

As Clay watched his father go, he reached out for Van and found nothing inside himself except meat. That made his father's worry etch itself into his brain, increasing his heart rate the way it did when the metal body was about to come forth. No metal body did, though, so his heart just kept beating faster.

"Come on," his mother said. "We have to go upstairs."

Clay shook his head. He tried to talk, but all he wound up saying was, "Rest. Ice."

His mother shrugged. Then she took him by the hand into the kitchen and made him a glass of ice water.

"Swish," she said. "Then chew on the ice. It will cool your mouth faster."

Clay did as he was told. His mother was right. The ice water did cool his whole mouth quickly. He let himself be led out of the kitchen and up the stairs as he chewed the ice.

The deadening cold in his mouth tightened everything without making it feel like it was going to crack, and it stopped the ongoing sting at the site of the actual wound. Forcing it against his flesh brought a new kind of acute pain, though, a cold that burned the way that snow did when he played with it barehanded. He had to space out his exposure, so he bounced the ice cube back and forth from cheek to cheek, letting the regular pain of the bite slowly push itself through the cold on one side while pushing himself to endure the perverse burning from the ice on the other.

He did not even notice he was still in his parents' bedroom until his mother climbed up on the bed and sat up, patting the mattress next to herself.

"Not sleepy." It was possible to talk a little around the ice as it melted, if he timed it to come immediately after he switched sides.

"That's okay," his mother replied. "Just climb up here and have a seat. I want to talk to you."

Clay climbed up on the bed. It was challenging to do it without spilling his ice water. After he settled into a seat, he said, "Talking hurts," through the ice.

"I know," his mother replied. "I can tell. Keep eating the ice, it will make things better."

Clay nodded and chomped on more chips.

"Did you know that there are places where people go to give themselves pain, so that they can offer it up to God?" Kitty asked her son.

Clay shook his head.

"It's true. There are islands where people crucify themselves every Easter, so that they understand what Jesus went through. Those people have only been Christian for a little while, because they did not know about God until the Europeans brought them priests, but when they decided to believe, God rewarded them by giving them these abilities and being willing to take their pain. I read about Mother Teresa's work in India, too," his mother continued. "She helps to poor there to offer their suffering over to God, and he saves them. Do you know why I'm telling you this?"

Clay shook his head. He was sure he was lying to his mother, but he did so anyway, because he knew that if he said "yes," then she would want him to explain, and his mouth hurt too much. Instead, he did what he could do to harden himself against her words. Without the metal body, it was difficult.

"I'm going to teach you how to do this," she said. "It's important, so that you know how God can help you when times are tough. The first thing we have to do is kneel. Kneel with me."

Kitty Dillon got up on her knees with her back straight, like she insisted on doing in church. Clay followed her. He did not want to, but this kind of prayer was something he was made to do every week, so he did not feel as if he could resist it without having to explain that he had never felt comfortable, and that seemed impossible even when his cheek was not bleeding.

Once they were kneeling, Kitty leaned over to the bedpost at the head of the bed on the side where she slept. She took the cocoa bead rosary that was draped there into her hands, holding it carefully, so that the crucifix dangled without dipping or spinning. She held it out to Clay.

"This was given to me by my priest when I was confirmed. He was a family friend from when I was little, and he came to my church just to do my confirmation ceremony with our regular priest. He got it while he was a missionary. It was made by the people he was sent to help. You need to take it. It's time to pray with a real rosary and not one of the ones they give out at church school parties."

Clay took the rosary. Something about his mother's story made it feel uneasy in his hands, as if he was being asked to use a tool that he knew was wrong for the job. He wanted the real rosary, the one that had the jagged plastic edges, not one that had been made by some child who probably didn't know very much about it, who did it just because someone told them it would make a priest happy. He didn't particularly like the idea of sending priests out to make people talk about God, either, because it seemed like the people who wanted to do that could go to the priests, and he really didn't want to think about the kinds of things that had to be said to one of those poor kids before he would put the time in to make such a finely worked and well-finished piece of jewelry "for God."

Of course, he thought, *the priest might also have just bought a nice rosary and told my mom a story to make her happy*. People did that. He knew, because his father and uncles had done it to him, and so had his mother's friends, back when Kitty still talked to friends.

"Are you okay?" Kitty's voice cut through her son's memories.

Clay nodded.

"You know what to do. Let's say each prayer together."

"Mouth hurts," Clay replied.

"I know," Kitty said. "We'll have you eat the ice to keep bleeding down and help with the pain, but you need to do this. It will help."

Clay shook his head.

"Say a *Hail Mary* with me to start," she said. "And offer your suffering up to God."

He shook his head again.

"Do you want to go to Hell? Or do you want to learn to have a relationship with God?"

Clay wanted to scream that they seemed a lot like the same thing just then, but his scream was gone. He was not only voiceless, but when he tried to reach into his stomach and provoke it forth, it would not come. He was just empty instead. He tried to summon Van, but he was also gone, to wherever the metal body was at. Clay was alone.

"Hail Mary," Kitty Dillon said. "Repeat it."

"Hail Mary," Clay said. He tasted iron.

"Full of grace," his mother said.

"No, it hurts," Clay said.

"Offer it up!" Kitty shouted. "Now we have to start over."

They did. In fact, they had to start over twice, because during the third decade, Clay started crying in the middle of the *Glory Be* and his mother decided that God would reject that rosary. By the time they got to the fourth decade on their final pass, they were out of ice. When Clay's bleeding could no longer be controlled with a single rag and his snotty tears mixing into the blood running down his chin made Kitty Dillon start to worry about infection, she decided that they had prayed enough and cleaned him up.

In the bathroom, as she ran the washcloth over his face, she asked him if he understood what it meant to offer his pain up to God.

Clay spat blood into the sink and then swished a mouthful of water before swallowing it. He opened his mouth, allowing his mother to see inside. Then, he closed it again, found his open wound, and used his tongue and upper jaw to tear loose a jagged piece of flesh that would not stop flapping loosely inside his mouth.

He spat it on the floor, directly between his mother's feet. He did not answer her. After a moment, she continued washing his face.

❖   ❖   ❖

Secrets of a Silent Earth

Clay stuck his tongue into the ice cream and wiggled it around, trying to numb its surface. Ever since biting through part of his cheek, he felt like his tongue was dried out and covered with some kind of rusty cake. He just could not get all the dried blood out, and it also made him feel queasy because he was constantly tasting blood, and the flavor of it was old. It made his entire throat and sinus cavity smell like a scab.

Ice cream helped. He tongued a piece of it off the cone and brought it into his mouth, tucking it between his gum and his cheek so that it could soothe the wound.

"Good, yeah?" His father held his own cone out.

Clay smiled even though it hurt the inside of his mouth. Then he took a bite, feeling the shock through his front teeth and holding it until his knees jerked him to the side and his body forcibly swallowed, taking the melting block of ice cream into his gut where it could sink through him like a melting blade.

"If you eat it too fast, you'll just feel bad and you won't taste anything," Mark said. "Slow down. It'll be good."

He smiled at his father again. He wanted to thank him, but talking was just too painful. After the rosary session the day before, his speech had fled him, and things were actually easier without it. Neither his father nor his mother talked to him in ways that demanded he agree with things that he despised. Instead, they just told him stuff and left it at that.

He toyed idly with ways to chew out his tongue so that they would not be able to go back to the way they talked before. All of those ways made his stomach hurt, and the physical reaction his muscles made when his mind showed him the blood that would come... No. He was done drinking blood. It was not good for him, and it made other things hurt.

Clay watched his father work on his own cone for a moment, and then he did his best to imitate the way the older man was eating. He figured doing that would please him, since it mattered so much how ice cream was eaten. The two sat together and ate for several minutes without any other communication, but when they were about halfway done eating, Mark Dillon broke his silence to speak to his son again.

"You're really doing everything you can to hold yourself up right now, and I appreciate it. Your mom is having trouble, you know, and it's affecting things."

Clay nodded.

"Not just her ability to do chores and go out," his father continued. "Her decision-making abilities are also getting to where they need a rest. You know what I mean? Like, she has had to do so much, and we were really young when you were born, and now she has trouble focusing. So if she is going to be able to think clearly about what is best for Baby Sis, then she needs to be able to stop making decisions about other things, right?"

Clay nodded again, but he was lying. He did not think his mother's decision-making skills had changed at all, and to him it meant that she had just started to treat his father the same way she had treated him. He wanted to be able to say so, but he was glad not to be able to do it.

"Anyway, I appreciate you doing what you can. And I want you to know that we had a talk about the rosary thing. I don't think it's right for her to make anyone pray, and she won't be doing that again. If you pray as a punishment or you pray because she makes you, then you won't know what it's there for when you actually need it."

This time, Clay did not nod along with his father. Instead, he sat completely still, frozen by the realization that his father thought there was a good reason for prayer. Clay had no idea what it could be, but the fact that the man could look so deeply into what his mother was doing and decide that the problem was just that she was doing it wrong, that hollowed out his core. It made him into an empty expanse, as quiet as the plains around his castle without the scream, and as dark as its unlit corridors now that Van was not to be found.

He sunk his teeth into the ice cream and left them there until he heard himself crying.

"What was that about?" his father asked.

"Seeing if I could." They were Clay's first words since the afternoon before.

"Well, you did," his father replied. "You don't need to keep crying. You won."

Clay wiped the tears from his cheeks and nodded, wishing that his father had not noticed the tears. He turned away from him and repeated the action, driving his front teeth down into the ice cream until it squished against his gums. This time, he did not stop the pain when he felt the tears begin. He waited until he felt them end instead.

When he was done, his father spoke.

"All the changes to the family can be a little overwhelming, but it will be nice to have a little sister. I think you'll get along well with a girl. And A.J. will have to learn to be responsible for someone."

Clay shuddered.

"You ate that ice cream so fast you gave yourself a chill," his father said.

He stuck his teeth into the ice cream again. This time, he left them in place until he heard the scream return, and then he relaxed into it, letting it howl away until his tears were summoned. When his father took his messy, drippy cone away and lectured him for acting like a baby, Clay did not even hear him. He was safely ensconced in the steel shell of his metal body, and nothing could make him come out until the warmth of the sun made it melt away and left him wriggling and exposed where others could reach him.

❖   ❖   ❖

Still in Saigon

After they finished their ice cream, Mark Dillon drove his son home. Since the boy was not feeling talkative, he did what he usually did to give the both of them something to do. He decided to teach his son about music by putting a tape in the car's deck.

"This is the Charlie Daniels band. They did a lot to make country rock really move, and to make sure the instrumentals pushed the envelope like hard rock bands did. This first song, it's a good one, but the later stuff gets deeper."

The singer was crooning about the devil going to Georgia. Clay liked the beat, but he was not yet sure about what his father's motive for picking this music was.

"The really good songs, like "Still in Saigon," they tell you something about the time when they were made. You can listen to them to learn about what people were worried by and what the range of views about it were. Music gives you that, like books do. And that song gets me, because it's kind of about that. About being stuck in a place, you know, where even when things are okay they're never going to be."

Mark looked over at his son. Clay stared at him, making eye contact almost immediately, and their locked gaze felt unbreakable.

The child refused to relinquish him back to driving even as he tried frantically to watch the road in his peripheral vision.

Eventually, Clay broke the stare. Mark looked back at the road. They were, thankfully, still in their lane and not going very fast. He was sure his son knew exactly what he had been talking about, which felt wrong because he himself did not know that he had exactly said what he had meant about the topic. That gaze, though... Clay had that gaze that said that whatever his father had described, it had been real. Somehow, he had experienced it already.

Mark ejected the tape and slid in another one.

"Let's try this instead," Mark said. "This is Billy Joel's album *The Stranger*. I think you'll like it."

As the first chorus of the title track hit, he saw his son's lips twitch.

◆   ◆   ◆

Somehow, his father had restored Clay's metal body back to full function, so now he could feel Van with him. Even the scream's battering, impulsive threat was there, and it felt right. Maybe it was because Van could only exist with an ultimate evil to fight, so needing Van was the same thing as needing to scream. Maybe it was because destruction was a natural part of life, and it was natural to sometimes be the destroyer. Either way, Clay was even thankful to have the scream. It was familiar, and in his metal body he was secure. He knew that he could protect himself without losing control and having someone call his parents, so the scream was nothing but a fixture on the landscape. He could turn things over to Van and sit in the castle, secure in the knowledge that the metal would obey orders and soldier on.

Until he lost it briefly, he had not even realized how central it was to his daily way of being in the world. He knew now, though. He would protect it more carefully, going forward.

Thoughts about music and the metal body held onto him throughout the rest of the ride and continued to occupy his attention as he worked his way through the house. He moved quietly, to make sure that whatever his mother was doing was not disturbed by his passage. All he wanted was to remain safe within his regular space, and he felt the best way to do that was to leave the smallest impression possible. Even attention would intrude on him, so he worked to fold his mother's attention around him, letting it would slip away into the background to latch on to a tree outside or a passing tune on the radio.

That goal was shattered when he stepped into his room and felt the first few LEGO pieces dig into the soft meat in the arch of his foot. Before he knew what was happening, he grunted and kicked. That was when A.J. yelped. Clay still did not really see him, but he felt the child's motion.

"Bang! Crash! Got it. Getting it for you."

As Clay looked at the scene underfoot, it slowly registered that A.J. was tearing apart everything he had built. Buildings were being dropped from head-height, then stomped apart as his brother panted half-sentences that were clearly the best he could do while in such a wild state. As he realized exactly what had happened, his legs started to burn.

The plastic embedded in the bottoms of his feet fueled his metal transformation, and he reached down, taking up the first block of LEGO bricks that he felt. He took it in both hands, and he did not think about what that meant. Not until the castle, free of a baseplate and half its interior structure, broke into three pieces in mid-air.

It hit A.J. with enough force to stagger him, battering his cheeks and forehead. Clay caught his breath as he realized what would have happened if the structure what been whole and complete when it hit. His brother took advantage of his moment of regret to start screaming, so there was only one thing to do and that was to stop the sound.

When Mark Dillon pulled Clay off A.J., his fingernails had already drawn blood from the younger child's neck and his cross-face control of his brother's head with his dominant hand had torn the child's cheek open against the loose plastic bricks on the floor. Blood trickled out of a jagged line in the middle of A.J.'s cheek at about the same place where his older brother had chewed himself open.

An hour later, Grandpa Harry came and took A.J. away. Nothing was said to either boy. In fact, nothing was said to Clay for the rest of the night, by anyone. He came down the stairs to the main level of the house only once, when he heard the oven timer go off, and then his father slid a plate of food across the counter toward him before stalking out of the room.

Later, when he got tired, Clay put himself to bed.

❖ ❖ ❖

The Wall

In the dark, Clay felt his mind reaching out for something other than Van and his imaginings. He felt around inside himself, groping his way through his skull to find anything left out and lying about. It was difficult with no eyes to help steer him toward objects. His sense of himself was reduced to just feeling, roaming free and loose and disembodied. He did not know how long he had been in bed, eiher. He only knew sleep was not coming for him. Loneliness was there instead.

Even though Clay mostly wanted to sit with people in silence, he liked being there with them. Knowing that his father did not want to even look at him was painful. So was not knowing what would happen in the morning. The last time he hurt a member of the family, he got to go live with Grandpa Harry for a while. Part of Clay hoped the same thing was about to happen over again, but part of him suspected that if it did, it would come with an accusation that he was attempting to use violence to get his way.

Am I? He wondered.

Van said nothing back.

Van was something he had made up. He could not rely on the cyborg. Clay understood this, but he also understood that Van was real and that the cyborg gave him a way to take breaks when he was overwhelmed. He did not know which he understood more.

I'm not going away.

Suddenly, Clay was arguing with Van in a way that was very intense but that lacked words, and then he felt the empty hole again, the one he had fallen into when Van was unreachable. He allowed the fictional part of himself to win out. The cyborg was right. Even if he was made up, he was necessary, and banishing him would be a loss that the rest of himself was not prepared to face.

◆ ◆ ◆

Drifting through the darkness inside his eyelids and wondering when sleep would come, Clay reflected on everything he had learned about the afterlife. He could not imagine how having no body and all his memories could be a good thing. After all, when it happened in real life, it meant sleepless nights spent in worry. Who wanted to spend eternity locked inside himself, contemplating things he had already done and seen? Even the good memories would eventually turn pale and boring, and the bad ones were already enough of a problem. He did not need them to become the only thing in the universe.

Part of Clay wanted to read the Bible more, because it would at least give him something to think about. Still, when he tried, he felt like the inconsistent moments and the breaks in the narrative, along with the sections that contradicted earlier sections, all came together to make it irredeemably flawed and impossible to reason with.

Eventually, he turned a light on and opened the book anyway, because he simply could not think of anything else to do to bring himself some sleep. When he checked his bookmark, it was only in John. Recent months had not given him much chance for progress. As he read, he was impressed by the way the story in John seemed more consistent and linear with itself, but he kept noticing changes from the other books. New stories he could understand, because no one writer knew all the stories of a life, but the changes to the other stories confused Clay and made him wonder why the four books were brought together when it was obvious that one should have been selected as the most accurate representation and the others rejected.

John seemed to revel more in the miracles than the other books, and Clay, knowing that there was no way the book was anything other than one person's idea filtered into his own mind, felt like it was the best one. Those miracles seemed to mark it as make-believe in a way that communicated the author was not intending for it to be viewed as anything else. The other books sometimes pretended to be history, and the pretense bothered him. John, on the other hand, seemed to be honest about the real work of God being in the listener and not the text. It made seeing how the story might be worth thinking about much easier, and it helped the reader see why it was worth reshaping and repeating and making into a part of his thinking. He still did not want to do it, but he appreciated the difference in this gospel after reading the others. He suspected that his mother would misinterpret his acceptance of the gospel as a belief in its history, though.

At one point, he had hoped for his continued obedience to eventually result in some kind of fitting acknowledgment. He imagined it would be something like his parents finally being willing to admit openly that the religious stories were just like television, only they were used to explain real life instead of explaining jokes. Instead, his mother's actual reaction to his Biblical study made him increasingly more suspicious that she thought the Flood and the Fall had specific dates like Gettysburg and the founding of the KKK did.

Clay sat with the fact of his mother's belief and the fact of her control over his life as he tried to read, and after a page or two his head jerked itself out, away from the wall before his whole body exploded in motion. He felt a collision that rattled his jaw and made yellow flashes in his eyes, and then came the headache. Moments later, he was asleep.

Seated on his bed, his back against the wall, with the lights on and his Bible open in his lap, he snored. The next morning, when

Clay woke with a stiff neck and a headache, his father lectured him about how reading for long periods in a book with such small print was going to make him need glasses.

He shrugged, but the pounding in his eyes made him wonder if maybe there was something to it after all. Even so, he felt like he must have needed to read the Bible, because whatever had been bothering him the night before was gone, and he could not even remember what it had been.

❖   ❖   ❖

Dawn of the Dead

Clay was grounded to his room all day Saturday, but that was fine. The dizziness that had greeted him on waking stayed with him, making reading almost impossible and sapping his motivation for anything requiring more strength and focus than scanning pages.

Every now and again, he paced the room for a while, straightening the odd item and organizing his dresser between other small chores. When he tried to tell himself to clean the whole room, though, he stopped and went back to bed, no matter how good an idea it seemed to be. There was simply no way into it; there never had been. The meticulous organization and construction of sprawling LEGO cityscapes popped into his mind, but he was unable to do anything about it because his LEGO had been taken away from him as part of his punishment. The relatively simplistic spatial organization of his own and his brother's possessions, however, remained irretrievably inaccessible in his mind, so he was unable to get into any real deep cleaning and sorting.

Losing his LEGOs had happened just after his father scolded him for falling asleep while reading and told him he would need glasses. Without waiting for him to wake up or get out of bed, Mark launched into a discussion.

"You know your brother was wrong. That's not being debated. You can't hit him, though."

"He hits. And he breaks things that aren't his. When was the last time he was left alone in a room all night and overnight for losing his temper?"

Mark Dillon nodded. "You have a good point. But you have to remember, your brother is only four years old. Some of the things you understand, he doesn't understand yet."

"He understands what is his and what is mine. He tells me every time I touch something he built with my LEGO sets that I have to leave them or he will break my stuff."

"And do you? Did you, this week, leave the things he built?"

Clay's head spun. Why were they talking about this?

"Why are we talking about this?"

"Well, you know. As the mature one, you've got to be the one to think about the consequences that might come from your actions."

"A.J. didn't even play with my LEGO stuff this week. Or if he did, it wasn't while I was home and he didn't leave anything put together."

"Are you sure about that?"

Clay nodded. "Besides, I didn't even take anything apart. Not for a long time. I just built some stuff onto other stuff."

His father was holding him down even though they never touched. The questions that kept interrogating him about his responsibility for his brother's actions confined him, and even though Mark kept telling his son that he understood A.J. had done wrong and also needed to be punished, Clay began to feel like he was being lied to.

As the man kept talking, the feeling just kept growing. Eventually, it led to this:

"What was that?"

Clay stared at his father.

"Answer me."

"I don't know what you're asking me about." It was true, Clay did not know. He was angry and felt trapped; he was just waiting for his father to give up and leave.

"You sneered at me. Like a little punk." Mark straightened himself and leaned over, putting his face directly in front of Clay's. "I am your father. You don't sneer at me."

Clay shrugged.

"What does that mean?" his father demanded.

"I don't know. I can't remember sneering, but I guess I did. What is my punishment going to be?"

Mark stood up. "You're already being grounded for the week because you can't control yourself. If your mother or I catch you with LEGO of any kind, it doesn't matter why, you will lose them forever. LEGO will just not be a thing you do anymore, because we won't be able to trust you with it. Got that? You screwed up. You get one do-over. One."

Clay nodded.

"Since you can't get along like you're supposed to, you can also spend today in this room. There are disposable cups in the bathroom if you need a drink. I don't want to see you further down the hallway than that. And you're not peeing every ten minutes just so you can look out a different window. Got that?"

Clay nodded. At least he was getting rid of his father. He focused on that goal, and asked Van to help make his face metal, even if his current headache was too strong for his whole body to be converted to metal.

Mark glared down at his son. The boy knew better. He had practically memorized everything he'd ever read, so he knew what he was doing. He had to. With the deliberate way he did everything from organizing his bricks to his articulate and minutely detailed recounting of the inconsistencies between Bible stories, he had to know. Probably better than most adults. That meant he had to learn what happened when adults who knew things still did wrong.

Mark nodded to his son, and then he left the room.

The door clicked shut a few seconds later. Despite the sneer that he could not control, Clay knew better than to slam doors.

◆   ◆   ◆

The day passed slowly, but it did pass, and the headache at least kept him from feeling the boredom that was inherent to his situation. At some point, when the sun outside was high enough that he could not see it but the house was not yet throwing shade outside his window, Clay finally wondered what time it was. His curiosity peaked because he did not know how long the sun had been high before he noticed it, so it could have been ten-thirty in the morning or five at night.

As he contemplated the time, he tried to listen for sounds in the house that might tell him when it was. Despite his best attempts to strain for noises, though, he heard nothing but a lawn mower from a few doors away. His mother, of course, should be silent. She was supposed to stay in bed, and the television that his father had put in her room was not loud enough to carry around the house. Still, he heard no sounds from his father, and he wondered if that meant he was gone or if he was simply being quiet.

Clay stared at the door. He might be able to go to the bathroom as a way to see what was going on downstairs. If he was caught, though, it was not likely to go well, so instead, he made a game of trying to get to his castle. It was a way to distract himself from his headache, and it was something to do without having to move.

Eventually, his bedroom door opened, and his mother stepped over the threshold. She carried a tray with her, and on it there sat a glass of orange juice and a plate with a sandwich on it.

"I am supposed to stay in bed, but you need to eat. This is lunch. I didn't realize that your father forgot to give you breakfast until I asked, but I can make you another sandwich if you want."

Clay eyed the tray. His mother set it down on the bed and stood over him.

"You'll have to sit up if you are going to eat," she said.

"I have a headache," Clay said. "I don't know if I'm hungry."

"Well, you didn't eat yet, so try a bite and see what happens," his mother's voice was cheerful but plain. Clay did not hear anything other than her words in her words, so he sat up and took a bite. The sandwich was peanut butter and jelly and it tasted mostly of the white bread it was on, but he did want it. After he finished eating, he took down the juice in a gulp.

"Do you want more?" his mother asked.

Clay shook his head. She picked up the tray and left.

He did not get up to close the door after her. He did not want to remain cut off from the rest of the house. A little while later, his mother came back and sat on the bed. When she sat, she did not make Clay move to give her space, but she also did not ask or announce what she was doing. He pulled the blankets close around himself as she began to talk.

"I am worried about you, Clay," she said.

He stared at her. He was worried too. Nothing about the exchange felt the way things felt when they were about to go bad, but since they usually went bad because of her, he could not relax.

"You used to tell me what was wrong," she said. "You don't talk a lot anymore."

Clay closed his eyes. He did not understand what his mother was talking about.

"Tell me what's bothering you."

He threw ideas across his interior sense of self, trying to find the one whose arc seemed the least likely to make his mother cross and mean. Honesty was out of the question, always, and had been since at least the beginning of his first grade year, if not longer. Lying was dangerous, though, because the lack of improvement in his mood after they gave him what he "wanted" was likely to be used as an excuse to start being mean to him.

Clay felt that the best thing he could do was to try to simplify things as much as possible.

"I'm having trouble with the Bible, and I don't think it says what you think it says. In fact, I've noticed that there isn't a whole lot of it that we actually even read in church, and a lot of what we don't use contradicts what we do. If it's a history, how does it contradict itself?"

"Well, that's the Old Testament," Kitty replied. "That's why we have a New Testament, to update us. The old part is important, but the new part is what really counts. It shows us what went before and how we live now, so we read both. But you only follow one. Get it?"

Clay shook his head. He wanted to ask about the differences between the Gospels, but his mother's words made it hard to think because they made his headache loud.

Kitty continued.

"The old covenant is over, because of Jesus. So we need to know what it was, and it's important to remember what it meant, because it was part of the world. But we need to know it was replaced, too, so we need the new one, otherwise we don't understand how we need to be."

"What about the afterlife?" Clay surprised himself, because he did not want to speak but the words were there.

"What about it?" his mother asked.

"In the Old Testament, they keep talking about the land of the dead and about Heaven, but it's like they're different places. But in the New Testament, they talk about Heaven as a paradise, and they promise we will go there. Sometimes they say we will go there instead of the land of the dead, sometimes they describe other punishments like Hell. What happened there? Did people used to go someplace other than Heaven and Hell? Are there still people there?"

Saying it out loud made it better, especially since Clay had not known that anything was bothering him in particular. His problems with the Bible were a constant, running irritation, like an itch or a garment tag made out of plastic.

"Oh. That's a good question," his mother said. "Let me see if I can remember what I learned back when I was in Sunday school. It's not something that we talk about all the time, because it doesn't have a lot to do with everyday worship."

Clay waited. His mother reached out and stroked his arm. He managed not to pull away, and he was glad that she did not look into his face and ask questions about what it was doing, because he did not know.

"The land of the dead is where people used to go, before there was a covenant about salvation. It wasn't like Hell or anything, but they waited there. You see, Jewish people believe that they don't get into heaven until their messiah comes. He's supposed to throw open everything and save them. Until then, they just kind of wait."

"Where is it then?" he asked. "Hell is supposed to be underground, but it's not really. But it's supposed to be, even if it's not under the Earth we're on right now. Right? So where is the land of the dead?"

His mother finally looked at him then. She was frowning, but not the way she did when she didn't like him. She was frowning the way she did when his father announced that no one had to eat the dinner she had just made because he had the money to get them pizza.

"It's under the ground. Like where people get buried, you know? And they used to be much more serious about burial grounds. They were taboo, and people didn't go there because they knew that the dead had to wait. Does this make sense?"

It did. It made too much sense. Just not the way his mother thought.

You know what you've read, Van said. **She's just making stuff up at this point.**

Clay shivered a question he did not have words to ask.

"What's wrong?" His mother prompted him. "You look like a ghost ran through you."

❖   ❖   ❖

Glory Be

Even though he knew Van was telling him the truth, and even though he remembered everything he had read about the land of the dead, Clay's night was still filled with visions of animated corpses and haunted valleys where mounds and cairns established the fact of human interference, despite there being no sign of ongoing habitation. The dreams came to him from nowhere when his mind was otherwise calm and his body was so far away there was no hope of a metal deployment.

The place where the land of the dead caught him was like the place where his castle existed, except that since it was in a dream and Clay did not consent to participation, he felt stuck. It was a Nintendo game with unconventional controls and a special controller he did not have. He kept pushing and pulling, leaning into the effort of escaping the dead things with their hollow mouths and grasping hands, only to find himself somehow folded back over and dropped into their grasp as soon as he got away. More than once, he woke up panting and tried to stay awake, but no matter what Clay did, the night came back into his head and forced him to sleep. Then the corpses of his ancestors came to visit him, showing him the skeletons and dust of bygone centuries going back to when small groups of people gathered in quiet places to discuss the problem with the Romans. In his mind, there was no grandiosity, no celebrity figures from history books or movies. No Charlton Heston. Instead, all of the corpse creatures were anonymous passers-by, people who would only be remembered for as long as the ones their age still held on and counseled the young. They were legion, though, and they all wanted to pull Clay toward something he did not want to be part of. Eventually, their grip overcame his resistance, and darkness took him. In the last moment before it did, he realized his own capacity for thought was about to vacate his mind, and he wondered if the dead things were sent to protect him from his mother.

♦ ♦ ♦

The next morning, the nightmares came back to him as he awakened. Coming up through hazy layers of unconsciousness and feeling his muscles slowly begin to twitch as they responded to the light and heat of the sun coming in through the window, he felt every moment of his brain becoming aware enough to project images of papery skin, stringy, dirty cobweb hair, and degraded faces with sunken cheeks.

When his eyes finally opened and the land of the dead fell away, he could still feel it behind his eyelids, just like he often felt the metal body ready to deploy from his joints and the scream in his stomach. He wished it away, but when he blinked the dead things in his darkness reminded him that the only way to keep them at bay was with open eyes.

Clay rose and dressed himself before going downstairs to find out how his parents were going to approach Sunday mass. No one had told him when to be ready, and they had not brought him to the Saturday night section. Nor had it sounded like they were leaving to go without him. At least, not as far as he had been able to tell from his place in his room.

Once he was downstairs, the kitchen clock showed him that it was only just getting to be eight o'clock in the morning. That was about the time when one or the other of his parents started to stir on the weekend. It was a little early to expect them to be up and moving toward breakfast, but only a little. Clay's stomach growled. Dinner the night before had been a single hotdog in a bun with a little macaroni and cheese on the side. At the time, it seemed like enough food; being alone all day with nothing to do had stifled his appetite. Now, with the prospect of a day of movement and freedom, it seemed like a starvation ration. He followed his instincts toward the breadbox and the jar of peanut butter in the pantry.

While Clay mostly did okay with pouring his own cereal and milk, he did have accidents just often enough to want to avoid causing a situation that would result in his parents finding him in the midst of cleaning up his own mess. Especially with the way things had been going lately.

He put his bread in the toaster. Peanut butter was better warm. It even spread better that way. Two peanut butter and jelly sandwiches later, his father found him. Mark smirked when he saw his son polishing off the last of the second one as he came into the kitchen.

"I was going to make us all pancakes for breakfast today, but it looks like you won't be hungry," he said.

"Sorry," Clay said.

Mark tousled his son's hair.

"Don't worry about it. As long as your mother doesn't know that she missed her surprise, she won't miss her surprise."

Clay smiled. His father sharing little secrets they would both keep from his mother made him feel like he was back on the right path.

"When do I have to be ready for church?" Clay asked.

Mark shrugged. "I guess I'd better go wake your mother up to make sure we're going. She was really tired this morning."

Clay watched his father retreat, and he wondered why it was that his mother being well would determine whether they went to church or not. It definitely mattered, because it determined whether she would be along, but he knew from being with Grandpa Harry that church happened and you were supposed to go unless you were the one taking care of a sick person. Maybe his mother needed more help when she was sick. Maybe she was finally weak enough that she could not be left alone. If that was true, though, then why did she bring both of his meals yesterday? He hoped that she had not overexerted herself just for him.

When Mark returned, he sent the boy back upstairs to change into his best church clothes, explaining that since he had already eaten a starter breakfast, they were going over to 9:30 mass with Grandpa Harry, who would then take them out for a lunch of pancakes and eggs.

Clay clapped his hands and ran upstairs to find the clothes in his closet that looked the most like Grandpa Harry's suit. He did not even take the time to notice that his father seemed a little upset about the news.

◆ ◆ ◆

Mass was terrible, and Clay could not keep himself from twitching all through the homily. It was worse than when they spent an extra twenty minutes reviewing the church budget in the middle things. It even made enduring a multiple baptism seem easy.

It was a day where they read parables about the afterlife.

Cobweb hair and parchment skin rubbed itself against the inside of Clay's eyelids as the gospel selection was read aloud. Before that, during the Old Testament reading about the Passover plagues, he had sworn that he could feel hands on him.

Things got even worse during the homily.

Usually, that was Clay's favorite part of the service, because it was when the priest told jokes and explained things with stories about present-day life, and that somehow pierced his confusion over the Bible's inconsistencies and just made things easy to put together. Today, though, that time was being spent discussing the visions of heaven that were granted to various saints over the years, and the things that were known about existence on that plane, things that had come from their narratives.

"We exist in order to exalt God," the priest said, "and in our return to him, we will be returned to our original essence and embody the word of his excellence. What does this mean? It means nothing but that we were created as adoration, and it is in adoration that we will find the perfection of our existence."

The words made Clay dizzy because they seemed pregnant with meaning that could not be derived from knowing what each word actually meant. If he had possessed a concept for drunkenness, he would likely have thought himself intoxicated by their interplay.

"There is nothing more than his presence, nothing greater, nothing that will make us happier. So, similarly, it is not that Hell is necessarily a place of gory or gruesome torment, but rather the lack of his presence and the inability to conceptualize one's true nature and purpose in the universe. It is simply living without God, without grounding, without the ability to discern whether one is being nourished or poisoned. We need only look at the reward of heaven to know the punishment of Hell, we do not need any further hyperbole. And we need only to accept our role and embrace obeisance in order to understand how eternity will unfold without trauma or pain, and how we might be fully realized in God's love."

At the word "obeisance," Clay's knees buckled and he fell to the floor.

In his mind, he was untouched by the priest's words because he could sense the divide between what had actually been present in the reading and the charged yet externally nonsensical diatribe coming into his ears. At the same time, though, his body reacted, twisting as if to evade the claws and grasping finger bones that reached through the veil of his imagination to pull him back toward the land of the dead.

"He's crying," someone said.

"He's just overwhelmed," another voice. Older, more male than the first one. "This happens. If we take him outside to get some fresh air, he'll be able to calm down."

"I'm his father, I'll take him," Clay knew the third person talking was Mark because of the words. He wondered if the other two were his mother and grandfather, or if the people around him had noticed his problem.

A tug on his arm helped him stand up.

"Come on," his father said, "let's go to the bathroom and get you cleaned up."

The bathroom was in the opposite direction from the vestibule, located right next to the daycare center in the church basement, and to reach the stairway going down to it Clay was forced to march down the center aisle of the church and across the walkway in front of the altar where the priest paced and waved his hands, never breaking in his description of the perfection that would exist in an eternity of complimenting an immeasurable being with nothing better to do with its power than build an army of sycophants. Clay wondered, as he passed, how it was that people were not killing themselves to go straight to Hell as they listened to it. There was nothing more profoundly nightmarish to him than the idea that he would be confined and left with nothing to do forever, except perhaps the notion that he would somehow embrace it as perfect.

As his father held his shoulder and steered him to the stairwell, Clay closed his eyes and let the corpses pull him along. The sleep they could bring him into was better than confinement, because annihilation at least promised an end.

"Stop monkeying yourself all over!" His father's bark brought him back to the world before the skeletons took him completely out of it. Clay realized then that only his father's grip on his shoulder had stopped him from toppling face-first down a flight of stairs.

The entire space twisted around him then, and Clay felt his feet get runny. A moment later he was lifted and in motion, flying. His father did not set him down again until they entered the men's room, where the mirror helped him realize that he had been crying for some time.

When he saw his face, he immediately ran cold water and started to get it wet. He knew that was the only way to eliminate the redness before his father's patience ran out.

"What the hell is going on?" Mark asked.

Clay hyperventilated.

"Stop it! Stop carrying on. Stand up straight. You can cry and fix your face, but if you throw a tantrum like a baby, I will bend you over and spank your ass like you're a baby. You got it?"

Swallowing helped stop his crying.

"What bothered you so much about Heaven?"

"It. Was. So. Terrible," Clay had to take a breath between each word. He splashed more water on his face at the end.

"That wasn't terrible. Maybe it wasn't playing with toys and reading about a spaceship, but someday you will realize that there are a lot more important priorities in life, and then maybe you'll think twice before you freak out over God having plans that you don't control. You want to know what terrible is? Terrible is Hell. Terrible is the way that flesh smells when it burns, and having that in your nose and knowing it's you. The priest doesn't want to scare you, but you know that the church burned witches at the stake because it wanted them to know what they had signed up for. That's what you can count on if you try to tear yourself away from your purpose. The priest was just being nice. Hell isn't some gloomy pit where you can't tell up from down. Hell is the stink of yourself dying forever, without having the hope that eventually you'll just be dead. Do you know what that would be like?"

Clay stared himself in the eye through the mirror and nodded. His tears were gone. He understood the message, and he wanted his father to see that he understood.

His gaze didn't waver until he heard a stall door close, followed by his father's belt unbuckling. Then he knew he was alone again, so washed his face while he cried. His father would never see him rebel, but he would not stop either.

❖   ❖   ❖

Fight or Flight

The next Tuesday, Grandpa Harry picked Clay up from school and brought him home. Not to his mother, Kitty, but home, to his own house, where the two could watch *Twilight Zone* reruns on WGN and eat s'mores for an afterschool snack.

At first, Clay resisted the change. He was sure that his mother did not know about Grandpa Harry's plan, the same way she had not known about Bayleigh's, and he did not want to be accused of going against her wishes again. When he said as much to his grandfather, though, Harry insisted that he had already cleared things with everyone, telling him that his mother expected this. It was not until Mrs. Hudson saw the two arguing and intervened that he accepted what his grandfather was saying. She was able to confirm that his father had called the school about the situation. It had, apparently, happened just as they were getting their coats and bags, and she had not yet had a chance to say anything.

Satisfied that even if his mother was uninformed, his father was in control, Clay left with his grandfather, and they did watch television and eat s'mores.

At first, he was glad that his grandfather was taking care of him, but after a little while, he started to become wary. Grandpa Harry was not exactly questioning him, not like his father did, where they sat down and Clay was directly interrogated, but he would start conversations, usually by telling a little story about something he or Grandma Doris had done during the last week. Soon after, Clay would find himself discussing his feelings about how his mother wanted to give him directions more than she really wanted chores done. Each time he slipped like that, he felt anxious. If his grandfather tried to help him by talking to his mother, then the words would come back to him the next time they were alone together. He knew this was the case; it had always been the case, ever since he learned to talk.

Each time he caught himself giving things away, the fluttering in his stomach became a little more like the scream and a little less like the s'mores settling.

"Why didn't I go home to my mom?" he finally asked.

Grandpa Harry shrugged. "I thought you could use a break. Your dad and your mom both tell me how much you do to help out around the house. It sounds tiring."

"But what about my mom? Is she okay alone? Who is going to help her if she needs things done?"

Harry put his arm around his grandson and pulled him close. The boy's frozen posture worried him, because it felt as if Clay was flexing his muscles against a possible hit.

"She's okay, Clay. You're really tense, did you know that? Kids should not tense up like that. Are you feeling all right?"

"No."

Clay's blunt answer shocked his grandfather.

"I have no idea why you keep talking to me about the things you want to talk about, because they don't seem like any of your business. I don't want my parents to think I'm untrustworthy. And I didn't ask to come over here. I just want people to leave me alone, or to tell me what they want so that I can do it and then get left alone. Why doesn't anyone just tell me what they want?"

"All I want is to find out how to help you, Clay. You always seem upset, and I don't know what is happening that makes you hurt so much."

"You do!" Clay's voice escalated to a screech as he worked through the syllables. He felt them lift him as they pulled themselves out of his mouth, and he had to begin moving his feet to avoid falling down. By the time he realized what his body had done, he was downstairs in the bathroom, clutching the hammer that his grandfather kept in the toolkit. He locked the door and climbed into the spot between the toilet tank and the wall. If he stayed there, he could hit anyone who tried to pull him out.

He was only in his hiding place for a few moments before his grandfather found him. Clay supposed that it was probably fairly obvious where he was at, because the bathroom on the basement floor was the only room with a lock in the whole house.

At least he was the one with a hammer. And the door was locked.

"Clay, I need you to talk to me," his grandfather's voice was slightly muffled as it filtered through the door.

He remained silent.

"I know you're afraid of getting in trouble, and I don't want that. I just want you to know that I am working to make sure your whole family is taken care of, because I remember what it was like to have kids and also have kids on the way. This is the first time your mom's had to do it, but your other grandma did it, and Doris and I did it three times. We all just want to make sure she has everything she needs, to make it easier on her."

Clay held the hammer with both hands. He believed his grandfather, but he also knew that he was only safe as long as he kept himself someplace where they could not make him do anything. As long as they could not reach him, then they could not march him in different directions. They could not lie to each other about what he said and did, so it was safe to close his eyes and let himself go away.

The decay was barely even repulsive anymore; the dead seemed more inconvenienced than anything else. Perhaps if he went with them quickly, they would be gentler.

◆　◆　◆

Clay's eyes snapped open as the bathroom door fell inward, its hinges popping.

"That's a solid door," the voice sounded like his Grandpa Clif, not Grandpa Harry. "Pity it had to go. It's really rare to see this kind of woodwork on the inside doors of a house."

As his eyes focused, he saw that it *was* his Grandpa Clif talking. Both grandfathers stood in the doorway with a toolbox between them.

"Well, what else could we do but break it? He stopped talking a long time ago," Grandpa Harry sounded like he had been crying.

"Still a shame, though. Do you know where your builder sourced his materials? I have most of the catalogs, and I can borrow others. We can order you a new one."

"Thanks," Harry said, stepping into the room. Then he locked eyes with Clay.

Clay lifted the hammer and held it between them, forcing his grandfather to look away from his eyes, to the threat. It stopped him from coming further into the room.

Then he felt the fatigue and the cramping that came with falling asleep between the toilet tank and the wall. Every muscle in his body twitched at once, and he cried out as one leg shot out in front of him, contorting with alternating spasms and rigor.

Harry's face went pale at the sight of his grandson's distress, but he did not move. As Clay let his scream fill the bathroom, he hoped that it would eventually call forth his metal body to stop the cramps, and he wondered if he was the one holding his grandfather in place.

Then, suddenly, Grandpa Clif was close to him and reaching for his body.

Clay swung the hammer wildly. It connected with something that made Clif grunt, but a second later it was ripped from his hands. He heard it bounce off the tile, but by the time he thought to scramble after it he was already over his grandfather's shoulder and kicking at the ceiling.

He swung his arms and legs, but however Grandpa Clif held him, it not only kept him from breaking loose, it also managed to keep him from putting any power into his hits. His arms were pulled behind the man's shoulders, and he could not kick anything except what was above him. He kept kicking, though. Partly, it was because his cramp was still forcing one leg to move, but it was also because kicking against the air only served to make him angrier, and he wanted to build himself up. Then the cramp started in his second leg, and he screamed even more.

Grandpa Clif carried him outside through the patio door in the basement's main room. They stood outside together, towering over the aluminum furniture, and he kept Clay in that peculiar kind of restraint until the boy stopped moving and relaxed against him. Then, he laid the sleeping child in a chaise lounge and stepped inside to see how Harry was doing.

❖   ❖   ❖

Cautionary Tales

Clay woke up in his own bed with only a foggy recollection of having been at Grandpa Harry's. He also found himself with the conviction that his Grandfathers had both been there, ganging up on him. Everything else about the previous day was transmuted into a kind of dense fog that hovered around the spaces in his imagination where he usually figured things out. Flashes from inside the fog told the stories it obscured in an abstracted way, and from them, Clay knew he would be in trouble once he left the bed.

He was not mistaken. Almost as soon as his feet touched the floor, he heard movement in the house, and it was headed in his direction.

◆   ◆   ◆

When Kitty walked into the room, her son was already wearing jeans, and he stood in front of his dresser, hurriedly picking through shirts as if he knew that there was exactly one right choice for his particular pair of the same blue jeans she always bought him.

He looked at her. His eyes were huge.

"When you're dressed, your dad and I want to talk to you about some of the things that have been happening over the last few months," she said. "It's time we started making some changes, because what we've been doing just hasn't worked out."

◆   ◆   ◆

Clay nodded. He felt exposed, and the shirt in his hands did not seem like it would do the job of covering him. Nothing would, though. His mother believed that she could see into him, and she would act as if that was true whether her words were accurate or not.

That is how she remakes you and how she remakes the world, Van said. *No matter what happens, she will tell a story that the others will hear, and the story will be what happened.*

"I'll let you get dressed now," Kitty said. Then she left, closing the door gently behind herself.

When he reached the bottom of the stairs and saw his parents holding hands on the living room couch to his right, Clay almost felt better. The way they released each other and sat forward, as if he had caught them with their guard down, was all that prevented him from actually relaxing.

After both of his parents settled into their alert postures, he approached them, but he made sure to stand with a wide gap between himself and each them, one that could not be crossed with an impulse.

"You might want to sit on the couch with us," his father said.

Clay shook his head. "I just got up. Can I move?"

"You can stand if that's what you want," his mother replied. "Just remember that we're trying to have a talk with you."

His legs itched when he heard her words, and just like that, it became difficult for Clay to avoid pacing.

Pay attention, Van said. *If you don't learn how this works, you cannot fight.*

"You've been doing some things lately that have us really worried. Swinging a hammer at your grandfather, for instance. Chewing open your own mouth to get out of school. Changing plans with family members and not telling us," Mark ticked off the items on his fingers as he went. "And it's not like this is the beginning. Last fall, after we paid extra to make sure you got into that church school and we did all the paperwork to get you on the bus schedule, you tried to just skip everything because you didn't feel like going. Those kinds of things are not going to happen anymore."

Clay stood, stunned. His legs became pillars of marble. He reached for Van, but the cyborg seemed to be frozen and unable to respond to the complexity of that last statement, even though they could both feel that it was exactly the kind of thing that they expected. They just expected it from Kitty.

The world shifted around him, and Clay struggled to keep himself from falling over.

"You don't need to carry on about this," his mother said. "It's not going to earn you any points, and we already know that you like to act out your disapproval. We can wait until you're done."

Old faithful, Van said. *Bringing us right back to the expected agenda.*

Clay said his own mental thank-you to his mother for her consistency, and then he tried to refute what his father had just said. Except he *couldn't.* He wanted to, but in the end, even if he had not chosen some of those things, what his father said was true. He was less disgusted by the pain and the doctor's visits that came from chewing open his own mouth than he was by the catechism class. And he really did want to manipulate his parents, because it was the only way that he could make them stop hurting him. They called it sass every time he bothered to tell them he was in pain, so what else was he to do? Of course he was trying to do manipulate them.

If he said that, though, he knew his words would be used as proof of his disrespectfulness, and then he would be lost to whatever machinations they had already cooked up. He could practically taste the lemon soap on his tongue already.

Fight or lose, Van urged him.

Clay fought the cyborg back, and then the metal body encased him. When his father spoke again, he was glad that it was so.

They want me to look closely at something that only makes sense when you keep it at a distance, he told the cyborg, *and they think that making me examine it closer is the way to do it. They are too dangerous to fight. We can only run.*

Deep within him, the groan of metal under pressure sounded quite a lot like a shrug.

"You remember Billy, right Clay?" His father was winding up for something. Clay could hear it.

He nodded.

"I told you he'd remember Billy," Mark said to his wife. To Clay, he added, "You might have only met once, but we know you don't forget anything. Anyhow, you remember your mom told you that she was worried that Billy was a bad influence? And that was why she didn't want you to be too happy about him coming to visit? He's in jail for burning down churches now. That's where your little rebellion gets you. That's where hating catechism and throwing temper tantrums is headed, in the end."

Billy had been sixteen when Clay met him, and already married. He had just gotten out of juvenile detention for stealing a car, and Bayleigh made sure to invite him to the family reunion because she was hoping someone would help him get settled. Clay remembered all of that. He also remembered that Billy had been in love with his young wife, and that the two of them had also been in love with something called "November Rain," so much so that they were asked to take both their love and their music outside. More detailed memories stayed at the fringes, but he did not remember Billy having a particular thing to say about churches. Apparently, they were something that he had learned to hate, though.

Clay understood why. He also understood why it was important to send people to jail for setting churches on fire. Even so, he could see how Billy might have gotten to the church-burning point. It scared him that he could understand it so well, though, and it made him sick to think about the smell of the fire, the danger, all those firefighters risking their lives...

His mother's arm on his elbow held him up, but he fought it anyway, and then she let him fall. Afterward, he climbed onto the couch with them and they continued telling him stories.

"It's not just Billy," his mother continued. "There was a girl that I knew from Catholic school. When we got to the high school level and we had to go to a regular public school, she decided she wanted to be popular and tried out for the cheerleading squad. She was really good. She got to know everyone, until she started getting invited to the kinds of parties that happen when people's parents are out of town. While we all thought she was sleeping over with a church friend, they drugged her drink and beat her with a tire iron. Then, those other girls wrapped her up in a blanket and drove around with her in the trunk all night. Close to dawn, the cheerleaders who had gotten together out of jealousy realized they had to get rid of her, so they laid her in a field, covered her with gasoline, and set her on fire. Do you understand the story?"

Clay did not, but he understood that he was expected to nod.

❖   ❖   ❖

Over the Rainbow

Clay felt a burning sensation in his knees.

It was good. In fact, it was the reason he was still saying the rosary.

His mother only lingered through the first decade before wandering away, bored by her own requirements for virtue and satisfied that he would continue to maintain her standards while she was gone.

After their talk a few weeks ago, she had hovered and kept on him about following every step of every process she taught him for a while, but within a few days it was apparent to her that he had learned the importance of paying attention. Now, she left him to himself, and his ache.

He let his hips ache, forcing them to hold him perfectly straight until the tension spread up his back and through his shoulders. The agony matched the pitch of his mental recitations perfectly, and the words no longer mattered. Whether they were the *Glory Be*, the *Hail Mary*, or Clay's personal list of crimes he wished to prosecute various people for perpetrating, the words were not the point.

The fire in his body was a kind of burning that did more than just consume his language, it also brought him visions. Visions like Patrick and him grown and living in a small house, a single-story one like in the development they were building down the hill from the school. There, they could watch TV together whenever they wanted, and Patrick could make video games on his computer while Clay wrote stories about Van and helped his friend design stories that worked in the games, too.

He had feelings about those visions when they came, but they did not feel like he and Patrick needed to be alone. In fact, Clay wanted more people; he wanted people who came together to live and to work on things that required their shared talents. It was easy to see, with the way Patrick and Aaron helped him, how easy it could be to make a work group that made things and held themselves together. It was also easy to see how this idea was so much better than a family.

His back knotted and twisted, hardening itself into a broad, tough shell of bunchy muscle, and he put all thoughts of being metal out of his mind. That process needed no help, it would now continue without him, now that it was finally safe to live inside it. The body would no longer retract, and Van would not be needed to negotiate it. Whatever part of himself had been speaking and teaching those things he felt in books and could not name, it had become him now, working the way it should, and that meant that the child was free to use his senses like a curtain, drawing thick drapes of pain around his hope until it was protected from the trampling feet of the people he could not escape.

That was how Clay Dillon entered the Complex, and why he allowed it to take him. Ironically, it was in those moments, just as he was feeling the tightening cords of flesh beginning to restrict his freedom of movement, when his mother found herself suddenly unsupported. Her own flesh, so neatly bound for over two decades into a compact and painful knot, found that it could no longer maintain its integrity in the face of the challenge that was her final pregnancy. While neither would know what it meant to move through the Complex in counterpoint for years, both felt the moment when their processes became intertwined.

❖   ❖   ❖

Part IV: War Nerve

Swallowing the Body

Clay felt himself swallow as the camera flashed. Ever since his tongue first practiced folding the wafer down the middle and flushing it into the back of his throat, the swallow reflex had automatically kicked in to signal the moment when he stopped worrying about details like his feelings, and it allowed him to do the things that needed done. In the last few minutes, that mostly meant posing for photographs with family members he loved, family members he loathed, and a few random stragglers he barely knew. He suspected his father invited them because they were casual acquaintances around town who understood that first communion parties involved cards with checks in them.

Before the photographs, that ability to swallow himself until the moment passed had also allowed him to navigate the final two months of catechism class. It had allowed him to simply sit without blinking for long minutes while Sully was telling jokes about "people who behave like this" while doing crude imitations of Clay's nervousness. It had even helped him down the aisle, just like it had helped him when he felt the dizziness and tension that signaled the need to throw himself into the wall or floor.

When that happened, he swallowed himself and let the moment guide him past the restroom, up the stairs, and into the kitchen behind the main vestibule where the carafe of wine from morning mass was stored. After a long draught that puckered his lips and dried his throat like clotted blood, the need to hit himself seeped out of his muscles. The fire that started in his knees and spread into his mind also dimmed, quieting the visions of things that were not happening and allowing him to focus on the things in front of him. By the time he swallowed his first draught of fully consecrated wine at mass, Clay had already realized he would need to monitor the size of his sip or the person holding the chalice might notice and talk to his parents about it.

Thinking about the wine now made him wish his party was at church so that he could steal away for more wine. His parents had beer for Grandma Bayleigh, but Clay could not stand to put it in his mouth. He knew because between photographs he had taken advantage of a moment when a stray can of something Lite was unattended, amazing himself with the size of the disgusted reaction he could perform without getting any attention.

His brain burned with the memory of the beer, angry that it was not like the fruity, cheap wine from church, which had at least tasted like rotten fruit instead of wet dough.

The urge to bash his head for being impulsive about stealing the beer formed, and then it itched its way down his arms, but he kept it at bay by cracking his knuckles. The more he wanted to hit himself, the more he remembered the wine, with its promise of a clarity and release of tension without cracking his skull against a wall or a bedpost. The longing made his chest tight, and for a moment, it made Clay smile. Then he realized that he would have no way to get into the church kitchen now that his catechism class was over, and he swallowed.

❖ ❖ ❖

Between the Essence and the Descent

"Clay, come in here."

His mother's voice startled him when it cracked out of the dim living room to catch him across the side of the face. He shook himself loose of his backpack as his brain began to churn out scenes from the day. None of them were anything to worry about, at least as far as he could tell. He had managed all his work early and read a book. Before that, he even managed to make his own lunch so that his mother, who should be having Baby Sis any day, did not need to fish in her purse for lunch money.

In the living room, she sat staring out the window. Her body was pointed at him, but she craned away from the direction of the entryway, more interested in the squirrels in the garden than the thing she had summoned him to discuss.

"Catechism class was today, wasn't it?" she asked.

"It would have been," Clay responded. "Before I had the communion."

His mother shook her head. "You don't get to just quit. The class is still going until the end of the school year, and you are still enrolled."

Clay shrugged. "No one told me that. All year, you told me I was in the class to study for first communion. First communion happened, and so I was supposed to go back to science class. If there was more, why did you tell me the class was for the communion?"

Suddenly, the squirrels were no longer fascinating. Kitty locked gazes with her son instead.

"Don't sass," she said.

The strangled, sibilant syllables slit Clay, and then he felt her metal in himself and shivered. There was no time for him to profess his sincerity before she spoke again.

"You know that you're not allowed to skip catechism. We had this talk months ago. I also know you remember it because you remember everything. The only question now is 'What kind of punishment is appropriate?' I don't think that we can just keep negotiating with you. Either you are lying about forgetting or you don't care enough about what I say to remember it, even though you memorize every episode of *Star Trek* your father watches. Either way, it means you need to know what it will cost if you do it again. You also need to know that when you do these things, we will just make it cost more and more until you stop. Do you understand what that means?"

Clay understood. The words echoed emptily through him, tearing at his insides. His ears throbbed with the absence of his internal wailing, and he wished for once that the scream would come. That feeling made him sick, which in turn made his bones ache. For a passing second, he wondered if his organs were rupturing from all the pressure. He had read about something similar happening to deep sea divers in the World Book Encyclopedia.

"Well?" she asked.

He nodded.

"We just can't have you thinking you can do anything you want. You know who does that? Criminals. The world is full of them, and they all think they can just ignore everyone else and do whatever they want. You remember us talking about your cousin Billy? Yes? You want to wind up in prison for burning down churches too? Keep your values right where they are. It can happen."

Clay felt numb. Why was his mother threatening to frame him for burning churches? How was that something that could happen for missing a week of church school?

He opened his mouth to ask a question, but all that came out was the scream. This time, it did not run through him and tear itself free. Instead, it seemed to flow out of his muscle, deflating him and carrying pieces of his mind out into the room where they discorporated, leaving a barely perceptible miasma, like soot from a crematorium being blown back down city streets. When it was over, his arms and legs hurt and he felt several new carpet burns in various places on his body. Everything was dark, too.

Clay opened his eyes and saw his mother standing over him.

"That's enough. If you think you can throw a tantrum like a baby to get your way, then that's how we'll treat you."

"I didn't—"

"Don't sass. I'm your mother. I know you better than you know yourself, and this manipulation is going to stop right now. Take yourself upstairs and go to bed. I'll figure out what happens to you later, but first I need to wait for my ears to stop ringing."

Clay thought about getting up, but his arms and legs remained heavy and unresponsive.

"If I have to drag you up the stairs I will... and you know what that will do to your baby sister. Do you want that?"

He felt himself moving before he could think about it. By the time he knew what had happened, the echoing sound of his bedroom door slamming behind him was in his ears. From below, he heard his mother bellow about opening and closing it ten times.

Instead of doing that, Clay found a wiffle ball bat in the back of his toy closet, and he beat it against the door frame until the plastic twisted and gave way, tearing at a point midway down its length where it kept making contact with the frame. By the time he dropped the wreckage of the bat, his mother's yelling was over.

❖   ❖   ❖

In the Closet

Clay fled down the hallway, barely noticing that the teacher's response to his request to go to the bathroom was "no, wait." When it did register, he was already two steps past the sound of the door closing, so it seemed like more trouble to go back and let the teacher correct him than to keep fleeing. The restroom was a no-go now, though. Clearly, if she thought he was going there, then that would be the first place she would send people. Luckily, St. Sebastian's parish had many buildings and community rooms, and they had many passages between them to allow for the pageantry of Mass without the visibility of the many stagehands it took to execute the performance. There were plenty of options, and even plenty of other bathrooms to seek. He bolted toward the exit at the end of the hall. The main church building had a side door that was exactly fifty feet away from the building with the classrooms and offices. All he had to do was run.

As Clay's arms and legs pumped, the motion disgorged images from before and during class. He wanted them to go away, but he also knew that they were the cost of the exertion. Something had to scream, so he let it course through his legs. They carried him across

the parking lot so quickly he lost track of the fact that he had left one
building and entered another.

There was a broom closet in the church's basement, across from
the men's room, and Clay stayed in it until he heard people outside
three times. The first time, whoever it was just walked by, and he was
happy that it was not the custodian coming to get anything. The
second time, there were voices, but they did not seem urgent. The
third set of people, though, were definitely adults looking for him. He
even thought he heard the priest, but he was not sure. After they
passed, there was nothing but the opening and closing of the heavy
door at the rear entrance, where Clay had first entered the church.

The closet was safe and dark. Being small, it was easy for Clay to
keep from feeling lost inside of it, even when there was no light to
help him see its boundaries. It was a spot where he could let himself
see the situation from the outside, and where he could tell what each
boy had done to him, in order to assess who to trust and who to
blame. The skill was one Clay trusted thoroughly, but it was difficult
to use. Most of the time, he felt its vague movements in the back of
his thoughts, but he did not understand its conclusions beyond the
fact that his body pulled him forward or back. Sometimes, he thought
that Van was this skill talking to him. Sometimes, he thought that
Van was proof that it was only a matter of time before they sent him
to the crazy house.

The scene that painted itself into being in the dark seemed
simple enough. Eight or so boys and three girls, and then Clay. They
sat around the Formica-topped folding tables the church set up in its
classrooms so that they did not need to buy real furniture. All of the
kids perched on metal folding chairs, too, the kind whose slick brown
paint reminded all of them of high school bleachers.

In the beginning, their taunts stayed boring and followed the
regular routine. Sully cracked on him for not knowing football. Noah
tried to tell them he was bored with the game, and the other boys
kept trying to say mean things that they hoped would be as funny as
the ones Sully let loose with. Clay told them repeatedly that he

wanted to know about football even if he never watched it, but no one would teach him.

That was when Sully decided that the reason Clay's father never taught him football was because Clay was really a girl. Once that was in the air, the other boys had no problem finding words that cut into him. Unlike their usual accusations that he was stupid or spastic or somehow in love with his friends, these words lodged in his skin and burned where they met his body.

In the dark of the closet, the pain was as fresh as it had been in the moment, making Clay lose his ability to explain things to himself. Once he could no longer tell himself things, the scene expanded around him, and he lost track of whether he was in class or in the broom closet. The girls across the table looked embarrassed. At least one seemed like she wanted to talk, but none of them ever did. Not then, and not since Hillary had moved away.

Next, the boys started discussing what kind of dress Clay should wear. He saw it in his mind's eye, and it was not the one they were describing, and he wanted to tell them they were wrong. Instead, he just felt fear.

Why was it impossible to talk back to them?

The scene felt just like when his mother interrupted him during nap time, when his pants were down.

Soon the teacher came in, and they stopped. At least for a while. Once the lesson was started, though, the notes started coming. They asked him what his favorite panties were and whether he had a favorite boy in class. That was when he had asked to go to the bathroom.

As soon as he fled the classroom, it folded itself up into a dream again, dropping him back into the dark broom closet where he spent several minutes trying to understand whether he was asleep or not. After he reacquainted himself with his surroundings, another projection came to him. This time, though, it played out somewhere inside him instead of projecting itself throughout his space. The new feeling was a beacon going off, pulling him toward the door and up the stairs. He could see the light from it even though it was inside himself, and Clay understood what it was, even when it was still too far off for him to make out details. Sour grape flavor hit the back of his tongue, and the word **Wednesday** floated into his mind from nowhere.

Wednesday meant communion, which meant the kitchen was open and the wine was, most likely, unattended.

◆   ◆   ◆

Clay drifted back into the classroom on wobbly cloud legs. The teacher's eyes grew wide as he did, and several of the boys snickered. Sully just looked surprised.

"What are you doing back here?" the teacher demanded.

"I peed and came back, like I'm supposed to. What's your problem?"

Clay liked how easily the words came now.

"My problem is that you were not given permission to leave, you didn't go straight to the bathroom, and you've been evading us for the last half hour. What's your problem?"

"My problem," Clay said, "is that the only person I know stupider than my parents is this clown they hired to convince me to believe in some book no one even reads. It's three thousand pages long, it's all about parents who have babies with their kids and kids who kill each other, and it's full of stuff like beating people to death with rocks. You want to guess what it's called?"

The teacher's face became very red before she responded. When she did, all she said was, "You should go tell the priest what it's called. And then tell him to call your parents."

"They should call your parents!" Clay screamed. "You don't ever stop anyone from picking on me, and you don't care if they call me names, and you suck at teaching because you just assign workbooks about stuff we already learned at church."

"Go, now," the teacher's voice was cold.

Clay looked around. The other children stared at him. When he made eye contact with Sully, the other boy grinned and held his hands up to his chest, like he was cupping a pair of his own breasts.

That was what it took.

Clay vaulted across the table, his hands connecting with Sully's neck at full speed and converting his intended strangle into a lunging throat punch. Suddenly, the air was full of hacking sounds and Clay felt hands all over his body. Someone asked him about the wine. He was unsure whether he nodded or lost control of his neck, but that was when he felt the teacher shaking him.

"Good one!" Noah shouted.

Sully, somewhere under the table, sounded like he was puking.

"Come with me," the teacher said. Then she marched him out of the room and down the hall to the main office.

❖   ❖   ❖

A Modest Proposal

Clay's head hurt, but his parents told him to stay on the couch, so he did it. He hated waiting out in the open, but since he already knew the teacher told them she smelled wine on him, he supposed that they could not only surprise him with the inventiveness of their punishment, not the fact of its happening.

He did worry, though. Previously, his parents had responded to problems at school by locking him up until they were done arguing. The fact that they thought they would finish in time to be inconvenienced by the need to retrieve him meant, to Clay, that his actions were anticipated by his parents. It seemed impossible that it could be that way, but why else would they be so quick to respond?

Luckily, they did not seem to have any plans to hold him in suspense. By the time he fully processed what it meant for them to hold him in the living room, they were back. Oddly enough, they did not seem angry. His mother wiped tears from her face instead. His father looked like he did when Grandpa Clifton pointed out some stupid mistake made during a home improvement project.

"Clay, it's obvious that you're not happy," his mother started. "That you're too unhappy to even learn properly. Your teacher told us about your accusations against Sully, and we want you to know that we believe you. In fact, it makes sense. It even explains why you started picking on your brother."

That was when his father chimed in.

"It's really common, when other people hurt you, to want to reach out and hurt them back."

The hairs on the back of Clay's neck stood up. In some far-off place, Lindo's windows opened, and he realized that they were describing what they were about to do to him.

"That's why we think that you might appreciate the opportunity to start over someplace where you won't have to worry about that gang of boys following you from year to year. The best part is, if you change schools you won't have to leave for catechism anymore, because St. Sebastian's has a partnership with a nearby school that incorporates prayer and catechism right into the curriculum."

Clay watched Patrick and Aaron fade into the sepia and become brittle in his mind's eye. He did not want them to be old pictures he could no longer talk to.

"The uniforms," his mother said, "they also help with bullying, because if everyone dresses alike, then issues like what you wear and which team you root for are gone. You can all just focus on the schoolwork."

"The work that is just catechism? What about science class? What about math?"

"Catholic schools are better about all those things," Kitty said.

"You *lie!*" Clay screamed. "They sent you there, and *you,*" he pointed at his mother, "can't even balance a checkbook. That's why dad has to pay the bills."

Mark stood. "You will not—"

Clay did not hear the end of his father's stale assertion of dominance. He screamed *"NO!"* and bolted before it came, making it four steps onto the lawn before his father caught him by the collar and dragged him back inside.

Over the course of the next hour, they held him to keep him still, and they talked at him about everything they were going to do. He threatened to fail intentionally, but they did not blink. He pointed out that his friends would be gone, and they just told him to make new ones, as if that was possible. Whenever his father let go of him, he bit, kicked, and ran, but still, he never managed to escape. Finally, when they were sick of reasoning with him, Mark let go of his son and pointed at the stairs.

"Go to your room," he said. "We'll talk about this when you're ready to do it without throwing a tantrum like a baby."

Clay stood and walked, but when he reached the foot of the stairs, something happened. He kept telling his legs to go up, but they did not move. Instead, he became very aware of the front door two steps away. He could see it without facing it, and his legs plotted their way to it even as he protested.

His resolve slipped, his foot rose, and his hips twitched, pivoting him away from the path to his bedroom.

"Don't even think about going outside!" Kitty shouted.

"*FINE!*" Clay bellowed. He was up the stairs in two bounds then, swinging his weight around the corner of the landing and into the hallway before his ears told him whether either of his parents were pursuing him. It was only when he slammed the door behind himself and caught someone in the face that he realized they were right there.

Unfortunately, his room was a box with one entrance. There was no escape.

When the doorknob turned, his hands worked ahead of his brain, throwing open the window that looked out over the back porch. There was no working storm window because it had been stuck open since they bought the house.

Once the pane was up, he caught the smell of the fresh air coming through in. Then, he heard his mother's voice, and he leaped.

Clay's heart stopped for a moment as he realized what he had just done. Then, the impact of his body against the porch roof started it beating again, even as that same impact took his breath. Throes of panic lit his chest up with bright flares of pain as he rolled down the slope of the roof, toward its edge.

Clay Dillon almost caught his breath before falling ten feet into the bed of gravel in his mother's garden. Almost.

His mother's screaming seemed far away as he watched the sky because it was so much quieter than the screaming in his back. The rest of his body was curiously numb.

Without words, he cried out for Van, but all he heard was the whistling of wind in the wilderness, like a far-away scream. Soon after, his father stood over him.

Clay tried to reach out, to say he was sorry, but his father would not touch him. Not until the paramedics showed up and made him watch their fingers move. Then, when they helped him onto the stretcher, he felt what had happened to his left leg, and he screamed until his father touched the top of his head.

"It will be okay," Mark said. "I fell off a roof once. I even broke my knee, too."

That was the last thing Clay heard before the feelings caused by his broken leg deafened him to any input from his other senses.

❖   ❖   ❖

Pattern Recognition

The hospital ceiling looked like a tombstone. Or, rather, it looked like a graveyard made out of the cheap prop stuff that the elementary school teachers used for various pageants, from the founders' graves in the Greenridge festival to the spooky backdrop of the Halloween sing-along. Those tombstones had followed Clay through both school years, hiding behind corners and manifesting themselves in new ways when he did not expect to see them. Today, they were the hospital ceiling: textured foam and cardboard, covered with some kind of flat paint or whitewash; spotty, with acoustic holes revealing the pale yellow insides and ruining the whitewashed stone appearance. Cheap stuff. Not real. Like his grandma's pizza, it was just hiding leftovers.

Time slipped away while he thought about gravestones and pizzas. Eventually, someone came in and saw he was awake. They adjusted something on the bag that hung next to his bed, petted his leg for a moment, and then left. He wondered who it was that just wanted to feel his leg for a second. He wondered if the person asked first and if he answered. That seemed like something he would normally remember, but for some reason, it did not seem like something he would remember right now.

While Clay was alone the second time, the room solidified around him. Beeping started, and soon he was clearheaded enough to tell which machines they came from and that they beeped things about him. There was no way for him to decipher all of the numbers and symbols. Besides, some machines had dials that were too small for him to read from bed. Still, he could tell from the rhythm of the different monitoring sounds that he would be okay.

Then he remembered that his parents wanted to take his friends away and send him to a new school, and he pulled himself partially upright. His feet twitched, ready to carry him away. As soon as his hip shifted, though, he felt a sharp, high-pitched pain that stopped his brain from communicating with his body for a moment.

The disruption was almost imperceptibly short, but since it was there, it forced Clay to re-think his commands to his body before continuing.

He rethought. Then he settled back down into the bed. His parents did not need to lock him in anymore. He had done that to himself.

Was this what my mother felt, when the doctors made her stay in bed? he wondered. *And will Baby Sis make it home before I do?*

The questions kept Clay busy until he dozed.

When he woke, it was an angry waking, but not for any particular reason he could pinpoint. His sleep contained no nightmares he could recall, and he did not see his father sitting in the corner until after the rage seized him. In fact, he did not move or open his eyes until after the hornets started to buzz in his brain, harmonizing with the scream as it tore at his gut.

He reached for Van and his castle, but they belonged to the past. He tried to create something new, but no visions came to him, just hornets in his head and screaming in his stomach.

"We won't be sending you to Catholic school," Mark said. "We will be sending you to catechism on Sunday nights. And we are changing churches. Your mother is too embarrassed to go back to St. Sebastian's."

Clay held himself very still so that he would not show how excited this news made him. After a moment, his father nodded at him. Then he looked away.

Was this as close as he would get to being alone now? For a few minutes, that was a daunting idea. Then, slowly, his father's ability to ignore him made him feel alone, and then he was able to think freely as if he really *was* alone, even if his free thoughts were still somewhat affected by his father's presence.

He could hear the man in them, telling him things about being strong, about fighting and sticking up for yourself. Clay hated the words, but they burned their way into him with a startling clarity:

His father had already taught him how to wage the next ten years of war. The secrets were all there. If A.J. was aggressive and still got to be coddled because he was younger, then that also meant that he didn't know enough to watch grown-up shows, and his baby ways should keep him with Baby Sis, not with Clay. He could use that.

If his mother wanted him to do just what she said, too, then he would. Just. What. She. Said.

If she told him to put peanut butter on bread, he would squash the loaf with the jar. They said that his sass undermined them? Then he would undermine them. They said that his behavior reflected on them? Then he would be a mirror. He had already been broken.

Now it was their turn, and while he threw rocks into them to reshape them into things like himself, he would send their fractured reflections back into their own faces.

In his mind, a vision shimmered into existence. It was catechism class again; it was the last day he had attended, too. Clay could tell because the writing on the board was the same. A moment later, he heard the familiar dialogue, too.

"Clay's just a girl. Don't worry about why she doesn't watch football. She's not supposed to," Sully said.

Clay lunged, just like he had before. This time, though, he kissed the boy. Hard. Then he punched him in the throat.

As the vision faded, he wondered whether he actually liked Sully, or if he just wanted the other boys to call him a faggot queer girl, and if that motivated the kiss. If so, then the best part was the fact that only he and Sully would really know, and what the other boys said would not change a thing, no matter what the truth was.

He laughed. In the corner of his eye, he saw his father nod. It was too dark to be sure, but Clay thought he saw the man smile.

In his mind, he cackled at the prospect of sharing his thoughts with his father, but he knew better. Instead, he tried to imagine what it was that his father thought he was dreaming about.

Then the room faded out again.

♦   ♦   ♦

Dreams bubbled around Clay, but none of them seemed to include him. Instead, they surrounded him, buffeting him and threatening to force him down into whatever kind of stream his dreams floated in, like so much flotsam. In one, there was a little boy named Michael who liked to wear his grandmother's makeup but feared to ruin her sample case. He spent days organizing the lipstick samples by shade.

In another one, a nameless human creature with giant old lady breasts and a man's lower body staggered around a shabby apartment, throwing beanbags and shouting in between long sessions sitting at a futuristic-looking computer and typing. He fled that bubble, swimming until he saw the neon glow of science fiction ahead. He approached that glowing bubble of dream-stuff and peered in, where he saw someone named Lynn being turned into a robot, like a

Terminator who was supposed to get married and have kids. Her screams were worse than the sounds of death in war movies.

Clay hunted for a bubble filled with LEGO, but there did not seem to be one, and none of the cyborgs in his science fiction dreams were Van. They were all fantastically animated things, like sparkling realizations of some future sequel to *Tron*, and they hummed, but they did not comfort him. They did not even reach out to communicate.

Eventually, the bubbles of dreams gave way to memories of books he had read, and then they were old memories from his outside life.

Clay replayed the last couple years of his experience, studying his parents' tics so he could understand which of his problems were likely to cause which eruptions. Somewhere in this would be a pattern, a pattern that could be reframed and then tessellated out into something new, something of his choosing. Or else, perhaps a pattern that could be disrupted if he kicked sand in the right part. Either way, the pattern was what he sought.

It was elusive. Often, he thought he had it, but he was wrong, and he had to set the false patterns aside. Soon, he lost track of which patterns were ones he remembered and which were theories about his parents, and he realized the truth:

War means never letting your enemy control the story.

❖   ❖   ❖

Clay Dillon will return in *Gaslight Village*.

Afterword: Calvin and Clay, the Protective Manipulations of the Unconscious, and Friends of Ambiguous Ontological Status
Nick Walker

The vast majority of human beings go through their entire lives without seriously questioning or examining their assumptions about what is real, what is imaginary, and where the boundaries between the real and the imaginary lie. Most folks operate under the rather narcissistic assumption that their own judgments about the distinctions between the imaginary and the real represent clear perceptions of objective truth —and that everyone who perceives reality differently, or who has a different understanding of the boundaries between the real and the imaginary, must be ignorant or insane.

At the same time, we live in a culture that loves stories in which reality turns out to not be what it seems, or in which the protagonist's sense of reality deviates interestingly from that of the audience. For most folks, I suspect, part of the pleasure of such stories is that they flirt with danger from a safe distance. Horror movies are fun because they provide the edge of fear without placing the viewer in real peril; essential to the pleasure of a good horror movie is that the hockey-masked fiend from the movie does not actually leap out of the shadows and disembowel you with a fire axe when you get up to fetch the popcorn. By the same token, most people enjoy *A Beautiful Mind*, *A Scanner Darkly*, *Fight Club*, or *Calvin and Hobbes* from a position of comfortable certainty that they themselves are in possession of a more solid grasp of reality than the protagonists of the stories in question —certainty that they themselves could never be mistaken as to which persons of their acquaintance are "real" and which ones are their own alternate personalities, hallucinations, or stuffed. Unreliable narrators (or unreliable viewpoint characters, even when they're not first-person narrators) give us the warm thrill of confusion, the intellectual adventure of having our minds blown in a small and safely contained way, without the terrifying existential disorientation that most people experience when their sense of reality is truly exploded.

Unreliable narrators and unreliable viewpoint characters are fun, but we like to imagine that our own viewpoints are reliable. Most of us read Bill Watterson's *Calvin and Hobbes* with an amusement at Calvin's antics that includes a certain sense of superiority. Calvin seems unable to reliably distinguish the real from the imaginary within his world, whereas we imagine that we *can* distinguish the real from the imaginary not only in our own worlds, but in Calvin's world as well. We imagine that our understanding of Calvin's world is more accurate or "true" than Calvin's. But how certain of this can we be?

Nearly every *Calvin and Hobbes* fan I know reads the comic with the assumption that Hobbes is a stuffed toy, and that Calvin imagines him to be real whenever no one else is around. That's how River, my currently nine-year-old daughter, understands the comic these days. But when she was six and I first introduced her to *Calvin and Hobbes,* she saw it differently: Hobbes was a real tiger, who had the magic power to turn into a stuffed tiger at will. He turned into a stuffed tiger whenever anyone but Calvin was around —because, as River explained to me, "If grownups knew he was real they would totally freak out." Where other readers laugh at the way Calvin's wild perceptions conflict with the ostensibly more "realistic" perceptions of the comic's other human characters, six-year-old River laughed at the way the clueless grownups kept failing to notice that their son was keeping a live magic tiger in their house. River's interpretation of *Calvin and Hobbes* might have been different from most people's, but it was perfectly valid; within the ten-year run of the comic, there's not a single strip that contradicts it.

The possibility that Calvin is a more reliable viewpoint character than most readers give him credit for, in terms of the accuracy with which he perceives his world, also suggests a second possibility: what if Calvin is a *less* reliable viewpoint character than we give him credit for?

We assume that the "real" version of Hobbes is the stuffed version, because we only see the live, unstuffed version in those panels of the comic strip from which the adult characters are absent. But how often do we see Susie Derkins, or Moe the school bully, in the same panel as an adult? How do we know that Susie and Moe are any more "real" than the live version of Hobbes, in terms of having an existence outside of Calvin's imagination? Surely an imagination as vivid and powerful as Calvin's, which can turn a stuffed tiger into a wonderful friend and companion like Hobbes, is perfectly capable of also generating imaginary friends (or foes, in the case of Moe) who look like human kids.

So is Susie Calvin's neighbor, or a manifestation of repressed and dissociated aspects of Calvin's own psyche? Perhaps a manifestation of what Jungians might call his *anima*? Is Moe an emergent alter ego, Calvin's equivalent of Tyler Durden?

On a bookshelf in my daughter's room, alongside her treasured *Calvin and Hobbes* anthologies, is an anthology of the one other consistently funny newspaper comic strip of the 1980s, *Bloom County*. This anthology includes an introduction by *Bloom County* creator Berkeley Breathed —and in this introduction, in perhaps the only truly serious moment in his whole body of published work, Breathed writes: "It took me years to discover that the most important dynamic in a comic strip is not shock and satire, but character and truth: the truth of Charlie Brown's anxiety, for example —a mirror of our own. The truth of Calvin's protective manipulations of his world."

Calvin's protective manipulations of his world. That gave me pause, when I first read it. Not Calvin's *impulsive antics,* or his *escapes into fantasy,* but his *protective manipulations of his world.* That phrase has stayed with me. It has the uncomfortable and unmistakable ring of truth. And it came back to my mind again and again as I was reading the manuscript of *Imaginary Friends.*

Clay Dillon, like Calvin, is an unreliable viewpoint character, a character whose own protective manipulations of his world significantly impact his perceptions of reality. Clay's protective manipulations are desperate attempts at survival by a sensitive young psyche under constant siege. Some of these protective manipulations are more or less conscious and intentional manipulations of his external relationships, his own sensory experience, or his rich fantasy life. But it is the *unconscious* protective manipulations —the complex of psychological defense mechanisms that Clay's psyche constructs instinctively, without his conscious awareness or volition —that impact his ability to distinguish the real from the imaginary.

Clay's psyche is fragmenting. The labyrinthine complex of defenses he's being forced to construct in order to preserve his psyche at all, in the face of constant assault from a psychologically toxic environment, also has the effect of dissociating various parts of his psyche from one another. This dissociation means that substantial parts of his psyche —facets of his personhood, essentially —are ending up split off from his sense of self. And because these facets of his psyche are dissociated from his sense of self and are thus no longer part of his experience of himself, he can only experience them and relate to them as if they were Others. As if they were external to himself.

Imaginary friends occupy a spectrum. At one end of the spectrum, there are those imaginary friends whom the imaginer intentionally imagines and recognizes as being imaginary. Perhaps we can describe these as *willed* imaginary friends; they are the product of the sort of conscious act of imagination to which the philosopher Gaston Bachelard was referring when he stated that "anyone who can imagine can will."

At the other end of the spectrum are those imaginary friends whom the imaginer does not recognize as being imaginary and instead regards as being "real," in the sense of having an objective external existence and agency. These imaginary friends are products purely of the imaginer's unconscious processes, without the imaginer's conscious intent; the imaginer is thus unaware of his or her role as imaginer, and mistakes the imaginary friends for external Others. We can describe these as *delusionary* imaginary friends.

Again, this is a spectrum: These two types of imaginary friends are located at opposite ends, and in between are various permutations that share qualities of both. As Clay argues, when he discusses imaginary friends with Grandpa Harry:

> "But Hobbes is real. Calvin might be imagining all the personality stuff and talking to himself, but he really does have a stuffed tiger. He's not just imagining the stuffed animal. He's only imagining the part where the animal talks. That makes it okay."

In other words, from Clay's perspective, Hobbes isn't a delusion (and Calvin isn't delusional, or "stupid" as Clay uncharitably puts it) because the stuffed version of Hobbes does have an independent external existence. Of course, Clay is somewhat missing the point here: the important question, when it comes to understanding what's really going on with Calvin, isn't whether Hobbes has a physical existence; the important question is whether Calvin is consciously aware that he's imagining Hobbes to be alive, or whether he genuinely and completely believes that Hobbes is alive and that the live version of Hobbes is an Other who has agency independent of Calvin's mind. This is a question that Bill Watterson carefully avoids answering, but I'm inclined to think it's the latter —and I suspect Clay's creator Michael Monje sees it that way, too. Imaginary friends who are entirely *willed* and entirely understood by their imaginers to be imaginary just aren't that interesting. It's the delusionary ones, like Tyler Durden in *Fight Club,* that make for the best stories.

Clay hits closer to home in this exchange:

> "I really didn't mean it," Patrick said. "I just couldn't help thinking like your mom should be in Calvin and Hobbes."
>
> "I think that too, only I don't think it's funny," Clay said. "I'm really worried that maybe Calvin and Hobbes is a warning. Like maybe Bill Watterson knows things, and he's trying to let us know about them too."
>
> "What kind of things?" Patrick asked. His voice was suddenly very quiet.
>
> "I don't know," said Clay. "But I think they're the same kinds of things that made C.S. Lewis think that the voices in

his head were demons instead of imaginary friends. Only, you
know, Calvin and Hobbes is for smart people."

This is a crucial moment in *Imaginary Friends:* a moment where
Monje hands us a great big hint as to what we should be watching for
throughout the book. Because Clay, like Calvin or the narrator of
Fight Club, is an unreliable viewpoint character —a character with a
fragmented psyche whose dissociated fragments manifest as
imaginary friends of the delusionary variety. And Monje herself, in
the role of third-person omniscient narrator, is a "reliable" narrator
only insofar as she reliably reports Clay's unreliable subjective
experience. Monje doesn't tell us, at least not outright, which aspects
of Clay's perceptions of the reality are more or less objectively
accurate and which aspects are misperceptions resulting from a
fragmented psyche. Monje drops hints, of course. Leaves clever clues.
But it's up to us to figure it out for ourselves. *Imaginary Friends* is a
puzzlebox of sorts, because the unconscious self-protective
manipulations of Clay's psyche have turned Clay himself into a
human puzzlebox.

We easily recognize Van as imaginary. The rogue psychoanalyst
Wilhelm Reich made a vital contribution to our understanding of the
human condition when he observed that the psychological defense
mechanisms we instinctively construct, in response to the unsafe
aspects of our developmental environments, manifest in the body as
largely unconscious complexes of chronic physical tension. Reich
called these complexes of tension *character armor.* Monje does a
brilliant job of vividly depicting the construction and functioning of
Clay's character armor, and what it's like in Clay's own subjective
experience. Van can be seen as a personification of Clay's character
armor: character armor conceived of and experienced as an actual
character.

Van, and the companions Clay invents for Van, are the most
obviously imaginary of Clay's imaginary friends, because Clay himself
experiences Van as manifesting within Clay's mind and body. Clay
experiences Van as having some degree of autonomy and agency, but
not as a person whose existence is entirely external to and

independent of Clay, like the existence of Clay's parents or Clay's friend Patrick. So we can recognize Van as imaginary even if we fail to pick up on Monje's various hints about the unreliability of Clay's perspective.

But if we do watch for those hints, if we look beyond the obvious and make the quite worthwhile effort of engaging with the puzzlebox nature of both this story and its protagonist, we begin to realize that Clay's psyche is so fragmented that Clay himself can't be trusted to keep track of all the fragments or to recognize them when he meets them. Which means that it's up to us, the readers, to figure out which characters are "real" and which ones are dissociated fragments of Clay, pieces of the Clay Dillon puzzlebox, manifesting as imaginary friends whom Clay mistakes for external Others.

Is Hillary real? If we could visit Clay's school, stroll out to the playground and observe Clay and Hillary with our own eyes, would we see a boy and a girl sitting and talking together, or a boy sitting alone and mumbling to himself?

And if Hillary is an imaginary friend, a fragment of Clay whom Clay mistakes for a classmate, is she the only one? What about this bit, near the book's end, when the bullies in Clay's catechism class are taunting him by questioning his gender:

> The girls across the table looked embarrassed. At least one seemed like she wanted to talk, but none of them ever did. Not then, and not since Hillary had moved away.

It's open to interpretation, and only Monje knows for sure, but I personally would bet money that if you and I could walk into that classroom and see it with our own eyes instead of through Clay's eyes, we'd see fewer girls in the room than Clay sees.

The strange and terrible saga of Clay Dillon begins with the books *Nothing Is Right* and *Imaginary Friends,* continues in *Gaslight Village* and other books that follow, and also includes *Defiant* (which takes place when Clay is 30 years old). The whole saga should be required reading for anyone who works in any capacity with the sort of young people who are often described as *gifted, disturbed, troubled, oppositional, defiant,* or *exceptional.*

One of the most striking and tragic themes of the saga is just how utterly clueless and constantly wrong all the adults are about what's actually going on in Clay's mind. In a way, Clay himself is an "imaginary friend" to the adults in his life, insofar as when they look at him they don't see him but instead see an imaginary child, a product of their own misconceptions and projections who has no resemblance (except in the external physical sense) to the real Clay Dillon. Every adult in his life is consistently one hundred percent wrong, all of the time, about Clay's motivations, needs, feelings, thoughts, and perceptions. No adult ever even comes close to being able to conceive of what Clay is actually experiencing. They can imagine neither the extent and nature of his difficulties, nor the complexity and sophistication of his thinking.

In this respect, *Imaginary Friends* constitutes a warning to any adults — especially those in "helping" professions — who are so arrogant as to presume that they can truly understand the realities of their young charges. The one thing that I hope every reader learns from the story of Clay Dillon is an increased sense of humility. Humility especially when it comes to our understanding of others, and when it comes to our assumptions about the imaginary and the real.

Read Clay's story with humility, and with an eye for subtle hints — for the twisty architecture of the puzzlebox, and for things that are not what they might seem. Michael Monje knows things, and she's trying to let us know about them, too.

❖   ❖   ❖

About the Author

By now, you should expect this address,
given that it's been a couple books
and the poetry has always been my biography,
A Portrait of the Artist,
and not a conventional cut-and-dried approach to me.

Forgive the indulgent self-comparison,
but you did just read a story
cut into four portions,
with each concluded by an epiphany.

Get me?

I told you about my three-way affair
with *Finnegan's Wake* and Rakim,
did you think *I* would forget about *them*?

No, the whole story is folded over
at the corners and then ordered
in just the right way to make the words
something clear to see
without ruining the origami
of the invisible movements
learned from careful study
and a diverse range
of artistic influences
invading, occupying,
changing my composition,
and fragmenting my identity.

They are all there for you to locate,
some in titles and some in scenes,
some in techniques,
and some in the structure
of the rhythm
between my beats.

Of course, this doesn't have to be
the shape of the conversation
between you and me.

This is a shared experience,
telling a story,
so even as I work with intent
to create you,
you can resist and renegotiate,
because my reader also
creates me.

The text is only as sophisticated
as you happen to feel like you should make it.

So now, we have another instance
where I stand before you naked.

Will you see the movement,
or ogle the spectacle
without seeing sophistication
in the choreography?

Choose quickly,
and be careful,
there are three paths:

One back away from me,
back to the things you always see.

One wide road, well paved,
with a downward slope
and an easy pitch,
and it will take you
into the *Gaslight Village*.

The final one would diverge,
a less traveled path,
difficult to pass by,
and it will continue this discussion.

In the end, where you go
depends not on what you want,
but what you see, so listen to me:

The road you choose to take
will make all the difference.

This conversation continues in

Teaching Languagings
To: Nonverbal Thinkers
——————————
The US Book

(**NeuroQueer Books, 2016**)

CPSIA information can be obtained at www.ICGtesting.com
Printed in the USA
BVOW05s0803150316

440112BV00004B/12/P